wreaking

Also by James Scudamore

The Amnesia Clinic
Heliopolis

wreaking

James Scudamore

HARVILL SECKER LONDON

Published by Harvill Secker 2013

2 4 6 8 10 9 7 5 3 1

First published in Great Britain in 2013 by
HARVILL SECKER
Random House
20 Vauxhall Bridge Road
London
SW1V 2SA

www.vintage-books.co.uk

Addresses for companies within The Random House Group Limited
can be found at: www.randomhouse.co.uk/offices.htm

The Random House Group Limited Reg. No. 954009

A CIP catalogue record for this book
is available from the British Library

ISBN 9781846551895 (hardback)
ISBN 9781409027133 (ebook)

The Random House Group Limited supports the Forest Stewardship Council®
(FSC®), the leading international forest-certification organisation.
Our books carrying the FSC label are printed on FSC®-certified paper.
FSC is the only forest-certification scheme supported by the leading
environmental organisations, including Greenpeace. Our paper
procurement policy can be found at
www.randomhouse.co.uk/environment

Set in Dante MT by Palimpsest Book Production Limited,
Falkirk, Stirlingshire

Printed in Great Britain by
Clays Ltd, St Ives plc

To my son and in memory of my father

PART ONE

1

In the garden he has trained roses through the frames of medicine trolleys and up stairwell cages made to thwart patient suicides. From the trees he hangs emergency eyewash stations filled with water, and seed dispensers that were once miniature incinerators mounted in every ward for the quick disposal of tainted materials. Sometimes he sits and watches the birds enjoying his hospitality, from a bench of wheelchairs lashed together with bathing harnesses.

He has ventured outside on this damp April afternoon to replenish the feeders and forage a little for himself. Pulling his oxygen cylinder behind him on its stainless steel caddy, he advances, a creeping shadow against the pale facade of Revenant House. He can feel cold soak spreading across his feet. Shouldn't have come out in his slippers.

He passes an apple tree and remembers how once, after some stupid argument, his daughter climbed it and wouldn't come down. She said she would stay up there until he apologised, and he was stubborn enough to shout at her that he never would. She was fifteen – far too old for that kind of thing – but that didn't stop her. He can still see the red trainers on her feet, hanging down like fruit, as he pretended to be getting on with his work inside, but checked the window every five minutes to make sure she was safe.

He stops by the lake to watch a thin band of mist rolling over the water, and listen to the babble of the birds as word spreads that he's replenished their supplies. He feels the wave of nausea that strikes whenever he forgets to have lunch: time to eat.

He grows tomatoes in an old hospital tour bus, which, when it was on wheels and not stacks of crumbling bricks, was used to take patients on excursions. He sows in stages, trying to achieve the longest possible crop, but it's still a bit early in the year. When he looks hopefully through the window he can see no red among the green. As usual the chickens are his best hope. He makes his daily raid on the coop, pondering all the poor souls whose lives played out in the hospital, and thinking that eggs are unrealised futures too – best-laid plans, hopes dashed and scrambled.

Three eggs, fragile in his pocket: now that he has them, he feels armed against the evening. Back in the kitchen he sits perched by the range on a hospital stool, letting the pan of water boil for longer than it needs to so that the steam will heat the air around him. He drinks sweet, strong tea from a pint mug. He melts some butter, and tips in the mixing bowl's marbled emulsion. A little whisk as they seethe into substance, and he eats the eggs straight from the pan, too quickly, enjoying the hot catch at the back of his throat.

A noise at the window makes him jump, and he wonders if it will be one of those days when trespassers are a nuisance. They still come, sometimes – local kids, pumped up on boredom, trying to spook themselves. He hears things in the night and goes down to find a bonfire lit, with bottles strewn round it, and a music machine throbbing nearby. The fleeing rabble taunts him from the darkness. He has become *that* old man, an object for their sport.

He wants to explain to them that he didn't intend to end up like this – that he moved here on the understanding that the hospital would be redeveloped in no time – but it would be pointless. It suits them to see him as a creepy adornment to the place: the patient who never went home; the mad, self-medicating doctor. When he braves a trip into town he can feel eyes on him in the supermarket car park, and a simple grocery shop can wreck his nerves for days.

Later, there will be evening hours with a bottle and a fire, and perhaps a copy of a small periodical he once edited called the *Milan Review*. For now, it is time to get back to work. Dragging his oxygen behind him, he makes his way slowly down the corridor to the ground-floor day room he uses as his study. He looks around him at the walls, where faded patient murals are peeling. He lowers himself into his knackered green armchair, and runs a palm down its lumpy fabric in search of the respirator pipe, which is kept in place by a table knife embedded into the stuffing. A cough is rising, but he tries to limit its expression to an extended clearing of the throat and a hoarse, high whimper. A full fit now would take too much recovery time. At the slow pace that he has learned works best for the avoidance of panic, he switches from his cylinder to the machine that is permanently installed at the chair's side. He fixes its lugs into his nostrils, and flicks the switch. It breathes for him with its soft thud and hiss, sending cool jets of improved air into his head.

Lying on a pad of paper in front of the armchair is the battered stainless steel pen he always writes with – a gift from his late wife. He takes out a new sheet of paper, and settles himself. Press on.

The project lasted a century, more or less. Now the era of Big Bins is over. And whatever we may think of places like this, we won't be seeing anything on their scale again.

Wreaking was huge enough both to feed and feed off its environment. Two adjacent farms supplied its food (and

provided employment to those patients deemed capable).
There was a butcher, a grocer and a hairdresser. A mortuary,
a coffin-maker and a graveyard. It had its own railway
station, and room for up to 3,000 patients. I can only imagine
how the staff here must have scoffed when it was announced
that their charges were to be relocated somewhere called the
Community.

The hospital is set in 180 acres of ground overlooking an
estuary, whose water tumbles into a widening shale mouth
as it approaches the shore. One bank of the river carries on
into the North Sea, becoming the bleached, bare arm of a
shingle spit known locally as the Ness.

The only way to get any sense of the scale is to pick your
way inland, across the water meadow that declines in wilder-
ness as the formal grounds take hold. From out there,
Wreaking is flat and vast, occupying an outrageous propor-
tion of the horizon.

Your approach will bring you in past the great perimeter
ditch that used to hide a sunken security fence, in the days
before pharmacological shackles made physical confinement
redundant. Beyond that, the detail of the hospital begins to
sharpen up: its follies and adornments; its long, dark-bricked
walls. Wreaking was built during a golden age of asylum
architecture, and even its most functional outbuildings have
ornate touches: spires and turrets; gargoyles and angels.

The hospital has long been a target for vandals. Thieves
have stripped it of its metal and equipment, and kids have
set fires there during mindless parties. The assembly hall, the
chapel, the wards: all now bare open wounds with charred
timbers and plaster that has sagged and collapsed, letting in
weather and all the life it brings.

I have done my best to fight the rot, though I am only one
man. I scour the corridors for relics. I hoard old papers. I
collect unbroken china and stack it carefully in my kitchen.

It is not a position I asked for, but I have become the curator of this place by default, because if I don't save these things then nobody else will. And in spite of all my best efforts, the grounds are still dotted with incongruous objects: walking frames, bathing chairs, a shoe or two (but never in pairs). The hospital contents have seeped outside as if in pursuit of the patients. The building is forlorn: its ground-floor windows are boarded up, and the whole, dark shell is defended now by spiked metal fences and warning signs. It is not what was supposed to happen here at all.

He still strikes out for the main hospital from time to time. It is riskier, with his breathing like this, but if he takes his cylinder and allows himself plenty of breaks, it's just possible to get around. The day rooms and dormitories may be empty, but their spongy carpets and levering floorboards are coming to life. Ivy that was putting out fine, exploratory tendrils against the wallpaper when he arrived here has grown thick, confident branches. Burnt-out chairs seem to be taking root where they stand. The innards of the building hang from the ceiling: tongues of dusty cladding; viscera of wires and pipework. Shapes are suggested by the constantly shifting textures of wall-mould: a cackling witch; an awful, leprous face.

His daughter worries. She assumes he is lonely, and she doesn't even know how ill he is. If she could only hear the portentous language his doctors use. They talk of his *lung burden*. He has been formally appraised that if he doesn't take it easy on his heart, he will be at risk of a *major event*. Cleo doesn't even know all that, and still she wants him to leave.

He can't leave. He has become addicted to the chatter of the past down those corridors. Corridors that once smelt of bleach and floor polish and gave prim squeaks under the footsteps of bustling nurses. Corridors with a hundred years' worth of linoleum scratches – all the marks of trolleys and wheelchairs and walking sticks and struggling boots, refusing to go quietly. Corridors where (he imagines, ghoulishly disregarding the facts) the light dipped as they administered doses of ECT. Corridors where consequences were addressed – sometimes even for the better.

Preserving the case notes seems particularly important: catalogues of lost folk, in folders that he has rescued by the barrow-load. Without his intervention the files would be gone by now, and there would be no record of these people at all. Some days he just picks a patient and spends the afternoon with them, trying to reconstruct the decisions made on their behalf, the direction they received.

. . . intelligent and pleasant young woman with a marked obsessional personality associated with feelings of guilt. In this she is a mirror of her father whom she describes as viciously strict and fussy to the extent that her house had to be kept spotless when she was growing up, and friends were never allowed in. She pictured herself as the perfect mother and fell short of this when her baby was recently scalded . . .

. . . patient is a single man who feels nervous and frightened all the time and is frightened of going outside. He says he is self-conscious and cannot talk to people. He is the youngest of six and was born when his mother was about forty-five. One of his brothers has already been treated at Wreaking for depression . . .

. . . saw this patient again this afternoon. She says she feels much calmer on the Mogadon and has been shouting less at her children. We discussed further the circumstances of her husband's affair, which she continues to attribute to the abnormal size of her nose. Nothing I say can stop her believing . . .

He wraps his dressing gown in tighter, hugging himself against the damp, and takes up his pen for another burst.

Revenant House was built later than the main hospital, as a sub-clinic or 'villa' within its grounds – initially run as a separate institution, then assimilated by the monster it adjoins. As Wreaking's acute unit, it came to house an ECT suite, a mother-and-baby unit and an occupational-therapy department. For the best part of twenty years, since its closure, it has been my home.

While I well know how cruelty can thrive in tucked-away places like this, it seems obvious from all the records that the founder of Revenant House was a good man. He gave it that name in the hope that within its walls, his patients would come back to themselves. To whoever they had been before the thing that deviated them. He was a great one for cause and effect.

For a while, after Wreaking absorbed it, I think the building was given a more anodyne name, like the Jasmine Wards and Petunia Courts so much in evidence elsewhere. But it takes more than a change of signpost to get people round here to forget, and the original name lived on, as did its curious local corruption, the Remnant House.

This building has a different atmosphere to the rest of the hospital. Larches loom, and generate a warm, coniferous hum. Their needles collapse in crackling footfalls as you walk. White walls and covered verandas distinguish it from the Gotham whose unthinkable domination begins just over the road.

This man, the founder – his name was Pym – developed an early, eccentric form of meditative therapy based around water. He identified a spring-fed pond at the rear of the building and fed it up into a small lake. He made a feature of it, and built pavilions enabling his patients to regard the water from every possible angle. It was a cornerstone of his approach to care, that there were near-unlimited ways of looking at a situation, and you just had to keep looking until you found the right one.

He even managed to build a pavilion beneath the water's surface – a dome of thick glass bricks, accessible through a tunnel off the hospital basement. Patients were allowed in by appointment, for contemplation and relaxation. They could see the shadows of carp nudging the glass when the sun was shining. There was room for a couple of comfortable chairs. The water created a dampened, close acoustic.

Sadly, it was only a matter of time before some unfortunate from Wreaking found her way over here and opened her wrists in the water with a piece of broken glass, weighing herself down for good measure with two pockets full of roof lead. Her body's black shadow drifted over the domed surface of the underwater pavilion, to the great distress of the poor soul whose special treat it was to be sealed in there for the afternoon.

After that, Revenant House came into line with the thinking elsewhere, which held, quite sensibly I suppose, that to build madhouses beside water was essentially a bad idea. The lake was fenced off, and left to choke itself with weeds, with the dome a curious polyp at its centre.

But I revived it. The first thing I did, before I even brought my family here, was to coax the old spring back into the watercourse and feed it up again. It is the only example of anything round here being restored. Everything else is going in the opposite direction.

One day, he decided to try and fish standing on top of the underwater room. He pulled on his waders and announced it.

'I bet you a million pounds you fall in,' said Cleo, who was never one to keep her thoughts to herself.

'You're on,' he said. 'You can pay me back in instalments.'

He had imagined she would set herself up at the side to watch him, in one of the waterside pavilions. But of course, she had a better idea. He didn't even know where she was until he was already stepping off the little rowing boat and placing his first tentative footsteps on the slimy glass of the dome, only to feel her, right there, thumping at the glass under his feet with a broom handle. She tapped each foot as it touched, and he could even hear the distant peal of her laughter under the water, and after that it was only a matter of time before he fell in. He can still remember the panic as he grabbed for a low-hanging branch and missed, as his waders started to fill up and he realised he had to get them off or he would go down. These days he tells himself that he let himself fall because he wanted her to win the bet. But he knows that's not quite true. He wanted desperately to be proved right, and he would have stayed on his feet if he had been able.

Incredible how Cleo can creep up on him, whatever he may think he is thinking about. It used to be her mother who did that, in the years after she died. Now, it is Cleo. Cleo who feels so distant from him that she might as well be dead herself.

He writes sometimes about how buildings like this one have memories. You won't ever catch him calling them ghosts, but he does imagine he can almost feel it sometimes – a kind of psychic residue from all the people who roamed these corridors, stuck in feedback loops of thought or behaviour. Unable to forget or abstract.

'Remind you of anyone?' he says to the empty room, and makes himself laugh.

'Fuck off,' he tells himself, by way of a rejoinder.

Oh well. Here we go again. He's written it so many times now that one more go won't hurt. He takes up the pen, resigned to it.

This is the same vile green chair I was sitting in on the day of the accident. One of many things left behind by the hospital that we said we were going to chuck out and never did. God knows what has been spilled into it over the years.

If I were melodramatic, I would write that Cleo's accident plays out in front of me every day. That when I visit the projection room at the back of the Wreaking assembly hall, and try to start the machine that sits there among curls of dusty, spoiling film, there is only ever one vision I see – the one that plays out in my head.

It's not like that. It was one thing that went wrong, and I don't think about it all the time. Some people – the cause-and-effect monkeys – they'd say it was everything, the accident. They'd have me acting it out in some ghastly role-playing exercise. But it wasn't everything. It was what it was, and it was nobody's fault.

Blunted September colours were taking over. We were leaving doors open, partly because we were still psychologic-ally in summer, and partly to try and rid the building of the smell of smoke from a house fire the week before. I sat at my desk, in this chair, watching a daddy-long-legs blunder into a wall, when in she came, breathless and bounding.

Her face then was a rehearsal of her adult features. The button of a nose, those thin, guileless lips with their first brash coating of lipstick. That mouth, free of worry, accustomed to burst open in proper, helpless hilarity at any provocation. The brow ready to furrow at any injustice. Those strong, green eyes.

And even though I had listened to her messing around outside with a full, pleading heart only minutes before, the act of her coming in made me feel encroached upon, and I snapped at her. She seemed hurt, but only mock-hurt, as she had been many times before. If I could just finish what I had

been doing – then, I thought, I would be in the right mood
to make it up to her later on.

How did it go?

'I want to ask you something. It's important.' Red-faced,
determined, a little out of breath.

'Ask me later.'

'I said it was important.'

'Ask me later.'

'But I might not want to later.'

'You'll be the same person, won't you?'

Except that she wasn't. When I saw her next, she had
become a different person altogether.

The ink is not yet dry but already he is screwing up the
page and throwing it aside. The machine taps and sighs,
but his ragged breathing is not keeping time. He reaches
inside the desk drawer, knowing they're here, tingling in
their box: cigarettes. He forces his hand to stop, and focuses
instead on the soft gargling of a pigeon outside. Time
to let go of himself for a moment, and try to calm
down.

Depersonalisation is the word the professionals use. He
experiences it here a lot: a kind of untethering of the
self. New mothers are depersonalised when the enormity
of their duty of care begins to dawn, and the great
myth of their own lives begins to lose definition. The
residents of large asylums were depersonalised, too, whenever staff got confused by their freedom and power, and
succumbed to the temptation to stop seeing their patients
as people.

He has no sense of how the disconnection feels to others,
but he knows that he can get very far away from himself if
he wants – so far that he wonders whether he will return.

All he has to do is stare at an object for long enough that it is stripped of meaning in the world. The stripping-off spreads, so quickly it is terrifying, to take from everything else around it, himself included. This room, with its peeling walls and damp carpets – it might be anywhere. And he might be anyone. Which is a good way of keeping emotion in check.

He closes the drawer and fumbles again for the pen, trying to keep his breaths in time with the soothing sound of the pigeon. What he is about to do will upset him, and that will lead to coughing. But that at least might make him tired enough to sleep.

The birds have moved in properly since I've been here alone. I think they know the place is theirs now. I can watch them for hours, from the grand display of an eye of starlings opening and closing in the sky, to the solitary robin pecking at one of my feeders. Even when I don't see them, I hear them: the soft clatter of wings as a dove flees the clock tower; the riffle of pages overhead as a strip of songbirds flashes through.

Starlings, glossy and sleek. Their flutter and commotion. The morning of the accident, they were everywhere. Edging the outbuildings with black. Ecstatic flashes of them bathing in the shallows of the lake.

I went outside to find her and tell her I hadn't meant it, to take it back and offer her whatever consolation she wanted. I called her name. Then I realised there was nothing to be done except to go back to my desk.

I sat here for two hours, trying to work. I heard the odd noise – a shifting of floorboard, a scuffle in the rafters – but that was always happening. Even then, the fabric was so packed with rats and birds that the house was never silent.

Then something made me turn in my chair – a tiny exhalation that sounded as if it was in the room with me. I noticed that a shadow on the wall had changed. And I saw it was her arm. How had she stolen in here without me even noticing?

The terrible thing had happened. It was right here, and I hadn't even noticed. She had gone to earth like a wounded creature, and I had worked on. She lay face down on the floor under the window. As I turned her over, I saw the blood that had flowed from her botched eye to coat her face. And though she remained silent throughout, I screamed and screamed.

2

As a child, Cleo feared that her own thoughts might bring down planes from the sky. If she somehow slipped, if she lost concentration, hundreds of deaths would be on her hands. Nobody had ever told her this, but she knew it was true. So, resisting all distraction, she kept to a silence of blazing, generous concentration, and balled up her energy to ensure the safety of every high jet she saw scratching overhead.

She is remembering this quirk of childhood as she sits at her new flat-pack dining table, hands bunched near her mouth, trying to tap her eye with a pen. This ongoing war of attrition with her vestigial blink has always been a good way to pass the time. When she succeeds, the brittle knock of biro-plastic on eyeglass sends a pleasing shockwave through the unseeing eyeball beneath – a seismic foreground event that stops her mind from wandering. But around half the time her eyelid intercedes, still thinking to protect the eye long after the damage has been done. She wants to beat the twitch for good. She imagines it will feel like progress.

The eye is not, as some suppose, a ball of glass – more a giant, artistic contact lens, projecting normality to the world, and sparing it the awkwardness of having to put words to a reaction. *Nothing to see here*, it says, in more ways than one.

At school – when she eventually returned to normal school – the various tricks she was already learning to play with it were useful defences. She soon learned to manipulate its position with her fingertip, pointing it in the direction of her teachers to make it appear as though she was paying attention, while the relevant one, the seeing one, looked at a book on her desk, or just into space, its true intent masked by a casual, shielding hand. And if that wasn't enough to fend off unwelcome attention, well, she was still getting to grips with the injury then, and found that nothing put people off holding out for a response like an ocular prosthesis 'accidentally' falling on to the desk.

She stares down at the pages of handwritten text on the table, at the cordless phone beside them. The phone seems to radiate alarm. She squints until it's almost hazy with it, wobbling with worry. He isn't picking up. And if she tries calling again and he still doesn't pick up it will make things worse. For now she has let the phone ring unanswered only once, which leaves a range of plausible reasons why he couldn't get to it. A second failed attempt will multiply her anxiety, square it and cube it into something to be reckoned with.

In swings the biro. Tap. Yes. Beat you.

People cotton on in the end, although it takes them a while to realise what exactly is different, apart from the scar. The glass eye lacks retinal depth. It betrays her in photographs. There can be no red-eye here: nothing sees back, so nothing reflects. So in fact, it's the real eye that looks demonic, the real eye that comes alive with mechanised intent in the flashlight. The prosthesis fools the camera, even though it never quite fools a human being.

Blink. The flinch strikes back. She drops the pen in frustration.

The wound healed into a striking red line on her lower right eyelid. She invites new friends to look closely at it on their first meeting so they aren't distracted later on. She tells the story of how a boy once approached her in the street and asked respectfully if she was a Terminator, or some other kind of cyborg.

'I wish,' she said.

Being able to make things disappear is a superpower of sorts. She stares down at the document, whizzing it from side to side on the glass tabletop, in and out of her blind spot.

She knows what this is. It's another extract. He has been sending them to her lately by post, with no accompanying note. She doesn't know whether she is supposed to be giving him feedback, or whether (as she suspects) he thinks that by virtue of working 'in the media' she will somehow be able to steer the thing towards publication. She hopes for the sake of his mental health that this book doesn't meet the same fate as its predecessors, but it probably will.

This one is called *Wreaking: Digressive History Of A Madhouse* – and boy, is it digressive. This section looks like one of hundreds of different beginnings that she knows to exist somewhere in the stacks of paper that are rising up around him in his study. The book starts itself anew regularly, and there is no end in sight. It's just what he does to fill up his days.

Excerpts like this used to be accompanied by one of the personal compliments slips he gets printed in town, which go into his letters to newspapers, or the batches of clippings he occasionally sends her to make unsubtle points about what he perceives to be her lifestyle. *With the compliments of Jasper Scriven, Revenant House*, they read.

They see each other rarely, and the good phone conversations – the ones when his guard is down and they fall towards a kind of intimacy – seem to be getting fewer and farther between. The pages have become vital despatches from the front line – her only way of checking in with his state of mind. But lately they have taken on a different tone, and he has started to write about events that they have never properly discussed in person. She isn't sure how she is supposed to react. And deciding just to give him a call and ask him, as other daughters might do, is anything but straightforward.

Her foster parents are as dumbly kind and cheerful to her now during their weekly chats as they were when she went to live with them. Fifteen to eighteen, they got – bad years. Unable to have kids of their own, they'd spent the money on a barn conversion outside a twee market town that was a healthy number of counties away from Wreaking, and populated it with troublemakers and outcasts. Cleo was not their first charge, and they knew not to ask her about the past if she didn't want to talk. Not to be seen to be trying to push buttons or get results.

She's a nicer person these days, and has been trying to make it up to them ever since. Still. The shit they put up with. They wanted a problem child, and they got one. One who made matters worse by being self-righteous as well as damaged. Harm quite definitely done, with a glamorous, emblematic injury to boot. It was far too late for them to do anything but live with her. So she broke things, and drank their booze, and embarrassed them by not locking or even closing her bedroom door when she brought boys home, when giggle and music and smoke flowed freely out through the beams above their softly lit mezzanine landing. None of which stopped Good Foster Father bringing two cups of tea to her room the next morning, and making eggs, and asking Cleo if her 'friend' was staying for lunch.

It endures, this implausible patience. Even though a succession of other bad kids has torn up their place since Cleo, they call her every week without fail. The conversations are easy and lively and full of mutual understanding.

Contact with her father is more complicated. Talking to him is like touching inflamed tissue. Their estrangement feeds itself. Any decision to call him must be weighed up carefully in consideration with other factors, such as how tough she's feeling when faced with the prospect of the aftermath of one of the bad calls. They have evolved ways of letting the other person into their lives, but there are ground rules, set by him, which are often altered and never articulated.

At the moment, one rule seems to be *Don't Call Back*. If she misses his call, by the time she calls him back the spirit he called in will have evaporated, and she will run into a different person altogether.

Then again, another rule at the moment seems to be *Don't Call At All*. When she calls him unprompted, it is highly unlikely that the conversation will go well. He has to be in the right mood.

She lifts her cup of tea, then puts it down again. Tea isn't what she wants. Fuck tea.

Music plays behind a televised disaster appeal: sad eyes; soft guitar phrases like flaked-off disappointment. Her professional eye admires the film as a piece of manipulation. She can't imagine having done a better editing job on it herself. More and more difficult these days to package information like this in a way that stands out without resorting to emotional bullying.

She picks up the phone, dials a familiar number and places an order with the local Chinese: plain noodles, bean sprouts, pak choi. It's enough of a step in the direction of dinner to justify a drink. She pours the steaming tea down the sink and goes to the freezer for vodka.

The best way to survive is to wrap a version of the world round yourself that you can live with, says her father, who is prone to aphoristic utterances. This is her version: a first-floor flat in a newly built block on the site of a riverside spice warehouse on the seaward side of the city. There are balconies made of metal posts with high-tensile wire strung between them, and huge windows in which she has never bothered to hang curtains. Inside: white walls, polished wood floors, mirrors, but no pictures – only television, shimmering on the wall.

She pulls open the top drawer of the freezer and the frosted bottle rolls forward obediently. From the same drawer, she plucks a heavy tumbler, which mists up when she sets it on the counter. She belts the draining board with an ice-cube tray, heaps chunks into the glass, and adds a big slug of syrupy vodka and a splash of tonic. She takes a slurp and winces at her own creation, slamming the freezer door with a nudge of her thigh. She should have known better than to attempt a reversion to tea after boozing at lunchtime.

She has been resisting invitations to have lunch with Emma for weeks now, and today she finally caved in. Cleo's producer and boss is only five years older than her, and lost her husband this year to a pop-up heart defect. Cleo has been dreading the big conversation she knew was coming, because she was afraid she wouldn't know what to say. She was careful to build a work-based excuse into the afternoon that gave her a cut-off point at which to leave. She didn't want the responsibility of getting Emma drunk. Not least because there's a vacuity to her grief that Cleo finds infuriating.

She switches over to the news to see if any of her work will feature. The stories play out. She enjoys the vodka's drenching effect on her brain. The way she can feel it behind her eyes. Here's a report she edited on yesterday's City demonstration. Things got out of hand, and somehow a pregnant woman was hurt in the crowd surge. An investigation is in progress to assess whether or not police brutality was to blame. Emma told her earlier at lunch that this was some of her best work. Cleo found the compliment embarrassing, because it was so obviously an expression of Emma's gratitude that she had consented to join her for the meal.

'I mean it,' said Emma. 'And I'll tell you why: because you managed to make it look like a real demonstration.'

'What do you mean?'

'These demos. It's work enough to edit them down so they don't look like massive press packs. If it isn't journalists, it's guerrilla artists and privately educated anarchists, and other supposedly creative individuals. The crowd surges are mainly caused by people with camera phones trying to get to the front. That poor woman was probably the only genuine protestor there.'

'So you're not allowed grievances if you own a camera phone?' said Cleo.

'Touché,' said Emma, which made Cleo inwardly cringe.

'They have an algorithm now,' said Cleo. 'I've been editing a feature on it. It can read a moving image to detect aberrant behaviour in a group.'

Emma put on her professional frown of concentration. 'What does that mean?'

'They use it in prisons to keep tabs on people who are on suicide watch. If an image starts moving in a way it isn't supposed to, it sets off an alarm. They developed it in battery chicken farms. If the birds' behaviour deviates from the rest of the dataset – like if they're attacking each other, or getting smothered – then an alert goes off. It cuts down on wastage.'

Cleo was aware of trying to establish a certain tone – something analytical, resistant to nonsense. A defence against what she knew was coming.

'What's it got to do with the demonstration?' said Emma.

'They'll be using it on demonstrations as well – the camera will seek out the people who aren't demonstrating peacefully, and identify the ones who are getting violent. The algorithm will sort of read the crowd and scout for problems.'

'They can do that?' said Emma.

'They'll be able to soon.'

'So now there's a right way and a wrong way to demonstrate.' Emma fingered the stem of her wine glass and looked sad. 'The world's moving fast.'

'What's wrong with that?'

'It's just cruel when you lose someone so suddenly,' said Emma. 'I can't bear the way that life carries on. Still, he's in a better place now.'

'You'll always have the past,' said Cleo.

She excused herself soon after that, fearing she might say more. It probably wouldn't have been wise, for the friendship or her career, to risk putting it to Emma that there was no 'better' place. Or that there was nothing 'cruel' about it, because 'it' didn't have a personality.

Back at her desk with a strong coffee, Cleo wondered where that fierce jolt of cynicism had come from. She feels sympathy for Emma, or thinks she does. But in that moment, nothing was going to suppress her urge to tell the unpleasant truth. Which reminds her strongly of a certain someone who is not picking up the phone.

Her father rails against all kinds of sentimental optimism, especially religion, with an emotion not unlike vengeance. She has never really known if he believes what he says. There is certainly more than a hint of symbol-worship in his attitude to her late mother, though he would never admit it. And more than a hint of it in the pages he's been sending her lately.

It was this atmosphere of identification that first made her consider breaking the rules and giving him a call. That, and she'd been drinking. A third reason was that the previous conversation they'd had was practically joyful. Three weeks ago. Saturday afternoon. She was in. Ran for the phone from the shower, trying not to slip on her wooden floors.

'I have to tell you about the badgers,' he said.

'What about the badgers?'

'I will never forgive them. You should see what they've done to my vegetable patch. Vandals. What were they hoping to find? I haven't grown anything there in ages. But no. They turned the whole lot over, and dug out a lot of my roses as well. What good does it serve?'

Cleo said nothing, knowing the best thing was to let him let him fly.

Then he laughed. 'But do you know what I did to them?'

'What?'

'I dosed them up.'

'What do you mean? On what?'

'Prozac.'

'Say that again?'

'I chopped up a whole packet of pills into a thing of mince, and left it out for them. They wolfed it – badgered it, I suppose – in about ten minutes. I've never seen anything go so haywire.'

'You did what?'

'And then I chased them down the drive in my car. Do you want to know how fast a badger can go on Prozac? I can tell you.'

'Dad – since when have you been on Prozac?'

'It's fast.'

'How long?'

'Thirty-five miles an hour.'

It was the best conversation they'd had in months, and it ended with laughter, and she knows that part of the reason they had been avoiding phoning each other since is that they both feared the next one couldn't be as good.

She imagines she can feel him sometimes. She feels the link wanting to establish itself, like an electrical charge summoned from the air. The impulse to call often strikes on a Sunday evening, but she rarely acts on it, for fear that if they do speak it will make her feel worse than if they don't. And then the feeling of connection goes, and she tells herself that he would say such feelings are just psychic rubbish. Projections of desire. That there is nothing super-natural in the world, just as he used to say how much he hated what he called *bourgeois happy endings*.

But the pages. The things they talk about. The way the last batch was screwed up and then re-flattened, as if he had tussled with himself about whether or not to send it. For all these reasons, and more, she called. Even though it was a clear breach of the telephonic etiquette that has evolved between them.

She stared at her editing console as the phone rang, wondering whether it was a good idea. The frozen frame of a dreadlocked kid running from a riot policeman filled the screen. She gently pushed at the glass of her eye with a fingertip, centring it, reminding herself of its existence. The phone was picked up, and she heard a sharp cough at the other end, then his ragged breathing came into focus.

'It's Cleo.'

'Hello?'

'It's Cleo.'

He paused. 'Cleo.'

Memories rushed back of why they never spoke in the afternoon.

'How are you?' she said, soldiering on.

'Fine, bar the interruption.'

'How is work?'

'What can I do for you?'

'I was hoping to kick off with some chat. The way people do.'

'It's quite a business for me to get to the telephone.'

'Yes, I know,' she said suppressing the desire to tell him once again about cordless phones.

'You do know I'm on oxygen?'

'Yes, you told me.'

'Well then.'

'Okay,' she said. 'I'll get right to it. The extracts you've been sending me. I just wanted to say that I like them.'

'Extracts?'

'Of the book.'

'But I haven't sent you anything lately.'

'Don't worry, I know you don't want to talk about it.'

'I don't know what you're talking *about*.'

'I just wanted to say thank you. And make sure you were okay. That you didn't want me to come down and see you, or something.'

'You mustn't come down here.'

'I just wanted to make sure you didn't want me there, but couldn't put it into words.'

'No.'

'Okay.'

'Really, don't come here. I'm not at all well.'

'That's exactly why I want to come,' she said, into the dead phone.

After a call like that she should have left it a few days. Eventually some little sonar ping of guilt might resound off his hull, and make him call her back. But today, that didn't seem like enough. She wanted to try and understand the terms of their latest contract renegotiation. So, when she got home, she sat down to call him again.

As the phone rang, she pictured the clanging bell in the hall, an old hospital thing, designed to be heard from a long way off, to alert nurses dealing with patients. She pictured him looking up from his desk, indignant, the pages in front of him instantly more urgent and important. She pictured his face. (A sharp face, with fine features, not much flesh on the bones. Topped by uncontrollably thin red hair that's beholden to the slightest current of air. A face that is prone to looking cornered. The face of someone who is more than capable of lashing out when threatened.) She pictured him sighing and dashing down his pen before pulling himself up and beginning the slow walk to the phone area, which they never bothered changing, like so much else. She pictured him taking his time, in the hope that the caller might have rung off by the time he got there. She stared at her green eyes in the mirror, one real and one false, resenting him for making her feel like this. And the phone just rang and rang.

She drains her vodka, which is diluted with melt water, and is about to refill the glass when she hears a moped outside. Noodles. She gets up, leaning too heavily against the glass table, making it tilt. The doorbell goes, and she grabs her purse before going to the buzzer. When she gives the delivery man a fiver, he grins and produces a red fruit from his satchel.

'For you,' he says.

'What's this?' Cleo hefts it, feeling the weight.

'Pomegranate. When people give me a tip, I am grateful.'

'Thank you.' Cleo notices him looking at her eye and trying to work out what's different about her as she closes the door.

Buoyed by the friendly gesture, she goes to the window to wave at him as he leaves. She sees movement beyond the street lamp outside, but whoever was there is walking in the opposite direction.

3

Roland steps smartly back into darkness as the scene in the window plays out, glancing once behind him to make sure nobody's watching him leave. He covers his tracks more carefully than most. Eats his boiled eggs without shelling them. Grinds and devours the bones of chickens along with their flesh. His cigarette ash is always wiped into the thigh of his trouser, and when a roll-up is finished, either he drops the end into his tea and drains the dregs or he extinguishes the coal on his tongue and swallows the scrap of paper and tobacco that remains. It is self-effacement verging on self-erasure: bodily material is chewed up and swallowed wherever possible, be it picked from his nose, bitten from his nails or scratched from his scalp. He carries all he produces away with him, and leaves nothing behind but the absence of things, and a faint odour of vinegary sweat and smoke. If he could snatch back the breath he has left hanging in the air of this unseasonably cold April night, then he would.

He is reluctant to leave Cleo so soon but it was obvious that there was nothing more to see: she was just getting on with her evening, and his rule is not to stay watching once he has confirmed there is no imminent danger. Leaving her is always hard, but he must think himself into it, or there will be paralysis. She is safe for tonight. Unless someone broke in. Or the delivery guy came back to hurt her. Or her heart – stop.

Keeping tabs on her used to be hard: her early twenties were peripatetic. He would lose her completely from time to time when she moved, and go through the usual fit of worry that she had left town. But he always found her again in the end: a helpful neighbour; a forwarding address.

She's had her hair cut into a bob. It looks good, but she's still thinner than he would like. He could spend his life watching her. He loves the small vanities that only he sees, like the way she checks herself in the mirror before coming outside, sometimes bolstering herself with what look like muttered words of encouragement. But he can't hang around: Victor needs him back at the arches so they can exercise some light persuasion on a crooked insurance broker who's having second thoughts about working for them.

There's another reason to leave, which is that Roland's own instincts unsettle him when he sees anyone new in her vicinity. Just the sight of that delivery boy made his blood flex, and he thought of flying up there and taking the guy apart if he so much as looked at her in a way that Roland didn't like. Roland feels a pang of jealousy at how comfortable he was, chatting away to her.

'Could sort you a better dining table than that, at least,' he says, walking fast to warm up. 'Something with a bit more life in it.' He shakes his head to stop the words. He must stop talking to himself. It gets him noticed.

He can smell the river – mineral mud, saline and kelpy – so he cuts down a side street to take it all in: the silky billow of the water; the angular glass structures of office blocks on the opposite side; the violet and blue of a cold night in the city. Light catches the wake of a boat, two glinting peaks in the ink. He keeps on walking, heading south, into less sanitised territory.

He and Victor operate from a network of arches next to a nightclub, halfway down a tunnel of blackened bricks, under a railway viaduct. As he approaches, he can see the insurance broker standing next to his idling car, suited, nervous, looking at the words on the wall and wondering if he's in the right place. The words are painted in careless white strokes to one side of the metal shutter, under the fierce yellow of a snaking line of halogens:

FURNITURE   FLATS
WANTED   HOUSES
    CLEARED

'Don't worry – you're exactly where you should be,' mutters Roland. 'Bad luck.'

The broker turns and sees him, and there is the usual look of alarm as somebody who has met Roland only briefly before sees him again, and remembers how big he is.

'Chris,' says Roland, bearing down quickly. 'Sorry I'm late. Had to pop out. Get back in the car and I'll open this up for you.'

'I've got my daughter here,' says Chris. 'Is that going to be okay?'

Roland looks into the car and sees a girl of about ten in the passenger seat. School uniform. Long, braided hair. Headphones. She isn't looking at them, but at a pigeon sitting on a ledge above the archway, peering between the fins of a broken ventilation fan. Steam pours from the gap, but the bird can't seem to find the courage to squeeze between the rusty white blades into the warm darkness. She looks as if she's talking to it.

'Of course,' says Roland. 'No problem at all.' He catches the girl's eye, then looks from her back up to the pigeon with his eyebrows raised, as if to say, *Were you just talking to that bird?* She smiles a little bashfully, and waves. He lets his fingers flicker in return, and gives her a nod.

Her father looks nervous. 'You're sure it's okay? She had a thing after school. I had to pick her up.'

Roland touches Chris on his neck, which makes him jump. 'She's got nothing to be afraid of, has she? Just let me open up, and you can drive straight in.'

He produces his key and slots it into the door of the shutter. He steps past Chris, stoops and enters. Through the shutter he can hear him talking to his daughter. 'This won't take long. Don't touch *anything* when we get in there. And don't talk to either of them unless they talk to you.'

Roland grabs the chain, his hands passing one over the other as he heaves, and yellow electric light from outside leaks in as the shutter flies up with a whoosh and a clatter. Chris drives his car up the concrete ramp and brings it to rest in an outer room of large metal containers and warehouse kit: power hose, forklift truck. He turns off the engine, and he and the girl both get out of the car.

It's quite something, this place, when you see it for the first time. Whitewashed brick walls tower up around you and meet in high, dark arches. Ventilation fans rotate lazily in their holes. It smells damp, but the air is kept warm by a giant gas heater in one corner of the room that jets fierce blue flame through a tube. Most seductive are all the doorways leading off this chamber, hinting at all the many others that lie beyond it. He can see the girl's attention starting to wander already.

'Stay away from that,' says Chris, pointing at the heater, so she looks in the opposite direction, towards Roland's beaten-up yellow Transit van that is parked in the shadows. The skirt of the van is uneven where its flanks have corroded.

Hammered into its side is a nail, from which a sign hangs that reads *Golden Sands Guest House*. He can tell she wants to look inside.

'Not there either,' says Roland, making her start. 'That's where I live.'

She stares at him, takes off her headphones, and nods.

In the silence, everyone's attention is drawn towards a scrawny man in a suit who is sitting in the mouth of a big, blue shipping container. The chair is an antique, dark wood with rich red material – and shrink-wrapped to keep it clean. Here is Victor, guarding his domain, enthroned in the gateway to his office, with its juddering metallic echo, its drawers of pointless paper, its dockets and stamps. Expired stuff, all of it – just like him.

'Christopher! How very nice to see you. And who do we have here?' The chair squeaks as Victor resettles himself, giving the new arrivals his full, unnerving attention. He is going bald, which makes him look older than he is, and he's been growing a scratchy, insubstantial beard.

'This is my daughter.'

'Sweet!' says Victor. 'Does she have a name?'

'Molly,' he says. 'She had an after-school thing. I hope—'

'Molly. What a fine name. Nobody's called that any more. Well done you. Your dad and I have a few things to talk about, but you make yourself at home, okay my dear?'

She nods, and looks uncertainly at her father.

'Listen to your music,' he says. 'Don't wander off, okay?'

Roland sees her taking in the metal briefcase at Victor's side, with its two chains leading from the handle – one to his ankle and the other to his wrist. She puts her headphones back on, and turns away, making for the safety of the parked car.

'Now then,' says Victor. 'What can we do for you, Christopher?'

The conversation begins, and Roland can tell already that it isn't going to go well for Chris. He wants out. He can't do the work any more. He's got his family to think of. He points at Molly to corroborate his point.

This is a new departure for him. Until now, Chris has been happy to supply them with information, because he's liked the feeling of being involved in something a bit dodgy. It excites him. Roland imagines him conspiratorially telling colleagues when he's had a few drinks that he *mixes with some pretty hardcore people*, but he can't tell them any more than that, because it would get him into trouble. Then after a couple more drinks, telling them about the softly spoken giant who lives under the arches, and his boss, the creepy man who never gets out of his chair.

High-end policies: the contents of houses. The information he's given them has yielded one or two good things, but it wouldn't be the end of the world if he backed out. Not that Victor is ever going to allow that to happen. When you've got information on Victor, he makes sure you stay on his side. And if you insist, he threatens you. He threatens you with Roland.

Roland keeps one ear on the conversation, in case he has to step in, and watches Molly. She takes her school bag out of the car and picks around in it for a while, looking for something. She takes out a packet of sweets, and leaves the bag on the ground. She skips around near the shutter, one foot then the other, but that quickly gets boring. She can't go near the roaring blue flame, or his van, or the conversation. Which only leaves one corner: the one with a low archway that leads deeper into the tunnels. He watches her, thinking she isn't being watched, glancing briefly over her shoulder, and disappearing. He looks over at Victor, who is calmly hearing the appeal of Chris, the insurance broker. It's getting tearful. Victor catches his eye, and motions for him to follow the girl.

The echoing chatter and the roar of the jet heater fade away. He watches her feeling up the wall until she finds the light switch: a cold metal lump with a downward-facing nub at its centre. She pushes hard on it with her thumb until it snaps up. High overhead, fluorescent tubes in rusty cages hum and flicker into life, and a new universe strobes into view.

In the first room are big metal lockers and heavy-lifting equipment. In the second, towers of rotting cardboard boxes lean and collapse into one another, spilling out wave after wave of paper. The third houses a high stack of computer junk: green-screen monitors; piles of clunky, beige hard drives. The fourth is where it goes mad: layers of dusty furniture in zigzagging angles, heaped and piled in such a way that you could never take it all in at once. And strewn on every available surface, things: hotel desk bells, oxygen masks, iron bedsteads, racks of test tubes, a medical skeleton, nurse's uniforms, clocks, sewing machines, tools, leather suitcases, stacks of steel basins, tables, chairs, golf clubs, a dish of scuffed cricket balls. He stays right behind her, tracking her as she advances, his presence masked by the tinny noise of her music. When she has gone far enough, he puts a hand on her shoulder.

She squeals, turns quickly, and rips off her headphones.

'Sorry,' he says. 'I called you, but you didn't hear me.'

'You frightened me.'

'Sorry.' He looks calmly down at her, letting her take in his face: the unevenly cut hair, the wide nose, the flat, calm mouth. He may have made her jump, but the actual sight of him doesn't seem to scare her, which is unusual. 'You shouldn't be back here. Victor won't like it.'

'What is all this stuff, anyway?'

'Back we go.'

Without thinking she offers up her hand to be led away.

He snatches his arm away from her and pounds off quickly back through the rooms, until the two of them are out front again.

'There she is!' says Victor, from his chair. 'We thought we'd lost you, my darling.'

Chris is looking down at the ground with a set expression in his mouth, trapping his right hand under his left armpit. A length of dirty cloth is wrapped round the hand. He looks furious enough to be on the point of hitting Victor, but at the sound of Roland's return, and the sight of him, his left arm falls back to his side.

'Your dad's cut himself,' says Victor. 'But he's all right, aren't you, Christopher?'

She runs over to him, and he pulls her into a tight, one-armed hug. 'I'm fine. Didn't I tell you not to run off? This place is private.'

'Do you need a plaster?' says Molly.

'Ah,' says Victor. 'That's a good girl you've got there. Looking out for her old man. I'm afraid we seem to have mislaid our first-aid kit, but you get a plaster on it soon my dear, that's a good idea. Did you like exploring back there in my tunnels?'

She nods.

'You want to watch yourself. They go back for miles. Some of them haven't been cleaned out in years. You know about the war, don't you? A bit? When they bombed the city?'

She nods.

'During the war, this whole place would have been stacked floor to ceiling with dead people. Imagine that. The Underground stations and the hospitals – they were all full of people who were *alive*. So places like this were the only places they could store the bodies until they had a chance to bury them. They would have been stacked up in here twenty or thirty high after some of those big air raids.' He lowers his voice. 'You wouldn't want to run into anything like that, now would you?'

She shakes her head. Her father pulls her tighter towards him, and spins her round in the direction of their car. 'We're off,' he says.

'Well, cheers then, Christopher, thanks for coming by,' says Victor. 'Can I offer you any vegetables before you go? We got the lot back here.'

Her father refuses with a shake of the head, staring back at him.

'Okay then. We'll be seeing you soon I hope. Pleasure to meet you, little Molly.'

Chris winces as he pulls the car door shut. As Roland is pulling up the shutter to let them out, he's aware of Molly staring at him through the car window. He turns away quickly to avoid having to look at her again, and steps into his van. The suspension flexes under his weight. Chris grinds his gears, then the car speeds down the ramp and out into the world.

'Come back out here and close this shutter will you? We're chucking tenners out the door with that bloody heater.'

Roland sits on his bed, a foam mattress heaped with packing blankets. He closes his eyes, wishing the conversation with Victor was over before it has begun. He steps outside, grabs the chain and brings down the shutter in smooth, powerful movements. Victor watches, waiting for him to finish. Roland wipes grime from the chain into his shirt and awaits instructions.

'That bloke. What a cheek. Think we persuaded him?'

'You tell me.'

'Oh don't come on all sulky. She was a tough little girl. I was only pulling her leg.'

'Whatever you say.'

'You're a self-righteous fucker, you are. And a hypocrite.'

'Was there anything else?' says Roland, un-looping the power hose from its yellow engine in anticipation of the instruction to clean up.

'Yeah. If he's really going to let us down, you need to scout for some new business.'

'Something always comes up.'

'I hope you're right.'

'Can't blame the guy for wanting to keep his job. Look after his family.'

'Oh, please. We pay him enough. He's just trying it on to get a raise.'

Nobody is allowed a conscience in Victor's world. Everybody acts for the lowest possible motive.

'And what a cheap stunt,' he says. 'Bringing that girl. I've half a mind to report him for child exploitation. Fetch my chair, will you?'

Roland steps past him and into the container-office. He brings out the folded wheelchair, throws it into shape, snaps it together and parallel-parks it next to the throne. Victor waits until Roland has applied the brake, then shifts himself over with strong, practised arms.

Victor has perfected his disguise. The suits, the turns of phrase, the frailty: to those who don't know him he communicates the notion of someone brave and sincere, who might bend a law from time to time, but only because life has dealt him a bad hand. The sort of man you might make yourself feel good by chatting to for an hour on a park bench, or offering a pint to in a pub – being careful at all times to communicate that no pity is involved. The sort of man younger people find endearing because they think he might be an endangered species, and because they can't fathom the idea of a bastard in a wheelchair.

But Roland knows the real Victor. The Victor who, like Roland, sleeps in the back of a van to save money. The

Victor whose briefcase is chained to him in two places to buy time for some last-resort act of violence if anyone should ever make a grab for it. The Victor who smells of vegetables and cologne, and calls people *darling* and *my old love,* including Roland – the most apparent, but not the only, outward manifestation of his broad, pansexual appetites. So far as that department goes, who knows? Victor would do anything. No, that's not quite right. Victor would *watch* anything.

'Give this place a good clean down tonight, will you?' he says.

'I'm already holding the hose. You don't need to tell me to do something when I'm just about to do it.'

'Yeah, but do it properly. We've got that director coming in who likes everything clean.'

Roland sniffs. 'Okay. I'll give it the works.'

Victor sits back in his chair. 'Doesn't quite float your boat, all our filming, does it?'

'You'll have to move if you want me to spray this room down and not get soaked.'

'Do it after I've gone. Let's have a natter.'

Roland sets down the hose and plants himself on a stack of wooden pallets to roll a cigarette.

'I might have a drop of wine.'

Roland nods, slots his cigarette behind his ear and gets up to fetch the bottle.

'Will you join me tonight?' says Victor.

Roland shakes his head. Victor knows he doesn't drink, but every night, he asks this question. It should feel like politeness but somehow it always ends up feeling like a taunt.

'You want to loosen up a bit. You're highly strung. When did a mouthful of wine ever hurt anyone?'

'I don't like the taste, that's all.'

'You and Oliver used to drink everything you could get your hands on.'

'I was younger then.'

Roland hands him the full wine glass carefully. Victor's hand rests on his for a second, cold and bony. 'Come on then. What is it about the filming you hate so much? I haven't noticed this ray of conscience shining in on any of your other dark, inner rooms.' He makes himself laugh.

'It's nothing.'

'You reckon we shouldn't be doing it though, don't you? You don't like that we make money off it.'

What to say? Of course he hates it. He hates every shriek and murmur and holler he hears from inside the van, and the visions they bring. Roland always hides away before the crews arrive, with their arc lights and their cameras, and doesn't come out again until it's over. He'd leave the tunnels altogether during filming if Victor would let him, but he is made to stay in case things need moving. The crews sometimes take advantage of all the stuff lying around back here to give period detail to their work – sideboards, animal heads – though if they want a bed, Victor insists on the use of rubber sheeting. It's Roland's job to mop the place down afterwards, as sweat and condensation run down the whitewashed walls.

Victor sends girls into the van sometimes to see how Roland will react. He pays them to stay unclothed, close the door behind them and flirt with him. Roland looks down at the ground calmly when they come in, at their invariably manicured toenails. Victor's most dangerous trait is his curiosity. For him to ask himself *what if* always works out badly for someone. And life has never told him that there are some things you shouldn't do.

'Your problem,' says Victor, 'is that you've got a stunted attitude towards women. And we all know why that is, don't we?'

Roland stares at the ground, smoking.

'How is she, then?' Victor says. 'I know that's where you were just now, so don't tell me it wasn't.'

'She's fine.'

'Good.' He leans back in his chair, cradling the glass, then something seems to occur to him. 'I saw something the other day you might find amusing.'

'What's that then?'

'Given your objections. The degradation, and so forth.'

'What?'

'Vintage material.'

'What do you mean?'

'Reel-to-reel orgy films from the seventies. Super 8. Very atmospheric.'

'Where did they come from?'

'Doesn't matter. Point is, you want to have a look at them. I think you'd be impressed.'

'How are they any different to what we have now?'

'Let me finish. You're so self-righteous. You always think you know what I'm going to say. It's not the sex I'm talking about. That bit's boring. A lot of hippies fannying about not knowing what they're up to: all sensuous, eyes closed and stuff. Nobody really going for it. No, the bits I love are what comes afterwards. Cause they kept the cameras rolling, see? And what you get afterwards is basically reel after reel of footage of guys crying. No sound at all, but they kept filming them, sobbing away. It's priceless.'

'Why are they crying?'

'You have to imagine the set-up. All these guys have obviously been persuading the girls to come with them and broaden their horizons, and it's the dirty seventies so you should try everything once, right? So of course what happens is that the couples walk in and the lady, even though she's not sure at first, starts to get into it. Then she sticks her arse up in the air like a skunk, and before you know it she's getting looked after by about ten fellas. Meanwhile *he's* all hopeful by himself in the corner waving it round, but nobody's the least bit interested in him, because the guy-to-girl ratio is about ten to one. But he can't complain, right, because coming here was his idea, so he just has to watch as his missus is done from every possible angle by great big seventies blokes with long hair. And that's why they're all so in bits afterwards. It's horrible. Slobber all over the shop. And all the husbands can do is sit in the corner, blubbing to camera. One of the funniest things I've ever seen.'

His laugh is the sound of a wind-up toy going mad. It inflames the high spots of red on his cheeks, and returns in fresh waves when you least expect it.

'What?' he says, when Roland doesn't join in. 'Why are you looking at me like that? I'd have thought that story was made for you. All your crusading for the girls.'

'I think you're missing the point.'

Victor shrugs. 'No pleasing some people.'

'Is that everything?'

'No. While you're wrestling with your conscience – we're short on cash. You need to get out there and see what you can pick up.'

'Fine,' says Roland. 'Tell you what: I think I'll do that right now.'

He pulls on his coat and lets himself out into the night.

4

Imagine how it must have felt to be locked up in a place like this. The justified fear of what you have to surrender. And I'm not even talking about the kind of struggling, shackled arrival of the popular imagination – straitjackets and syringes and all that. No. Let's imagine that this is a voluntary committal. That you are coming in because you think, or have been told, that a stay here will do you some good. To make it simple, let's also assume that you don't have an acute condition. Perhaps you are simply one of those people who is not at home in life. Unhappy with the narrow scope of what is expected of you. Suffering from what, in a previous age, might have been written up in the admittance log as Disappointed Expectations.

Maybe you're a young woman with nothing in her future but marriage to a local boy and a life of homemaking. The prospect depresses you. You are subject to panic attacks. You find yourself having dark, even suicidal thoughts. Rashly, you tell a doctor how you're feeling, and, as calmly as he might prescribe a course of throat lozenges, he suggests a short rest up here to calm you down. A week or so. No more.

Even though you're coming here by choice, it is an approach that makes you wonder what you have let yourself in for. The car passes between tall gateposts topped with sneering griffins, and you see the blunt red water tower rising up ahead. In the rear-view mirror, a porter is closing the gates and securing them with chains. The long, gravelled driveway sucks you in round a laurel chicane, with occasional windows on lawns, benches and pavilions. Some of the more harmless chronics are working the garden in their blue overalls. Others, less applicable to work, pursue their own personal agendas of muttering and shuffling. The perimeter fence is sunk into a ditch, which gives the impression from a distance that the patients you can see wandering around are voluntarily following some kind of prearranged pattern.

The brooding walls are visible in flashes as you pelt up the main driveway, suggestive of something so immense that it can never be seen in its entirety. The building thus takes on the scale of something show-stopping: the enemy mothership; the final-act monster. And now here it is, banking up before you: a high, wide abstraction of brickwork and glass. The car stops, and whoever has driven (because however placidly you came, you did not drive yourself) gives it a minute after turning off the engine before opening the door. To give the idea of the place time to settle. Then the doors are open, and the car is full of Wreaking air, a sharp compound of manure and woodsmoke and brine. Gulls kick up fuss overhead. Your first, hesitant step rolls a little on the gravel. And out you get, to see what you're dealing with.

The wings are two tentacular limbs, multi-jointed and unending. One male, one female. Down the middle, there is a central nervous system of offices and secretaries, of superintendents and visiting rooms, of laundries and workshops. But you can't see any of that from here: the pomp of the admittance block is performing its work on you. Planting and nurturing the thought that this place is formidable. Trustworthy. You look up the redbrick walls at rows of high, sash windows, noticing that none of the first-floor ones is

43

open. A fat gull stares from a roof gable with an expression that seems to say, What were you thinking? But it's too late now. They're walking you towards the front door.

A cupola throws a well of light on to the marbled lobby. Footsteps echo from distant corridors. You are taken to a reception desk recessed into the wall between a pair of dusty aspidistras. An admissions secretary nods curtly as your paperwork is completed. The wings branch off on either side. And it is here that you reach your first locked door. Which way you turn depends on sex. Left for women, right for men.

The journey to your ward might take time. Try not to let the cumulative effects of corridors and wards and colour-coded walls heighten your anxiety. Try not to be unnerved by any violent shouting or unpleasant odours. You might get glimpses of other wards, for different diagnoses. Acute. Chronic. Epileptics, at one time.

In general, the ground floor of each wing is for day patients and other low-risk inmates, and the first floor is secure. The ground-floor windows might be opened in the summer, but never the first floor. No matter how fugged up the air of the first floor gets with shit or stale bed linen or bad food, that lot have to make do with the view.

The view is the thing that's supposed to calm everybody down. The gardens, the marshes. Some days you can see the Ness describing its lonely arc all the way out to nowhere. Other days the mist drops over it like a theatrical curtain. Around it, visible from every rear-facing day-room window, lies the sea. What could be better? The sea, blazing there on the horizon! Everything about the topography of this place suggests to your troubled mind that now you are through that prim, evergreen tunnel of a drive, all will be well. The view screams liberty in your face even as doors are quietly locked by those who brought you in as they retreat, and your

possessions are boxed away in some storeroom. Just in case
it should take a little longer to settle you down.

You tell yourself to relax. This will do you good. It's neces-
sary. You will leave here a new person, and the thing to do
now is just let them do their job. And as if on cue, you realise
that a nurse is standing beside your chair, bearing a little
paper cup and a fresh glass of water.

Wings have been beating in intermittent, frantic bursts above
his head for at least ten minutes. The sound's insistence has
elevated it from dream-fuel to disturbance, and his curiosity
to find out what's causing it is steadily pulling him from
sleep. But he's too much of an old hand to make sudden
movements, or open his eyes, until he has remembered where
he's been sleeping. Picture it first, then look: surprise can
bring coughing fits, and he needs to be sure not only of
where he is, but of where he left the oxygen.

There it goes again: spasms of fluttering, as if a bird were
trying to take off, but can't because of some hindrance. As if
one of its legs were trapped. He opens an eye. A green door is
ajar, leading out on to some blue cobblestones at the back of
Revenant House. He remembers: he came in here after his
conversation with Cleo simply because he hadn't looked in here
for ages, and couldn't remember what the room contained. He
found a stack of horsehair mattresses that were chucked out a
long time ago and forgotten here. He pulled a couple out from
the middle, put his coat over himself, and lay down, with his
oxygen cylinder and a flat pint of whisky. Curious decision.

The pigeon is perched on the green painted door, looking
straight down at him. As he watches, it flaps its wings again,
sending dust into the air. He shifts on the mattress heap and
the pages to his side crumple and rustle.

'Go away.' He makes a pathetic shooing gesture with his
hand.

Speaking is a mistake. The fit buckles him, and he can tell it will be a bad one, because he's been drinking, and he's slept through the afternoon on a pile of damp mattresses in a fucking *shed*, so what do you expect, but there we go, it's happening now. The panic as he can't find the air. The uncontrollable noises. Every lung-shudder hurls out another gobbet of phlegm that rattles into his mouth, sweet and cloying, and mixes with whisky afterburn and bitter bile, and wouldn't it be terrific to cap this one off with a vomiting spell too, let's go for that, maybe scare up some blood while we're at it.

He coughs until he is dizzy, almost high. Until there are sparkling black shapes behind his eyelids. Until he thinks, once again, that he will die. He hears the phone ringing inside. He hears himself muttering the word *God*. The fit runs its terrible course, then he leans back and tries to concentrate only on his breathing. If he can do that, it might just calm down. But his inhalations are running into the sand, making his lungs clench with fear. Each breath feels like it is getting stuck somewhere, arrested by the fungus.

No, more than that – actually it feels as if the inhalations are somehow *feeding* the fungus. Substantiating it, in the way that breath is supposed to freeze solid in Arctic air. It goes against the science of what he knows is happening, but he pictures it anyway. The image makes him feel nauseous, makes his heart pound and his vision bruise. He reaches around him for the oxygen tube, which he knows must be there somewhere, trying not to panic, knowing he will find it eventually, but fumbling nonetheless. Desperate spittle froths at the corners of his mouth.

He reaches into his pocket for a handkerchief. (He is in the habit of carrying a billowing pocket square with him wherever he goes – not just to cough into, but also to hide his face in should he see anyone in the street he wants to avoid.) The smell and feel of cool silk are calming enough to make his search more methodical.

He finds the tube, fumbles it into place and reaches for the tap of the cylinder to turn it. But there's something wrong. The tap won't turn the way he knows that it turns to send the oxygen down the tube. And he knows it just before he knows it properly, as his synapses light up with the bad news – he knows that this is because he left the tap open all afternoon, that he fell asleep here with the tube on, and that at some point, either before or after the oxygen ran out, he knocked the tube away from his face. Now he has to try not to panic, and work out what to do. Or this could really be it. He lies still, rehearsing his next move, calculating the distance to the day room where the respirator is.

Brisk footsteps on the cobbles, and a voice calling his name: Carol. Thank God for Carol.

'In here,' he manages, taking in a lungful of dust. He starts coughing again, and bends over the mattress, hacking, his body involuntarily trying to dislodge something. A shout and a sudden liquid sound indicate success.

The footsteps stop. 'In there?'

The pigeon decides on a proper exit, and with a high whistling of wings, is gone. A shadow falls over the doorway.

'Oh dear, look at him now,' says Carol. He can feel her taking it all in: the cylinder, the pages, the empty bottle, the stained dressing gown.

'Good evening,' he murmurs, which leads him into another bucking, painful round of coughing.

'Golly. I thought we'd lost you there for a minute.'

'That would save us all a lot of bother, wouldn't it?'

'Wouldn't it just,' she says. 'Though I expect I'd have to pick up the pieces.'

'Don't worry about it,' he says. 'Help me get to the machine, and we'll have a drink.'

'I'm serious. You mustn't go disappearing like that. There'd be no end of trouble for me if you went and died on my watch.' She puts a hand under his armpit and strains with the weight of getting him up, grabbing his pages from the mattress with her free hand. 'Come on – I can't lift you by myself. I'm too old.'

He smells a fresh, floral scent on her, and inhales deeply. 'If I knew you were coming I'd have baked a cake,' he says.

She settles him at the kitchen table, and brings in his respirator from the study. He sits, chin to chest, recovering, taking deep draughts of the cooling air of the machine. Thud, tap, hiss. She makes tea, and disapproves.

'It's not far off tipping,' she says. 'From looking like some-where somebody lives to looking like somewhere somebody died. A while ago.'

'Stop tidying. I like it like this.'

She picks with a forefinger at the line of drying-out tea bags in the window. 'Is there a system here? How many times do you reuse these things?'

'Please sit down.'

She sits opposite him with her cup, setting the crumpled pages he's been sleeping on to one side. She reaches into her bag and takes out a small brown bottle. She taps out a pale yellow pill. She daintily picks it from the palm of her left hand and places it at the back of her throat, dry-swallowing, then chasing it with a mouthful of tea.

He puts a palm on hers. 'If something happens to me, it won't be your fault.'

'That's not what I'm worried about. I just don't want to go drawing any unwelcome attention to myself.'

'Oh.' He takes back his hand. 'I see. Well, I wouldn't worry about that.'

'I do worry about it. They could sling me in jail.'

Scriven is one of a handful of people in the town who

know Carol by her real name. To most, she is Mona. The name goes with her job, and it was available – the real Mona hasn't been using it for some time. Just occasionally, however, the fact that what Carol is doing is illegal gets on top of her, and she worries about being found out.

She puts down her cup, and looks away. 'You've got to change this. You can't stay living here. It's not hygienic.'

'You know,' he says, his breathing getting more agitated. 'That that. Conversation. Is off. Limits.'

'If I had any sense I'd have called Cleo long ago to tell her how you really live.'

'Don't let's. Argue. Let's talk about. Something else.'

'Okay,' she says. She looks down for the first time at the pages on the table. 'What's this?'

'Don't read it now,' he snaps. 'Sorry. I don't mean to be bad-tempered. I think I'm hungry.'

She is no longer conversing. He watches her eyes skipping from side to side, and spaces out his breaths to try and keep hold of them.

'This is about me, isn't it?' she says. 'You're imagining what it was like for me, arriving.'

'Not just you – for any number of patients being admitted.'

'It's too clear,' she says. 'It would have been more confusing for many of them. And frightening. They arrived in a terrible state, most of the time.'

He sighs. 'You write it then.'

She reaches into her bag. 'I've got something for you to read, too.'

'What is it?'

'Don't hold your breath, it's nothing exciting.'

He smiles. 'Are you taking the piss?'

'Just why I brought it. Now, what else do you want me to see to before I go?'

She bustles around: gets eggs in from outside; tidies away

the crockery, and tries to throw away some of the more ancient tea bags in the windowsill. Eventually, she leaves. He hears her going to the front door, and her little blue Renault 5 starts up and zips down the drive. She is long gone before he realises he should have asked her for his pages back. She can't just go walking off with them whenever she wants to.

5

How are you supposed to eat a pomegranate, anyway? Its halves sit bleeding into the crumpled foil tub her noodles came in. She has periodically explored it with her fork over the course of the meal, but the fruit remains basically undisturbed.

She catches sight of herself in the mirror. She is holding her drink to her eye as she watches television. She does this often. To her it is a perfectly natural, cooling place to rest the glass, but like many unthinking habits to do with the eye, this tends to unnerve other people and must only be done in private. The same goes for scratching accumulated salt from its surface with a fingernail, or casually repositioning it with her thumb.

For years, after she made the decision to leave him, there was nothing. Then contact was tentatively re-established, and she started going down to Wreaking at weekends to see him – an experience which, she suspects, always tended to make both of them feel worse rather than better. These semi-regular phone calls are a recent development in a very slow process.

There has even been talk of reviving an ancient ritual – the trip the two of them used to make every year to the patch of ground where her mother's ashes are scattered.

She can just picture them, meeting dutifully, staring side by side at the relevant area, then putting themselves through an excruciating lunch at a bad country pub, facing the uncomfortable truth that her mother is probably the one thing they have in common. And she's been gone for some time.

The site is pleasant enough: a riverbank outside a small Midlands town where he says he and her mother once had a picnic, not long after they met. Cleo is still able to conjure guilt from her earliest memory of being taken there. She remembers him almost having to drag her out of the car because it was so cold and wet, and she wanted to stay on the back seat watching raindrops slip down the window because she had a bet with herself about which one would reach the bottom first. Then when he got her outside, she remembers wondering why she was being made to stand around in this random place, stared at by anglers on the opposite bank. The sun must have cut through, because she can remember crisp shadows on the riverbank in spite of the rain. And then she remembers looking up and seeing that he was crying, and staring into the middle distance, and so she tried to stare ahead in the same way until it was time to go.

Somehow he managed to explain to her what they were doing there without making the information too upsetting. He must have done it well, because Cleo can remember understanding quite calmly that her mother had been an unhappy person, but was less unhappy for being in this location.

It has fascinated friends and lovers over the years that she should have an estranged parent, but she had allowed time to do its burying work and was able to forget. Paying him a visit was just something she had to get out of the way from time to time. But then these phone calls began. And before long, their new rules of conduct had brought them a fragile peace, and even a kind of mutual dependency.

Her imagination is not the kidnapper it once was. Age and experience have diminished its power. But that same immersive concentration that was its engine is still in use today, powering her memory. That one unanswered call has lit her up with alarm, and she knows, as if she had cued it up in her editing booth at work, that a highlights package of their best and worst calls will now play out in her head for the rest of the evening. This is how she frets.

That very first call, one Saturday evening just after she moved in here. Cleo had finally accumulated the money for a deposit, and not on just any old place, but this precious one-bed box in a riverside warehouse towards Rotherhithe. Her days of six-month leases and begged-for portions of friends' floors were over. House-proud, she had some cards printed, and sent one to him at Revenant House without even thinking. Three days later, her phone rang.

'It's me.'

'Who?'

'It's Jasper Scriven.'

She jammed the phone to her ear and left her boyfriend of the time, a functioning addict called Nat, browsing little plastic bags, setting out the evening's entertainment on the kitchen counter.

'For God's sake. You can call yourself Dad.'

'I wasn't sure if it was you. Do you know we haven't spoken for nearly a year?' He sounded bemused by the fact.

She shut the bedroom door behind her and left the lights off, to enjoy the water outside. 'You got my change of address card then.'

'Yes. Not that I knew where you were before.'

She scratched her head with tetchy fingers. 'Of course you did. How else did you know where to reach me?'

'I had a number. Nothing more.'

She closed her eyes, and pressed her forehead to the cold window, relishing the pressure. 'Seriously. Why are you calling?'

'I thought we might try to . . . *reconnect*.'

'Where did you learn that expression?'

'It was on the radio.'

And that was enough to get a laugh, or at least a smile, from both of them.

'So shall we speak a bit more from now on?' he said, audibly bolstered by having amused her.

'Yes,' she replied, and stayed in the dark room alone after the call, holding the phone, wanting the feeling all to herself.

He might as well have been resurrected from the dead. This was what she had to explain to Nat, who was hurt that it had taken her over a year to get round to revealing – and then only because she had to – that the people she referred to as her parents had only fostered her, and her real father was living in part of a derelict psychiatric hospital on the coast.

Whether to make up for the hurt or out of relief at finally being forced to talk to someone, during the late night that ensued she told Nat things she had never told anyone. The two of them were still on an upswing at this point, and defined by a mutually encouraged taste for abandon. And on that particular night, in the intensity of striking out for each other, in the fire of their own collision, they talked.

Possibly she did it in the knowledge that she wouldn't have to account for it later. That what she said could be put down to a familiar kind of narco-melodrama, and might not even be remembered by him the next day. Because let's face it, there were a lot of nights back then of which she remembers very little.

She was never as honest with Nat on subsequent occasions as she was on that night. Later, she told him different stories, which had the effect of diluting the first one and leaving him with a range of possibilities to believe in.

'Have I ever told you the story of how I lost my eye?' she would say.

'I think you have, yes.'

'Ah, but I mean the *real* story.'

And out it would come, the latest version. Her stories would always include some component of the truth, but she dealt him a fresh deck every time, like a croupier. Even so, she never forgot how much disconcerting truth her father's first call had elicited from her. Certain things were closer to the surface than she liked to imagine.

The next call, which she decided to initiate, went less well.

'What are you calling me again for?' he said. 'We spoke the day before yesterday.'

'I thought we were going to reconnect.'

'We don't have to speak to each other every *day*, though.'

But they had spoken again, quite soon after that. And through trial and error had worked out ways of having conversations that left them both feeling better, not worse. He lamented the state of his flowerbeds. She told him about her job. He joked about the things that were happening to him now that he was getting old, but even though he said once or twice that she would *not even recognise me now*, her invitations to go down there seemed to have dried up, and she learned that if she steered a conversation in that direction it was terminated quickly.

'There's a throb now, when I breathe,' he said one morning, when he called her just as she was leaving for work. 'It's *frictive*. I haven't taken a clean breath in I don't know how long.'

'You should see somebody about that. See the doctor.'

'They can't do anything. I asked. It's just stuff building up. You should hear some of the coughing fits when I go up and down stairs.'

'Living where you live probably doesn't help. All the damp in there. Mould, too, I expect.'

'You have no idea.'

'So why don't you move?'

Silence. The temptation, always short-lived, to imagine that he is not stitched into that building, and could live elsewhere, with anyone but his ghosts.

She had heard the coughing. It interrupted their conversations sometimes. Each bark and shout seemed to be an attempt at finality, at stopping the coughing for good. But there was always another cough after that.

'How about some better central heating?' she said. 'Wouldn't that help, at least?'

'I'll tell you what it sounds like: snap, crackle and pop. Do you remember? On your Rice Krispies? That sound comes out of my lungs all the time.'

'It's not like you to reminisce,' she said, unsettled by the reference to her childhood. 'Maybe you should go back to sleep. It's only eight in the morning. What have you got to be up for?'

'Waste of time,' he snapped. 'Work to be done.' But she could hear him perking up because of her willingness to spar with him, and, however briefly, wanting to make something of the conversation other than an end to it.

'I have been falling asleep in some funny places lately,' he said. She could hear him making himself smile.

'Like where?'

'Let's just say that I've been using my imagination. Carol can't believe where I end up sometimes.'

'You're still friends with Carol? How is she?'

'Fine. She comes up here from time to time to check on me, and make sure I'm taking my pills.' His textured breathing lurched into a cough.

'What pills?'

'It doesn't matter. I'm fine.'

'Dad.'

'Goodbye.'

If he didn't want her to probe him about the pills, why mention them, or his sleeping patterns? And now there is this new revelation, about the Prozac. Is Carol getting him the Prozac? What is he trying to communicate with all this stuff? Is it self-pity, or something more familiar – his old urge to present her with the facts, in all their cold reality?

One afternoon, when she was fifteen, he made her hold his ladder while he climbed the Revenant House clock tower. She stood obediently at the base, gripping a rung and fearing the responsibility.

'Catch,' he said, but he'd already dropped it, and the pigeon egg shot down right past her, too late to catch, although she got a finger to it as her hands flew up off the ladder, just before the wet crack as it hit the ground. She glanced at the yolk bleeding on to the cobbles, and grasped the ladder again, shocked at her own dereliction of duty.

'Ready this time?' The noise of the pigeons up there seemed to be intensifying, as if they knew what he was up to, as if word was spreading. 'Don't let go for too long, or I'll fall.'

Just as he said this he dropped another, which she was ready for, but it smashed in her hands, soaking them with slime. She called up to him, asking why he was doing it, trying not to sound as upset as she was, but all she heard was laughter and the sound of more pigeon eggs landing all around her.

★

A fresh drink, and more trusty television. There's a film on, but she isn't following it. She's staring at her phone, willing that still unfamiliar number to flash up on the screen. She pictures him sitting in the corner of one of those peeling rooms, and the impulse taking him, to dial her number. What freak chemical cocktail shoots through his brain and makes him decide to call? She should pay some mad scientist to synthesise it and get it put in his water.

But then there are the bad calls. Like the one she can't get out of her head. Only a month ago. A new kind of call. She knew immediately it was him, even though there was only laboured breathing coming down the line and no voice to begin with.

'What's wrong?' she said.

'I'm having. Trouble breathing. They say. It's some sort of fungus. In my lungs. Maybe from all those. Roofing materials we ripped out. Anyway. It's taken away. All my puff. I can't do. Long sentences. Any more. Or move around. Very much.'

'What can they do about it?'

'Nothing except. Put me on oxygen. For when it gets bad.'

'Oh dear.'

'They're delivering. The machine. This afternoon.'

'I'll be right down.'

'Don't even. Think about it.'

The phone was put down. Later, she mentally replayed it all and realised he had just told her how he was going to die.

Since then there have been breathless messages on her machine. Coughing, a hasty replacing of the receiver. Then, one of the worst ones. One of the last they had when she actually tried to challenge him on anything.

'Why should we speak more now just because I'm dying soon?'

'What?' she said, hating the smile in his voice. The readiness to fight.

'You seem to want us to speak more often because we know I'm dying sooner rather than later. Why?'

'What do you mean, why?'

'You don't need anything from me. And if we didn't know I was going to die soon, we wouldn't be speaking any more than we ever have. Maybe we wouldn't be speaking at all.'

'I know you're just saying this to be contrary.'

'I'm not. I actually think it might be less painful than trying to understand each other at this point.'

She tried not to let the tears come, but it was impossible. She was damned if she was going to let him hear her cry, though.

'But we might have things to say to each other,' she said. 'And those things we want to say might feel a bit more urgent now that we know that one of us might not be around for much longer.'

'If you ask me, that only really applies to you. Because, as you say, I'm not going to be around much longer. So you tell me: what do you want to say?'

She sniffed, trying to control her breathing. Blood filled her head.

'I'm perfectly serious, Cleo: what do you want to say to me? Ask me anything you want.'

She couldn't have said anything at this point even if she'd wanted to.

'You see?' he said into the silence, his breathing triumphantly unimpeded. 'All this wanting to make ourselves feel better. It's just . . . vanity.'

And this time it was she who put down the phone.

What, then, to do with the time? Soon there will be none of it left, and they will not have filled what they had with any great coming together. They know this but still they do nothing. And her worst fear is that maybe he's right. Maybe there is nothing they should be doing with the time but letting it elapse.

Her eyes alight on the pomegranate, which is still just sitting there. She grabs the half-cut fruit and squeezes, letting red juice run down her hand. When she lets go, it springs misshapen from her palm, shedding its mean little bullets on the table. She picks up both halves and dumps them in the bin, along with his pages, and pads off for a shower.

6

Roland advances quickly, with no wasted movement, looking in basements for unlocked windows, laptops on display, anything simple and costly and available. The pavements are largely empty, but a solitary woman walking up ahead gives him pause. He hangs back for a while so she won't fear he's bearing down on her, then thinks again, speeds up and overtakes. This might have caused her some anxiety – he thinks he hears her breathing quickening a little as he passes – but it's done now, and he can get on.

The tunnels enable him to avoid much of society, but he wonders sometimes about how he must come across to others, out here in the world. He suspects he is seen for what he is, which is someone stuck in one moment, whose life has left him stranded. A huge, mumbling character in a donkey jacket who busts past people on the pavement, having powerful, combative discussions with himself as he walks. He might as well have the word *AVOID* tattooed on his forehead.

He prowls one of the new residential docks with its polished glass boxes, its sheet-metal units, its sustainable wood flushing. These see-through hives have co-opted and erased the warehouses and factories they replaced, with all their damp and mould and vermin. But rats still own the riverside. They're just as happy among gleaming steel ducts and chipboard electrical cupboards as they were among lime-flaked walls and networks of lead plumbing.

The workers who come home to these buildings don't venture outside unless they have to. Roland watches them from the pavement, soaking in the blue wash of television. They order delivered food and put their feet up. They exhibit themselves to passers-by: their lives, their lamps, their empty shelves. For this lot, the future is dated. Now that everything is possible, there is nothing left to yearn for, so nobody does anything at all. The wave has passed, leaving this: flickering boxes; blank, glowing walls. This version of the end of the world doesn't come with any lively savagery or fire in the streets – only a kind of neutering, a death of desire.

But the old is still there, if you look. Lift the right stone, and the eyes of the old are there, pearl-bright in the grime, meeting your stare, unblinking. Roland loves the old so much that he will sometimes come to himself in the tunnels, touching something, trying to channel its history. He is at an advantage as a thief because he genuinely craves the things he is sent to steal.

With the past in mind he takes a detour past the Boar's Head Cemetery, a death pit uncovered during an extension to the Underground: commuter trains running into piles of prostitutes and plague victims, too damned and too many to be buried in consecrated ground. On the fence, people have affixed ribbons and prayers, many of them laminated against the weather, in memory of those whose bones are packed down there somewhere, while legal action proceeds in a room somewhere to determine whether the yellow diggers stopped nearby can be allowed to resume their work. There was a similar debate about the cemetery at Wreaking when it was thought someone might acquire the hospital for redevelopment. Then nobody bothered, so all the numbered patient graves were left undisturbed. Roland stops to read some of the messages: *In Memory Of All Who Lie In The Hoar's Bed*, reads one. Most of the messages are a bit tongue in cheek like that. Written by people who think the past is a theme park.

He is beginning to realise how tired he is, and is just on the verge of giving up for the night, when he spots the torched bag. Even from a few feet away it looks more like rubbish than a possession: something to walk past, an over-looked item lying crumpled near the edge of a yellow puddle of street light. But some echo of its former life speaks to him, pleading for it to be clocked as a thing of value.

He crosses the pavement and budges the charred shape with the toe of his boot. It looks to have been a man's leather satchel. It creaks and crumbles. It has been rained on, and it smells of ashes, but it's more resistant than he expected. He toes open the aperture. The pages of scorched notebooks creak open inside, on which Roland can make out hand-written notes and figures. A pack of business cards protrudes from a dedicated pocket. A fat stainless steel pen glints stub-bornly, hanging from what remains of a leather loop. He takes out one of the business cards and looks at the name. He carefully extracts one of the burnt notebooks, and there he finds it: a home address.

'Something always turns up,' he says, taking out his mobile, then thinking again and heading for a phone box.

You could get nostalgic about the utility of these things: no tiny buttons to diddle, no screens to squint at. Just a tough, black handle that bananas usefully around the face, large enough to be patient with the biggest, most fumbling hands. He unhooks it and punches in the number.

'Jonny Finer.'

'Mr Finer? Good evening, sir – I think I've found your bag.'

'Have you? Jesus. Er, thank you. Where was it?'

Roland tells him the name of the street.

'Round the corner from where they took it. I was having a drink, looked down and it was gone. Thank you for taking the trouble to call.'

'No trouble. It's not all good news, though – the bag's been torched. Burnt up pretty badly. Lighter fluid, or something.'

'Is there anything left?'

'I don't know what was in it before, but there are one or two things. Your house keys are here.' Roland flicks them round his index finger, being careful not to touch any glass surface of the phone box.

'That's something, I was going to change the locks. Do you know how much these people charge?'

They make an appointment for nine the next morning. And for tonight, Roland's work is done.

Victor's van is parked in shadow, down one of the side streets at the end of the tunnel. Against Roland's advice, he never sleeps under the arches himself. He says it's because he doesn't trust Roland. It amuses Roland to think that Victor imagines sleeping in a van could protect him if Roland wanted to cause him harm. Roland could go in there any time he wanted and stop his windpipe, and nobody would notice he'd gone.

Clubbers are beginning to assemble outside the archway next door, from which music is already pumping. It looks like a big night is on the cards. Roland moves quickly through the crowd, sensing eyes on him. He meets the gaze of three of them as he passes, all of whom look down and away immediately, knowing trouble when they see it. He knew it was hoping for too much to think that Victor might have already put himself to bed, and sure enough Roland returns to the arches to find Victor's shipping container awash with the wine-glass light of old film.

'You're back! Come in here – I've got something to show you.' His voice is clogged with booze.

'I'm fine out here.'

'Come on! You might like it.'

'No.'

'How did you get on, anyway?'

'There might be something,' he calls, opening the cab of his van and setting the burned bag on the passenger seat. 'I've got an appointment in the morning.'

'Good lad. Come and give me a hand, will you? I'm all fucked in here.' Roland closes his eyes, and leans heavily against the side of the van. 'Don't be such a prude! I'm turning off the projector. Okay?'

'Okay. I'm on my way.'

The atmosphere in the container is hot and damp, and it stinks of spilled wine. Victor is leaning back in his chair, and seems to be messing with the zip of his trousers. There's a smash as he knocks over the wine glass. 'Fuck.'

Roland turns on the desk lamp. 'Don't worry, I'll fix it in the morning. I'd do it now if you left this place unlocked.'

'Nice try, big boy,' says Victor, making himself laugh. 'No way I'm ever leaving you alone in here. This is the nerve centre. The *mothership*. Bollocks, I'm spinning. Get me out of here, will you?'

'Why don't you just stay in here tonight? You'll be warmer.'

'No fear,' says Victor. 'I like my own space, thank you very much. And there's no telling what you get up to in here of an evening when I'm gone.'

The wheels of the chair crunch on broken glass as Roland edges him backwards into the arches. His breathing is uneven.

'You'll go round, will you? Pop a rat or two.'

'Course I will.'

'I'm very lucky to have you. I do know that.'

'Going to get all sentimental now, are we?'

'Fuck off.' Victor padlocks the container messily, pockets the key and scoops the briefcase up to his lap. 'You know what I heard this week? Apparently there's a gang going round mugging women by throwing a rat in their faces. They get it all wound up, and hold it in a bucket of water for a couple or three minutes, then they chuck it at people and they scream and drop their bags on the floor. Can you believe that?' He gives a wistful chuckle. 'You're quite right to watch over her. It's a nasty old world.'

Roland opens the door in the shutter, and night air and club noise blast in again. He places Victor on the packing crate they leave outside the door. He folds up the wheelchair, which is a stupidly difficult thing to manoeuvre – the giant, bastard offspring of an accordion and an umbrella. Victor winces as Roland carries the chair across the threshold and shakes it down into shape. 'Bloody hell, that's chilly, coming out here. Like being *born*, coming out here.'

'Night then,' says Roland, settling him back into the chair. 'Don't pitch over on your way home.'

Victor's briefcase chain makes light metallic chatter on the metal of the doorframe. 'You want to worry about yourself a little more, not me. And stop fretting about that girl. She can look after herself.'

'I know that,' says Roland.

'She's had to, hasn't she? Everybody's let her down, that one.'

Roland gives the chair a shove, and sends Victor out into the night. When he's sure that Victor has made it safely past the club entrance, he brings down the shutter, and its deafening noise diminishing into all those damp, hidden chambers means that he gets what he has been craving: the sealed, church-quiet of the tunnels, blanketing him; the air, settling. He fires up the power hose, and the hum of its engine fills the silence. He leaves the jet heater on as he sprays down the room, so that the fine mist converts quickly to steam, and he is surrounded by water jets and indoor rainbows and vapours of cold and hot water, and can scour away the muck of Victor and his words for another night.

When do you make the transition from being a boy to being someone like Victor? Roland has known him, or been aware of him, most of his life, and he still has no idea how it happened. It was Oliver's idea to start working for him, of course. Oliver idolised his half-brother, in spite of the fact that even the father they had in common said that Victor was no good. Finding Victor and becoming his apprentice became their obsession after the accident. Roland allowed Oliver to persuade him that it was the only logical thing they could do. It took Oliver time to track him down – and when Oliver finally did, he returned with the news that Victor was now in a wheelchair, that he didn't like to talk about it, and that he had work for them if they were up to it.

He wasn't yet under the arches then, and wouldn't be for some time. But he already had plenty going on. Had a gig picking up Scottish newspapers from the overnight train first thing in the morning, and using his delivery route as a spine from which to hang a string of dirty deeds. Dropping off, picking up. Restaurants and clubs. Groceries and meat. Never drugs, because it *got you mixed up with people who can't take a joke*. This dark pronouncement was as much of a clue as they were ever going to get as to how he'd ended up in the chair, and it was probably all they needed.

Victor is always the enabler, and he always makes a profit. Roland would love to know how much cash he keeps in that briefcase alone, before you consider the accumulated worth of all the junk down here. Then there are all the other areas of his business. He is the proprietor of two market stalls, a snack van and a climbing wall. He also does archive storage, nightclub security, and a car valet service staffed by gruff, industrious Poles. Roland is never sure what the arrangement is – who Victor leases from, whether anyone even knows he is here. It's a labyrinth in plain sight: you can enter in one place and come up in any one of five different streets in the area. You emerge, blinking, among scurrying suits who pound the pavements sucking at tubes of coffee as if they were baby bottles, and know no better.

When all this got definitive, he doesn't know. But it's got momentum now, and it won't stop just because it happens to have gone too far. Roland has become the janitor of all the acquired mass back here. And the fact that it has turned out that he doesn't mind knocking people about suits Victor fine too. He never knows what he will find when he opens the door of his van in the morning: lights being erected; the piercing beep of reversing lorries; a rack of carcasses to be hung in the chiller. Victor can get you anything from a church lectern to a high-end camera to a baron of beef, and with Roland on his side, he's formidable.

Victor's our way in. That was what Oliver said. *We just use him to get started. We eat in from underneath, and before you know it we'll be living in the guts.* And of course, Roland followed him. If Oliver was around now, he'd have a plan to get them out of here. But Oliver isn't around. And is unlikely to be around again anytime soon.

Oliver. The state he was in when they came here. He had been impetuous enough before Cleo's accident. In its aftermath, he became unstoppable. Whatever safety measures had been in place before had been permanently removed, and there seemed to be nothing for it but to watch him burn. It was only a matter of time before he got himself into serious trouble.

When the hose is stowed, Roland enters his van and closes the door behind him. He twists himself around to make a well in the rag-heap of his bed. He lights a stub of candle stuck into the knot hole of an overturned wine box and sits, waiting for the van to steady itself on its springs. He spoons tea leaves from a tin, drops them into a saucepan of water and ignites the gas ring's tiny blue tongues. He sits back, concentrating on his breathing as the water heats up. He smokes, ashing on his thigh and rubbing it in with the flat of his palm.

On a small ledge near the flimsy orange curtain that shields his sleeping area from the cab of the van is a small dish of cherry tomatoes. He balances the dish on his lap and eats them one by one as he smokes, even the ones with grinning seams of soft grey mould. Some are sweet and some of them, the rotten ones, are bitter. He stops looking down as he eats so that it's at least a surprise, which is which.

He shifts, trying to get comfortable. Trying to relax. But he can't shake Victor's words. And now it comes to him, in the fug of the van, the steaming water wetting and heating the interior, all his vinegary smells stinking it out: here it comes. The memory that has been so used and reused that he isn't even sure he can trust it.

Roland is looking for Oliver. Neither of them are supposed to be coming up to the hospital any more. It's in writing now: they are officially banned from the site, and some fixed radius around it. But you don't tell Oliver he can't do something. Telling Oliver he can't be somewhere is the only reliable way to predict where he will go. The air is crisp, and smells of bonfires.

Roland keeps to the evergreens so as not to be seen. He knows his way round these bushes so well by now that he doesn't even have to think about it. Knowledge of the terrain is hardwired into him. He need never look down. He steps automatically over roots and bits of hospital debris. If it rained he would know in advance exactly where the water would puddle.

He takes up a position in a thick clump of laurel bushes that screen one end of the garden. Its snaking boughs are a puzzle of thick, leathery green. He watches her father emerging from the main entrance of the building. His usual manic energy seems diminished somehow. He looks tangled up with worry. He calls Cleo's name, then puts his hands in the pockets of the dressing gown and goes back inside, glancing over his shoulder before slamming the door shut behind him.

The smell of burning seems to be getting stronger, catching his throat. Trying to avoid picking up on her father's unease, Roland tells himself that all is well, that this building anxiety is nothing to worry about. That everything is fine. He should leave now, and not worry about trying to find her. It doesn't matter if he can't see her, because Oliver told him to stay away. Oliver told him she would be all right. And of course he can trust Oliver. Can't he.

The van is full of steam, and his pan of tea leaves has boiled almost to nothing, and is starting to smoke. He leans forward to pull the pan off the heat, and burns his hand. He presses a thumb to the burn, rubbing at it, thinking of her father, with his thin, spidery fingers, and his thin, fiery hair. The way he presided over events that summer.

Roland takes out his phone, gets out of the van, and walks over to the shutter, which is the only place down here where you can get a signal. The noise in the street is building. He thumbs his way through the address book until he finds the number he has for Carol, and fires off a quick question.

Everybody okay?

7

Locking the bathroom door makes spotlights spring to life, as if you were shooting the bolt in an aeroplane toilet. Given that the room is windowless, this means that unless you lock the door, you're in the dark. It is a system Cleo had installed at some expense after the demise of her relationship with Nat, and it is just one expression of her belief that the more her living space replicates the environment of business-class travel, the better.

She loves the way a hotel room is a space without context, and with that in mind she has consciously resisted any inclination to make the flat more homely, which is the main reason why she doesn't have any photos around. The towels should be white, there should be plenty of ice and the fridge should be virtually empty. She throws away bars of soap that are more than half-used, and finds the wafers that limp on for weeks in other people's soap dishes infinitely depressing. Maybe she should take things to their logical conclusion and have a telephone by the toilet, a down-lit minibar in her bedroom and a sign by the shower asking her to reuse her towels to save the environment.

She tips her head back towards the light and stares up at the ceiling. With the fingertips of her left hand, she widens the aperture of her eyelids on the right-hand side, before dropping her right hand in a practised pincer and pulling the shape away. She blinks down hard on the exposed, unseeing eyeball as a single, plump tear is expelled. She regards herself in the mirror – her real self, whose right eye colour is intensified by the strikingly pale pupil at its centre. Greener than green. She relaxes as her body remembers how much more comfortable life is without the invasion of a synthetic cap, however beautifully made, over a piece of itself.

She has a spare one. Although they are not easily smashed, they have a way of falling down plug holes or into toilets. And she did manage to crack one once, drunkenly stepping on it back in the days when she would take it out in pubs and pass it round for the ghoulish amusement of others.

There's one man left in the country who can make a proper ocular prosthesis out of glass: a German named Mr Engel, who has known Cleo since she was fifteen. This man, the last ocularist, has watched her grow from a child terrified of the world and what more harm it might fling at her into a woman proud of the person she has become, who would change nothing about her appearance, but is thankful all the same for the work he has done to make her less conspicuous.

'Try to stay a little reckless,' he said on their first meeting, when she went to get fitted. 'When people lose one eye, losing the other often becomes their greatest fear. But you must try to overcome that fear. It can make you very sensitive to risk.'

And it was he who advised her to keep a spare handy, warning that however beautiful and strong his creations might seem, they are not indestructible. Fissures are created in the glass over time – barely visible faults, caused by the natural fluids of her body. These becomes repositories for salt deposits left behind by her tears, which means that a well-worn eye can become uncomfortably abrasive, especially when it has been in too long. In the old days, when she used to stay up all night for recreation, the fissures would become conduits for an alarming brown gunk that would accumulate until the only thing to do was to remove the eye. Which would give rise to one of Nat's enraptured monologues about how much he loved the brighter colour of the blind one, thrown into sharper relief by the paleness at its centre – made more beautiful by its sightlessness, he said, than any he had seen.

Once, she turned up at an appointment with Mr Engel after such an all-nighter, and he turned her away. Her pupil, he said, was so dilated that making a copy of her eye in its current state would be a waste of time. 'I know I told you to stay reckless,' he added, 'but do try to stay alive as well.'

She drinks more vodka, steps out of her clothes and gets into the shower. Lit by carefully placed spotlights, she lathers her skin with a fresh bar of expensive soap. At times like this she likes to remember the tepid, murky baths of her childhood, and celebrate the present.

She knows better than to think that one past incident, however definitive, can dictate the path of an entire life. Better than to think it is the *only* reason why she and her father don't get on, or why she used to get lost of an evening with boys like Nat on pills and powders. You can't pin everything on one event, just because it happens to loom in the past. That's what happens to the past: most of it dies away, and what is left gains mass to fill the space available.

She doubts some of what she remembers doing in the shadowy echo-territory, the murk of her early twenties. But even if she may not want to, she knows it happened. There might be gaps, but you don't misremember stuff like that. The order of things might be clumsy, and there might be whole tracts of individual nights you don't remember at all, but you can't *insert* things like the things she remembers.

Visions of sex with Nat: the tight, hard clench; the sweaty, doomed melodrama of the drug-fuck. Something that would bring you up short if you walked in on it. As you sometimes did. Her teeth tasting the salt of his shoulder. And then the hindered stagger to the bathroom, cupping a hand under herself as she exited the bed so she wouldn't need to change the sheets. The feel of it on her fingers, warm then quickly cold. Flicking it into the toilet basin before reaching for the wad of tissue to press and soak. Relaxing into the soak, willing it away. Willing away thoughts of Oliver, which had a habit of popping up at times like this.

They were nights that often ended, as it was getting light, with Cleo staring at herself in a mirror, chest rising and falling, heart hammering, smoky, sticky, telling herself that this way of living could not go on. She had felt nostalgic, then, about its future demise. She felt this even though she could not see then how it could possibly stop. And then she would have a momentary realisation that if she didn't take steps, it was only going to stop when she, or someone she was with, ended up dying. Now she sits, still and composed, watching the news. Control is never lost. One day soon she may even win the battle with her vestigial blink.

The shower roars. She stands, scrubbing herself, to distract herself from the flashes of her old behaviour that are visiting her, and the guilt they bring. The things she did. Right here in this flat. She was frantic to escape, and created a sort of bracingly damaged persona that she imagined other people might want to explore. Willing to visit remote places. When she was with Nat, the two of them would even leave the curtains open sometimes, in case anyone should happen past. On four occasions, someone rang the buzzer and asked if they could come up. Twice, the answer was yes. (True reck-lessness, that – for which she wonders if she is still due one day to pay a price. Her doorbell still rings from time to time in the middle of the night, and there's never anybody visible in the street when she gets up to check.) It had to stop, though she could never have predicted the way in which it did.

The closer she got to Nat, the more he tried occasionally to ask her questions about the past. But whenever he really tried to get at the nub of anything that once happened to her, she dissolved and re-formed and was gone. And especially if it was the accident.

'It doesn't matter,' she would say. 'It was a long time ago, it was nobody's fault, and I don't like dwelling on it.'

Which was usually enough. Finding out about her was never Nat's main concern. He was far too distracted by her damaged state to find out what had actually caused it. He liked the lack of a brake, the wanting to go faster, the coasting to oblivion.

The last concerted effort he ever made to dig was when she had made some vague remark about how her father's mood swings were a bane on her childhood, and then ended off by saying, 'But we probably deserved it. We weren't very respectful of him. It must have driven him mad.'

'Who's "we"?' he said, when it became obvious she wasn't planning to say anything else.

'What?'

'You said, "When *we* were disturbing him".'

'Did I? I guess I meant me and my friends, growing up.'

'What friends?'

'I don't see them any more.'

She gets the urge to call Nat sometimes, and say to him, *Did we seriously do all that? Were we mad?* But she knows she will probably never contact him again. Not because it would be good or bad, particularly: she just knows she won't do it. She doubts she would interest him as much now as she used to, and their unsuitability for one another has been too comprehensively revealed.

The only problem with this bathroom is how much it reminds her of him. It waits in here, the memory, and is reanimated along with the lighting every time she locks the door. He was fascinated by her glass eye as soon as they met, and it took time for him to get used to it. Initially, for all the usual reasons, he found the idea of something so alien and synthetic living so close to the body off-putting. Then he seemed to warm to it, and even to develop an affection for it. She supposes at some point it must have occurred to him that if the eye could be taken out of her it could be put into him.

The definitive full stop came one evening when she wanted things in bed to be over more quickly than he did, and brought matters to a perfunctory, early conclusion. As she fell asleep she mumbled something about how she was sure he could find a way to amuse himself. She woke up to hear nattering from the bathroom – a conversation so real-sounding and one-sided that she initially assumed he had gone in there to make a phone call. When he didn't respond to her questions, she pushed open the door, and found him sitting there, his hands conjured in a complicated arrange-ment, talking to the creature that looked up from his groin – a creature that could not have existed if Nat had been circumcised. Mr Engel's work is so lifelike that you can put it in any casing and it will muster a personality. Any skin gathered around the piece of beautifully blown glass will resemble a living, seeing socket.

Her shower over, she stares at herself in the mirror as she pushes her toothbrush back and forth. The seeing eye only hints at green. In some lights it looks almost grey, a variability that the prosthesis struggles to replicate. But the green of the damaged eye is bold, stunning, incontrovertible.

8

Before bed, Roland does the rounds, moving from room to room turning off lights and checking for signs of vermin. He starts in deep, where water runs in unseen channels beneath the concrete and the damp floors sustain mosses and lichens. Victor says it's the course of the river Neckinger, and whether or not he's right, the sound of running water is a constant back here, and there are frogs to contend with as well as rats. The atmosphere changes the further out you go: from damp, to wet dust, to dry dust, and finally to the air of the outside world. He hears the deep boom of the ripening party next door. This one sounds like it could go on for some time. The road will be a horror show by the morning.

He makes his way back through the rooms, extinguishing one by one the worlds lit up by Molly, looking at all the accumulated material in here, and wondering how much the two of them could make if they just sold it all right now, cashed up and went their separate ways. Victor thinks everything should be hoarded, just in case somebody might want it in the future, and be prepared to pay. He's caught Roland throwing things away before now. It's not a pretty sight. The eyes widen, the white deposits in the corners of his mouth begin to liquefy, and desperate filth spits out of him that even Roland finds hard to ignore.

On the third chamber from the outside, his eye catches a ragged shape in the corner: a tatter masquerading as an animal. He returns to the van and brings out a gas-powered air rifle called a Ratsniper. He flicks on the night scope, and trains the rifle on the red darkness. The rustling movements are accompanied by a gentle trilling: that knackered pigeon from earlier has forced its way in through the fan above the ledge. One of its feet is missing, and bird is hopping on its one good leg, while the other one, which isn't much more than a ball of scar tissue, whisks around uselessly in the air. Roland relaxes and feels the butt of the gun settle into his shoulder, breathes in sharply, then out very slowly, and slots the bird. A dusty thud is followed by two weak flaps, then silence.

Before turning in, he sits on the side of his bed, fries five eggs in turn and eats them with a spoon. Each egg is cooked with a little oil in a pan on his gas ring and then splashed with Tabasco, like an oyster. One after another the fiery, slippery spoonfuls disappear. He crushes the shells up in a mug as much as he can be bothered to, then drinks them down with milk, chewing until they are crunched to nothing.

It is no wonder he ended up down here. Some of the earliest memories he has play out in a network of cardboard-box tunnels that his mother made his father build to contain him when he was little. Stacked flat-packed in one of the attic rooms, the boxes were part of the sales promotion business his father ran from their home, when he was still around. He had taped a whole load of them together, tops to bottoms, to create a kind of hutch. Roland remembers the smell of the cardboard and the sense of enclosure. He remembers how occasionally light would flood in, and the head of his father or mother would appear in a gap above him to say something, before disappearing again as they closed him off once more. The only memories he has of his father's face are from below like this, framed in cardboard.

When he asked his mother about it later, she claimed he'd made it up. But even then – before the last few switches were thrown in her engine room, and her recollection began to power down for good – even then, Mona was hardly a reliable source.

There were long plateaux, intercut with abrupt falls, as undiagnosed mini-strokes wiped the ground from under her. The plummets were unexpected: a sudden, vicious personality change in a café; a night-time disappearance; being found on the other side of town in her dressing gown in the middle of the day.

Carol had a solution, though. She proposed it to Roland quietly, one day. The idea that would make things less traumatic for everyone, and enable them all to carry on doing what they were doing. Roland could stay in town with Victor, and Carol and Mona wouldn't have to leave their home. It's a precarious situation, and there are any number of ways in which Carol could be rumbled. But for now it is working. Technically the guest house in which they both live is still run by Mona. It's just that most of the people who work there, and many of the people in the town who haven't known her a long time, think that Carol is Mona, and Mona is Carol.

For a while, Mona resisted the change. She would shout for help out of the window, and tell anybody who would listen that she was incarcerated against her will. Now she sits quietly, with the forefinger of her right hand placed constantly on her left wrist, monitoring her own pulse. Her hair is a shock of white, and her skin has thinned so much that it is nearly translucent. Roland calls to make sure that Mona is happy, and Carol tells him she is. As far as Mona is concerned, she has never left home.

Communicating with her is difficult. Not least because,

to cap it all, she has gone deaf. And Mona is not about to start trusting any of the equipment that might rectify the problem. When Roland was growing up, she kept the milk wrapped in tinfoil in the belief that this would shield it from the effects of the local nuclear power station. But in senility her technophobia has become more understandable – it feels like a philosophy rather than a defence mechanism. Roland has tried sending her hearing aids and special telephones to enable them to communicate better. Carol reports back that Mona's reaction is the same every time – she drowns the devices in a bucket of water. She has decided, it seems, to remain unreachable, a serene white witch who will no longer allow the world to trouble her as it did for so long.

Not so for Roland, in spite of all his defences: he's down here like this every night, hauling himself through the past, converting the night-time noises of the outside world into memories. Tonight, it's the crowd queuing for the club night next door, whose shouts and hollers are being effortlessly transformed by his mind into his mother's screams as she calls from the window of the Golden Sands Guest House, telling the world she is a prisoner.

Comfort is never usually a problem, but tonight the foam mattress bothers him. He sighs and shifts. The hot fug of his body in here. He gets a sense sometimes when he walks into the van of how he must smell to others, and it's not nice – cheesy, fungal. But he has given up trying to get properly clean under the dribble of water they have that passes for a shower.

He hears the club queue intensifying outside, the building sonic violence. A fight breaks out over a car. He can picture what's going on: the crowd in the clubbers are gaining confidence, starting to feel like they own the road. A driver has taken exception to the obstruction of a load of drugged-up kids, and probably finds it scary too, the manic energy of the fucked young, so he has sounded his horn. And the revellers have reacted badly. Someone is taunting him. *Drive on. Drive on.* Other cars honk too, and are met with gales of sarcastic cheers from the crowd. Someone is rattling the front shutter. A thrown bottle punches at it, showering tinkling shards. Roland shifts, and the van rocks on its suspension.

A tinny buzz, a vibration, a pale green illumination on the roof of the van: his phone has mustered the energy to pull something in from out there. He reaches for it, and holds it up to his face.

Just been up, says Carol. *He's in a bit of a state, but okay for now. Not well though.*

What about Mona? types Roland, but the signal has gone, and he lies there, prodding away at the button, while the question gets lost under the arches.

9

After breakfast Scriven sits in the kitchen, listening to the breathing of his mechanical lung. Everything he does now must be backed by the rhythm of its shallow *in-out-tap-thump*. It's fitting that Revenant House has found a way to finish him off: the two of them have been locked in a death dance since he first laid eyes on the place.

He took hammers to it, that first summer. Tried to turn the building to his purposes. He cut down trees, and ripped out fire doors. Then he got more ambitious, and graduated to knocking through walls and smashing ceiling tiles. Thankfully, Cleo was mostly elsewhere, so she missed some of the toxic avalanches that whooshed down on him from ceilings, and did not see the ghost who wandered back from the frontier, covered in fine, light-catching particles. Now there is fungus in his lungs, planted by a building's spore, and no amount of machinery will stop it from killing him.

The day stretches out before him. He should take it easy after yesterday afternoon, but he feels fine. Better than fine. Without thinking, he runs water into a glass from right at the back of the cupboard, enlivening three dead woodlice that swirl and dance in the liquid. He almost drinks it anyway, then leaves it on the side, watching the bodies settle. He looks down again at the leaflet Carol left him last night.

Coping With Lung Disease.
He flicks it open to the first page, headed *Diagnosis.*

Prognoses vary considerably. Don't assume the worst when you first receive the news, as the progress of your condition can be greatly altered by a few changes in your home environment. You may be surprised at how many unpleasant symptoms of your disease, including breathlessness, coughing and chest pain, can be alleviated when you take a few simple steps to avoid dust, damp and excessive exertion.

Mustn't laugh too much. It would lead straight to a fit.

You should by now have undergone some kind of chest imaging scan (X-ray, MRI, CT Scan) so that the extent of any scarring of the parenchymal tissue of your lungs can clearly be seen. It is on this – the amount of scarring – that your prognosis will heavily depend.

The doctor was a young man with a pocketful of plastic biros. He looked nervous as he clipped the results into the bright box of bad news on the wall. Scriven told himself not to get carried away working out what he was to be told in advance, but he could tell it wouldn't be good. The map of scars was unnavigable. He listened only vaguely to what the doctor was saying as he traced his finger along some of its lines, wondering where each branch had been seeded: wondering if you could map the damage over a plan of Revenant House, and work out exactly which corridor had wrought which pathway of damage.

'Have you got someone you can tell about this?' said the doctor. 'Someone who can take on the responsibility of looking after you?'

And he did think of Cleo to begin with. She would have

come if he'd asked her. But he dismissed the thought as soon
as it arose. She would probably want to do something grand
and self-sacrificing, and he couldn't consider the prospect of
living with her again.

'If not, we can always arrange visits from the district
nurse,' said the doctor.

'No nurse,' he said. 'There is someone who can help me.'

'One more thing,' said the doctor. 'This is a little irregular
– but the other thing I'm going to do is write you a prescription for some Prozac.'

'Prozac?' said Scriven.

'You look like you could do with it,' he said.

He took one, and gave the rest to the badgers.

When he called Carol, he tried hard not to make it sound
as if he was blackmailing her into taking care of him. Which
he could easily have done. He is one of only two people
who know about the switch, other than her and Mona, if
Mona does know. There was a ghost of the old fear, then.
Carol's terror of responsibility. Of things getting on top of
her. Carol is pragmatic, detached, and she would never do
anything to make him change his lifestyle, whatever she may
say. But today he wants to defy her, and her advice. He's
feeling *up to it*. And if he should expire up there, away from
it all, then so be it.

He goes to the fridge, throws provisions into a bag, and
heads outside. He lingers under the front door, looking up
at the stopped clock in its tower, remembering the day he
made Cleo stand at the bottom of the ladder while he
dropped pigeon eggs into her hands. A time when he took
measures to stop things living under his roof – the thought
seems laughable now.

He remembers how mortified she was when the first one
hit the ground. The way she found a way to move her cupped
hands as each new egg arrived, to compensate for its velocity

and keep the shell intact. He can still see the determination on her face as she tried to catch them. Hear the squeal when they broke in her hands.

He came down the ladder, took the bowl of intact eggs she had collected and flung it against the wall. Hadn't she realised that the idea was to kill these pigeons, or potential pigeons, to stop them becoming pesky squabs? What notion had been in her head? That the two of them were moving the birds to more suitable quarters?

As usual she did a stern job of hiding the upset, swallowing the revelation so quickly that he almost missed the hurt, and then even joining in the egg fight that came after, when they started hurling them at each other. When it was over, they trooped inside together with drying yolk in their hair. He suggested a swim in the lake but she disappeared quickly for a bath, and he didn't see her for hours.

That night she made an omelette. It didn't occur to him at the time that she might have been back out here to scout for survivors, or even to scrape the yolk off the ground in places, but it occurs to him now. It is the sort of little vengeance she would have loved.

He has made excursions like this before – bold journeys, dicing with death (and breath). He travels to distant parts of Wreaking with his oxygen on its caddy, picturing himself as an astronaut or an undersea explorer. But he's never made quite such an ambitious play as this. Best not to think about it too much and see what happens.

He snatches a breath and looks up at the inside of the water tower. Six ladders connect six mezzanine floors. No one has put a foot on any of them in years. He knows that one of the rotten rungs could betray him at any time, sending him down to the platform below with enough force to snap that one too, and possibly pitching him all the way to the ground in the process, rung fragments pinging off as he cartoonishly slides down to a broken neck. But he gives each rung his full weight all the same. These little games of roulette with the building are some of the most thrilling parts of his day.

Halfway up the first ladder, he has to stop. His throat is closing around his breath, and his lungs are whistling. He closes his eyes, breathes in the cool, shuttered air of the tower, and imagines it. Just letting go. But even though they are shaking, his hands keep their selfish clutch. Just as the instinctive half of him won't let him *not* panic when the lungs start fizzing, the other half won't let him let go of this ladder to do the job properly. So he makes it up from one level to the next, from ladder to attic to ladder to attic, until he's high up, and the only damage he has to show for it is a palmful of splinters.

His bag contains a flask of tap water, a screw-top bottle of German white wine, a service-station pork pie and a small jar of English mustard. The bag weighs on his hipbone as he climbs. He takes it slowly, stopping to rest on the attic platforms between the different ladder wells. On the boards of the top floor are the feather-explosions of two dead birds. He reaches the low door that leads on to the roof, and leans, panting, against the tower wall. Opening the door, he disturbs two pigeons, which fly off, their wings snapping like wet linen.

He looks down on the bones of the hospital – its intersecting corridors; its grand geometry. Wreaking was built to a scheme known as the compact arrow plan, which linked different wards with central services more efficiently than before. It is credited with creating environments with greater natural light, which were easier to navigate. The network of corridors looks endless even from up here, where you can see their beginnings and endings. They link gabled towers, and zigzag their way around to cover all possible corners of the available space. Inside, they are unknowable. It's a ministry of madness, its colour-coded passageways getting warmer or colder as you approach the correct destination. *Getting Warmer. Warmer. Very warm. Boiling.*

He looks down on the airing courts where patients paced, stuck in cycles that only they could discern, condemned for the sins of pattern recognition and magical thinking to a lifetime of pharmacological confinement. It makes him angry. Nobody should be damned for disbelieving what some other group claims to be the prevailing wisdom. Because don't we all have days like that? Days when we talk to our dead, or fear we might do something awful, or can't get out of bed because it's too much? This place should be given a taste of its own medicine. The hospital itself should be lobotomised, its memories set free, to avenge all who were categorised here. The compost of anguish and torment this place is built on. A geology of sadness. To think people used to worry about the nuclear power station. What about Wreaking, with all its psychic pollution?

The paperwork was done, they said. The site was sold, and redevelopment of the hospital would begin any minute. He shouldn't think twice about buying Revenant House: it would be the *jewel in the crown* when the work was completed. They showed him a brochure printed expensively on thick, blue card, with artists' impressions of happy families at play in Wreaking's 180-acre grounds – the Largactil shuffle replaced by the dashing of gorgeous children. The chapel was going to be a yoga centre. The patients' high-walled airing courts would be opened up and dug into formal gardens. The hydrotherapy block would become a water park. Kids and dogs would fly kites together in the grounds. On the wards, women in white linen would relax on taupe settees, listening to expensive-looking hi-fis. The brochure referred to the building as a 'Victorian gem' without saying what it had actually been.

This place was what did for Cleo. She shouldn't have ended up spending the formative summer of her childhood playing among medical equipment and straitjackets and padded cells. They should have just stayed where they were before – the rented suburban semi with its clapboard frontage, its rock garden, its anachronistic, flat-roofed carport. How did he manage to smuggle this plan through, to bring them here to disaster? That moment before, of not knowing what was to come – you can crave it so badly. You can crave wanting to get back there so hard that you can believe just for a second that it might be possible, like walking into a photograph.

He crosses his legs and sits down on the roof, eating the pie and swigging the wine. He is amazed he can still cross his legs. The last time he even tried was probably twenty years ago. Being on the roof reminds him of that day, at the old house, when he brought home Ursula for the first time. Cleo never made it easy for him to have girlfriends, but her hostility towards Ursula was the most embarrassing reaction yet. He had forgotten his keys, and she hid on the roof of the house, pretending not to be there, so she didn't have to come down and let them in. He can remember standing at the front door with Ursula while she brazened it out, stubbornly refusing to come and let them in, the brat.

He should call her.

No. She should call him.

Yeah. That's Jasper Scriven. Never one to get over his own self-interest.

In the flat days, the dark days after he finally lost her mother, he would have nightmares about being told that Cleo had gone too, that even after all that he didn't have her either. He would wake in a pit of breathless panic, and have to go to her room to steal a glance, and a hit of the safe smell of her sleep. And the awful thing? The *nature* of the relief. Because it was not simply relief that she was alive. It was relief that he would not have to live with the guilt of having lost Cleo as well as her mother.

His feet are cramping. He gets up and looks down on his peculiar little universe. The hospital. The roofs of the town. The Ness, snaking off into the mist. He glances down, and like something coming up to bite him, he sees it. Scratched into a flap of roof lead, right here in front of him. Her name, and those of the two boys. Roland's crude, serious writing. Cleo's whimsical hand. A filthy doodle that can only have been drawn by Oliver. They had been up here, all three of them, and he never even knew it.

PART TWO

10

The Golden Sands Guest House was created with the last of Mona's redundancy money and a loan she secured on the promise that once a few more years had elapsed, her husband's life insurance policy might finally cough up something meaningful. She used the cash to get it tricked out with all the right kit: emergency cords, wipe-clean surfaces, rounded edges, and plenty of locked doors.

It is one of a row of Victorian seafront houses, whose first floor overhang is so steep that they seem to have produced the peeling beach huts before them, like hunched crones pushing dodgy sweeties. The buildings on either side are flyblown – one seemingly empty, the other an occasional halfway house for the homeless – but this one is in business, of a sort.

Roland remembers the way people used to address her when she worked at Wreaking. He would overhear the chatter of the ward as he waited outside for her to finish for the day. *Yes, Nurse Lamb. No, Nurse Lamb. If you want permission to come on the excursion, you'll have to ask Nurse Lamb.* He remembers the sense of purpose in the house; the smell of disinfectant; a line of blue shirts hanging to drop their creases in the front window. Mona was someone then. Now she is small and tight and sad with worry. Roland looks at her from time to time and wonders how he can possibly have come from that. She is his mother. But to him she will always be Mona, as she would be to anyone else who knew her, if anyone actually knew her.

All along the coast are similar towns that, like it or not, have been revived with the money of second-homers and city commuters. Here, it seems to have been a case of *Do Not Resuscitate*. Some lament that the branch line was never upgraded, while others celebrate the fact – but whichever side of the fence you are on, you can't deny that this town is on the slide. It is home only to the old and the unimaginative, especially now that most of the mad folk that used to define it have been farmed out elsewhere – which is not to say you can't still find them, muttering on park benches or nursing tea in tolerant cafés.

There are three funeral parlours, and the mobility centre does a steady, trundling trade. The house-clearance centre always has fresh stock in, and there is brisk turnover in the many charity shops on the high street. You can't see the sea from here, though it is close by. The only evidence of it is a briny sharpness to the air and the fat, bolshy seagulls that squat for warmth on every chimney cowl.

The town reaches a kind of gathering point at the blunt, granite church, where the notable deceased lie under heavy stone slabs, many of which are heaped with decorative glass pebbles. The graveyard is full, but you can have a commemorative bench for the right price. The more recent bench tributes have taken on a competitive edge, as widows and offspring try to adorn their farewells with character to make their dead stand out: a simple epitaph, like *Stanley Cooper, Who Loved This Place*, or *Betty Thompson, Always In Our Thoughts*, is no longer enough. One recently departed Frank Hordupois – *(pron. 'Warboys')*, as the plaque helpfully informs – has a tribute formed of cryptic crossword clues, staking a claim on wordplay as well as the spot. Soon there will be no views left that haven't been bagged by one dreary dead person or another.

There is a lifeboat station, too, as if to prove to outsiders that it isn't all death (though it mostly is): a reassuringly modern cabin down at the shoreline, whose steep runners spit a sturdy orange tug on to the water in times of crisis, and good men drop everything to pull on their oilskins and take the form of heroes. It doesn't matter what their day jobs are: no house fire or supermarket coronary has the scale of the ocean. The lifeboat offers them a grander scope, and they grasp it eagerly, revving up their engines at every unconfirmed sighting of a stricken sailor or a washed-away dinghy.

Wind swings in low and fast over the North Sea, battering the pier and flaking rust on to the brown water that churns under the boardwalk. It pummels the creaking sign that hangs off the Golden Sands Guest House, and rattles the windows of its exhausted siblings. It barges through the double doors of Arcadia, disturbing the *Reserved* signs on flashing, burbling fruit machines that wait for their players to return, paused in agonising possibility, surely, *surely* ready to spit this time. It travels easily across the marshes and through the broken ward windows of Wreaking, agitating tattered strips of curtain and slamming doors.

To the south, a nuclear power station sits like a toxic puffball. Some can't get it out of their heads, and will not be persuaded that its rays aren't mutating their bodies or tinkering with their minds – none of which seems to make them want to move. To the north are marshes that lead out towards the Ness, where perspective is tricksy, where you might imagine a ghost on your tail amid the chatter of the oystercatchers, and where escaped lunatics from the madhouse behind it must once have raved at the moon, down among the reeds and wraiths and bog-spirits.

Lack of demand did away with pier-side donkey rides years ago, but casual visitors still feel entitled to expect them, as if it were incumbent on the past to live on indefinitely in towns like this just to sustain their nostalgia. You see them sometimes, remonstrating with blank-faced locals, wondering aloud where *the spirit of this place* has gone, lamenting their disappointed expectations. They probably imagined that there would be knotted handkerchiefs and Kiss Me Quick hats and What The Butler Saw as well.

Roland and Oliver smirk at these idealists from their stoop in front of the public toilets and wonder what they were thinking, to visit this place for pleasure. This collective delusion they arrive under – it's mad – but it carries on sustaining them right up until it won't hold any more. On occasion, the boys are around to see it crumble. People stand on the beach staring at dishwater surf rinsing the shingle, and experience a kind of awakening, looking behind them as if suddenly noticing how forlorn the town really is. You can see them in real time, beating themselves up for their nostalgia and resolving to go somewhere hot in future.

What to do in such a place before the pubs let you in? What to do with all the afternoons in limbo, waiting to be able to drive away and not look back? Go to Arcadia. Hang out on the pier. Get drunk on the sly. Cycle around. Peddle local legend, and add to it. Deck places with mythology to make them less dreary: the bomb shelter, the marshes, the pillbox – and of course, Wreaking, which has been the spring of lore for as long as Roland can remember.

Call the yellow van! Someone's escaped from the bin.

Send the freak to Wreaking!

Rumours are passed round of what has been seen there. Who had a relative in there. Who went visiting and saw straitjacketed patients running around the place being chased by doctors with tubes and syringes. The conversations come and go so naturally that Roland sometimes forgets it was Mona's place of work. Not that he had ever been allowed in – whenever he ended up there for any reason, he was made to sit in a long, echoing corridor lined with coat hooks, waiting for her to finish, and furnishing a picture of what lay beyond the locked door from the noises he heard. Even back then, in the old days, when they used to test-fire the escape siren once a month, sending its cold wail over the town and the marshes – even then, Roland had never really associated the hospital with her. With all its potential for crazed escapees and straitjackets and lobotomy, the hospital has always shone far too brightly in the imagination to accommodate something as mundane as his mother.

A vicious wind is rattling the sash windows, and it's Roland's turn to check on Carol. Working for his mother used to be a holiday job, but the more the talk fades of him going to the sixth form, the more it is taking on the feeling of some-thing permanent. He and Mona have an agreement now to share the workload between them equally, so tonight it is her turn to relax, if she can manage it.

Mona does not so much watch the television as supervise it, keeping a vigilant eye in case it makes any sudden moves. As with all electronic devices, she is wary of its power and reach, and when it is on she sits alert, rigidly perched on the sofa's edge – which does not stop her from relishing and lamenting the worst news stories that play out on the screen. Tonight, again, it is famine. She's fretting at a piece of tissue whose origins are somewhere up her sleeve, working it into thin, tortured ropes, as she sits, pinned to the spot by bad news, hunting ever more tragic and unjust detail with which to flesh out her version of the world.

'God, but it's awful.' She glances at Roland to see if he is watching, then turns her attention back to the television. The short, grey hair on her head is silhouetted against a backdrop of exhausted, desperate faces. 'Have you seen this? It's the flies round their eyes I can't stand. Oh turn it off, I can't bear it. No, leave it on. Will you look at that poor girl. She can't be any older than nineteen. That's her baby, look. There, in her arms.'

'I know that's her baby,' says Roland, getting up to look outside. He is expecting Oliver any minute. They have planned to go out.

The window judders even more unnaturally as Oliver appears outside, miming being pinned up against it by the wind. His look of shock and terror goes through various different phases. He then manages to convert the movement into a swift lowering of the trousers and starts rubbing his bare arse against the windowpane.

Mona doesn't take her eyes off the screen. 'Get that foul boy off my window.'

Roland opens the front door with a meaningful look already composed, to communicate to his friend that his mother is not to be conversed with. You have to move fast with Oliver, or he would be off before you knew it, announcing himself to the room in some loud or disruptive way. His arrival anywhere sets Roland on edge because the possibilities are suddenly ramped up: if he is bored he will make the room more interesting, in any way he can. Oliver nods to show he has understood, and crosses the threshold quickly to get out of the wind.

'What kind of God would let this happen?' Mona is saying now, to the screen. 'How can you say that *this* is fair?'

The two of them cross behind her and take to the stairs at speed.

She hasn't always been like this. He can't pinpoint the exact moment, but it has got a lot worse since the day when they were out walking on the cliffs, and Mona developed vertigo. Out of nowhere, she was on her hands and knees, screaming at him to get away from the edge. For a few months he tried to work out where it was coming from – whether it was a delayed reaction to the departure of his father, or whether it was something to do with not having enough to worry about now that there was no Wreaking. After a while, realising it would do him no good to know, he stopped wondering where the new anxiety came from, and got on with ignoring it.

Mona initially railed against the hospital closure. She protested that it would take away her livelihood, not to mention remove a safe haven for all sorts of unstable people. She muttered that patients were no longer called patients or even inmates but were now known as 'service users'. *What's that even supposed to mean?* she demanded. *No wonder they're shutting us down. The whole world's gone mad.* Then it was explained to her that under the new system she was well placed to open up a home of her own, making private money, and could even solicit any patients she might know from the old days to come and live with her – at which point her sentimental attachment to the old place withered demonstrably.

Other patients come and go but for now there is only one permanent *lodger* at the Golden Sands: Carol, a manic depressive in her forties who has been in and out of Wreaking since she was nineteen. Two other rooms take residents who come and go, but at present they are empty.

Oliver loiters awkwardly, reluctant to mire himself in it. Not so much, he claims, because he finds Carol difficult (which he does) – more because anything that looks too much like work makes him edgy. He is fanatical about keeping his sights beyond the town. His quasi-mythical brother, Victor, told him at some impressionable age that looking for work in the town was a trap, and Oliver has taken the advice to heart. Victor left as soon as he could and, according to Oliver, is making a killing in the house-clearance business. All they have to do is ask, he says, and Victor will get them work. As soon as the time is right. Oliver doesn't say when that time will be.

Roland knocks on the door, and they wait, careful to maintain the illusion that Carol has control over her privacy. It's like a garret under these top-floor eaves: bubbly linoleum that puts a spring in your step; a plastic fan cut into one of the dusty windowpanes; the murk of the North Sea outside, studded with the yellow lights of dismal, freighting industry.

For the most part Carol is quiet, but sometimes she has a bad spell, and must be watched. Sometimes it's more than a bad spell, and her scream is like a fire fed with oxygen, and she becomes a different person. One who would bite you, and kick you. And then things get difficult, and some-times Roland has to hold her down. He tries not to listen to the things that come out of her mouth when he does. Expressions it does not do to think about too much, that come from somewhere unknowable inside her.

Roland knows more about her life in the hospital than he lets on to Oliver. He has heard about it from her during the conversations they have on their long afternoon walks. It took time, but eventually he plucked up the courage to ask her about it. Everything from the food, to the other patients, all the way to the shocks, and what they did to you.

'I'm old enough to remember what they call *unmodified* ECT,' she said.

'What's that?' said Roland, already regretting having decided to pry.

'These days they give you a muscle relaxant or a general anaesthetic. They never used to do that when I first started having it. You had to go through it all.'

'All what?'

She talked about the fear beforehand, even if you wanted the treatment, which of course you did sometimes, because a lot of patients knew that without it they'd be a mess. But, she said, no matter how much you thought you wanted the shocks, or knew they were doing you good, the idea of them was always scary. How could it not be, with a build-up like that? She told him about the smell in the room, of fuses, and the high ozone burn of electricity. She told him about the businesslike expressions of the nurses.

Oh yes, said Carol, to the look on Roland's face, and the question it implied. Yes, she remembered Mona, looking down at her as if she were a thing to be processed, like the biscuits on the chocolate biscuit factory production line where Carol had worked in her teens.

The fear always took over at the last minute, she said. Everything gave in to it. You knew like a condemned person that it was going to happen, that it was imminent, that time was running out, and that there was nothing you could do to stop it. Strong hands would overpower you and strap you down. You'd smell the alcohol they rubbed on your temples. Your tongue would be stopped and your mouth gagged to stop you from hurting yourself. Your mouth would dry out.

And then SNAP.

Reset.

Nothing to feel but the blind fear of nothing.

All the reassurance of your self gone.

Like being born.

Things were going on at this point, she said. Things you never saw or knew about. You never saw yourself thrashing about, having your seizures. You weren't there. She didn't know where you were, but you weren't *there*.

Carol said that after the shocks she would walk stiffly in the gardens of the hospital, trying to loosen her muscles again, and that for up to an hour afterwards she was unable to remember the names of any of the things she saw outside: not just the names of flowers, but the very word 'flower', or the word for 'earth' or 'grass' or 'sky'. And you were never *quite* sure, she said, if you would get back safely or not.

Roland said it sounded scary.

It was, said Carol. But a little wonderful, too.

Roland knocks again at the door. The silence does not bode well.

Sure enough, she looks terrible. Her pretty, elfin face looks beleaguered and sorry and scared, and she's fretting with her clothes and glancing from side to side in a hunted way.

'I'm not my best self today,' she says. 'Not my best self at all.'

'Can we come in?' says Roland.

'You boys have better things to do than to sit around with me.'

Roland puts what he hopes is a calming arm on her shoulder, which she tries to hold, but some impulse in her makes her snatch at it and throw it away.

'Shall we go for a walk tomorrow?' says Roland. 'Up to Wreaking? Would you like that?'

'That might be nice,' she says, looking down at the floor, brow furrowed in concentration. The comfort she derives from the hospital buildings is often unimaginable to her when she is somewhere else.

Roland closes the door. 'We'll stay and chat to you for a while, shall we? We'll do a jigsaw together.'

'Fucking hell,' mutters Oliver, his evening plans falling away. 'This place.'

11

She is lying in roof tar, duffle-coated, eyes wide open, keeping a plane in the sky. The tiny speck up there; the thin scratch of exhaust it is drawing: the responsibility of keeping it safe is dizzying. But she must concentrate: the moment when the plane slips off course will be worse than anything she has ever felt, and the realisation that it is her fault as the flaming pieces break off and plummet towards her will be even worse.

And really, the jet is only one of four things to concentrate on. Her whole body is involved. With one eye she must keep the sun at bay. With the other she is directing the jet. Her right foot is keeping up the roof hatch, since (she now knows) there is no peg to hold it up. The fourth thing, which is more in the region of something to try not to think about, is that bitumen from the roof is starting to coat the back of her head.

It was cold when she lay down, with a thin frosting of ice, but the waves of sustaining energy she's been aiming at the plane have directed fierce heat down into the roof tar. She can feel it absorbing her hair, strand by strand. Her body is melting a shape beneath her into the tar, whose oily smell is getting stronger as it warms. Her coat will be ruined, and trying to get up will involve struggling like a bog creature – if indeed she ever rises again.

None of that matters. Only the plane is important. Though it is barely visible. Though it is a toy that she could hide behind a cloud of her own breath if she so chose. She pictures them up there – all those people, oblivious to the girl on the ground keeping them aloft.

There will be no word of thanks, and that's okay – the point about powers like these is not to boast about them – but her pivotal role in the universe is not always easy. This banging on the front door could not be worse timed.

She heard the distant thumps without comprehending them at first. Then they were joined by the calls of a cold voice that rebounded off frosty, hard surfaces. Then the voice was calling for her by name. She shifts. Her hands move in her coat pockets, disturbing tissue fragments, pens, sweet wrappers, string.

Here is an opportunity for righteous anger, if she wanted to take it. They have a clear agreement – one that is etched into their father–daughter contract – that allows her a certain amount of time to herself. A scenario like this one is exactly why they have rules in the first place. He's meant to give her an exact picture of his comings and goings in advance so that she knows when she will be alone. Excursions like this are her privilege. And she sees quite enough of him at school without him pitching up at home unannounced.

She can always tell what kind of mood he is in by his knock. And this was a good-mood knock to begin with (of course she heard it). A *something to tell you* mood. A *let's have some fun* mood. The jaunty rat-a-tat-tat of the homecoming father with news to spill. What a shame to spoil it.

'I won't ask you again,' he says, in that *getting bored of this* sing-song. 'It's *cold.*'

'Okay,' she shouts. 'You don't need to ask me again. I've got the message.'

'Now.'

'Okay.'

'Why aren't you moving?'

'Why haven't you got your key?'

There's a pause to accommodate a set of physical movements she can picture precisely: a furious hand clapped to the forehead; a stifled roar of frustration. But for some reason the pause is short today. What is the moderating force?

'I haven't got my key,' he says, trying to control the quaver in his voice, 'because I forgot to take it with me. Will you let me into my house now?'

'I can't, Dad.'

'Is there something the matter?'

'I just have to finish something.'

The plane has a way to go yet. She has to give it at least three more clouds before she can hope someone else might be on hand.

'Is it something embarrassing?'

'No, Dad.'

'You're stuck on the roof again, aren't you?'

'No.'

'Why can't you tell me what it is?'

'The longer we keep talking, the less I'll be able to concentrate on finishing what I'm doing.'

'How long will it take?'

The plane is maybe three-quarters of its way across her field of vision. But there's no way she can leave it alone yet, and recent patterns suggest that his general mood at the moment can take something like this. She can get over anything he can dish out – or has been able to until now – but she can't have a plane crash on her conscience.

'Difficult to tell. Longer if you keep distracting me. Can't you go for a walk around the block?'

'Jesus Christ, Cleo—'

It's almost gone. Just a little farther and it will be out of her jurisdiction. She's become used to breaking off her focus when he needs her, but it has to be done carefully. To snap out of it too quickly can be fatal.

'Can you please hurry up? There's a good reason for this.'

He's getting self-conscious. She pictures neighbours gathering at windows, unable to see her, only him shouting at his own front door. They will assume another episode is in progress.

She closes her eyes and sits up, fully expecting the tar to come with her, pulling ropes of roof-treacle between her back and the surface. But sitting up is all too easy. The crown of her head is wet from meltwater, some of which has started freezing again in her hair. Most of the frost around her hasn't even wilted.

A dark shape bruises out the vision of her left eye. She rubs at it, and it throbs, and doesn't go away. This is the cost of keeping the sun at bay. She blinks, enjoying the way the shape remains, enjoying its dull, local pain.

It takes time to get back. You can't rush it. This is exactly why they have the agreement that he will warn her when he's coming home. She must shut this down before reaching him: she's still in a place where anything can be modified. Grinning trolls spit yellow fire in the gold world of the stair carpet. Waves break beyond the beach-house clapboard of the banister slats. The only thing for it is to go down the well. It's a trick she does: descending towards herself, growing up with each step down, arriving back at fifteen as she hits the bottom stair.

With each footfall the colours dim, the world gets smaller, the house more drab. Boring thoughts help. Will she cook him eggs or beans tonight? She's sick to death of both.

Through the frosted glass of the front door she sees him shifting from side to side, and shielding his eyes to look through. Something's different. That suit isn't very Friday afternoon. And what is the shape behind him? She opens the door.

'Finally.' He's actually smiling. Still trying to keep a lid on it, even though it's chilly out here. Why is he trying so hard? He looks her up and down to make sure nothing was wrong, then pauses to re-establish his composure. 'I suppose there's no point in asking.'

She shakes her head. 'I did say it was important. And you weren't due back now.'

As she tries to close the door after him he says, 'Cleo, there's someone else here.'

A woman looms behind him – a stately creature Cleo knows only as Miss Morrell. She is well groomed, and normally wears her hair up, but not today. People at school think she's lonely. What is this about? Staff sometimes come home with him when they have some parents' evening to go on to, but never on their own like this.

'Cleo,' she says, with an unpleasant widening of the eyes that seems meant as an overture of friendship. 'You can call me Ursula if you like.'

Cleo closes her eyes, then reopens them and turns to her father with a hard expression. 'Come on. Seriously?'

'What?'

'Do you have any idea what this will mean for me?'

He's never actually done this before, in spite of all the playground allegations. He's never actually got together with one from school before. And – potentially more devastating than the inevitability that word will get out – this one will know how picked on she is, and undo the careful lies she has told her father to keep him out of it.

It's not just because he's a teacher that they get at her – it's not even as simple as that. It's the fact that they know that the children of teachers get their fees paid by the school. In other words, it's more because she is poor than because her father is there to supply them with endless ammunition.

They would go for the daughter of any teacher. This is what she tells herself during pep talks in the mirror, sometimes even persuading the sceptic who looks back from the glass. But, on the other hand, he is one of their favourite targets. His classroom persona – a manic, ratty force of nature – is routinely ridiculed. The pushier ones mutter that he shouldn't be kept in his job given how unpredictable he is, and how far he strays from the syllabus. She tells herself that it isn't their fault: that they have a lot working against them in a place like that. A lot of distracting pressure to compete and feel superior.

The rules of conduct are complicated, and nobody has ever told her what they are. She has worked them out by making mistakes. This is a place where bossy girls take you aside into a classroom and make you agree with the poisonous things they say about one of your friends, before opening a cupboard door to reveal that the 'friend' was there all along, listening, to test your loyalty. Early on, after this happened to her, Cleo decided that a clever way to get revenge might be to hide in a cupboard and eavesdrop on them herself. But when she did, she was so shocked at the level they operated at – actually talking methodically about the ways they were going to *kill* her – that opening the door and revealing herself was an impossibility.

She has invented a new word. *Unclude.* It's worse than excluding someone because they go out of their way to devise things specifically to keep her out of them. And are very careful to ensure that none of their special treatment is ever witnessed by her eccentric, unpredictable father – about whom they make jokes in her hearing about giving him erections in lessons by showing him bits of themselves, and say to her over and over again that he looks down their tops, and tries to grope them when she isn't around.

The names they call him are bad enough already. And it is amazing that it has never happened before at one of the other places. But at this school – not wise. For her or for him.

And *Ursula*. Really? With a name like that she should have seen this one coming. Ursula. Gloria. Josephine. Must he always go for women whose names are at least fifty years out of date?

'You can't do this,' she says, notwithstanding the fact that Miss Ursula Morrell is still right there beside them. 'You can't.'

12

Oliver is ranting again. It's a favourite topic, about small lives and the injustices they entail. Some of the rant is learned from his wayward brother, and some of it is his own. Nobody in the room is hearing it for the first time but, as with Roland, it looks less and less likely that Oliver will be going anywhere near the sixth form, and fear of the world has made him strident.

'*Just take this*, they say. *For now. Until something good turns up.* And that's how you die. Not in one big go, but in all the little deaths that happen every time you say that you'll just do it *for now*. Before you know it, it's four years later, nothing good has happened, and stacking up the DIY place or the supermarket is your own personal forever.'

He gesticulates with pieces of bread, as if he were facing firm opposition from somebody else in the room, though nobody is saying a word. His hands are on their usual nervous quest, ranging the tabletop in search of something to shred. Three slices of white bread were left in the basket after dinner, and he is tearing them into small pieces, and dropping them one by one on to the table.

'Each little death rolls into one great big death. And then you die for real. 'Cause believe you me, mate, there is nothing so lethal in the world, nothing that has fucked over so many people, as that *for now*. You ask Victor. He'll tell you.'

Everyone knows it's better not to interject when Oliver is on transmit. Better to let him fly, to let the jets of nervous energy that sustain him blast off at random. If it can be made to blow itself out smoothly, in one go, then he'll be properly spent, and more relaxing to be around. And something about his close scrutiny of the world is terrifying. There is always the possibility, it seems to Roland, of ending up on his hit list yourself, and being found wanting. The expression on his face shows you that he is mainly concentrating against himself, in any case – negotiating the fizz and start of his internal whims.

After a while he'll have less contained within him and might be able to bring things a little more under control, but the dangerous cargo of his nervous energy must be jettisoned first. The ship doesn't stand a hope of being directed, much less hitched to another, with all that volatility in its hold. It's worse the more time he has spent on his own. And Oliver has usually just spent a lot of time on his own.

'That's how it happens. All the days we say, *Yeah, okay, that'll do, that's enough for me.* Well it's not enough for me. None of it. No sir. No thank you.'

Mona has come in from the kitchen to clear the plates. 'Nobody's making you stop here for tea if you don't want to, Oliver. I can happily do without another mouth to feed. Especially one that isn't paying for it.'

This is a rare thing: Mona relaxed enough to poke fun at someone. It has not been seen for some time, and should be celebrated.

'That's not what I mean,' says Oliver, getting frustrated. 'You know what I mean. You all do. This town is a trap, and anyone who says they're here because they want to be is either fibbing or round the bend. No offence, Carol.'

Carol has left the table, is working on a painting at her easel and says nothing.

As abruptly as it kicked in, Mona has lost her sense of humour. 'Watch it, young man. You may think that kind of remark is okay because Carol is nice enough to let you get away with it, but you won't get that kind of treatment from me.'

'Sorry, Mona.'

'Coming in here ranting and raving and spoiling everybody else's evening. And how dare you? I live just where I want to live. If you don't like it, you can always spend time somewhere else. And you can owe me a loaf of sliced white while you're at it.'

Roland has given up wishing that what Oliver said could be made to pass through some kind of filter. That would be to endow him with tact. And then the universe would be altered fundamentally, and who knows what else would be destabilised in the process?

'My lodgers pay their way,' says Mona, nodding her head in Carol's direction. 'What do you bring to the party, apart from a lot of pointless noise?'

'You want food? I'll get you food,' says Oliver. 'Consider it done.'

'What food?'

'Chickens. I'll bring some next week. I'm due a visit to the broiler house.'

'Believe it when I see it,' says Mona.

'Does that mean I can stay?'

'You can come and do the dishes and earn it like everybody else.'

'She drives a hard bargain, this one,' says Oliver, getting up quickly to dodge an incoming swipe from Mona's dishcloth.

A wet day at school, years before, some sap of a supply teacher trying to control things, and the dirty kid nobody had spoken to came in with emeralds to sell. He was still recently arrived enough to be called 'new', though he'd been there almost a term. On the day he started trying to tout his gemstones it was the first time many had even heard his voice.

Reverently taking out a handful of the green glass pebbles, which anyone could see weren't real even if they hadn't lately been by the churchyard to notice its desecrated grave beds, Oliver brushed away threads of damp moss and disclosed that they were emeralds, and that he'd stolen them. Their sparkle and gleam was offset by the dirt under his fingernails, and the farmyard smell on his hands.

'Friend of mine's mum,' he said. 'No way she'll know I took 'em.'

The other kids looked down hesitantly at his dirty handful of beads, then back at him. They didn't know what to say. The boy was outside their understanding. Until that moment he had only been known for being smelly and weird. He stank: a festering combination of wet pond scum and scalp. He wore the same shirt for weeks at a time, during which it would build up a repellent combination of smells and stains. He liked to beckon to people when the teacher wasn't looking and direct their attention to something disgusting in his pocket: a dead rat, a handkerchief stiff with snot or blood, and once, when his pocket lining had gone, his fiercely erect little penis.

But Oliver had a secret weapon: he was beautiful, and he knew it. However off-putting his behaviour, he could stop people in their tracks with the right smile. His eyes were so blue that people sometimes thought he was blind. It was a beauty that you couldn't lock on to for long, and it would help him get away with a lot in his life – right up to the point where it was no longer enough.

He would sit in class, saying nothing, drawing heavily inked, violent scenes on books and desks. He would rock backwards and forwards, and giggle in a way that was meant to sound mad, and did. Teachers ignored his behaviour, as if they knew something nobody else did (which fuelled the suspicion that his derangement was official) and when other pupils turned to look at him, they were the ones who were told to concentrate and face forward.

Nobody was even prepared to be spoken to by him, let alone to be offered the opportunity to buy emeralds. But having decided to sell them, he seemed to get more and more frustrated that people were laughing at him. And then he pushed it too far. He went up to some of the older boys and told them they had to buy his emeralds or he'd kiss them.

The first time, they laughed it off. But Oliver hated not getting a reaction. When he leapt up at one sixth-former, curled his arms round the boy's neck and pecked him on the cheek, the joke was over. Oliver had stepped out of the scenery and become a target. The pack chased him, and grabbed him, and he kept laughing even as he fell, and the kicks began firing in at his head and stomach.

Even when every last kid in the school had pointed out that they weren't real emeralds, still Oliver insisted. So Roland went up to him at the end of the day and said, 'How much are your emeralds, anyway?'

Oliver looked up warily through swollen eyelids and said, '5p each.'

Roland bought four of them. He and Oliver were eleven years old.

From then on, Oliver always seemed to be running. Roland would be quietly parked somewhere, eating, not wanting anyone to notice how important his food was to him, and Oliver would hurtle past, shouting insults so vile over his own shoulder that you almost wanted his pursuers to catch him and shut him up. Roland would watch as he streaked

away, meeting trouble eventually, his clothing torn, his possessions dashed to the floor. Roland would listen to him where
he fell, screaming for mercy, and the pity would come back,
and those beating him up would stop. Then, breathing heavily
on the ground, regaining his composure, he would say something so provocative they would be too taken aback to begin
again before he was back on his feet.

There was no explaining him, but that didn't stop people
trying. Everyone had their own version of the inside track.
It was said that his father knocked him around. That he had
fallen into a grain silo and never been the same. Kids spoke
of his life ban from the Leisure Pool for pushing so hard on
another boy's goggles that he had created a vacuum, sucking
the boy's eye from its socket. His family farm was said to
be a disgrace – a place where cows staggered around the
yard with bulging udders, having been for days without
milking. His father was known to empty the cash and carry
of whisky at regular intervals, and his mother was said to
be in with the gypsies, welcoming them on to the farm in
return for chickens and horses and other dark assistance.

Now, adults utter his name in a wary tone of voice. They
look into his strong, blue eyes and see themselves appraised
with no deference or respect. They react to him like water
to oil, and hope their kid isn't his friend. He is the first
suspect in the pettiest of crimes, even when he is nowhere
near the scene. He makes everyone uneasy, usually deliberately. But not Roland. Roland just sees someone as bored as
him, with as little money, who is only trying to find ways to
stop those two problems colliding with each other.

When Oliver gets himself into real trouble, it is Roland's
cue to make himself noticed. He waits until the last minute,
until the point when Oliver is at serious risk. Then Roland
steps in. And if on occasion someone doesn't understand

what that means, and enters Roland's space with a swagger, they soon see their mistake. He is not to be threatened or played with. He is gathered intent, awaiting direction.

Some of Oliver's behaviour at school already feels hard to believe. Did he really sell speed in the playground and punch a teacher and negotiate his way out of imminent expulsion on three separate occasions? All of that and more. There is so much of him that memory will always hesitate to trust itself. He will never let anything stay the way it is. He is in too much of a hurry to mark the world. To commit to defend him as Roland has, no matter what – it is quite a thing. But what else is there to do? The boy is his friend.

13

Whenever there is famine or abduction on the television Cleo makes her father hot chocolate. In the future her powers of consolation will be stronger, but this is the best she can manage for now. As the fading hopes of starving children or desperate parents play out on the screen, he gives her a barely perceptible sideways glance, which is her cue to slide neatly off the sofa and get the milk on.

Whatever the story is, however bad, it never puts them off as they blow on their drinks and take comforting slurps, and Cleo eats the skin off both hers and his by scooping it off with a fingertip and dropping it into her mouth. The world may be a bad place, but at least they are in it together.

And when, as sometimes happens, he loses his temper, perhaps even on the same night as a shared intimacy like this, she does not feel let down, because he has told her so often how these lapses have nothing to do with her. That they are just the fault of life, and all it has thrown at him. Or taken away. Or something. She does her best to help without feeling responsible, secure in the knowledge that however violently rejected her assistance might be, nobody else is offering it but her.

But all of that has changed.

How has Ursula won him so quickly? For days there have

been low voices in adjacent rooms, that come to a halt when she walks in. She gets quite enough of that at school. And it isn't just the talking: it's all the ways he has been trampling on their habits. He blocks off her usual position on the sofa beside him in favour of Ursula. He no longer asks for Cleo's advice, and the idea of her cooking dinner is now a joke and not a necessity.

Ursula seems to fill out the house, and make it smaller. You can't get past her in doorways. This in spite of the fact that she is self-conscious about her shape, and can move out of the way with unexpected speed when she wants to. Even these awkward sideways shifts Cleo has stopped finding endearing and started to find irritating.

The woman smells of coffee and make-up, and there is a slick sheen to her skin that makes Cleo think of butter melted then re-formed. She can use her stature to be imposing or absorbing, depending on whether she wants to get you to do something, or to bestow random, unasked-for comfort with one of her melodramatic hugs. During these embraces she tends to cry, which annoys Cleo because it feels like a demonstration. Any real emotion Ursula may feel is always blown up into something false.

She enjoyed meeting her father's girlfriends before, when less was at stake. When he brought someone home, the implied understanding was always that Cleo was in charge – that the purpose of the visit was to present the latest candidate to her for approval or rejection. And there was also a time when she thought she needed them. Motherless pup that she was, she latched on to the first two or three serious candidates, craving their intimacy, persistent as a muck-heap fly. When one of them told her she liked roses, Cleo spent three nights with a gardening encyclopaedia, and wiped out her bank balance on one rare-breed stem in a pot. She was inescapable. She got into their lives with incessant questions. She asked them what their favourite food was, then tried to cook it for them, with endearingly comic results.

The others were determined in their ways, and there were plenty of them: a procession of widows and other last-chancers, who broadly fell into two categories that Cleo labelled Props and Droppers. Props were worthy souls who wanted to save him – the ones who, God help them, believed all the fantastical stuff he fed them about his future. That he was going to publish books and set up institutions and *make* things, when the time was right. Some of them even seemed to have concluded that one day his *ship would come in*, and by extension, theirs too. Into this category fell Gloria and Maggie, both of whom he met at libraries, and both of whom retired hurt in the end. Droppers were those who didn't care what he did for himself so long as he could save them, and these were the most disastrous matches, that tended to end in the most riotous arguments and even (Jen and Josephine) in threats of suicide.

She wonders which category her mother fell into, if any. The dazzling light of his enthusiasm when it splits the clouds is sufficient to lull all kinds of women into thinking that for all the apparent chaos he lives in, this is someone who will be okay, who can therefore look after them too. By the time they discover that the enthusiasm is not only a finite resource but also, much of the time, a cover for blind despair, it is too late, and they have to fight their way from under the relationship before they turn into its crutch.

What makes Ursula different is the way she seems to have understood that danger from the start. At no point does she look panicked by him, and – more terrifying still – her complicity with him seems to be gaining mass, lathering up between them.

They are sitting over omelettes and salad in the kitchen. Ursula seems to be trying to break down barriers and make the conversation more intimate. Cleo doesn't want to acknowledge Ursula's growing influence by allowing that to happen, but Cleo's guard against her is down – partly because Ursula was unusually kind to her this week after Cleo burned her arm in a chemistry accident, and partly because an episode at school two days later has muddled her opinion.

The three of them eat in silence. Her father is dispatching his omelette in quick, slippery forkfuls. Ursula cuts prim triangles of hers, which she has made with no filling, and in between swallows she mounts her terrible campaign.

'That was a tiresome episode yesterday, wasn't it? I'm sorry I didn't see it coming. I hope you didn't feel that I let you down.'

'It's okay,' says Cleo. 'Forget about it.'

Her father looks up. 'What happened?'

'Please forget about it.'

'It was nothing, really. Just a silly joke where some girls got me into a room with Cleo and made a few comments.'

'What sort of comments?'

'You know. About you and me.'

'Oh God. Cleo. I'm sorry. What did they say?'

'It really doesn't matter.' Cleo piles into her omelette, and tries to think of another subject, remembering how her insides had curdled the first time one of them had shouted out the word *Mum*. Ruining it forever with vile associations. And the sentence that was said to her next, by, what was her name, she can't even think of her name, well, good: that sentence was even more corrosive, because she kept repeating it, like a mantra. *Think of him licking her out. Think of him licking her out.*

'Don't you think it is time you came clean with your father?' says Ursula, mercifully cutting off her train of thought.

'About what?'

'About the fact that you are being rather badly picked on at school?'

Here is a familiar feeling, though not one she is used to at home: the world weaponising itself against her; the air turning prickly and dangerous.

'What do you mean? No, I'm not.'

'It's nothing to be embarrassed about.'

'You two are always asking me if I am embarrassed, as if you think I should be. What are you saying I should be embarrassed about?'

'You're changing the subject.'

Fire can be returned if she wants. She has stuff on this woman. She knows her nicknames. She knows that girls at school say she has webbed feet, and repeat a horrible chant about the size of tampons she uses. *Super Plus, Super Plus, Super Plus.*

She shoots a nervous look at her father, who has put down his fork and seems genuinely concerned. But there is something incomplete about his expression. And as he goes through the motions of pushing her on it, Cleo realises what it is: this revelation is not new to him. Which means that the two of them have rehearsed this conversation.

'I think it would be good if you admitted it,' Ursula is saying. 'I think it would be an important step.'

'I don't know what you're talking about.'

'Listen, darling, I've seen the graffiti. In the girls' toilets.'

'What graffiti?'

'It's silly to say you haven't seen it yourself.'

'Stop this.'

'And I know what happened this week in Adam Wilson's chemistry class. I spoke to him.'

Her father looks up at speed. 'What do you mean?'

'Her arm. It wasn't an accident, Jasper.'

'Don't do this,' says Cleo, picking in spite of herself at

the still-painful rough patch on her arm, that has yet to scab over properly.

'They dropped sodium into her schoolbag, then poured water in it. The bag caught fire. She got burned in a sort of fight that happened afterwards.'

'It wasn't a proper fight.'

'And someone did that to your arm on purpose?'

'Well.' She allows herself a smile. 'You should see what I did to her.'

'Cleo.' Ursula gets up, threatening to take the table with her. 'I'll get the pudding. Talk about it between yourselves.'

'Is it true?' her father says, looking her straight in the eye with an old honesty, a directness that makes her want to sob because it has been gone for so long.

'It's just one way of looking at things,' she says.

She is trying to communicate without saying it out loud that all she wants him to do is change the subject, that this is not the time for deep chats or big revelations. Instead all she can think of to do to distract him is to make a sort of imitation of the side-to-side wobble Ursula did when she got to her feet. But although he starts smiling he catches himself quickly, and cautions her with his eyes in a way that shows where his new allegiances lie.

'Of course it's true,' says Ursula from the kitchen. 'You should hear the things they say about her. The way she's talked about. I can't count the number of times I've found her bike impaled on the railings, or had to tell someone off for writing stuff about her.'

'Why don't I know about this?'

She's back, with bowls of a bought trifle. 'Everybody keeps it from you, because they don't want to hurt your feelings.'

Cleo's vision of the world is starting to break down. Devils taunt her from the grain of the tabletop wood, from the material of Ursula's white apron.

'It's okay, you can admit it. There's a reason why I am saying this.'

'Which is what, exactly?'

'It's the fact that we may not be staying here.'

She looks up. The world has pulled itself back into very sharp focus.

'Do you want to tell her, or should I?' says Ursula, in triumph.

14

'Do you know,' says Mona, warming to the topic as her second vodka takes hold, 'what an odd little boy your friend here was, growing up?'

She's talking to Oliver but pointing at Roland, as if he were an object. He looks up from his plate into her pointed finger. Carol has left the table to watch television, though tonight's tea is still very much in progress: blistered turkey legs, surrounded by livid pools of economy beans. Roland has boiled some eggs to add bulk. He is in the habit of augmenting Mona's meals, which rarely fill him up these days.

'When he was little, he used to go skulking round people's houses,' says Mona.

'When did I do that?' says Roland.

'Don't tell me you don't remember, because I know you do. After Dad left.' She turns back to Oliver. 'He was quite the peeping Tom. Women used to find him in their gardens looking at their undies on the line, and ring up to tell me. Bet he's never told you that before.' There's an unpleasant note of triumph in her voice, as if she were jealous of how close Oliver is to her son, and wanted to get one over on him.

Oliver looks up calmly from the wreckage on his plate,

where everything has been dissected but hardly any of it eaten. 'I can't blame him. Got to do something in this place to keep yourself entertained.'

'What a strange boy,' says Mona. 'Playing with himself in the bushes, looking at women in the bath.' She gives a lewd shriek.

Roland drops his fork. 'I never did that.'

'Aha!' Mona pounces. 'So you do admit to the spying part?'

There's no point getting involved. You just have to let her say what she wants. He has been peeling three eggs, careful not to disturb the white, only to remove every last scrap of shell with his thick, clumsy fingers. Now he places them all wobbling together on one slice of bread, rolls it up into a fat cylinder and eats it in quick bites, enjoying successive yolk explosions as he progresses, and sucking to ensure that not one drop of good stuff gets away. His hunger is distracting, but he has learned not to disregard it because of what that does to his mood. His new body is proving useful in terms of the respect it has brought him, but it comes with imperatives that you ignore at your peril.

It wasn't like she says it was. He was only ten, and he can't remember ever thinking about sex then, not that he does much now either. No – it was about browsing other people's lives. The magic of a winter window. The things you saw when the nights started drawing in earlier, when people carried on watching their televisions or dishing up their tea without drawing the curtains. There were terraces off the high street that were like whole banks of television screens for him. Then there was the added layer of excitement that someone might step out to light a fag or fetch in more coal, chancing upon him pressed to their window or behind their bins, and – following a crucial pause for fear and disbelief that gave Roland the head start – start chasing. Nothing like that jolt of adrenaline, that hammering in the chest. It put colour behind his eyelids even in the dark. The town is where he served out his skulking apprenticeship; where he learned his craft; where he graduated to ghost-hood.

He still walks at night, though for different reasons. Now he walks because he has grown so fast that his bones hurt, and getting out is the best way he has found to deal with it. At night he seems to itch on the inside – an excruciating feeling that makes him want to stretch to the point of dislocating his limbs. Temporary relief can be found in the kind of full, joint-popping stretch that causes his hands and feet to meet the coffin-ends of his bed. But when it's really bad, he just has to walk. Walking is a way of working his body loose of it.

Muscle is piling on to him around the arms, on his thighs and calves. It is gathering at his shoulders. It has turned the loose-limbed movement of his boyhood into an awkward lope that he is stuck with until his bones catch up with the rest of him, and his knees ache constantly under the pressure of a body that is developing too fast to be supported. The doctor who told Roland this jovially asked him if there was any way he could 'slow things down a bit'.

Sometimes he walks out to the Ness before dawn. He doesn't take a torch, because torchlight makes you feel more in the dark. And this way, he gets to see every change as the sun comes up. The view gets more hypnotic the more you know how to look: a fishing tug surging through the swell; the golden patch of a sandbank; the texture of a bird-flock in the air, agitating like water in a bath. He likes it when they come inland to pour on to a patch of beach or a piece of driftwood, and fuss and flutter before another impulse shocks through them and off they stream again, ribboning out to sea.

It's the shipping lanes that really get him: supertankers

oozing across the horizon, moving things on a scale bigger than ordinary life, to impossibly northern destinations like Oslo or Shetland. However slow their progress, they transfix him – especially in darkness or fog, when their strong yellow lights turn the ships into recumbent giants, queuing feet first, wearing miner's lamps. They lie back and push forward, secure in the knowledge that nothing on earth can stop them.

'Cor blimey Mona, that was delicious,' says Oliver, putting on a cockney accent, and covering his own near-full plate with the empty ones he has collected from the table. 'You should open a restaurant.'

The plates are nearly swiped from him by Mona's fast, cuffing hand. 'You should never, ever say *cor blimey*. Do you know what it means? It means *God please blind me*. Is that what you want, Oliver? Do you want God to blind you?'

'Not when you put it like that.'

The three of them move to join Carol in front of the television. Mona is hiding the vodka, but Roland knows it's around here somewhere.

'He still does it, you know,' she says to Oliver. 'Goes out at nights. He thinks I don't know, but I do. Peculiar.' Her nostrils flare as she says it.

'No more than me or thee,' says Oliver.

Roland feels a wave of love for Oliver, the intensity of which is embarrassing.

'So you say,' says Mona. 'But what does he do out there? What does he get up to? He's got this, I don't know, this *secret* streak. We'll never know exactly what he's about.'

Tempting at this point to tell Oliver just how much Mona talks about him when he isn't there. That, for example, she quite often says he is *hypomanic*. That he could do with *a good dose of lithium to box him in a bit*.

'Well,' says Oliver. 'I don't care what he does at night.

Whatever keeps him out of trouble. Got to find something to do round here until we find a way to get away.'

Mona aims a finger at him. 'Remember who you're talking to, young man. I live in this town by choice.'

'No you don't,' says Oliver.

But she's lost the will to contradict him because the local news has come on, and two missing kids have turned up drowned in a quarry pond.

'Oh good Lord, here we go.' She closes her eyes to focus grimly on the details. 'You couldn't live with yourself, could you?'

As the story plays out, with police divers, discarded clothing, distraught parents, Mona screws up her eyes to focus right in on it, in dialogue with the horror, punctuating the narrative with horrified interjections.

'Stop. They didn't. Oh Lord.'

'Don't. I can't bear it.'

'You couldn't go on, could you?'

'Well, that's their life over,' she says, finally.

'Of course it is,' says Roland. 'They're dead.'

She turns on him. 'Not the children's lives, you idiot. The parents'.'

'What?'

'You've never seen pain like that. Trust me, I have. It sends you to a place you never come back from.'

'All I meant was, it was pretty bad for the kids who died.'

Mona is still staring at the screen but her mind is elsewhere. 'Up at Wreaking there was a woman whose son had accidentally throttled himself in the ropes of a swing. She never got over it, of course. How could you? Snapped his neck like a bird's. Every time I see a playground, I think of her.'

And that's it, isn't it? Her fear is not disaster but being blamed for it. It's the terror of something happening on her watch. The thought keeps Roland awake for hours, until finally, before 5 a.m., when he can bear the itch in his bones no longer, he slips outside.

The night is just beginning to bow out. He crosses the road quickly, through the pooling yellow of three beachfront street lights. A milk float is out, bottles jangling. He takes the gnarled concrete steps down to the beach. His feet pound through shingle as he forces on across the marshes and out to the Ness, his movements becoming more confident as he gets away from the town. He pulls his jacket in tight, gets his head down, and walks. He has always found the simplicity of the spit comforting – you walk out to the end, then you turn round and walk back. And while you walk, you know there is nothing on either side of you but waves breaking on grey stones. It's like setting out into the static of a detuned television.

He will see the sun coming at him when it rises. He likes having the dark behind him. He likes imagining that he could turn around at any time and see it at his back. He likes the birds that make hidden noises out here and the otherworldly red plants that grow in the shingle, belonging half to the sea and half to the land. He likes the rods of night-fishermen planted in the shore. He likes hearing snippets of their conversation as he tramps unseen behind them and watches the glow of their cigarette ends.

Once he has gone very far out, further than any other people, he sits in the wet shingle, waiting for dawn, listening to the sound of tidewater pawing at the stones, beaten and submissive. He stares at the surface of the water, hoping for the thrill of a bird-flock to flash past, skimming the surface, silent as smoke. He replays a worn old fantasy about being adopted; a foundling; not of this peculiar place at all.

15

'At some point, later on,' says Cleo, 'but only when I say so, we might be able to talk about the idea of me calling you my stepmother. If you like.' She can barely choke the words out, but her father has told her to make Ursula feel as welcome as possible.

With improbable poise, Ursula is kneeling on Cleo's bedroom floor trying to finish her packing. The movers came and went yesterday, and Ursula supervised the loading up of everything in the house before embarking on a long, deep clean in advance of their departure. It was at this point that Cleo 'remembered' the chest of drawers behind her door – a mirrored, sparkly dumping ground that she kept as a place to forget old things without having to throw them away.

Ursula takes mangled wedges of clothing out of the chest and sets them down on the floor one by one. She tries to disentangle the garments one from the other, identifying and categorising them. She holds up a tight twist of denim, and says, 'Tell me: is this trousers or a jacket?'

Cleo sits cross-legged, staring back at her. 'Didn't you hear what I just said? I said you could become my stepmother. That was a big thing to say.'

Another wedge of clothing emerges – this one shelling

out a clatter of lipsticks, nail polish and cassettes. 'I know dear, and I'm grateful, but your father was quite specific about which train we had to catch, and I had no idea you had this whole chest of things left. Are you sure you need all this?'

'Hang on. What I said doesn't mean you can start telling me what to wear, or when to wash my hair and stuff like that.'

'It wouldn't be the end of the world if you dressed more smartly from time to time.'

'I give you notice here and now that I will do what I like in all such areas.'

'Can we have the rest of this conversation on the train? We're running very late.'

'I don't understand why he had to go ahead of us in the first place.'

'He wanted to get it ready for us.'

'Shouldn't we be helping him to do that?'

'We should let him surprise us. That's the kind thing to do. We're the ladies, and he wants to put on a show.' She has opened the final drawer and is frowning at the nest of pants and bras intertwined inside it.

We're the ladies. Please.

He does like to take charge when he's on an upswing. But in Cleo's experience it's good to be on standby for the times when things go the other way. Ursula seems tough enough to make herself happy without needing him to do it for her, but Cleo still hasn't seen how she is going to be when things turn the other way. It's all moving too fast – as things always do when he is on the up.

She looks around before leaving the house. She tries to divert energy into the banking of details, to archive the quirks of door handles for posterity, to record the creaks of dodgy stairs. She stares at herself in the bathroom mirror, trying to fix the moment. Then Ursula is calling her from downstairs to tell her the cab is here, and that she should post her key through the letterbox on her way out.

The taxi is a luxury. Then again, Ursula would probably pay anything to avoid carrying her luggage on the Underground. On the train, Cleo takes out a paperback to try and head off any conversation. But that doesn't stop Ursula, who waits until they are settled in a carriage full of silent, eavesdropping people, and opens the discussion.

'I didn't know your mother, of course. So I don't know how she'd have liked her money spent. But if Jasper thinks this move is right for us, and that's how he wants to spend it, then I think we should trust him.'

Ursula clears her throat and swigs from a bottle of water. She tries to do it without touching her lips to the aperture, and the lack of a seal over the bottle means that its contents spill down over her front, soaking one flap of her silk scarf.

'Don't you have anything to say about that?' she says. 'It's your inheritance we're spending.'

Cleo stamps a hole in the floor of the train carriage with her foot, and looks down at the blur of track flying past. Ursula's words fly away down the hole, and are instantly forgotten. She wishes. But she knows now, and there's no way of unknowing it.

'What inheritance?' she says.

'Of course,' says Ursula. 'I forgot. Sorry. You should talk to your father about this. But in a nutshell, it's money that comes from your mother.'

'My mother?'

'Yes.'

'Why haven't I heard about this?'

'You should really talk to your father.' They are passing a field with a windmill on a tower and a red-brick barn stranded in the middle. 'He knows exactly what he's doing.' It is the last thing Ursula says to Cleo as the train pulls in at the station and they see him waving from the platform, jiggling one leg and grinning desperately.

It's not even March yet, but the air is still smoky, and it smells of muck being spread on fields. This will be her memory of arrival: the smell, and the damp that seems to chill her bones as they get off the train. And the fact that one of her father's arms is bandaged up, against what looks like a nasty injury, with a brown, dried bloodstain coming through it.

'What happened here?' says Cleo, trying to break up the pathetic, devotional embrace that Ursula is receiving.

'Bit of DIY. No harm done.'

He has bathed and attempted an erratic shave, but he has sweated since, and his shirt looks soaked. His breathing is ragged and fast. As he walks along, trying to pull Ursula's two huge pieces of wheeled luggage, he knocks the daffodils he is carrying into the side of a bin, decapitating several before he's even had a chance to present them to Ursula.

On the journey Cleo looks at papers strewn on the back seat of the car. They may want to keep this a surprise but she wants to be as prepared as possible. There are documents that look like they are from the Health Service. She wonders if someone is ill. She throws her head on to the back seat of the car to see if the clouds out to sea are doing anything interesting. Then she pipes up.

'So where's this *money* come from that we've suddenly got hold of?'

She's in a good position to see the panicked look he shoots at Ursula, and the firm reply it receives.

'I need to talk to you about that.'

'It's from Mum? Why only now?'

'It's complicated. It's to do with the liquidation of a trust. I can explain it to you.'

They rattle through the town – a new context for their

familiar estate car with all its smells of sweets and fluff. He fills the awkward silence by enthusing wildly about a pier and some haggard seafront amusements. Then they are leaving the town behind them, heading up the coast.

'Originally it was just a private place,' he says. 'Then it got assimilated. Then I think its purpose must have changed several times.'

The water tower is visible from a distance, looming closer on the horizon and finally sinking into the trees like a descending periscope as they draw close. Then they pull in at the gates and her father leaps out of the idling car to fumble with a padlock and throw them open. The signs remain: some in ancient stone-carved script; others in faded sky blue: *NHS WREAKING*.

As they pass the hospital's immense walls of red brick, and its ranks of high windows, he explains that the place is shut down. They skirt the perimeter, then take a turning down a separate driveway to a whitewashed building that is much smaller, but has a clinical atmosphere all of its own. Her father brings the car to a stop in a parking space where moss and weeds are taking over but you can still make out the painted word *DOCTOR*.

She will know the structure so well in the future that it will be impossible to imagine not knowing it, but on this first day it is confusing: the clock tower, the entrance lobby, the two wings sprouting off it.

'*This* is where we're living?

'Come with me and all will be revealed.'

When he is like this, the persuasive energy is unstoppable. It fills him, and comes out in uncontrollable bursts. Obstacles bounce off him. But this is as much of a test of his irrepressibility as she has ever seen.

In the flat afternoon light, she sees grimy windows, the stopped clock in its turret. A lone pigeon is working away in a knackered dovecote with peeling paint and dilapidated entrance holes. The dank smell of standing water makes her think of problem drains.

She stands near the front porch in her tough uniform of jeans and trainers, ready for anything, staring up at the building. And when she sees the silhouetted figure moving away from a window, she doesn't question who it is. She just offers it a request that this should work out, that this quantity of Up will not be followed by something terrible.

16

Oliver has promised to make good on his offer of chickens, so Roland goes off to meet him, leaving the two of them sitting there: Carol sitting quietly at her jigsaw table; Mona, sucking her teeth at a page of the newspaper headlined *MY BOY IS GONE AND I'LL NEVER GET HIM BACK.*

He wraps himself up, takes the bus out of town, gets off at a stop flanked by ridged fields, and walks the half-mile track to Oliver's house. It is understood now that Roland will not enter the yard, not even to ring the front doorbell, so he waits outside, staring at lichen on the drystone walls, waiting to be noticed. The air is cold and filled with the tang of muck.

After five minutes he hears a door close, then quick footsteps in the slop of the yard, and Oliver comes out through the gate looking businesslike, and touches Roland briefly on the arm by way of greeting and apology. Soon they are walking up the shoulder of the broiler-house hill, the leather of Oliver's rifle-strap creaking at his shoulder.

They climb, two dark shapes against the sky, braced against life, with low expectations and no contingency plans. They approach the barbed-wire fence that marks the end of Oliver's family farm, and the perimeter of the broiler house.

'How's your dad?' says Roland, referring to the fact that he still isn't supposed to go anywhere near the house.

'Doing okay, I think. Still not quite right.'

He hasn't seen Oliver's father since he stopped by the farm the morning after a late summer thunderstorm last year, to find a house in mourning. Oliver's mother was in a back room with the television on silent, doing needlework, while his father sat at the kitchen table with a long, dirty tumbler and a bottle of cooking brandy, staring into the stove and silently weeping.

His prize bull and nine cows had been sheltering from the storm under the broad canopy of a Holm oak when the lightning struck. The electricity was conducted directly into the puddle of water in which they stood, and in which their smoking bodies were found. He had been drinking ever since, in a reaction both Roland and Oliver thought was over the top, but they knew him well enough to know that they should stay out of his way. The two of them sat trying to talk, trying not to raise their voices over the ticking of the coal stove and his father's soft sobs, but they were not quiet enough, and at a certain point, when the boys were laughing too hard at some stupid school story, Oliver's father dashed his brandy glass against the wall with one swift sweep of his arm. He carried on staring straight ahead, tear-trails shining in the stubble of his cheeks, but Roland knew it was time to leave.

'Next time I'll come to you,' said Oliver, showing him to the door, and they had to stifle bonkers, inappropriate laughter.

Their breathing rings out against the cold, hard ground.

'So you're still taking Carol for walks up to the hospital?' says Oliver.

'It's a big deal for her.'

'She can't go on her own?'

'I leave her alone when we're up there. Then I meet up with her and walk her down again.'

'What do you do when she's away on her own?'

'I don't know. Just . . . walk around.'

He doesn't like that Oliver knows he still goes up to Wreaking. The place is old hat now.

'Bet it's not as fun as it used to be. We were the lucky ones there.'

Oliver is talking, with a nostalgia he has learned from older kids, about the parties. That first summer, two years ago, straight after the closure, has acquired legendary status. People are already lying about having been there. And it's true, the parties were good. The building seemed inexhaustible, and so did the summer.

They were fifteen, and just finding out about the good stuff. The hospital was still full of its furniture, and it wasn't even fenced off. It felt like it had been vacated for their benefit, with interesting things left deliberately for them to find in every single room. They marched on it, the young of the town, as if it were the palace of a deposed dictator and they wanted to show they no longer feared it.

They were tentative to start with, but they got bold quickly enough. He remembers people daubing what they thought were satanic slogans on trees and walls. Wearing straitjackets. Looking for the morgue. He remembers the first fires being set inside, and kids dancing round them to the music, and the wave of panic when the floorboards burned through for the first time.

'Remember the bathing chair?' says Oliver, breathing hard against the gradient of the hill.

You were nobody if you hadn't had a go in the bathing chair. You were strapped in by the restraints on its arms and legs, and people poured booze into your mouth until you'd had enough.

'And what about that girl? Claire something. Remember her?'

'Not sure,' says Roland.

He remembers her well. He will remember her for years. She was older than them, maybe seventeen. Surging round from group to group in Doc Martens and a wide brimmed hat, drinking Southern Comfort and making it known that if anyone told her they had never been kissed then she would rectify the problem. Roland was one of the first people she approached, but would never have dreamed of making such a declaration. So she had turned to Oliver, who, unlike Roland, was no stranger to kissing all manner of people, and he had put on his sweetest grin, batted his eyelashes and said that he was 'untouched'.

By the light of the fire, he watched Oliver taking one long, drunken snog, converting it to another, and then capitalising further on the situation. This is his way: you make one audacious move, then use it to advance your cause before anyone gets wind of your determination. He watched Oliver suggesting something to her, and her laughing, and the two of them disappearing towards the old assembly-hall stage. Then, cursing Oliver for having dosed him up with drugs just before abandoning him, Roland stormed off to find more drink.

He remembers his heart belting with the speed Oliver had made him take – the gritted-teeth intensity as he looked down from a balcony at the mob rioting in the hall. They were right down in the throat of the music, where it was at its most penetrating and abrasive. The sound filled the chamber with harsh echoes. Bigger fires were being set.

He assumed when he first saw it that Oliver would be at the centre of the group piling up the chairs and tables to be torched. That the party had reached that stage because of him and his destabilising energy. But when he scanned the crowd there was no sign of his tiny, dangerous form. Instead Roland saw that he was leaning up near the stage behind a load of stacked metal chairs, near some old scenery, with the girl. Her legs were apart and he had a hand up her skirt. Before Roland turned away for the last time he remembers being surprised by the tenderness with which Oliver seemed to be operating, for all that any observer could have seen that his objective was just to steal whatever he could get away with. Oliver was no tourist: he was here undercover, to topple the regime.

And then savage envy kicked in, and self-hatred that Roland could have been stupid enough not to tell her the truth, because if he had it could have been him getting the goods, and he sat there on the balcony talking to himself with his teeth gritted, saying let it go *let it go let it go* but knowing that the more he obsessed about it the more it would be impossible to let it go at all. And all the while, look: could you fucking believe him down there, surging on to third base? He turned in disgust, and left the back of the gallery through the little hut that contained the old movie projection room. He sifted through the rolls of film for a while, then made his way outside down a precariously corroding set of waffled metal steps.

He walked down a long, sealed corridor, outside the building but connected to it. He found a window-board on a distant wing that hadn't been touched, and levered it easily away from its window, screws protesting in the chipboard. He ducked inside, and pulled his sleeves over his hands to climb over the broken glass on the ledge. He crossed a square room lined with green metal bedsteads, then found himself in a blue-carpeted corridor. He passed a record office stacked with a huge wall of index cards. And then he heard it: the calm sound of someone whistling an absent-minded tune, coming from somewhere inside the building.

He went further in, the building soaking around him as the party's noise fell away. He carried on, his footsteps crunching on broken glass, following the whistled tune. He opened the door to a bathroom, where a dove sat on a partition between two toilet cubicles, cooing. Still, the whistling carried on next door.

He pushed open the door to find an old man with wild, white hair, sitting next to an unmade bed and painting a picture. Beside him were chocolate bars and a large bottle of lemonade. Leaning against the wall were a broom whose bristles were almost worn to nothing, and a garden fork with only two tines. How long had this relic of a man been living here?

It was Roland's first meeting with Geoffrey the Gardener.

The staff at Wreaking had done a good job of keeping him busy – put him to work not only in the gardens, but in the kitchens and corridors as well. He was so well integrated that when the hospital closed down, it was just assumed that he would find work elsewhere. It went completely overlooked that his official status was that of patient. When Roland found him, he'd been living there for nearly a year, taking his fork and his brush out to the gardens every day, awaiting further instructions.

He came to live at the Golden Sands after that, only to die seven months later from what Carol described as 'underuse'. She wasn't upset, though. She waited until after Geoffrey's funeral to mention it, but she claimed that he'd 'pestered' her at night throughout his time with them, but that she hadn't wanted to say anything to get him into trouble.

'Still,' she said, 'after the time he had of it, it's no surprise.'

She went on to explain how Geoffrey had been difficult with the opposite sex ever since his original admittance to Wreaking, which was caused by a fight he'd got into with the man who was sleeping with his wife when he came back home.

'Came back home from where?' said Roland.

'The war, of course,' said Carol.

They reach the outskirts of the broiler house – two long barns with a pair of grain silos at each end. Oliver motions for them to lie down on their fronts near the hedge.

'What time are they coming?' says Roland.

'Around five, this time of year.'

'And you know it's today?'

'Course I know it's today.'

They lie there, getting cold. The wind carries the smell of ammonia and the sound of muffled indignation.

Oliver taps Roland on the shoulder, and jerks his head towards the driveway, where a red pick up is arriving. It backs up to the entrance, and two men in donkey jackets get out. The back of the truck is stacked high with identical wooden crates. Roland can't hear exactly what they are saying, but he can hear the intonation of a joke, and brief chuckles. The men put on thick gloves, and clamber over their truck and into the broiler house. The simmering sound of 5,000 chickens comes to the boil.

'Phase one in progress,' says Oliver.

'Do we go in now?'

'No. Phase one is when the chicken catchers are here. We move at phase two.'

'Which is?'

'When they've gone.'

'It's cold lying down here.'

'You want free stuff you have to pay for it somehow.' Oliver settles himself and takes the air rifle out of its slip. 'Here.'

'What?'

'I bet you can't hit one after a whack on this.'

Roland looks down to see a familiar little brown bottle, with a lightning-flash label. He sighs. 'Really?'

'Got to keep things interesting.'

It's a cold afternoon, and the poppers make it colder. After the first deep hit of the fumes Roland is staring uselessly at a patch of ground as his head swells with blood. Then comes hard, gut-shaking laughter tinged with desperation because they're laughing for no reason but still can't stop, and fear that if they did stop there would be nothing but a headache and the sadness. The beautiful toxicity of it; the swimming-pool-soak of those fumes that swell your brain to bursting point.

The chicken catchers work fast, grabbing four or five at a time by their necks and stuffing them into the wooden crates they carry before slamming the lids. It isn't long before they are getting up and driving away, and sure enough, though they've locked the doors behind them, the men have been clumsy, and several birds can be glimpsed pecking around in the scrub by the shed.

When the van's lights have safely receded up the bumpy track, Oliver gets busy. He breaks the barrel of the air rifle and inserts one of the pellets from the tin in his lap. The gun makes a dull tapping noise and the pellet hits home. A stringy stalk of cow parsley wavers nearby, and the chicken drops into a flapping mess in the dirt. Oliver leans back to reload.

They end up with three, which Oliver puts in his satchel, and they walk. Oliver drops into the farmyard to leave a bird at the back door for his parents, then they get the bus back into town.

'What about your dad?' says Oliver, as they stare at their own reflections in the darkening bus window. 'Ever think about him?'

Tyres hiss outside. He says it calmly, imposing no obligation on Roland to reply, and not taking his eyes off their pretend version of the view. But the question is still hanging in the air when they get back to the Golden Sands, and hangs over the party atmosphere in the house brought on by the chickens they produce.

They pluck the birds, and put them in to roast. Mona opens a bottle of sherry. She and Oliver are still at the table, laughing about something, when Carol comes into the kitchen to help Roland with the potatoes.

'Sorry to put you out,' she says. 'But I'm still keen on that walk.'

He kisses Carol's forehead, which feels damp with the sweat of stress. 'We'll go tomorrow, okay?' He feels for her. Being mentally ill seems to involve a lot of sitting around.

Later, after the meal has been cleared away, Roland stands over a chicken carcass on the counter, roving it expertly with both hands, reaming out muscle meat with precision where it remains. His fingertips walk over it as if he were playing it like an instrument. He eats the wings, and turns it over to get at the oysters.

'Hey. I was planning on making soup with that,' says Mona, dropping an empty bottle in the bin, and going to the cupboard for another.

He licks his fingers. 'Sorry.'

'He's always had an appetite,' he hears her saying in the next room. 'As a baby he fed so hard that I couldn't get out of bed afterwards until someone had brought me a cup of beef tea.'

He found treasure once, in the garden, glinting. He was digging out a flowerbed, and there it was: a silvery seam of ring pulls – the archaeological evidence of his father's sales promotion business. Tokens dutifully amassed by punters in pursuit of the useless gifts he sent them in return. Roland dug deep – there were years' worth of them down there. It was the first proof Roland had that his memory wasn't making things up.

Now, wiping the last of the dishes, he allows himself to think again of the way they boxed him away. He strains to see his father's face, as if by opening his eyes to the memory the features would spring down out of the light. But all he can see is the room as it was then, before the Golden Sands, with a suggestion of his father present in aftershave and laughter. The face is looking in, but he can't see it. Then the flaps come over again, sealing him quickly back into the muffled darkness.

17

He has strung coloured lights over the front door. A trestle table is set up over the two *DOCTOR* parking spaces to the right. On the table he has put out drinks and a portable radio.

'Everything but bunting and a marching band,' says Ursula.

They get out and stand around acclimatising themselves to the damp in the lea of the building, to all the undisturbed smells and sounds. It's a little fresh to be hanging around outside, but he has thought of that too. He puts a match to the contents of a red metal bucket-bin by the front door, and the insides – carpet remnants, paper, wood – take quickly, burning up into a viable brazier in no time. The three of them stand around it drinking glasses of sparkling wine with some kind of ginger liqueur in it, while he briefs them on how to behave.

'I just want to say a few things before we start. One is how excited I am to be setting out on this journey with you, and the other is how much I love you both for having the faith to come this far.'

Love you *both*? Steady now.

'The point is,' he says, warming to his audience, 'that this tour of the building needs the assistance of your imaginations. You have to try and see what this place *will be* as much as what it is now.' He reaches for the bottle on the table and clumsily slops fizz into their glasses. 'Leave your bags in the car. Just bring your drinks and come with me. And remember: it's not what it is, but what we're going to make of it. This is, if you like, a tour . . . *of the future.*'

'We get it,' says Cleo.

The lobby has four waiting rooms leading off it, two on each side. Wood-panelled walls are broken up with noticeboards scattered with clinging fragments of hospital information (safety notices; meal rotas), and one or two calming pictures of landscapes: mountains, fields, streams. The recessed area behind it is not unlike the reception of a small hotel: it contains a desk backed with cubbyholes and filing cabinets, a couple of fire extinguishers and two dead ferns in pots.

'The two wings were called the Utterson and the Enfield,' he says. 'Female and male, just like at Wreaking, but on a smaller scale. To start with we'll live in the Utterson. The Enfield is a bit run down.' He produces a large key from his pocket. 'So. In we go.'

He leads them down corridors, past common rooms with tables and chairs strewn around them. The carpets are peppered with cigarette burns. A chair hangs down from the ceiling, embedded in the ceiling tiles. They pass a room with a thick door painted medical green, a spyhole looking in, and a sign that reads ISOLATION. Cleo lingers long enough to see that the window inside has a lockable shutter drawn over it, as do the radiator and the light fittings.

'Revenant House was built later than the main hospital, originally as a private clinic – then later it catered for certain specific requirements. Mothers and babies. Shock therapy. Its function changed over the years. This was where patients made phone calls.'

They've reached an area of green shag walls and pin

boards with biro graffiti on them. A little well in the floor is lined with brown, fabric-covered benches, where Cleo guesses you would have waited for one person to get off the phone. A patch of different coloured paint and some drilled holes in the wall show where the pay-phone had been. She reads the graffiti drawn among the scratches and phone numbers.

remember someone's always worse off than you are
I love Bill
if Mary had a little lamb, why wasn't she arrested?
this is my Mum's number DO NOT rub it off
because the little lamb had fun – it hadn't been molested
I don't want any more cheese I just want to get out of the trap
address here is Revenant House, Wreaking, England, The World,
The

'Just remember: all of this can change. We can do anything we want with it. Keep your eyes on the future. But for now . . .' He throws open the door on to a long, ground-floor day room, walking quickly, hoping to blind them with it. 'This is where we'll live.'

He's laid another fire in advance here, around which some of the familiar furniture of home has been arranged, and he crouches down to light it. The wood is damp and the chimney smokes, but the smell of the stuttering fire dispels the close, institutional pall and brings in a bit of nature. He has made it as cosy as he can, but the room wins out, and their furniture looks lost in it. She imagines sitting here with a rug over her, staring out of the window at the fir trees outside. In one corner of the room, a torn flip-chart lies on its side next to a broken overhead projector. Cleo rights the chart to see a heading, in red marker: *ASSIMILATING LONG-TERM CLIENTS INTO THE COMMUNITY*. Some bullet points are written underneath.

Next he shows them into a long kitchen, which is bisected

by the deep trench of a metal serve-over counter. The strip-lights overhead are fogged up with grease.

'Sadly the parquet floor that was here before has been stolen,' he says, looking down absent-mindedly at the zigzagged patterns of the stolen blocks, which are still there, traced by mould. 'But that's an opportunity to get the floor we *do* want. Cup of tea?' he offers, as if it is something spectacular.

'What about bedrooms?' says Cleo.

He puts the kettle down again. 'Right. Bedrooms. Come with me.'

The stairs are enclosed in metal cages all the way up, so nothing can be thrown down the well. She runs her fingers along the rusty, latticed metal. They pass a room with a sign on it that reads *Occupational Therapy*. A room of long benches with the odd half-finished bit of woodwork or needlepoint: coffee tables; cushion covers. It smells of paint.

'Try not to focus on what it is now,' he says. 'In a year or two, we'll be living in the most desired residence of a very fancy area. The developers will be publishing their plans any day now. There will be flats and shops. Cinemas. Leisure centres. Swimming pools. You name it.'

Off he goes, the time traveller. Leading them from room to room of his imagined version of the building, setting it before them relentlessly, never pausing for long enough that they should accidentally stumble across the here and now. This will be their sitting room. Here is where they will sit by the fire after wet winter walks. In the summer they will set out deckchairs here. This is where Ursula will go when she wants to be alone. Will. Will. Will.

It is hard to keep her mind off the notion that this building *wants* to rot away. That it is quite happily going one way, and that trying to do what he wants to do is like trying to throw a speeding car into reverse.

149

He shows Ursula their new bedroom, which he has set up in a day room done out in hot, Bagpuss pink.

'That's quite a colour,' says Ursula.

'I think this was part of the mother-and-baby unit,' he says. 'They went in for bright colours. We can change it.'

'Lovely,' says Ursula. 'And what are the paintings?' She's pointing at a wall done out in murals of grinning teddy bears, and flowers with eyes and noses. Everything in the painting has a face.

'Patient art,' he says. Do you like them?'

'Not much,' says Ursula.

There is so much to see that they wouldn't be looking in her direction if they couldn't hear the wobble in her voice. But they can hear it, which means that they are able to understand quite quickly that, with the slow collapse of a monumental edifice, she is starting to cry. The tears are slow-moving but they are acquiring mass, sheering off flakes of make-up in their path. This thing is going all the way down.

'I'm fine, I'm fine. Take Cleo on.'

He pauses, and turns. Ursula is lost for now, but not his loyal little girl.

'Come with me,' he says, leaping on, as if the prevailing mood were one of glee, as if everybody knew it.

They leave Ursula sitting on one side of the bed, teasing a tissue from a plastic packet. Cleo follows him along another long corridor of closed door after closed door, box after box, boxing away into forever. And still he keeps on talking.

'This one we can make into a bigger living room when we get round to it. Then when we get settled we can start to think about the Enfield wing. Classrooms, staff rooms, a canteen. We'll have the place filled up and making money in no time.'

'Dad?'

'Yes?' He stops and looks at her.

'What do you mean, classrooms?'

'You didn't think we were going to live in a big place like this all on our own? Ursula and I are planning to open a school here.'

She looks down at a wide-panelled lever on the door beside them that reads *PUSH PAD IN EMERGENCY*. It is broken.

'A school?'

'We'll open in a year or so. It's all planned out. When Wreaking is developed fully it will be full of parents wanting to send their children to our school. The catchment area will be huge – and right here on our doorstep.'

'Are you serious?'

'Before you say anything else,' he says, 'this is for you.'

They have reached the end of the corridor. A spiral staircase leads upwards from a corner. White lettering punched into a black sign on the wall reads *NURSES' QUARTERS*.

'Up you go,' he says.

'It's dark.'

'You can feel your way up using the banister.'

The staircase turns several revolutions so there is no way she could look back and see him even if there was any light. There is a musty, almost sweet aroma she recognises as the smell of mice.

'Well, have the stairs run out?'

Foot forward, sliding from stone to a rougher texture: floorboards.

'Yes,' she says.

A short pause, then it lights up: a yellow galaxy in attic rafters, clustered round her lovely old green bed. Even as she recognises the old Christmas lights from home the breath is knocked from her by the love of it.

At the centre of the room, her desk has been set up in a bay window. He's left the curtains drawn for theatrical effect, and put a side table with a reading light by the bed, and her other possessions are up here too, though mostly still in boxes to give her some unpacking to do, some ownership.

'Do you like it?' he says, from the top of the stairs. 'Because if you don't we can always put you in one of the day rooms, nearer us.'

'I like it.'

He is frowning, almost shaking with the worry. The loss of Ursula so soon has unseated him.

As she undoes the curtains, light pools at intervals down the length of the room. She looks down on the careful clumps of laurel outside, on the rhododendrons and firs that fret the edge of the garden. She sees the marshes, and beyond them a glinting thread of sea. The garden is losing itself. Spring is here, and things are about to get riotous. She sees the shattered surface of a tennis court, and for the first time, she sees the lake, sulking down to the left of the Enfield wing, its edges dotted with decrepit pavilions.

What are we doing here? she thinks. But she knows what must be said instead.

'Okay. I can see it,' she says.

He beams, and hugs her, a little too tightly, as usual. Too keen to transmit – making the connection so intensely that it hurts.

'It will work, won't it?'

'It will work.'

And now he is the one crying. Which is usually a bad thing, but not, she thinks, on this occasion.

18

Even though he's known the building for this long, there is still a hangover of the old days that makes him fall silent; still a point at which the approach stops being a walk and becomes a bated-breath creep instead. It tends to coincide with the moment when hospital contents start appearing in the woods: armchairs wedged in the elbows of branches, a soap dish in the brambles, signs sinking into leaf-litter. Carol's gaze snags on these things as they walk, and whatever conversation the two of them might have been having always falters. Roland knows that this is his cue to start giving her the space to have whatever thoughts she needs to have when she comes up here, and he drops back from her side in preparation for their arrival.

Sometimes her mood is subdued. Sometimes, as today, it is triumphant, in a complicated, fragile sort of way. When moods like this one take her, she gets Roland to stand with her in front of some ruined facade, and hear her proclaim her victory.

'Once people told me I couldn't even walk on this grass,' she says. 'It was all mown and out of bounds. Look how scrubby it is now. I could do what I wanted here, couldn't I?'

'You could.'

'I could drop my knickers right here and go on the lawn.'

'You could.'

'There's no being late for dinner now, is there? No locked doors at night, either.'

'No, there's not.'

She looks over her shoulder. 'Thanks, dear. Meet you in about an hour?'

'Course. Where?'

'Maybe the boiler room?'

He leaves her staring up at the building like an awestruck mountaineer, and sets off on a new tack, towards the white building by the lake. He hasn't got that close before he realises that something has changed. Normally every sound round the hospital site is muted, because anybody who is here is wary of getting caught. This is different. It's the proud noise of entitlement: the prattle of a portable radio, the sputtering of an idle chainsaw. From a distance he can see a scrawny, red-haired man stripped to the waist at the front of Revenant House, clearing out some of the screening shrubs that border its garden. He has ripped out the chipboard window covers that previously made the building inaccessible to all but the most diehard explorers. There is a smell of wood shavings on the cold air. He has set up a trestle table by the front door, which he's laid with a clean, white tablecloth. It is littered with tools, fragments of wood and nails, bowls of snacks, and a bottle of water covered in dust which the man swigs from intermittently.

He looks away as he leans over with one hand and picks up the saw, which is still running. He approaches a densely overgrown shrubbery, holding the chainsaw above his head with both hands. Roland knows how you are supposed to hold a chainsaw, and this isn't it. He is at least wearing a helmet with a built-in face guard, which he draws down as he begins to work on a branch.

Roland doesn't see exactly what happens next, but he does

see the saw kicking back and flying in an uncontrollable arc towards the man, glancing sharply off his upper right arm. There is silence. He wonders if he should show himself and see if the man is all right. Then Roland can see him. He's fallen into a crouch, and is holding his hand to his shoulder, bucking and rocking on the spot. He lets out a furious scream. He stands up to take himself inside.

Roland emerges from the bushes and goes over to the site of the accident. He sees gobbets of dark blood on the freshly cut wood. Blood, too, on the white cloth over the trestle table, and in the bowls of snacks. From inside he can hear the agitated sound of the man chastising himself. The chainsaw is still idling, so Roland switches it off. He takes it over to the bushes, opens the fuel tank and empties it.

He places the chainsaw back where it fell. The lights strung over the table are powered using an ancient extension lead whose plug is lying in a puddle. Roland kicks the socket away from the water and secures the wire to a nearby tree branch to make sure it doesn't fall back in. He hears more swearing and the sound of someone's approach, and makes for the bushes.

The man returns with a cloth crudely wrapped round his arm. Hearing no engine noise, he glances down at the chainsaw. His attention is diverted by the blood on the table-cloth, and on the bowls of snacks. He swears again, and swipes at one of the bowls, which flies off and smashes against a wall of the house. Roland watches long enough to see the man cleaning up, and bunching away the tablecloth, before stepping backwards into the bushes. It's time he went to find Carol.

The utilities block: boiler room, water tower, workshop, laundry. This area interested them initially, before the more complex pleasures of the wards won out. Roland enters the dripping boiler room, where a single mushroom grows in the centre of the floor. A ghost of diesel lingers in the air.

There's a bit of old machinery here that is one of the most interesting things around, which is why it was one of the first things to get trashed: a console marked *THYMATRON*, with switches and dials on it that look capable of delivering and regulating current. He always notices it, though he has never mentioned it to Carol.

The floor here has been reclaimed by dirt. He kicks at it to try and disturb the surface and find what's underneath, and in doing so, he unearths something. He bends down and pulls out a heavy, envelope-sized square of metal from the floor. Roof lead? Whatever it is, it's soft enough to be kneaded. He enjoys the feel of it, and makes it hot in his hands as he stares at the machine. Soft it may be, but few people could mash this metal like he can, he knows that. It might as well be wax. He is still working it when he hears Carol's footsteps approach.

'Ready?' he says.

'Ready,' says Carol, giving the machine a glance as she takes his arm.

The two of them walk across the yard. Roland kneads the lead, and waits for her to speak.

'I can't believe the old Thymatron's still here,' she says. 'You'd think somebody would have wanted to take that somewhere else. There was a lady on my ward who got the willies just hearing that word, Thymatron. Or anything that sounded like it. She set about one of the nurses once – it might even have been your mother – just for asking her if she wanted an *eiderdown*. Doesn't even sound like it, does it? She used to get in such a state before her treatment.'

'What was she called?'

Carol stops and stares at the ground. 'You know, I've absolutely no idea. Isn't it awful?' They carry on walking, past some overgrown flowerbeds. 'I do remember that she went berserk once because they wouldn't let her drink her orange cordial undiluted, straight from the bottle. They said it would make her sick, and took it away. She started ripping out her hair. Then she beat her head so hard against the taps in the sink that she ruined her face. There was blood every-where, and a flap of skin hanging down above her eyebrow. And a letter C from the cold tap was marked on her head, the wrong way round, of course. Everyone said it would have been better if it had been an H, because her name was – Harriet! That's it!'

'We got there in the end,' says Roland.

'We did.' Carol smiles to herself. 'Poor old Harriet. I wonder where she ended up.'

'Tell me again what it felt like afterwards,' says Roland. 'If you feel like it.'

'It's hard to describe. And some of it I don't much remember. But it's a sort of . . . refreshing of the world. You lose the links between things and what they're called. Which can put the wind up you, as you can imagine. Headaches, too. And then, hopefully, your mind joins up the dots, and you start remembering what things are called, and that blankness goes, and you begin to feel weighed down again. But calmer.'

He looks at her to see if she's feeling uncomfortable, then decides he can venture further. 'I can't imagine losing my words like that,' he says.

'I used to love that bit,' she says. 'So they told me. I don't remember. They recorded me once with a tape recorder, to show me what I was like after the seizures. My words were all flying around trying to find one another. No idea what they were for. All liquid. And I was laughing at myself all the while. You should have heard the nonsense that came out of me.'

'Like what?'

'I don't know. Rubbish. Free association. *Echolalia*, the doctors called it. Or *word salad. Flaming silks the pear sands her frail tail avail the whale snail a Braille beware the stare pear a dare care.*'

'What did they record you for?'

'To show me where I'd been. So it wasn't so scary. She was very resourceful, your mother.'

'That was Mona?'

'Of course it was. She was my ward nurse. Without her, I'm not even sure I'd be here. Whatever you may think of her now, she's been wonderful to me.'

They are somewhere off the network of corridors on the women's side. The lawns are turning into meadows. The setting sun lays gold on to the fragments of smashed windowpanes.

'Do you even know which ward was ours?' Carol says. 'Come with me, and I'll show you.'

She leads him to a broken sash window, which they step through and come to a staircase.

'I was up and down these stairs the best part of twenty years.'

'That's longer than I've been alive,' says Roland.

'Is it?' says Carol. 'What am I putting my trust in you for? You're hardly born.'

She sidesteps broken glass on the floor where a reinforced glass security window has been smashed, shattering safety glass into cubes that cover the carpet like spilled ice.

They make their way up the stairs, Carol clutching at the low banister as if physically diminished, as if just entering the place has aged her, or drugged her, or otherwise slowed her down. A hysterical face with its skin half-flayed off screams from the landing wall halfway up. There are other graffiti: tags, insults.

Ten identical doors lead to individual bedrooms. Some of the doors still have names on them.

'This was Rachel. She was the only one here anywhere near as long as me, seven or eight years.' A bare room with a bedstead and a mattress up against the wall. 'This one was a poor girl who'd lost her baby, but I think she was schizophrenic before that anyway.' Browning magazines in piles on the built-in desk. A fragmented mirror. A sock on the floor. 'This one seemed to have someone different in it every day. Short-term acute cases, but not dangerous. *This* one – don't get me started on poor old Kathleen, she was nothing but trouble. And this one was me.'

She stops dead, as if someone has thrown a switch. She just stands patiently, staring at the door and waiting. Roland steps forward to push it open, and she crosses into the room. Orange floral curtains. Desk. Dressing table.

'I used to sit on a little blue stool here to put on make-up,' says Carol. 'Wonder where that's gone.'

Roland remembers some charred blue legs fanning out from the remains of a bonfire near the entrance, but says nothing.

She reaches forward, opens a drawer of the dressing table, and takes out a clip-on earring with a plastic pearl dangling from the end. 'I've still got the other one at home.' She laughs. 'I keep this one here just to remind me.'

'Carol,' says Roland, thinking that he will just go ahead and ask. 'How did you end up in here? To begin with.'

She puts the earring back in the drawer, and closes it. 'I had a headache.'

'Really?' he says, as images fall away in his head of murder, infanticide, loss.

'Well. That's not far off the truth.' She looks out of the window. 'There were a lot of headaches. I suppose I just didn't like the way things were looking for me.'

'Why not?'

'You don't know what it was like.' She turns and prods

gently at him with a thin, penetrating finger. 'For someone like me. Nothing to look forward to. I knew the whole story from the beginning. I was to do some terribly boring job until I met a local boy. Then I was to marry him, and that would be my life. I could see it all stretching ahead of me, all of it, as if it had already happened. It was all so . . . predictable.'

'Right.'

'Then there was this lad creeping round me, son of a friend of my dad's, and I didn't take to him one bit. And then at some point after that, I started having the attacks.' She clutches at her cardigan, pulling it around her.

'What kind of attacks?'

'Panic attacks. Couldn't breathe. Couldn't see straight at all. Felt like I was going to pass out. Started screaming. It was just part of being unhappy, I knew that. But it worried my folks no end. So the GP had a look at me and said I should come here for a week to sort myself out.'

'A week.'

'But it was ever so confusing, what happened to you on all those pills. I didn't take to it at all. And one way or another, my stay got extended. Then one morning they came and collected me, and took me off for my first dose of ECT. And it was in the confusion after that when your mother first suggested I try painting. Do you want to see my old day room?'

They go through a door into a waiting area at the top of the staircase, and Roland's world shrinks and time contracts as he sees that it's where he used to have to sit and wait for Mona to finish work. The long line of coat hooks stretching away down a curved wall over a dark wooden bench.

The day-room door has words painted on it above a large white X that read THIS WARD IS NOW CLOSED. An older sign on embossed enamel reads ALL VISITORS MUST REPORT TO THE NURSE IN CHARGE. Roland pushes the door open and they enter a long room with twin fireplaces at either end, and the usual floor-to-ceiling windows looking out towards the Ness. The walls are a teeming collage of patient murals, with the odd painted sign or slogan over them, some of which might be in Mona's hand. Some are day-to-day housekeeping notices, while others must date from the days leading to the closure of the ward.

Place Broken Glass In Clear Plastic Bags
Absolutely No Smoking In Here
Stop Health Service Cuts
Goodbye Cruel Ward

This last one has a smiley face next to it and a load of autographs underneath along with a date. Mona's neat, businesslike signature, so regularly deployed back then on permission slips and prescription forms – he can almost see her being badgered into a little frivolity by her patients on that last day, in the end-of-term spirit. The signs hint at indulgence from her – a display of tolerance and lenience that she chose to put on then, when it still made a difference.

'I used to love my pictures,' says Carol, running a finger along the wall. 'I painted quite a few of these ones. *Seclusions*, they were called. See that one of the train? That was mine. Your mum was strict about some things, but she was very kind when it mattered. A lot of other nurses would never have let you paint the walls like this. I'd love to have some of the other pictures I did, too. On paper. They're all gone now, I expect.'

'I can't believe this was where Mona worked,' says Roland. 'It doesn't *feel* like her.'

'There's a lot you don't know about your mother. The other nurses would treat patients like children. Smacking them around, and saying things like *You dirty girl* if they did anything wrong. They made it worse if someone was having an episode. Not Nurse Lamb. She was no pushover, of course, but if there was ever anything seriously wrong, if anyone had a proper turn or something, she wouldn't get as tough as the others. She'd calm right down, and talk to you, and hold you if you wanted, for as long as it took until you stopped. And as for what she did for me . . .'

'Tell me.'

'I'd been in here a while before I met her. And I was going through a very bad spell, so she had me on what's called close obs.'

Roland knows better than to say anything now.

'People always talk about their parents,' she says, 'as if that has something to do with it. Well, I can make that argument if you want. My father was a funny man. Used to raise his hand to me if I hadn't done all the housework. Never let me have any friends round. Hated my putting on make-up. He was most peculiar, really. One of the reasons I kept coming in and out of here was because of him.'

'You never told me that.'

'And then for a while I became a bit of a problem patient. Bet I never told you *that* either. Fighting. Drinking, when I could. You probably don't expect that of me, do you? Anyway one day it all came to a head and I went down to the end of the grounds, to the river, found my way out and stripped off to have a swim. Well, you can imagine what they all thought. I wasn't trying to hurt myself, but there was no way of explaining that to them. That was when they assigned me to Mona.'

Roland sits on the windowsill.

'And by this stage I was very difficult to deal with. Very aggressive. I felt the whole world was a trap, in here and out there. There was nowhere that wasn't going to hurt me. Mona seemed to understand that. And because she had me under close obs, she busted me in the end.'

'Busted you doing what?'

'Stockpiling. Keeping my pills back. Saving them up so I could take a proper overdose and have done with it.' Carol stares grimly at her own brushwork on the wall.

'What did she do?'

'She did a very clever thing. She made a pact with me. She said if I promised her I wouldn't ever try and do anything so stupid again, then she wouldn't make me take the medication when I didn't want to. And so that's what we did.'

'But still you ended up in here all that time?'

'Of course.'

'Even though there was nothing wrong with you?'

'There was less wrong with me for being in here than there would have been if I'd been out there. If you're not strong enough, the outside world will blot you up like a raindrop.'

She reaches inside the pocket of her cardigan and takes out a crumpled paper bag.

'Mints,' she says. 'Want one?'

'No thanks.'

'You ought to try one of these. Most places don't sell them any more. They take a lot of getting hold of.'

They are heading down the stairs now and out into the oncoming night.

'Did you notice what the button says on the Thymatron?' says Carol.

'No,' says Roland, watching her extricate one of the sweets from its position inside the paper bag.

'It was always the last thing I looked at before they strapped me down. Know what it says?'

He shakes his head.

'Treat,' says Carol. The word is distorted by the mint in her mouth, then flowers into a bitter laugh.

19

After lunch on the second day Ursula announces that she thinks the three of them should 'walk the grounds'. Cleo's father falls on this scrap of enthusiasm and jumps up to get the coats and boots.

They end up in a no-man's-land of woods between the garden of Revenant House and the grounds of Wreaking, walking a path edged on one side with yellow sprays of gorse, and on the other by a fence of drunken old palings held together by rusty wire. The coconut smell of the gorse mixes with the ferrous odour of nettles and spring ferns.

Ursula comes to a halt, and tells him to walk on so that *the girls* can have a pee in the bushes.

'Both of us?' says Cleo.

Ursula gives her a meaningful look to suggest that she wants Cleo to hang back too, and since this day seems to be about giving Ursula what she wants, it looks like staying here and peeing with her is what she's going to do.

Nettles glance off her ankles as she looks for a place to squat, bringing up peppery heat through her thin socks. What with the gorse as well it's hard to find a spot where nature isn't going to bite you, but Ursula is soon installed on her hams, gazing straight ahead, her mind on higher things, while a surprising, pungent gush issues beneath her. Cleo tries to ignore that, and the globelike buttocks that threaten to crowd out one side of her field of vision, and to concentrate on her own affairs.

'Do you need a tissue?' asks Ursula, producing a packet of Handy Andies. Cleo makes a remark about dripping dry that earns her a sour look.

They rejoin the path to see her father, far ahead, concentrating hard on a patch of bluebells. Ursula puts a hand on Cleo's arm to stop her rushing on.

'I think you're doing very well,' she says.

'What do you mean?'

'I think we're both doing a very good job of not showing him how we really feel.'

'About what?'

'About this *place*, of course. We both know the whole thing is potty. I mean. It's sweet in a way that he thinks all he has to do is dress it up with fairy lights and we're going to see something that isn't there. But it is still just an abandoned hospital, no matter what you do to it.'

'I don't think it's potty.'

'No. Of course not. We would never tell him that.'

'But I don't *think* it either. You lie to him if you want, but I'm not doing a *good job* of anything.'

'I'm sorry to have mentioned it,' says Ursula. 'I was only trying to pay you a compliment.' She exhales a little through her nose, casting around for another subject. 'Tell me. What is that strange thing you do on the hall carpet?'

'What do you mean?' says Cleo.

'I've seen you. You avoid the flowers in the carpet when we go inside. Why?'

'I don't like flowers.'

'That's odd for a girl. What *do* you like?'

'Aeroplanes.' She runs off, calling to him, haring through

the damp woods, enjoying the crunch of spring flowers under her feet.

From the moment she stepped over the threshold of Revenant House Cleo knew that she and the lobby carpet were going to have a problem. Fitted, hard-wearing, unavoidable, it is a violent medley of implausible flowers that must have been thought to provide a cheery sight for new arrivals, before they had their details taken at the reception desk and were bustled off to Wreaking. In fact, she imagines, it must have terrified them.

Slender, thorny stems hold goblet-cups fretted with bursting seed heads. Compact pods of red radiate toughness and resilience. There are pendants, bells and hoods. At the centre of it all is a giant purple bloom with dark recesses, whose petals flare like arrogant nostrils, and which can barely be looked at, let alone stepped on. Cleo stopped dead as soon as she saw it, knowing she needed to work out its rules. Better to spend time on it now than risk being burned later on. She stared, finding its recurrent shapes and the regularity with which they occurred. It didn't take her long to reach some important conclusions: you must confine your steps to the yellow sunflower heads, and avoid most other shapes, especially the red and orange seed clusters: if you don't, bad things are sure to happen. As for the purple monster at the centre: to tread there would bring certain disaster.

Or would it? She doesn't know any more. Now that more of the general worrying has been taken on by her father and his ocean-going companion, she feels her superpowers on the wane. It makes her unsure of herself. Maybe her instincts are childish, and there is nothing dangerous about this carpet. But she can't risk it. Not with this much at stake. Her worst fears have been proven right many times, and the chances of the carpet doing damage are so great that she must never tread carelessly there.

There's still a toxic atmosphere because Ursula cried yesterday. Cleo decides that the best thing to do is excuse herself for the afternoon – partly because there is much to explore, and partly to leave the two of them alone. The sooner they have a chance to confer and come up with a united front, the better. At least then she will only have to deal with one lie at a time.

She sits dutifully in each lakeside pavilion, appreciating the different angles they give on the water. She picks around in the gardens, browsing hospital detritus. The objects look so abandoned that their sadness is infectious. When she crosses over to Wreaking, she gravitates towards the assembly hall. Rooms like this, it seems to her, have melancholy in their DNA too: stacked canvas chairs; dusty light; the drowned notes of a detuned piano.

She walks around the echoing hall, putting her imagination to it, picturing a grand sheen on the woodblock floor, and chairs arranged in neat ranks for some function or address. A pigeon takes wing with a round of sarcastic applause. The wood is scorched and tarnished by rave-fires and other misdemeanours. She lies on the floor, imagining she has just fallen from one of the holes in its ceiling, and thinks she sees a figure stepping over one of the gaps. Ursula will surely stick it out for a bit. She has to.

When enough time has passed she makes her way back to Revenant House, wondering what she will find. Against all expectation, the party atmosphere has been ramped up rather than dismantled. There is music from a portable radio, and he's got some coals burning on the lawn in the basin of what she will realise later is a commode. There is reconciliation in the air. There's grilled chicken and potato salad. A bottle of wine is open, and a table has been brought outside even though it isn't quite warm enough, and green-rimmed hospital china has been set out. Both of them look up when she appears, wearing expressions that tell her they must have agreed to focus on her – which is about as much as she can hope for. Cleo is not one to bear a grudge in a situation like this, and she throws herself behind the mood, hell-bent on adding to it in a way that's almost competitive. She is damned if she won't be making everyone feel good if they're trying this hard.

They sit at the table and crack jokes, and ask Cleo if she saw any ghosts on her walkabout.

'I want to apologise for crying yesterday,' says Ursula. 'I'm still behind the project. I just started to find some of these rooms a bit creepy.'

'You should see some of the rooms on the other side,' says Cleo.

'Actually,' says her father, 'there's one room here you haven't seen yet. I've been saving it up.'

He leads them downstairs into the basement corridor, which smells of damp and gives a flat echo to his voice.

'That's the thing about this place. The water. In most institutions it was considered to be a hazard. Dangerous to let a patient anywhere near it. When you think that some of these people couldn't even be trusted to exist safely in a padded room without restraints, you can see why. And then of course, later on, the thing about the water didn't matter. Because everybody was restrained chemically instead of physically.'

The tunnel they are in seems to lead to somewhere she knows can't exist. Unless her geography is letting her down, it's heading straight for the lake.

'Think of this as like an early version of a therapeutic fish tank in some psychiatrist's waiting room. Designed to calm you down.'

'Think of what?' says Cleo.

'The underwater pavilion,' he says, throwing open the door.

It's green inside. Many of the bricks are too dirty to see through, but some are not – she can see the dark outline of a fish grazing the outside. Nobody speaks for a while. They just walk around, touching the glass walls.

There's barely room to stand in the dank, damp chamber, but later, they bring down a stereo and more wine, and play music so loud that the dome echoes, and the three of them waltz around it like the occupants of some doomed bunker. The moment does not last long, but it is a moment, and sometimes that's all you get. She thinks this to herself later as a distraction from childish fear of her new bedroom, pulling the covers over herself under her halo of fairy lights. When she feels something solid under her pillow, her imagination flares, and she wonders what creatures might be up here. It is not a creature she finds, though, but a piece of lead, folded carefully and surely into the shape of an aeroplane.

PART THREE

20

It's not a fantastic painting by any standards, but he can lose himself in it. A bright green hill curls to the gently sloping shore of a pretty fishing village. Train tracks follow the gradient and arrive at a station where a locomotive is pulling in, trailing a whimsical curl of smoke. All the murals in this ward hint at escape in different ways – gardens with open gates; a path leading to a mountain summit; a pod of dolphins making for open water – but this one in particular is the one that Scriven can live in. He comes here to find her. He stands before it, transported. Then, when enough time has elapsed, he trundles off again with his oxygen tank, leaving her somewhere inside.

He might be misremembering this but in his head, the body of the train was all silver. You had to climb two or three steps to get on it. It was making its slow way down a portion of the southern Spanish coast. There were many open windows, slammed down to let in scorching air and dust, but in weather like this there was nothing to be done to the heat but embrace it.

The two of them were enjoying the fact that the carriage had compartments. It suited the anticipated glamour of their first trip to Europe. They sat side-by-side on the brown leather seats, holding hands. She held an open novel in her left hand. He did a crossword with his right, one of an envelope full of crosswords he had cut out of the paper before their departure to keep him occupied during the trip. Both of them wore a nonchalance acquired in the last few weeks – each had now relaxed into the dirt and the discomfort of the voyage, even though neither had ever done anything like this before.

Outside, the coast came and went. The train seemed to flirt with it. One minute they were up close, so near that you could smell the salt, and the next they were back inland, thumping across bridges and past scrubby fields that throbbed with cicadas. It was a compartment for six, but they only had two travelling companions: an older lady, dressed in loose, black clothing, and a boy who they took for her grandson. As the train stopped at one sun-smacked platform after another, the lady fed the boy, distracting him from the comic he was reading with proffered foil packages: tomatoes; boiled eggs; roughly cut pieces of dark, oily ham. The couple did not speak Spanish, but they could understand enough of what was passing between the woman and the boy. They exchanged glances and smiles with the woman as she tried to push her food on the reluctant boy, and a complicity sprang up between them.

The lady then started offering her food to the young couple, who for all their studied comfort with the situation had not planned ahead enough to bring any lunch for the journey, and eventually, they accepted. He was peeling one boiled egg while another waited on the crossword at his side. She had a lapful of tomatoes. Both had greasy fingers from the ham. The old lady passed round a salt cellar and a plastic bottle filled with tap water. This camaraderie established, the two groups made more concerted attempts at communication. The young woman used rudimentary words and hand gestures to establish that the boy behind the comic was indeed the lady's grandson. The young woman said that he was handsome, and the boy smiled from behind his thick glasses, and coloured a little. Everybody laughed.

The old lady pressed more of her picnic on the couple, and when they tried to communicate that she had been too generous already, she insisted. Especially, they understood – there were more hand gestures – especially since the young lady was carrying a child.

'Oh no,' said Scriven. 'She's not pregnant.'

'*Segura?*' said the woman, looking only at his wife with a puzzled expression.

'Quite sure,' he said. This was exactly what they didn't need. They had come here to forget all that. To forget the ones that 'didn't take' (her mother's expression). The trip was relaxation, and distraction. The last thing she needed was witchy old ladies in black smocks conjuring the ghosts of lost children from some animal intuition. It was too complicated a notion either for his Spanish or his hand gestures.

'Not pregnant,' he said. 'Not pregnant.'

The train was going through a cutting in the rock, reinforced with concrete slabs. The effect was of a slatted tunnel, whose darkness alternated with perfectly framed shots of blue seascape and spray off to the left. He held her hand as postcards flickered in and out of existence: a beach with kids in the surf; a whitewashed village where washing hung from the windows, and more sea-spray hitting the rocks. Hot air pumped through the window.

She held his hand back, pressing eggshell fragments into his palm, tightly enough for him to turn and look at her.

'Actually . . .' she said. And he saw the whites of her eyes, and the white of her smile.

This was his first news of Cleo. When she was an abstract and very welcome idea. A relief. A hope which they put faith into, but upon which it never occurred to them to put a face or a name.

And then, before he knew it, she was there, incontrovertible. He remembers the wave of buoying familiarity with which he saw her for the first time. Scraps of clotted blood on her cheeks. Eyes dark with a kind of certainty she had brought with her – a certainty that seemed to fall away over time as the eyes went green, and she learned the fear and guile involved in being a child. *Oh it's* you, he thought. *It's been you in there, all this time. Well – now I understand.*

His own reaction to the fact of her always felt dangerous – something he knew he could never really control or predict. Love was too simple a word for it. It was more than love. Love, with extras – one of which was a kind of terror at the sight of himself. At how instantly he understood that the only important thing he had ever done was to supply his genetic material to be spliced and repurposed in this powerful new context.

And if, by a freakish catastrophe, the other contributor to this bewitching confection should be destroyed, then what remained would be his best reminder of what was missing. For better or worse. And love was certainly too simple a word for that.

The wind is up. During weather like this, you can get the impression that the hospital is actually breathing. Distant parts of it groan. Sash windows shudder in their frames. Doors slam in sequence like controlled explosions. Curtains are inhaled and exhaled through windows, whose jagged glass frets them into tatters. The building tells the truth, and is exposed for what it is – stuck in one moment, endlessly repeating itself.

At the end, individual wards were emptied, then tied off like gangrenous limbs. The large white X marks they painted on doors are here to prove it, forbidding entry to specific corridors as if they were plague houses. You can tell that the final death throes took place at the end of a year: here is a plastic Christmas tree collapsed in a doorway like a drunken reveller; nearby, a box of unused cards, labelled *Hospital Chaplain*.

He's upstairs, making his way down a women's secure ward. Patches of copper-coloured fungus seep down corners, reclaiming the colour scheme. On these upper floors, the corners are all curved. No hard edges to hurt yourself on. The rounded surfaces make you feel like you're going mad anyway. Losing definition. Losing purchase.

He makes for the assembly hall, for old times' sake. The last few pieces of scenery are still knocking around from the play that was staged here just before it was shut down. Painted flats with rocks and waves on them. A staff that breaks in half and remakes itself thanks to a cunningly inserted piece of elastic.

There were dances in this room – chaotic events from the sound of things. He read one account of such occasions that said that as the music started the men and the women just ran at each other across the floor, like opposing teams. Now, holes gape in the floor and an effigy of some kind hangs from the remains of a light fitting. The gangs of kids who come up here in search of fright are wont to leave things like that. They don't get how important it is to be alone if you really want the place to talk.

He takes to the stage, picturing the first superintendent as the last century began. He would have stood here, declaring his noble intentions for the building, perhaps proclaiming it *An Asylum For The Twentieth Century*. Then, a hundred years of blind alleys and advances. Hosing patients down. Putting them in comas. Shell-shocked soldiers playing billiards during the first war. Bombs striking the building twice during the second. New and terrifying treatments. The randomised violence of the pre-frontal leucotomy. The chemicals. Thorazine, to make them drool and shake. Lithium, to box them in so tight that there were no more highs and no more lows. The anti-psychiatrists, who decided maybe their patients were on to something after all. A new language of 'service users' and 'cost-benefit analysis'. And throughout, the thousands of souls who roamed the corridors on continuous playback, greasing the prayer-wheel, charging the place up with anguish. Personalities altered. Thoughts subject to transubstantiation. Sometimes, as he walks these corridors, he imagines he can feel them: the vapours, the gaseous remains of burnt-out memories.

He heads for the central record office, even though he knows there aren't any papers left because he personally removed them and filed them away in Revenant House in case anyone should ever come asking. He offered them back to the Health Service in the early days, and was told to destroy them, so now they are his personal archive: story after story, typewritten on bible-thin paper, of losses and worries and fears. It always amazes him just how many of the problems seem to start with children. With wanting them, or not wanting them, or not liking them once you acquire them.

> . . . *patient has been depressed and tearful and complains of feelings of unreality. In spite of the fact that she has been sterilised she is afraid she might conceive and she has asked to remain at Wreaking and not be discharged so that she won't have to see her husband again, and risk relations . . .*
> . . . *has a long history of psychoneurosis, to which I would attribute in some part his background, as he was his mother's first child but his father would not marry her and he was brought up with a stepfather and five younger siblings . . .*

. . . understand she had become increasingly tense and depressed since the birth of her last baby, and been overworking herself completely. I recommended a course of outpatient electroplexy, after which . . .

Sometimes he spends time with a medical dictionary trying to label his own disorders. Apophenia is one. At various other times he's been tempted by bipolarity, dementia, hypomania, schizophrenia, syllogomania. He wonders sometimes which of the old Victorian diagnoses he might be awarded if he were in their shoes. Uncontrolled Passion. Metaphysical Speculation. Mortified Pride.

The air takes on a coniferous edge as he leaves Wreaking behind him, and walks between the banks of evergreens that flank the drive. Clods of soaked fir needles damp down his footsteps. Scattered debris in the leaf litter looks as if doctors and patients had fled the place in some urgent wartime exodus. As he turns in the direction of home, it starts to rain.

Which for some reason makes him want to stay outside, and nearly an hour later, following a spin round the lake and several other unnecessary detours, he finds himself shivering before the mirror in the Revenant House bathroom. The Decision Mirror, as Cleo called it.

It was a game they had. He would stand behind her and the two of them made decisions together. What to eat. What to do. Stay or go. You find one of the marks in its smoky world and you position yourself so that it sits over the reflection somewhere. Then you ask it a question. The thing he can't remember is how you work out what the answers are. When Cleo used to do it she always swore there was a new shape she had never seen there before, and that it told her what to do.

'Should I call her?' he asks, feeling stupid. But he sees nothing new.

He thinks of standing behind her as they looked at one

another, his gaze settling on hers. How he rested his chin on her head, and smelled her scalp. How when she was a baby, her whole head rested in the palm of his hand like a grapefruit. If he squints now in the right way he feels he might almost see her, standing here in front of him, wearing her beaten-up red trainers, telling him not to worry.

'Stupid man.' What is he thinking – if she was here now, she'd probably tower over him. She's a grown woman, and he's a shrinking troll.

He unhooks the plastic lugs from his nose, and pulls at the nostrils to get things moving again, to remind himself what it is like to breathe as he was meant to. He unbuttons his soaked shirt and dumps it on the floor.

Look at him, haggard and dyspeptic. He looks hollow. Grey. Green, even. Maybe he's been dead for years, but somebody forgot to tell him. Against all the odds his plugged valves manage to relax enough to admit a squirt of blood from time to time, but essentially he's running on vapours. His limbs seem cast at funny angles, as if he has been thrown off a high building, then somehow reanimated. He'd give anything to be shot of this traumatised body and see it all through some fresh eyes. He's sick of all this dread. Sick of fearing sirens, and knives, and scissors, and matches, and pens. His scared heart. His scarred lungs.

In the window there is movement, high and fast, and he jumps before his ears even register the bright smack as a bird hits the windowpane. The shock makes him leap towards the mirror, jolting it at the base. His feet are slippery from the rain, and panic leads to overreaction. He grasps the sides of the mirror in such a way that contributes to its slide rather than arresting it. He falls forward into the mirror, which topples forward on its shelf, top-heavy after years of stability, and crashes on to his head, so that his arms must leap up to grip the frame if it isn't to take him down.

He stands, breathing heavily, unwilling to move in any direction for fear the mirror will overwhelm him, the cold weight of it bearing down hard on his crown. He emits a high-pitched laugh at the ridiculousness of the situation. Eventually he summons the strength to heave the mirror back towards the wall, and manages to topple it over so that it is righted more or less under its own weight to the position it occupied before.

He steps backward, his arms spread out before him, as though he were trying to persuade the world that if the mirror did indeed topple forward he would be in with a chance of catching it. Eventually he believes it will not move again.

His breathing is fizzy. Something sharp stuck into the frame has cut his hand. He's aware that he's muttering. An object fell out from behind the mirror when it moved, and clattered on to the floor. He bends down to try and find out what it was, and finds two broken halves of a crude toy aeroplane, made of lead, that must have been back there behind the mirror all this time.

21

She had forgotten the luxury of waking up slowly. She was woken early by birdsong, and little hooks of worry got into her before she had a chance to drift back off. If she couldn't sleep she decided that she would at least come to as slowly as possible, and has been watching light fall across a landscape of crumpled white linen for the last hour.

She misses her old self sometimes – the way she and Nat almost conned themselves into making a life together. And it might have worked, you never know. She will never know, because that ripcord has been pulled.

She remembers mornings when he had early flights to catch: the noise of his cab idling outside, which made the moment feel more precious. The way he would throw an arm over her, and come in close, both of them taking pleasure in knowing that the car was being kept waiting.

Sometimes their breathing was so close that it reached the stage where the two sets of breaths were intermingling in that self-advancing way – the co-conspiracy of arousal, when excitement was transmitted from one to the other. They were good at that.

'Don't go,' she would mutter, sometimes. And in the early morning, with her coping mechanism down, it would feel so desperate, the ache for him not to be gone, that she truly does not know how things might have panned out if he had, one day, stayed.

This is not the time to make a ghost of Nat. He is just one old life among several. There are others she could miss if she chose to. Like the pre-Nat days, when she was adrift. The days when she went from house to house. She had plenty of friends who didn't mind, back then. You could pitch up anywhere and grab a bit of floor or a sofa. She used to pride herself on having the spontaneity to decide to drop her bag and bed down for the night on the spur of the moment.

Life is no longer like that, and won't be again – and not just because the floors of those friends she has left are now littered with baby toys. She looks back on the person she was with hardly any recognition: a young woman who made her friends pull their cars over so she could dance on the bonnet when her favourite song came on the radio, who was known for being nakedly predatory when she wanted to be and ruthless when she decided to move on. Then one day she had felt herself abruptly but unmistakably wanting to anchor herself to someone else. And that someone became Nat. She coiled round him like ivy, then realised how much randomness had been involved in the selection, and cut herself free. And now what.

These prattling birds have taken her by surprise. Can it be that close to summer? The seasons are shading into one another again. You can't see much evidence of it here, but at Wreaking the hedgerows will be filling out, the branches will be budding, and what is he *doing* about it? He seems to have decided to keep his head down right to the end.

Her father sounded better yesterday, almost back to his old, brittle self – albeit a self broken up by terrible episodes of thick, congested coughing. He apologised for not picking up the phone before. He didn't say why he wasn't able to.

Just said he was fine. He is not fine. He's weak. She knows it could happen at any time. So does he. She stretches and moves to the cooler half of the bed, hoping for fresh thoughts.

She has noticed in herself over the past few months a new urge to mend things. She spends evenings at the table fixing tiny rips in clothing. She glues mugs back together. She is assembling an old box full of buttons and fabric and patches, and putting them to use.

A memory surfaces, of how he used to go around the place with a button in his mouth the whole time. During the renovations, with Ursula, but afterwards too. It was just a habit, she supposed. Then one day, poking around in his room, she found the rack of her mother's clothes, with all its missing buttons, and understood that it was better not to ask.

After a long shower and some coffee, she opens her bedside drawer, and her hands crab around inside for a while, selecting and discarding objects, before she finds what she was looking for – his watch. A seventies stainless steel thing. Japanese.

He gave it to her after their last trip to her mother's riverbank. He was looking around desperately to give her something of himself, and fumbled for the watch on his wrist as a kind of afterthought. He joked that he didn't need it any more because all his days were the same. They both knew it was a way of trying to make a connection. To put some-thing on her that would stay on her for as long as they were apart, which might be some time. It was still warm when she had put it on, and flecked with house-paint from years before, when he repainted the corridors of the Enfield. She had meant to have links taken out of the bracelet, but wore it anyway for a while, until it flew off her wrist on to the pavement during the course of one of the lost nights, and its perpetual motion was replaced by a queasy sound of shot springs whenever she tried to shake it into action. It has been in this drawer ever since.

She slips it into her jacket pocket, enjoying the way it drops and tightens the fabric with its weight. She looks up at the ceiling, parts her eyelid, and fits her eye, blinking back the single, sharp tear. She takes a final look at herself in the mirror to confirm that she is armed against the day, and heads to work.

She stops at a cashpoint on her way to the bus stop, and gets an amused look from the guy in the queue behind her when she thanks the machine for her money. She would habitually project personalities on to inanimate objects when she was little. She remembers instructing her father to buy a charity shop hat stand because it was 'lonely'. Later, they took it back again because she had decided that the same hat stand had become 'bossy'. It must have been infuriating.

On the bus, she holds the watch, enjoying its weight. He made some remark to her recently about how these days he lost track of all time, and she asked if he wanted it back, half hoping it might be a cue for the two of them to meet. He replied without thinking that these days it would prob-ably slip off his wrist as well. Another abrupt deterioration in the call, as he heard her voice, realised he had shocked her, and tried to backtrack. The subject was changed. And then, in some other context she can't now remember, she ended up saying to him, *Life's too short*. And then felt so bad that it was she who terminated the call.

She can't decide whether it's better or worse now that the two of them only have awkward telephonic encounters, as opposed to the real ones that used to fill and ruin her week-ends. Sinking into a cab from Revenant House to the station following their latest attempt to pretend that the obstacles could be overcome, she would wave at him, hunched over under the front-door portico, looking in need of such care, her own dereliction of duty screaming at her. The agony, every time. *Was that okay? Would it be all right if that was the last time? Was my final glimpse of him as I drove away a happy one, or did he turn back reluctantly under that sad white porch?*

It is hard in retrospect to decide which version of him was worse when she was growing up: the one who was up because he'd fallen for somebody new (or persuaded himself that he had), or the version that recurred at intervals, sodden with renewed grief over her mother. This usually appeared after the latest relationship had collapsed, and it was his way of atoning to Cleo for having strayed from her mother, and his way of telling himself that nobody ever mattered as much as she had – which supplied both with justification for his latest collapse, and consolation that the cause of it had left.

Cleo's talent for consolation is something she feels she owes to him. It was forged in the desperation of trying to keep him afloat during some of the great troughs he went through back then. At that time, the best she could do was to make him hot chocolate, but now she has more sophisticated ways of moderating the influence of the bad things in the world. It is, after all, her job.

She strides across the office lobby, swiping herself in at the glass turnstile that doubles as security barrier and time clock. She takes the lift down to her floor, and sets off down the dim corridor to find a spare editing suite. There is the usual harsh note of machine coffee in the air. She gets the thing to squirt a measure out for her into a skin-thin plastic cup, carries it to the desk, and fires up the equipment.

She has been telling other people's stories in booths like this for years. Raw footage comes in, with instructions from producers or presenter, or the accompanying report itself, and she assembles the pictures that tell the story. She's good at it: fast, clever and capable of compartmentalising the traumatic things she sometimes has to watch: bodies gushing blood; eyes that will never see again.

Today she has been asked to edit some footage of the aftermath of a bomb in a marketplace, and eliminate that which is unfit for broadcast. Scraps of clothing are all right, as are pools of deep red on the ground, snaking towards gutters. As usual, she must screen out actual body parts, or scraps of flesh. Any lips burned open around gaping sets of teeth. Most of these things she is inured to, but the amount of blood involved in explosions is always a surprise. It's as if people were just bags of liquid, ready to go pop.

In films, when bombs go off, there's often someone in shot calmly walking the other way – the nasty person who planted it. Cleo doesn't think those people ever exist in real life. Bombs are messy, for those who plant them as much as for their victims. And why don't they ever carry the bodies properly in these bits of aftermath footage? There's always one arm hanging down off the stretcher, knuckles grazing the floor, or a bare leg juddering off to the side. She cuts the pieces to tell a story. The horrified screaming. The facts hitting home. The beating of chests.

She focuses momentarily on her reflection in the screen, where a miniaturised version of the scenes she is viewing sparkles in her glass eye. She knows no peace like the peace she feels in the editing suite. She finds it hard to enjoy most conversation out in the real world, but she can make clips of film tell any story she wants. She calls it the Youngster–Monster scale – trap a child down a mineshaft, he's a 'youngster', put him on a charge of abducting a minor and he graduates straight to 'monster' – and she is a master at inserting the visual cues for whichever direction the story calls for.

She's not quite the gatekeeper she once was – what's the

point, when any boy or girl can view confusion and terror and blood if they know what to type into the machine? She thinks of her job now as to sit behind this bank of instruments and turn complexity into easily digestible chunks of story. To suggest a bit of right and wrong. A bit of cause and effect. Exactly what her father would despise.

I feel as if my heart has burst, says the woman whose husband was eaten by a bear on their Canadian honeymoon. *What did we do to deserve this?* she asks.

My heart has burst. She will edit that out so the grief comes over more naturally, without the distracting cliché. The poor girl is only saying the first thing she can think of. It's not an accurate representation of how she feels. She finds footage earlier in the interview of the same girl, having been asked to talk about what her and her husband had been doing that day.

He'd just made me coffee, she says. *I thought there wasn't any coffee left, but he kept some back to surprise me. That was the kind of thing he did.*

There it is.

Over years of fiddling with the dials and buttons on this console, and its predecessors, she has worked out ways of scanning whole tracts of news, hearing the expressions coming off the reports in little snatches. Scan the dial of all the cued-up reports, and you can get a whole picture of current events, phrases floating before you like bingo balls.

swell ripped though the town, making toys of cars and shops
body will be repatriated this afternoon with full
gunman has been identified as twenty-three-year-old
cockpit fire following an aborted take-off at

She spins the dial on from that one fast – she still feels an old pang of culpability, a hangover from childhood that she can't seem to kick, every time she hears anything about an aircraft in distress. Magical thinking, it's called. That terror of responsibility for your thoughts. He told her that.

Here in the horn of Africa it's hell on earth. For now they die of hunger. In a few weeks they will begin to die of disease.

She remembers sitting with him to watch the great famines of her youth. How he would sit and stare bleakly and not know what to say. How it would be down to her to tell him it was going to be okay, and get the chocolate on.

Sometimes, sitting here, she sees her life in compilation, cued up like a sports montage, with powerful music and significant highlights. *All the hits, ladies and gentlemen, in one glorious package.*

A metal train runs down a bright blue coastline.

A father is told of the death of his wife.

A fifteen-year-old girl lies on a rooftop staring at the sky.

A sixteen-year-old cranks up the volume of her stereo to get at her foster parents.

A lost, skinny twenty-year-old dances on the bonnet of a car.

A boy in an amusement arcade breaks away from kicking a fruit machine to stare at a girl as she steps over the threshold.

A kiss on a shingle beach that tastes of cigarettes and cheap vodka, and is both bitter and warm.

A pot of paint falls, coming to rest upside down on some attic floorboards.

Cleo swivels her chair away from the console, towards the computer on the adjacent desk. She takes her father's watch from her pocket, and types in the make and serial number to see if there's anybody out there who can fix it. There must be someone.

22

Roland wakes up with a start, early, before six. He reaches for the Ratsniper. His van door is open, and he can hear something moving around by the shutter. He can't see what it is, but he's ready to fire a shot all the same, and if it hits some saucer-eyed refugee from the club next door then so be it, he's not feeling patient. Then he hears a familiar sound of wheel-spokes clattering against metal.

'What are you doing in here so early?' he shouts.

Victor is sideways on in his chair, frozen in profile, trying to get inside. 'Cold out there. And those kids are tearing it up. Couple of them started trying to tip my fucking van, if you can believe it. They ran away when I coughed.'

'Do you want me to see to them?' Roland shoulders the rifle and steers Victor to his office. Victor's hand trembles as he reaches into his pocket for the key to the container padlock.

'No. Leave it,' he says. 'And don't bother with the usual routine of telling me I should sleep in here.'

'Come and get warm. I'll start the heater. Do you want a cup of something?'

Roland settles Victor at his desk. He stares ahead in the gloom, without reaching for the lamp.

'Are you all right?' says Roland.

'Fuck off with you, I'm fine.' His fingers drum on the desk. 'Little bastards. One of them offered me crystal meth just now. It's nearly six in the morning, for God's sake.'

'Tell me if you want something. I'm heading off in a minute.'

'Heading off?'

'I told you. My appointment.'

Victor nods, pretending to look through bits of paper. 'You're a resourceful boy. Get us something good. Make the hairy cripple proud.'

Roland busies himself boiling up water for tea. He is aware of some laboured movement behind him, but doesn't look to see what it is, so doesn't see how Victor manages to drag himself to the top of a pulpit that was ripped off from some church or other and has been hanging around waiting for a new home.

'Here beginneth the lesson,' says Victor. 'In the name of your father, who popped off God knows where and left you to look after your batty mum, and the son, funny tunnel-creature that you are, and the Holy Ghost, which is me I suppose. What would your old man think if he knew I was your *in loco parentis*? He'd have a kitten, wouldn't he?'

Roland takes a deep breath. 'I think that if he knew there was barely eight years between us, and saw the state you're in, he might not agree with the description.'

'Ha!' Victor leans forward to consult his imaginary congregation. 'What do we think, children? He's probably right, isn't he? Would I survive the week without him? Maybe not. Little Roland Lamb, the biggest boy underground. And surprisingly eloquent with it, isn't he, boys and girls?'

During Roland's early childhood his father was simply *missing at sea*. He can't remember the point at which an accumulation of rumour supplanted that notion with something more cowardly, but he knows it now. It doesn't matter.

All that matters is that one day he was gone, and his boat too, with his business caving in behind him, and Roland's mother was never the same. The version Victor feeds him now is nothing like the truth, but that doesn't stop him. Feeling threatened always puts him in a nasty mood.

'Which is *not* to say, boys and girls, that Mr Lamb is by any means the only missing person in this young man's life.'

'Have you quite finished?'

'We all know who the real Holy Ghost is, don't we?'

'Obviously not.' Roland feels in his pocket for his earplugs – when Victor gets like this, quietly inserting them is the only way to deaden the impact of the ranting – but he must have left them in the van.

'A big, Oliver-shaped hole in the world, and nobody knows where he is. But you do, don't you?'

'I know where he is, and so do you,' says Roland.

This is true, up to a point. Oliver's last-known whereabouts are a campsite in Spain, where he was working, servicing family-sized tents under bug-infested conifers that smelled of drains. Neither of them have heard from him in a long time.

Roland stops pretending to be busy and looks directly at the face in the pulpit. 'You should come down from there before you hurt yourself.'

'Is that a threat? My Lord, I think it is. What's he going to do with me, boys and girls? Am I going the same way as my poor little brother?'

'Mind if I step into your office?' says Roland, hoping this will unnerve him. Victor doesn't like anyone rooting around in there.

But the voice from the pulpit carries on. 'Poor little Lamb. Lost his best friend in the world, and stuck here with nasty old Victor. But don't you worry about me, boy. I won't let you down like Oliver did. I won't be hurting anybody you love.'

Victor's dusty lamp throws light down on to the surface of his desk, but leaves the rest of the container in the murk. Roland is on the verge of giving up the tactic of incursion when he spots a tatty, pink schoolbag hanging from a cabinet in the corner. On the outside, correction fluid has been used to draw neat letters that spell out the word *MOLLY*. The bag gives off a smell of pencil shavings and ink and food. He goes back outside, clutching it low, out of sight. Victor is still declaiming, gripping the pulpit like an evangelist, and then a pleading note enters his voice.

'Just tell me what you did.' The words smack of desperation, but there's an equal measure of fascination in the way he delivers them. 'What did you do to get rid of him? Did you pay him? Is that it? Did you give him money to stay away?' Vicious pause. 'Did you hurt him?'

Roland extends his arm and holds the schoolbag out at arm's length. 'What the fuck's this?'

Victor does a show of squinting his eyes as if he doesn't know exactly what Roland is holding in his hand, then steadies himself again on the pulpit's dark wooden sides. 'Obviously she left it behind, didn't she?'

'And what exactly are you planning to do with it?'

'Safekeeping. She might come back for it, you never know. Maybe I'll give her a call.'

'Really.' He might just be doing this to get to Roland, but you just never know with Victor. Roland's seen the way he looks at children sometimes. And there are memories he has of waking up in the early days, before they slept in separate vans, and hearing the kind of videos Victor was watching while he slept. Nothing concrete, but definitely stuff Roland didn't want to find out any more about. Ah fuck, who knows?

'Anyway, if she does come back,' says Victor, 'it's not me she's going to be afraid of.'

'What do you mean?'

'I told Christopher stuff about you, boy. Told him he better keep working for us, or you'd go looking for his little Molly. It was that more than any cut that got him back onside, I reckon.'

Roland closes his eyes.

'What?' says Victor. 'My Lord, the hypocrisy. You're pretty sinister yourself, you know. I know you went spying on that poor girl again yesterday. Why not let poor old Cyclops get on with her life?'

Roland keeps his eyes closed and says nothing.

'What's done is done. Let it go.' Seeing that this isn't going to get him the result he wants, Victor tries a different tack. 'And what about her old man? Checked in on him lately?'

'I haven't had time.'

'He didn't sound too clever, last I heard from you. Might be in all sorts of trouble for all you know.'

'He's all right. I get reports.'

'Reports? Hadn't you better check? I know you, boy. Always looking for something else to beat yourself up over. I know you'd never forgive yourself if anything happened to him and they hadn't made it up.'

'I'm sure he's fine,' says Roland.

'Poor old fucker. Can you believe he's *still there*? Do you remember what we used to say at school about people like him? We'd have said he'd *gone Wreaking. Been bundled in the yellow cart. Taken the number 7 bus.* Do you remember that one?'

'Vaguely.'

'You better check in on him. You don't want to lose another one on your watch, do you? You haven't exactly got a very good record in that department.'

'Say one more word,' says Roland, quietly. 'Go on.'

Victor looks at him from the pulpit, eyes shining, his wet mouth doing a *my lips are sealed* expression that makes Roland want to kill him. Victor makes a grab for the satchel, falls head first down the pulpit steps and strikes the concrete. The sound of real skin and bone connecting with hard surfaces. Roland springs forward, and puts a hand under Victor's arm to help him up. Drops of blood hit the floor. Victor hisses without looking up, 'Fucking TOUCH me.'

Roland slackens his grip, lets Victor fall slowly back, and withdraws to have a shower.

The roars from outside have settled into a low, toxic buzz as the dregs of the rave seep out into the world. He snaps the switch and the damp chamber stutters into light: a series of redirected pipes cover one wall, coming from many different origins – the little sources of hot water that Roland has managed to find and divert over the years into a pipe over a drain.

Roland stands naked under the shower pipe, trying to get wet enough to be able to generate lather from the wafer of soap that is kept slotted behind the calcified water pipes on the wall. His feet are great blocks of flesh on the concrete, untouched by the water. When the hot dribble has nearly soaked his hair, he soaps as much as he can, trying to cover some areas neglected in his last wash. He shuts off the tedious trickle, then moves to the opposite side of the bathroom, where he has rigged up a wall-mounted toilet cistern over an upside down copper funnel that he found out the back somewhere. He pulls the chain and air is shocked out of him as the numbing gush hits his body. He stands waiting for it to fill up one more time, flicking cold, soapy water from his skin with his fingertips.

Trying to get dry with a damp towel, he sees Victor's toothbrush sitting up in its grimy glass. He can hear him getting back to his chair. There was a time when Roland had to be on his guard at moments like this in case Victor 'accidentally' wheeled in on him after his shower, but those days seem to be over. Either he's beyond that kind of thing now, or Roland has gone to seed.

If he can make it after that fall, he'll be in here before long for his own ablutions, whatever form they take. Mercifully he has never asked for any assistance. Roland picks up the toothbrush and thinks of scrubbing it around some of the floor's grimier corners, where there are lines of rat shit. Then he thinks better of it, returns the brush and walks naked back to the van, feeling reptile eyes on him from the darkness of the container.

He dresses quickly and checks to make sure Jonny Finer's torched bag is still on the passenger seat. He packs a few essentials and removes his mattress and the wooden board it sits on, leaving the back of the van all but empty. He settles into the driving seat and turns the key, and the shuddering beast is awake. He beats the dashboard until it coughs hot air, which warms the interior with smells of plastic and ash. He plants his foot on the accelerator pedal, filling the arches behind with smoke and fumes.

Starting the engine before opening the shutter has exactly the effect he wanted. In his rear-view mirror he can just make out Victor having a coughing fit, waving and slamming at his desk with his palm. Roland revs the engine some more.

He guns the engine and the van shoots down the ramp, sending another black fart of smoke up in the direction of Victor. He jumps down at the front door and passes the cold chain swiftly hand over hand. The steel shutter flies upwards and fresh air hits his face.

'Like being born,' he mutters, breathing in a deep lungful.

A few early-morning taxis grumble down the tunnel, their wheels crunching through a tide of discarded plastic cups. Clubbers emerge bewildered, morning-shocked. Some sit on the pavement together, coming to terms with it. Some are still nodding to the music in their heads.

To one side of the crowd at the door is a more fundamentally dishevelled man. He has dropped his trousers and is shitting on the pavement, one leg manically pumping, while his friend with a dog on a string looks on, laughing. These two will be on their way to the shelter for breakfast. They barely notice the clubbers, who are not so messed up that they don't know to steer clear of *that*. Watching the shitting man, and the way he seems to be talking, but not to the man who's with him, Roland notices something that speaks to him of psychosis.

A tall guy with long, straight hair wanders up, sweating, carrying a bottle of water and a fur-lined parka over his arm. His pupils are enormous.

'Hello mate,' he says to Roland, holding a crumpled fiver. 'You still open?'

'Whatever it is you think I am, you're wrong.'

'I just want, like, some water. My mouth's so *dry*.' He smacks his lips by way of proof. 'And a paper, if they're in.'

'Drink the water in your hand.' Roland flicks him round and shoves him away, to the sound of woozy protestation. Time to get moving before more turn up.

He moves the van outside, and pulls down the shutter to box Victor in with the last of the fumes. Once he's free of the tunnel, his phone throbs in his pocket, and he hopes it will be a message from Carol, reporting on his mother. It could even be a message from Mona herself, who takes it upon herself to call sometimes, leaving confused messages that make him very sad. Her voice, lost in the static, asking if anyone is there. Saying that she has been kidnapped. That only her son can save her.

The thought is so distracting that he doesn't react to the sound of something falling off the van before it's too late, and he knows that the *Golden Sands Guest House* sign he forgot to remove has clattered off its rusty nail and into the gutter, and it's too late to go back and look for it now.

23

He smelt it properly on himself for the first time a couple of days ago as he stooped to weed the airing-court roses: the musty, crotch-waft smell of Old Man. The silt left in dried-out pores when the pheromones have died. Sexless, stale, and resigned to be both.

The smell summoned a gallery of childhood ghosts, from the benign to the sinister – crumbling old specimens who feigned indignation at his grammar or spluttered complaints in his direction from the edges of games pitches. They always seemed unconvincing to him, however frightening their performance, because he had thought it impossible to be as inflexible as they all pretended to be. It must have been an act, he thought. Now, he understands it.

To start with, everything is within reach. And then, however much you don't want it to happen, the view gets crowded out. Before you know it there are barely any ways forward, and you're choosing between remaindered options.

'Pretentious git,' he mutters, wiping his mouth with a handkerchief.

What a laughable thing it is, to live long enough to become a *difficult man*. What an indulgence, to sit here taking up space, with thick hair bushing out of his nostrils, and egg yolk on his lip. It's time he was done away with. Clear the decks for someone younger and less dried into shape.

But, as usual when he has eaten, there follows a rallying surge of optimism. A feeling that things could be different. That all he has to do is call, tell her to come and put down the phone before the atmosphere has a chance to curdle. It would all be so easy if it wasn't for this noise in the walls.

Things are coming alive again now that spring is here. He knows it, because when he turns off the machine, he can hear creatures massing in the fabric of the building. Insects teeming, making the walls tinkle like soda water in a glass. While his territory is constantly reduced, other beings, sensing weakness, are on the march. He used to go round with a tank of pesticide and pump it through holes in the walls at this time of year. But now he is beaten. The building is theirs now.

There are times when he can't hear the noise, or is sufficiently distracted by other things to forget it. And then he will remember it. And he will go to the wall just to check if it's still there. The temptation is almost irresistible, in spite of the anxiety. But he won't do it this morning. He'll go to his study, and get some hours in, and go nowhere near the walls.

He fills his mug with the last of the coffee, and takes it to his desk. He thinks he sees movement by the skirting board, but tells himself to think his way out of that one. Let them come, the mice and rats. Just get some hours in, and you'll feel better.

What a *day*, though. Calmed by rain that kept up a steady beat all night, his body let itself shut down properly for once. Balled up on a favourite two-seater sofa, under a bedspread, not too far from the kitchen range, he slept. And now the rain has cleared. It's a day for cracking things open, and letting in air. He reaches under his desk for the bottle, and pours whisky into his cooling cup of coffee. He drinks it quickly, then pours another. He sits, raising and dropping the pen on to the clean page before him. The pen his wife gave him all those years ago.

Sometimes, when he's dropping off in this chair, he can think she is right here in the room with him. Just out of sight. And he knows that if he were to talk to her, or look directly, she would be gone. It is enough to stare at one spot, and know it, and feel warmed by it.

Once, he dared to speak.

'You're back,' he said. 'Was there something you wanted to say?'

There was no reply, but he decided that she must be smiling.

He thinks of how terrified he used to be of being alone with Cleo. How the trauma of what was happening to her mother was compounded by the fear of being in charge of such a fragile, unknowing creature. Only when she was asleep could he give full vent to his emotion, which he did by drinking. And then he would remember her, upstairs, undefended, and he would panic, and fear that something had happened to her while his guard was down. Even when he went in, and saw her, he would worry that his boozy, smoky breath was going to harm her.

Later, he would watch her striking out to do some new thing – exploring a beach or a wood, or climbing a tree. He would keep his distance, willing her to turn just once to look back at him, and maybe, if he'd earned it – kind gods – to give him a wave. The sun in her eyes as she turned. His chest ready to burst. His legs set to send him flying at anyone or anything that dared touch her. The helplessness of that feeling.

But all of it nothing next to the helplessness when you were told she had asked to be taken away from you.

'No,' he says, shaking his head and pouring more whisky as the noise in the walls gets louder.

When she was a little girl she used to like packing bags. Tissues, a doll, a toothbrush, pebbles. She would put seemingly random things in one of several shoulder bags she owned, and come to him to say goodbye. 'Bye,' he would say, casually, through the pain at knowing that one day it would happen for real. He can't look back now without seeing her rehearsing. Everything about the past seems to lead towards its awful closure. To the moment when she lay back in bed, in the casualty department, with bandages round her head, and told him that she would not live with him any more.

He remembers staring down at his watch in the days after she was born, his palm to her chest, timing her heartbeat, while her mother was away in another room, facing up to her demons. He wonders if Cleo has any idea that the watch he gave her was once used like this, to reassure him she was still alive.

For years, everything seemed harmful. One day she held out her little palm in wonder and he saw a drowsy bumblebee flexing its abdomen and its sting, and could not see her palm again for the rest of the week without seeing the bee, lurking there, ready to harm her.

He picks up his pen, and writes a sentence.

This is the same vile green armchair I was sitting in on the day of the accident.

Not again. He yanks the tube from his nose, and turns off his respirator. Which is how he hears the sound in the walls.

It seems to have been intensified by the rain. The pocking and percolating and scratching. He gets up to the wall, flattens his ear against it as much as he can, and hears what's really going on. The toxic, buzzing commotion of wasps.

They're building an army in here. Calling for reinforcements. Massing out of sight, to *take him down*. Time to get out of here.

He picks up the phone and squints at the wall, where he has written Carol's number, boxed in with permanent marker.

'Well, it's me,' he says when she picks up.

'Yes?' says Carol. 'What's the matter?'

'Are you coming up here today?'

'You know I am.'

'Can you bring some outdoor wear?'

'Come again?'

'I thought we might try and go for a walk.'

'A walk? Good Lord.'

After the call, he limbers up with a little internal wander. When he reaches the blue tarpaulin that marks the end of the habitable building, he pulls it to one side, to see the blackened bones, the swallowed floors of the Enfield wing. The jagged edges, so stark in the years after the fire, have mellowed and softened as the weeds have moved in. From here you can see not only the fireplace of this floor but the green-tiled fireplace directly above it, stranded up there in the wall. Fifteen years since the fire, and still these timbers are as charred as they were on the day he got back to find the wing being soaked down by the fire brigade. Fifteen years since the beginning of the end.

It seems impossible that he has been kennelling his rage down here all this time. And yet he knows that there are great passages of time that pass when he drops out, and comes to, and has no idea what he has done with his day.

These down times aren't new. Cleo's mother used to say that when he disappeared like that, he was *in the care of the angels*. She would ask him *what news he brought* when she realised he was back. She meant it, too. Although she took her time in mentioning them to him, her own angels, it transpired, had always been there. And they become his angels, too, at the end. She even confessed to him eventually that her angels had names. The Drill Sergeant. The Sniggering Aunt.

There are times when he thinks he can almost see what she meant. When fatigue makes his sight crawl, and the texture of things comes alive. Then, he feels he might see them as she did. Maybe even her, too. But he never does.

He goes to the phone again, and dials Cleo's home number. He's smiling as it rings. She answers. His heart dips like electric light in a storm. He hears her voice, a little agitated. He holds his nerve, staring straight ahead.

'Dad,' she says.

'Correct.'

'Are you okay?'

'You know, I think I am.'

'It's good to hear your voice. I've been missing you.'

'I . . .'

That's all it takes to stump him. It doesn't detonate until he's already embarked on his sentence, but he can't finish because the sob is rising at his throat. He can't think of anything to say that won't fracture into something emotional, so he keeps his mouth shut, breathing through the nose for a while, until he finally finds the composure to get it out without wobbling.

'Me too.'

'Well then, why don't we see each other?'

'I'd like that.'

'Great. Listen . . .'

'Yes?'

'Something odd's going on here. I can't talk now. If I call you in an hour to tell you about it, and fix up a way for us to meet, is that going to be okay? You're not going to go weird on me, and tell me not to come and see you?'

'No. Is everything okay?'

'I'll tell you all about it.'

'Okay.'

'I got another package from you today.'

'You did?'

'About someone arriving at Wreaking for the first time. What it must have been like.'

'Did you like it?'

'Yes. I'll call you back, okay?'

And like that, it is done. Quite a thing to catch.

That call has given him the energy. And for some reason today the drink brings more clarity, not less. He will capture this moment, get it right, put paid to all this thwarted communication for good. And he won't read it back to himself either. He'll capture and get out. Right now, when it counts, he won't be unknowable to her ever again.

He writes calmly, drinking steadily, the pen familiar as an appendage, letting memories surface to help him. Memories of the two of them together. Memories of her mother. He writes until it seems to him that he has written the best version of this letter he could possibly write. He does not risk reading it back, and eroding its power. It must feel perfect. He collects up the pages he has written, puts them in an envelope, writes her name on it and leaves it near the top of the papers on his desk.

All he has to do now is hide the evidence. He brushes his teeth and hides the empty bottle. He combs his hair and pours a glass of water. His breathing doesn't even seem too bad. By the time he hears Carol at the front door, he's almost managed to persuade himself that everything is fine.

'In here,' he says.

He hears her approaching footsteps, and she stops in the doorway. 'What's the matter?'

'Nothing.'

'What have you done to your hair?'

'I want to go out.'

'So you said. Are you sure you're in a fit state?'

'I'll drive myself if you won't take me. By the way – Cleo got your latest package.'

'I see,' says Carol, not even looking particularly embarrassed. 'And you're sure about this walk?'

'You're always telling me to get out of here. I thought you'd be pleased.'

'Can you *go* for a walk?'

'Of course I can.'

'And what are those scratches on your hands?'

'A mirror fell on me.'

'Tut. Seven years. What do you need?'

She makes herself busy around him, and he gives her directions to the hooks in the hallway where his coat is, and the rack beneath them where she will find his boots. When she has left the room and he can hear from her voice that she is by the coat rack in the hall, suitably far away, he slips his hand into her bag to remove her mobile phone, and tuck it safely under the cushion he is sitting on. By the time she's back, it is hidden.

Her ancient blue Renault 5 is outside. It isn't long since Carol got her licence and he knows she is a nervous driver. But there are many things Carol can do now that you wouldn't have thought she was capable of before.

'Where to, then?' she says.

'The Ness,' he replies.

And in her silent surprise she manages to put the car into gear and set off down the drive without even asking him why he hasn't brought his oxygen.

24

It's early enough, so Roland's first stop is the back lot of a sprawling supermarket on the way out to the ring road. He needs to find somewhere and calm down after all that shit with Victor, or he won't give due care to the job in hand.

He turns off the rattling din of the engine and coasts to a halt by some red refuse bins. Sometimes they lock them, sometimes they don't. This chain has a policy of leaving its bins unlocked and stacking the waste food neatly in date order, for those in the know. Roland lifts the domed lid of the bin to check out the lay of the land. Some tired bagged salad. Yesterday's éclairs. And – bingo – three packs of smoked streaky, only two days past.

At this time of day it doesn't take more than an hour to get to Jonny Finer's house, with time for him to park up in a loading bay and breakfast on tea and bacon, and soon Roland's van is parked in a street lined with white stucco mansions bordered by tight banks of box hedge.

He waits, watching the house, until Finer emerges – a healthy-looking man in his forties, carrying a blue holdall that must be the replacement for his briefcase – and gets into a broad, maroon 4x4. Roland makes a note of the registration number.

He sits in the van, smoking with the windows closed,

flicking ash on to the thighs of his trousers and rubbing it in. He stares at the walls of the house, trying to work out how many people there are inside. The way to proceed here is just to sit like this, calmly, smoking on it. As so often before, a little patience and he gets his reward. He sees what can only be the mother, floating efficiently between a pair of breakfasting children.

Things are accelerating. Things for these people are about to change.

He leaves it another half-hour before calling the house number, in case Jonny Finer has forgotten something. He uses his mobile phone and one of a bag of twenty SIM cards he got from a market stall the week before.

'Mrs Finer? I work in A&E at St Michael's Hospital. Does your husband drive a maroon off-road vehicle? I'm afraid he's been in a serious accident. He's unconscious. Can you get here quickly?'

'Oh God,' she says. 'Is he okay? What happened?'

'Head injuries are complicated. We'll know more soon. Please don't panic, but if you could get here as soon as possible we'd be grateful. Time may be a factor.'

There is a little guilt pang, especially when, after a very short while, he sees Mrs Finer coming out of the house, looking flinty and strong. Look at her now, coping with it, her set lips the only outward sign that anything is amiss. Her frilly yet sexy blouse. Her tight blue jeans, showing off her sleek, toned calves. She's holding it together beautifully for these children. And yet, at the same time, in there some-where, she is probably wondering how this moment will impact on their carefully constructed existence, with all its trappings and accessories. All the habits that have become indispensable to them. She's probably already enacting some mental contingency plan. She leads two children to the car, one of whom is trying to finish a piece of toast. And

– hallelujah, there it is – she leaves a floppy golden retriever at the door. A totally non-threatening creature, which at the same time precludes the possibility of her having set an alarm.

What a waste of that resolve it is to test her like this. If something terrible does happen in the future, she will never again approach it face on, with the determination he can see now. She will always think back to this moment and wonder whether it's for real – whether, this time, disaster has finally come for her and her family. That may happen one day, and, unlike today, her weapons will be rusty, because she won't fully believe it.

But the guilt passes, and soon, when he's certain there is nobody else in the house, Roland parks his van right up in their driveway, leaving the engine running. He takes Jonny Finer's keys out of his pocket and opens the front door.

Nothing hangs suspended like this moment when you're waiting to see if a house is empty. There is a burglar-alarm box, but it's over ten years old and that dog has the run of the place. It comes clattering down from upstairs, pausing when it sees him, panting, and he wonders whether things are about to get interesting. But he manages to lead it into a toilet on the ground floor and shut the door.

There is always the chance of someone else. A cleaner, perhaps? Roland calls out, and there is nothing. Only the close quiet of the Finer house. He shuts the front door behind him and immediately feels he can't breathe. How do people live in these airless places? Nothing but air freshener and furniture polish, trapped under the stifling cloak of double glazing: every fart flying round looking for an exit.

Roland never enters a property if he thinks it might be occupied. But even if you think you know where people are, or aren't, you can be surprised. Once he entered a bedroom and counted not just one, or even two, but three different snores. He stood in the doorway, trying to work out the arrangement. It was only when the third snore rolled smoothly into a snarl that he realised they had a dog on the bed. That was a hasty exit.

There have been other lucky escapes. He once thought he was going to have to thump an old woman in her nightie who met him in her living room at 3 a.m. He had already begun to rationalise to himself why he had to hit her, and to hope he wouldn't have to do it too hard, when she spoke to him without fear.

'Do you have a message for me?' He stared at her. 'If not I assume you can let yourself out. I'm very tired.'

He only realised after she'd gone that she had assumed he was a ghost.

Mrs Finer is house proud: not a mark on one of these surfaces. Not always a good sign. The best stuff is often in the filthiest places. Roland feels his sympathy for her beginning to wane. He never warms to those who are too allergic to dirt, and this looks like the home of the sort of woman who would pursue you everywhere you went with a wet wipe.

Jewellery first, of course. He zips up to the master bedroom, and finds it quickly, on a dressing table. He doesn't linger.

The hallway contains artfully arranged painted and lacquered sticks in a pot. Nothing on the walls of any value, as usual. You sometimes get modern art in a place like this, but this lot are more in the reproduction poster category.

A vibration in his ankle. He reaches into his sock for the phone, which brings Victor's words into the frame: *WHER FUCK U GON ASUME YOUV HT JAKPOT.*

He composes a quick reply – *on to something back in a few hours.*

With one finger he flicks open a box of chocolates on the

kitchen table and begins eating them as he wanders round, muttering at the furniture. The chocolates are dense pralines, that fill his mouth with a cloying sludge. But he forces through them all anyway as he makes his way around, talking himself through the strategically deployed antiques of the Finer household. 'Occasional table, nineteenth century. Faux panelling. Bureau, Georgian, could be. Credenza, worth a swipe. Heavy though.'

A painting on the wall stops him. It's not all that good, but something about the composition gets to him, and it doesn't take him long to work out why. There is water, and woodland, and the hint of a brick-built tower beyond.

'You're coming with me,' he says.

Within ten minutes the painting is stored carefully in the back of his van along with jewellery and furniture, including a nicely solid oak table. He supplements them with an enormous television that he unscrews from a hinge on the kitchen wall.

He takes one last look round the kitchen before leaving. It's a glass atrium of an extension, with black units and white walls. Key clusters and dog leads dangle from a home-made rack with a child's picture on it of a crocodile by a watering hole. The wall is taken up by poster-sized photos of the family, posing on a ski slope. Jonny Finer – dashing, reliable, athletic – stands at the centre of the group, holding it together. Look at this Lego man with his model family. This is a man who would be calm in any conceivable storm, grinning with his gleaming teeth, which match the toothpaste white of his sunglasses frames.

Roland goes right up to the photo and eyeballs it. 'You died, for a bit, this morning. How did that feel?'

There's one of them on a boat as well. The kids, younger here than they were up the ski slope, less self-conscious, less *too cool for school*, are here laughing delightedly in their lifejackets, while Mr and Mrs Finer share loving glances and a bottle of white wine. (Who is taking these pictures? Do they travel with an official photographer?) Just look at them. Look at the design involved in it. Who are they trying to sell this to? Themselves? Who's meant to be buying it? What would happen if you just started to tear little bits off it, like old wallpaper?

It is then that Roland sees what's written on the wall. The family keeps a chart of who has grown and when. Who has overtaken whom. It is their one daring concession to spontaneity and untidiness, and it's hidden round a corner, so that guests don't see it when they first walk into the kitchen. So it doesn't spoil the wow factor of this showroom of a place, with its glowing family portraits. Names have been carefully applied to each mark, with gags and comments beside them, the scrawls gaining in confidence and maturity with advancing years:

27th April '04. Watch out Dad! Daisy closing in!

5th March '05. Lily takes off! Must be the spinach.

22nd September '10. Lily chasing Daisy like mad. But what's going on up here? Can Dad be SHRINKING?

1st March '11. Red Letter Day: Daisy overtakes Mum.

Roland pokes around with a finger in the rough ceramic mug of pens in the windowsill, eventually selecting a sharp enough pencil. Positioning himself against the wall he takes the pencil and holds it straight across the top of his own head. His line comes a good foot above any member of the family.

He stands there, breathing, staring at the mark on the wall. Then, from the pot, he takes the blunted stub of a pencil eraser, half a dinosaur, the other half rubbed away leaving only the trunk and the tail. He reaches forward again and rubs out his line. And as he rubs at the mark, erasing his own contribution to the chart, he keeps rubbing, taking away the little increments of Daisy and Lily and all of them, until great worms are shearing off the eraser in his hand, and you can't even make out the indent in the wall where the marks had been. Now there are no marks on the wall. All is clean. And nobody can smugly look back on how they have plotted their advancement.

She will probably have got to the hospital by now and found no sign of a brain-injured husband. Her husband, meanwhile, will be sitting waiting for Roland to turn up at the café they agreed on. It won't be too long before one of them phones the other. Roland leaves the empty chocolate box on the kitchen table, places the charred satchel and the house keys neatly beside it, and heads out to the van, whose engine is still ticking over nicely.

25

As they set off she looks worried, as if she knows something isn't right. But Carol wants to be seen to embrace the new initiative, so she doesn't say anything. The Ness today is simple, naive as a child's collage: a strip of gravel stuck on a blue background. Their steps dislodge clacking stones as they lean into one another like a pair of old lovers. He opens his eyes wider than is natural, to try and exercise them, to stretch them enough to take it all in: this tongue of slate-grey shingle; the indigos above; the complex greens in the water. The exposure has startled him.

'We wouldn't have been able to bring the oxygen down here anyway,' he says.

'We could have found a way.'

'And this air's probably better than the stuff in the tank.'

'If you say so. Just tell me if you start to feel breathless.'

He pulls her in closer. They're making good progress, alternately slipping along and getting good purchase on the stones. The promontory stretches out ahead. His breathing is getting shallower, and his heart is yelping, and sending up danger signals that he must coldly ignore, and most definitely hide. She is anything but stupid.

'Why here, particularly?' she says.

'Because I haven't been down here for ages. And I think I should again, before it's too late.'

'Excuse me,' she says, pinching his side, where she is holding him tight to help him stay upright. 'We'll have none of that talk, thank you very much.'

'Seal.' He points at the flat, bobbing head in the water beside them.

They walk on. Waves sigh against the shingle banks. The seal blinks, and he entertains a brief but comforting fantasy that this is his wife, batting her eyelashes at him from the other side.

'Why are you smiling?' says Carol.

'I can't remember the last time I came out here. It's lovely.'

'So you spoke to Cleo?' she says. 'How was that?'

'Fine. Surprisingly.'

'If I had a child, I can't imagine falling out with them. Life's too short, isn't it?'

'It's complicated. We've done some nasty things to each other over the years.'

Waves arrive in gentle, depleted slaps.

'Why can't you just forgive each other?'

'I can't be anybody other than myself, can I? No amount of knowing what I'm like can stop me being the person I am.'

'All the more reason to forgive.'

A coarse back-noise has started to accompany his breathing. Noticing it, she stops walking, and tries to turn to him. 'I think we should go back now, old man.'

'I'm fine.' He grips her tighter, and strides forward, forcing her onwards.

'It's not a good idea. I don't want to have to call the coastguard on you.'

'You won't have to.' He keeps marching, trying to get them to cover as much distance as possible on the shingle.

'Let me go. Stop.'

He lets her go, and carries on as far as he can, until he can feel it, the tightness in his chest, and here it comes, the waves and waves of it, the bilious bitterness at the back of his throat, the inability to take a breath, and the fear that brings.

She doesn't speak as she watches the fit take him, and watches him sinking to his knees on the stones. He sees her looking up and down the length of the beach. But there are no fishermen here, not today. No one except the two of them.

'Try and breathe slowly,' she says. 'I'm calling the lifeboat. They'll be here any minute. How I let you bring us out here I'll never know.'

She unhooks her handbag from her shoulder and begins sifting around in it for the phone. Her movements get faster, more jerky. His fit has subsided enough to him to be lying on his side, drooling. He can still barely take a breath, his lungs are so constricted. It hurts.

'Hang on. I know it's in here. Keep breathing. Steady as she goes.'

She looks at him, and he can't help giving a sad smile. 'Sorry,' he mouths.

Whether it's the smile or the apology, something makes her realise.

'You didn't,' she says, her expression changing from one of fear to one of anger.

She bends down towards him to try and heave him back on to his feet and get him walking again, but he bucks and hacks against her shoulder, and his vision has started to change.

'Sorry,' he says.

Fossils of fish and shells down here among the pebbles, calcifying, pulverising themselves to nothing. Having the good grace to let themselves be erased.

'This wasn't your fault,' he manages. 'Don't go thinking it was.'

He falls on to his back on the cold, wet stones. Carol is fleeing away down the Ness, and he's waving her goodbye, and muttering the word *sorry* over and over. He pulls the cigarettes out of his jacket pocket, and fumbles with the box, shedding them on to the pebbles. His sour, old man's trousers are getting wet. From the water, the seal continues to watch.

He can just make out the figure of Carol, receding down the Ness. Fast. Determined.

No regrets. Regrets are a waste product. It happened. That was the story. No use trying to unmake it. For some reason this thought brings to mind a repeated, half-remembered line from something classical that must date back to school, playing like the final chorus, everyone on stage for the big show-stopping finale. *Things are as they are, but it is useless to say more.*

After two or three attempts he manages to light up. He inhales deeply, feeling the soft detonation in his chest, the stuff hitting his system. His blood flexes with the impact of the nicotine.

Smoking has never felt better than it does now. Places once horribly defiled but years clean recoil in dumb shock as fresh bombs of tar start falling. Just for a moment it is how it used to be, free of dread. Then the sharp, merciless consequences strike.

26

It's a short day's work – she's owed a half-shift after several late nights last week. Her main job of the morning is to provide further supporting footage for her report on the universal algorithm, which, it is said, *can accurately predict the patterns of cause and effect, enabling us to understand precisely how one thing leads to another.* It requires three years' worth of data in any given scenario in order to *eliminate false patterns,* and is now in use in a variety of extreme contexts. If you believe this report, it can be used to predict the behaviour of enemy insurgents, to monitor and forecast earthquake activity, to prevent the suicides of prisoners in solitary confinement, to read the movements of a crowd or a shedful of battery hens, and, most fruitfully, to anticipate when and where burglaries will occur. The algorithm is so established as a policing tool in some American states that it has even been incorporated into the latest iteration of a popular, violent computer game. The report concludes with a vox pop from a stern Texan police chief with sunglasses and a bulging neck: *If you understand how one thing leads to another, you can act in a preventative way, and be there to stop bad things happening.*

She splices stock footage of broiler-house hens with some up-to-the-minute pictures of the demonstration she edited yesterday, which has been in the news more and more as the condition of the woman who was hurt in the crowd surge has worsened. There's a strong narrative, some suitably chaotic scenes with chucked bottles and riot shields. She edits it so that when the reporter is talking about the algorithm's capacity to 'read aberration from a set', there's also a brief shot of the injured woman looking bewildered just before she went down.

There's just one more task to do before she goes: a science piece about in vitro fertilisation. Footage of the needle piercing the egg. The bubble breached and popping back to shape with the intruder inside. It reminds her of Oliver, stamping on frogspawn in the shallows of the Revenant House lake. The squelch and burst of it under his shoe.

She doesn't quite dream of Oliver, but he's there as a presence in her subconscious, all the time. Once, when she was in bed with Nat, she had a distinct sense that Oliver was watching from the corner. She has no reason to think that Oliver might be dead – but experience has shown her that death has no bearing on whether or not ghosts appear.

It's time to get home.

On her way out of the office, she nearly trips over the figure of Emma, who is on her knees in front of a vending machine.

'I lost my pound,' she says, sounding a little desperate. She is still in the kind of state where everything is the end of the world. Maybe she's always in that state. Maybe she lives her life at the end of the world.

'Let me have a look.' Cleo lies on her front near the machine. One eye is helpful here – whereas in many situations it makes her unable to triangulate properly and messes with her perspective, it's great when you only need to look at something straight on. She spots the coin, reaches forward, and feels something cut the back of her hand. She shunts her body right up against the machine and plunges her arm forward, making the cut worse, until her fingers feel the coin, and she teases it out, and passes it over, winning a quick bet with herself that Emma will be too self-involved to notice she is hurt.

'I've finished the algorithm story,' says Cleo. 'I think it should be fine.'

Emma fingers the dusty pound coin. 'You almost feel sorry for them. These burglars. Thinking of committing a crime, and arriving to find the police there waiting for them before they've even done anything wrong.'

'Well,' says Cleo, moving uneasily from one foot to the next. 'They're only wreaking what they've sown.'

'Sorry?'

'Reaping.'

She makes her excuses quickly and leaves.

The bus home in the middle of the day; an agreeable feeling of bunking off; of going home to hide. She'll close the front door and put herself to bed, make up for that early start, get some equilibrium back. She feels in her pocket for his watch, which nobody online seems to be able to repair. She takes her phone from another pocket and checks it for missed calls, then leans her head against the window.

This isn't right. This isn't how it's supposed to go. If he must leave, she should be by his bed until then, going over all the things they did together, playing it out, the highlights package, the compilation of hilarious out-takes as the end credits roll. Not this blockage. Everything silted up like concrete poured down a hole.

But even as her anger swells, something in her rises coolly to defend it. To defend them. This is who they were together, however it made them feel, and that, ladies and gentlemen, is family.

As the bus passes a launderette, she realises again how precarious her mood is. Anything that suggests loneliness, or even just solitary people looking after themselves, is enough to make her well up at the moment: a lone diner; a girl on a bike. As for the sight of harmonious interaction between parent and child: she saw a man tousling his son's hair in the street last week, and had to look away. Small kindnesses like that are lethal.

Things burp up from time to time. Different aspects of his conviction on a particular subject, surfacing at random.

No, I don't want an apple! Sour, mean little things.

Bloody twitchers. Why do they have to watch *them? Why can't they just leave them alone?*

Why should I be held to ransom by a pear?

She smiles to herself as the bus stops and starts, and people get on and off who have no idea that such a confusing man might exist, and probably never will.

On the rare occasions when she can't sleep, this is what comes for Cleo: her father's voice in the night, gaining momentum, getting into his stride about something, raving and countering away until it could drive her mad. The insistence on rejecting everything, just to show he could. Repeating himself over and over, to invest things in her. Bank them. And – by virtue of this powerful, constantly wrong-footing memory of hers, she has been able to hold on to them until they matured. Now, his sayings have become priceless. Even the ones she doesn't agree with, that smack of cant, which she finds endearing because of what they tell her about him, and because they help her to engage with the ongoing mystery he represents. He plumbed them down into her, like an oral tradition, like a water table of mythology, so that they are here for her now, and she has the luxury of being able to judge them for herself. What does it matter that the two of them don't speak in real life when she can hear him speaking from within at a thought's notice? In that sense, he is always with her. So it shouldn't really matter if he dies.

Should it.

In the hallway of the apartment block she sees a packet sticking up out of her mailbox. He's sent her another one. She rips it open on the stairs, and there it is again, another load of pages that can only have come from her father's study, since they are extracts from his Wreaking book. Which he swears blind he is not sending her.

She opens the front door. And now she really does think that someone is fucking with her.

She wanders forward into the apartment, not bothering to close the door behind her, because what's the point of doors, when something like this can happen.

'Is someone here?' she calls, to a silent flat. The air of the place has barely been disturbed. She can still smell her own sleepy sheets in the bedroom. But *this*.

The dining table has been replaced. The glass-topped, flat-pack item that was here before has disappeared, and in its place is a magnificent oak thing that would not be out of place as the centrepiece of a medieval banquet. Her chairs have been carefully arranged in the positions they were in before, and even the fruit bowl has been carefully set down in its rightful place in the middle, but the table makes everything else look flimsy and absurd.

Her gaze drifts up to the wall, and her skin seems to shrink round her skull. Hanging on the wall is a charity-shop-standard oil painting of a lake, with a hint of red-brick wall behind it, secluded in trees. And if she wasn't certain of the fact that she's going out of her mind, then she would admit to herself straight out how much this painting reminds her of . . .

Her phone rings and she snatches it out of her jacket

pocket, and doesn't bother to look at who's calling, so when she hears her father's voice she doesn't have the will to make anything up. She's too freaked out by it all to come up with any kind of smokescreen or strategy, and she just tells him what she's thinking. And says she will call him back later.

As she walks round the flat, to try and find out if anything else has changed, she can barely remember the conversation she's just had. She pours herself one vodka, then another, roughly squeezing a lime wedge over the glass in an effort to sharpen things up, and work out what is going on. She runs fingers up and down the length of the table's cold, polished surface. She stands in front of the picture. She takes it off the wall, rehangs it, and straightens it up.

She is standing there for so long that night begins to fall, and she doesn't even think to put on the lights, with the result that it's nearly dark when her father rings her back again, wondering why she hasn't called him back as promised. But it isn't her father. It's someone whose voice she doesn't recognise, *asking* her about her father. Whether Jasper Scriven is her father. Why are they asking her whether Jasper Scriven is her father? In the gap before she composes her reply, she can't work out for the life of her why anyone would be ringing to ask her that.

27

Rearranging Cleo's flat has left him hungry, so Roland parks near the greasy spoon at the end of the tunnel for some food before heading back to face Victor. The café's yellow-on-red sign hangs suspended across the dark mouth of an arch near the end of the viaduct. Many of the other arches in this row have been tidied into gyms or offices or wine bars, but not this one. Pigeon spikes sprout from the top of the sign in skewed clusters, but no longer keep the birds at bay. Several blinking birds sit massed on the letters, watching the entrance in the hope of a chicken bone or a scrap of bacon. In the window are pictures of food: the usual pig-and-egg combinations; patties; pies; chips; livid pictures of red things on yellow sticks.

He orders tea and a fried breakfast, and parks himself awkwardly in a corner, struggling to settle into the aperture between the bolted-down chair and the bolted-down table. He grips the mug and takes big, scalding gulps, trying to wash out the dirty feelings swilling around him. He was in and out as quickly as he could, but the shame is powerful. The heady smell of her strewn bedlinen nearly knocked him out, and its seductive disorder made him think for a moment that he might get in it for a bit without her noticing. Even contemplating a decision like this is the sort of thing that scrambles Roland for hours. He finds it hard sometimes to distinguish between real memories of the things he has done and the nightmares he has after feeling the urge to do them. His dread makes memories of his fears. He'll come to sometimes, in the van, panicking at what his imagination has served him up. He'll think he has hurt her, and must check immediately to make sure he has not. The fear has caused him to end up at her flat more than once in the middle of the night, finally ringing the doorbell to get her up if he can see no sign of life. Anything to be sure that he has not done what he thinks he might have done.

His food arrives, and he piles into it quickly with his head down, and the meal is almost finished when he hears a girl's voice at the counter asking for a Coke, and looks up to see her, standing with her back to him, her schoolbag slung casually from her shoulder, the word *MOLLY* on it in bold Tipp-Ex letters.

She pays, turns to leave, and sees Roland for the first time, the hulk stuck here at his table. He sees her seeing him, then he sees her eyes widen, and she puts her head down to make for the door.

'Molly,' he says.

'I need to go,' she says.

'What's the matter?'

'My dad's office is only round the corner. I can call him any time I want.'

'What? Just wait a minute.'

'He warned me about you. He told me if I saw you anywhere, I should run away as quickly as I could. He said I should call the police if you came near me.'

'How long were you in there?' Roland says, quickly. 'Did you go in alone?'

'Get away from me.'

'Did Victor . . . are you okay?'

As she turns to leave, Roland reaches and grabs her arm. He knows he's doing it too tight. He can't help it.

The scream is high and loud, and so surprising that it sounds fake. Roland tries to put distance between himself and Molly, but he can't move because he's wedged into this prison of a table, so all he can do is raise his hand in the air, away from her.

Having let out the sound, she looks almost embarrassed, but she doesn't speak or leave. She just stands in the doorway looking at him, and at his hand, which is resting on the Formica tabletop. The café has fallen silent, and he feels his face prickle with rushing blood under the settling attention and judgement of other diners.

'What was that for?' Roland says.

The owner of the café is standing behind her in his apron. 'Are we all right here?'

'It's fine,' says Roland. 'Just let me talk to her.' He puts another hand out and the scream is so loud now that people get up and stand around her.

Now she has her audience, she hams it right up – shoots him a wide-eyed, wounded look as she stands behind this seedy-looking character with his stained apron for *safety* or something, and the thing to do now is just get out and not lose your cool or make yourself even remotely conspicuous, which is all he wants to do. But already the talk is all *I think it would be best if you* and *are you okay dear is there someone you'd like us to call* and it takes as much strength as Roland can muster to lever himself out from behind the table and get to his feet, nearly toppling a spider plant.

'I'm going,' he says, willing the café owner not to be a fool, but there's a look of defiance there that is fuelled by everyone standing with him, and the look seems to firm up rather than diminish when Roland gets to his full height.

'I think it might be time we called the police,' he says, brandishing his palette knife.

'I'm leaving,' says Roland. 'And you need to let me.'

As he steps forward, Molly lets out another scream, which steels the café owner into stepping forward. Roland grabs him by the apron and flings him quickly against the wall. This sends him into the path of a table of plates and cutlery, and elicits a collective sound from the diners which is halfway between a gasp and a scream, and then Roland is out on the pavement, fumbling for his van keys, hoping he can get away and park up inside the arches before anybody spots him.

He knows he's talking to himself as he walks along but there's nothing to be done now.

stopping to hide tables in people's flats and look what happens, stopping to hide tables, with your priorities got to get your PRIORITIES straight, and telling him you were going to be a few hours, oh that was good wasn't it, that was something, well just do it now, just get it done now

The van judders and rumbles into life. He struggles with the gearstick, and it makes, what is it, a sort of *barking* noise, because he's in such a state he can't put it in gear.

Oh no. Not now. Not now, you genius.

He makes a fist and mashes it into his thigh two or three times, until the leg is so dead he risks having trouble keeping pressure on the accelerator. The van lurches down the tunnel towards the entrance to the arches, with Roland massed at its quivering wheel, trying to slow down his breathing, trying to remember one of his cardinal rules about not acting rashly. But even as he tells himself that, he realises that he is calm, and this is not an impulse, but something he has been meaning to do for some time.

He brings the van to a halt outside the shuttered door. He takes out his key and unlocks the door. He could bang on the shutter, but this way he gets to make more of a surprise entrance, and get closer to finding out the unpleasant truth of what Victor gets up to when he's on his own. He steps inside the shutter and heaves it up from the inside. He shoots the van up the ramp and brings it to a halt in its usual spot, brings down the shutter. He leaves the engine on.

It's darker than normal, and inside the shipping container he can make out Victor sitting in his chair, bathed in the light of projected film. He's not quite sitting in the right place, so parts of the image spill on to the back of his head and catch his face, lighting up bits of his cheek and teeth in segments of colour: blues, reds, yellows. Hearing Roland arrive, he turns, no doubt preparing something nasty to say.

Try and remember how it happened later, because what will happen is that you won't get it right, and the guilt will kick in, and so it's very important to remember how much you want to do this now, and how right it feels.

Victor's right hand strays to his fly in the crook of his groin, bundled over down there in the chair, and he makes a big show of leaning back, so far as he can, to zip himself up. 'Sorry about that. Flying low. Didn't know you'd be back.'

Roland says nothing, but slams the inside of the container, sending a great shudder through the metal.

He looks amused to begin with, but it doesn't last long. Every time Victor starts to say something, Roland delivers another powerful blow to the metal, sending loud booms reverberating round its interior. Full-on anger sends Victor to a calm sort of place, where he relaxes back into his wheelchair and calculates what to come back at you with.

'What do you care if she's been here?' says Victor. 'What's it to you?'

Boom.

He smiles sweetly. 'Poor old Roland. No matter how hard he tries, he's never in the right place at the right time.'

Boom.

'Cleo.'

Boom.

'Sweet brother of mine.'

Boom.

'Little Molly.'

Boom.

'And what about your mum? Heard from her lately? How's she doing?'

And of course he's far calmer than Victor thinks he is, because this is what he wanted to do. It's the way he's always planned it. Roland is far too methodical to get as angry as Victor thinks he is, but he wants Victor to think he's cross because that's what calms him down, twisted fuck that he is.

Roland steps forward neatly into the container, with that speed he has that has always surprised everyone because of his size. He leans down and plants one on Victor. He's never put everything into a punch before. Always been far too afraid to do that, because Roland does know his own strength, and that's what scares him.

Hitting a man in a wheelchair is complicated, turns out. The angles are all wrong. Especially when the confined spaces of defunct shipping containers are involved. But Roland is nothing if not versatile. You just have to lean down a bit, and into it, to get the right cut.

Roland has hit more people than most, but something about it always comes as a surprise. The release of the energy. The levels of adrenaline involved. Even when you're only thumping a weak, soapy-skinned jaw like Victor's.

The look on his face is priceless though. A look of disbelief. A look of *Hit a man in a WHEELCHAIR, would you?*

Victor buckles. The chair clatters back and to the side, bunching and swerving and coming to rest with one wheel still rolling like the aftermath of a road-safety advert.

What Roland does next does surprise him, because it

wasn't part of the plan, but he knows he'll go through with it now he's started. He walks calmly to the van and returns with a pair of bolt cutters. He steps back inside the container and leans down towards Victor, snips both bits of briefcase chain, the one from his wrist and the one from his ankle, and plucks the bag away. He sets it on the passenger seat of his van, among the ashes of Jonny Finer's man-bag. After all Victor's tough talk about the briefcase, he doesn't even notice.

Roland steps back away from the pathetic jerks and shuffles of the creature in the shadows, and he closes the doors of the shipping container, bringing down the great blue bolt which is secured to the outside. He does a once-over of the area, and loads the van up with one or two important things. He discards the remains of Cleo's dining table and the less valuable objects he took from Jonny Finer's house. He steers the van calmly back outside. As he's lowering the metal shutter, arm over arm, he hears the deep detonations of Victor's fists from inside the container.

As he drives away his phone rings, and the residual guilt is so profound that he thinks it will be his mother, so he's surprised to hear Carol's voice on the end of the line, and he thinks that at least she will be able to give him an update on how his mother is doing. But something's wrong. She sounds different – like she used to years ago, when she was the old Carol, and everything was not all right, and even though he's telling her to calm down, he can tell that something has tipped her terribly badly, which at least solves the problem of where on earth he should head for now – not that it was ever going to be anywhere else.

PART FOUR

28

Roland sees it all. From his vantage point in the shabbiest
first-floor ward of the Enfield wing, surrounded by rusty
bedsteads and fungal horsehair mattresses, he watches them
arriving: the car pulling up to its skittish halt; the nervous
welcoming ceremony; the illumination of the porch; the fête
for three. Even this far away you can feel a man's fear when
it's as loud as that.

The man in question – whose name he still doesn't know,
but who will soon be hitched for good in Roland's memory
to the name of Jasper Scriven – brakes too early, so the car
skids on the drive, before doing a final lurch forward and
coming to rest halfway between the two parking spaces by
the front door. Then he's out, shouting at the people inside,
stilling them, telling them not to emerge just yet. He runs
round and into the entrance hall to throw a switch, and the
lights over the front porch come on. Thanks to Roland, they
do not electrocute anyone.

A theatrical bow follows, and the man opens the passenger
door to let out a fat woman. Then a girl leaps out, and
something tips Roland on his axis, enlarges his understanding
of what's on offer in the world.

She's a year or two younger than him. He notices her
battered jeans, her bright red trainers. Instinctively he

crouches down at the sight of her, and this movement draws her darting eye, and she looks straight up at his window, which he had thought was a good place not to be seen, because the man has only been operating in the other wing.

He's ready to punch himself for being so visible, but her gaze travels on, alighting on a different window on the other side. She stops here, as if seeing someone else, and Roland scrambles to look over and see what she is seeing. She seems to say something to herself, still staring at the other wing, and then she smiles.

He tracks them as they tour the place, from room to room as far as he can, and quietly escaping when they get too close. The girl has a way of stopping and turning round suddenly, as if she is trying to catch sight of something that disappears as soon as her eyes find it. Several times, as he tracks them, she seems to look straight at him, with no fear or hesitation, and then to turn away again. He becomes convinced she knows he is there, until he starts to notice that she is doing the same thing when looking in other places as well – places where nobody else could be hiding. She is talking to someone, but it isn't him, or anyone else who is there.

On the second day, he watches Cleo and the fat woman urinating together in the woods. The sight is fascinating, and a little unnerving. He shakes his head to try and scatter visions of what would happen if he was caught watching something like this, and it got back to Mona.

But if you see something like this, you aren't going to not watch it. And he craves more evidence on her. Ways to understand. All he has to go on for now is this thing she shouts about aeroplanes. Even as he hears her saying it, his hand strays to the piece of lead in his jacket pocket. He is working it without thinking for the rest of the day.

Later he returns as soon as he can slip away from home. He can't see any people, but the front porch is still lit up with coloured bulbs. He smells barbecued food. He keeps to the shadows and goes round to the lawn at the rear, where he finds their abandoned plates and two candles wavering in old jam jars, and strewn cutlery. He finishes somebody's piece of chicken and swipes a finger in a leftover blob of mayonnaise, before going up to her room to plant the aeroplane. He looks around at her things – the beaten-up paperbacks, the jewellery.

He's getting ready to leave altogether when he becomes aware of the music. Something from the twenties – skittish, joint-jumping stuff, with fiddles and banjos. But the noise is not coming from within the building. It's somewhere else, outside. He heads down to the lake to try to understand more of what is going on by seeing the building in its entirety. He can perceive the outlines of two pavilions: one in a nook set back into the rhododendrons, the other placed behind the mist on the water so that it might be floating on it. Their texture seems to be frayed, crawling. It is decay, more visible in this more honest light than it would be in full glare. And still he can hear the music.

From the edge he can make out an illuminated bubble under the water, clotted with pond murk. Its glow is bright enough that he can make out the dark shapes of suspended fish backlit in the pea-green water, and the moving shadows within. The only thing for it is to get in closer, so he walks into the lake, feeling its slow, intimate soak around his legs and waist. He stares at the glow, and as he gets closer, at the shape inside the glow. Dancing people: the adult couple, clasped together, and beside them the girl, jerking wildly to the music, lost in it. He wishes they could see how otherworldly they look from out here in the dark – spinning, optimistic, impregnable.

The family photo album is decimated now. Roland wasn't around when all the images featuring his father were torn out, but he's not about to ask her where they are. Of the photos that remain, only two feature Mona as a young psychiatric nurse. In one of them, she stands in a pub at the centre of a group of three men and two women, all of whom are at different stages of erupting into laughter at something she's just said. While the rest of the group all try with greater or lesser success to keep their eyes on the camera lens, Mona looks calmly off to the left, and the flash that catches the eager teeth and eyes of her companions only finds on her a composed little smile, downward-turning, mischievous, satisfied. The second shows her looking bored at a staff party in the hospital assembly hall, raising an eyebrow at the camera as if daring whoever was behind the viewfinder to liven things up a bit. In both, her hair is long rather than practical, and there's even a suggestion of make-up.

It is probably wrong to assume on this evidence alone that Mona's younger days were spent briskly ministering to the mentally scrambled then laughing it away all night – some of the later, careworn person must have existed then too – but it's hard to discern any trace of that person in the Mona of today: bitter, edgy, sad with worry. And certainly not in the Mona of this afternoon, who is sitting at the table, frowning at a shrink-wrapped ham. He watches her from the door, and pictures her younger self in the photo album, shrugging up at him from under her dated hairdo as if to say, *What can you do?*

'Where are you going?' she says, without looking up.

'Carol asked me to take her out.'

'This says it goes off tomorrow,' says Mona. 'Maybe you should pick up something else. Tonight could be cutting it fine.'

'Tonight it will still be on date. You've got that, about Carol?'

'If I froze it today that might buy us some time.'

'I'll see you later.'

'But then I'd have to start defrosting it again almost straight away.'

'Bye.'

'What do you do up there, with her?'

He stops in the middle of reaching for his coat. 'What?'

'Don't think I don't know what goes on with my patients. I don't mind – but I'm just wondering what you *do* all the time.'

'We just walk around. It calms her down.'

'You should be careful. It could be traumatic for her to keep going there. To be so attached to the building when it's falling down.'

'What harm can it do?'

'You wouldn't have any idea about that, would you?'

He closes his eyes. 'I'm going now.'

'You wouldn't have any idea about it,' she repeats.

'I'm just trying to be nice to her.'

'She's not your friend, you know,' says Mona. 'She can't be.'

'What do you mean? Of course she's my friend.' Roland is mortified to see Carol standing right there, at the bottom of the stairs, staring at the front door and pretending she isn't listening.

'Come on,' he says, shouldering his coat and offering Carol hers. 'It's starting to rain.'

'Lovely,' says Carol.

'I don't think we can serve this ham,' he hears Mona saying to no one in particular, as he and Carol leave. 'I couldn't bear to poison anyone.'

On the way, Carol stops him, just as they are emerging from the woods into the water meadow. 'Your mum told you you shouldn't, but you're bringing me anyway. That's really something.'

'You like coming here,' he says. 'And so do I.'

She touches his cheek with the palm of her hand. It feels warm and soft. 'You're very good to me, Roland. You make me my best self. I'm lucky to have you.'

This is the moment that he will isolate later on – the one when he should have realised something was wrong, and taken Carol straight back home. But he does not. He is too excited at the prospect of seeing Cleo again.

The rain is falling steadily by the time they make their way back, and Roland doesn't notice how quiet Carol is – how her features have set in a grim and different way, how her hair is messed up, her clothes differently arranged. He doesn't even reply when she says to him that she thinks they might go on a different walk next time, because he is too busy thinking about what has just happened to him.

He can't sleep this evening – but it isn't like the not-sleeping of normal evenings. This is different. This is because he is already missing this day, because he knows how important it will turn out to be. He wishes you could plant a stake in the ground when you had a day like this, and sacrifice the rest of your experience in exchange for never letting it go, and say to whoever was in charge: *I'll take this one, thank you. I'll stick here.*

The rain had set in after he left Carol. A cool, sharpening, early summer rain. He stopped for a while in one of the waterside pavilions, listening to its wet chatter on the lake surface. At Revenant House her father was off somewhere with a visitor, and the fat woman was on the other side going at walls with a blowtorch, but Cleo didn't seem to be around. And then he saw it, on the wall. A chalk arrow, that had not been there before – with a small sketch of an aeroplane beside it.

He followed the markings for twenty minutes, from building to building, then across a small courtyard where overflow was swamping gutters and clattering on to the tarmac. One or two of the arrows were being diminished by the rain, and a couple of the planes weren't finished, but the trail was intact. It took him to a low, flat-roofed extension to one of the women's wards, where, looking through the window, he found her.

The walls were covered with photos cut from old magazines, showcasing different hairstyles and looks. She was reclining in a barber's chair, one foot lolling and shoeless, reading a trashy-looking paperback novel called *To the Tower*. There were bits of hairdressing equipment around: one of those domes that blue-rinsers sit under; a mirror with light bulbs round it. The madhouse beauty salon.

She might have been waiting for her appointment, so nonchalant was her pose. She'd positioned a paint tin to catch the water that dripped from the ceiling. He watched her. Her shadow against the vivid greens of the courtyard creepers that were starting to cover the windows. He took in the detail: the thick sock round the ankle at the top of the red canvas trainer she was wearing. The swirls of dark hair on the nape of the neck. Her thin frame. The mole in the indentation above her hip bone.

Broken glass crackled under his foot, and with a shock of adrenaline he sprang to one side, keeping himself down, breathing heavily. When he dared a glance back into the room to see if she had heard him over the steady fall of the rain, or worse, had actually seen him, she still had her eyes on the book.

But she was smiling.

29

'Up!' he shouts, from halfway up the stairs, which is about as much warning as you ever get, both that he's coming, and that he's up, and that means he has to shout about it, regardless of who might be asleep, because when he's up, everybody else has to be up too.

'Up!' The footfalls approach, and she can hear his breathing, then the door is kicked open.

The *volume* of his voice when he's like this: it's a sound so driven by its owner's need, for his own sake, to project a clarion call of positivity into the world; a sound so harsh and glaring and uncompromising that if, as often happens, she is asleep when it bursts in on her, it shocks her awake so hard that her skin feels seized all over, her heart rips into action and she nearly falls out of bed with panic and fear.

'Blow-torching! Paint-stripping! Sanding!' He snatches aside the curtain of her turret window, disregarding the pool of water that has collected on the sill overnight. The white noise of the rain has been the delicious backdrop to her sleep for the last few hours. She's been keeping herself awake for it. But not that awake.

He dumps a cup of tea on her bedside table – no milk and the bag still in it – and there is an unsettling clatter as her lead aeroplane is knocked on to the floor.

She raises her head and plants her face in the palm of her right hand, rubbing and propping at once. 'I thought you had a visit from the bank manager this morning.'

'And you thought that meant you got to lie in bed? I want you and Ursula to carry on with getting rid of all that paint in the ground floor of the Enfield. I want that banker to see a hive of activity!'

This thing of everybody getting behind his plan is wearing very thin. With every new morning there is another rota, and another few hours of looking the other way to help him carry on blundering towards his buckled, implausible future. The three of them spend their days blowtorching paint off walls, ripping out stairwell cages, taking down ceiling tiles so toxic you have to handle them wearing gloves and a mask, building bonfires of safety doors and paper and bric-a-brac. Cleo prides herself on being a believer, and if it was just her and him she might be able to sustain it, but the presence of Ursula shatters his credibility rather than augmenting it. Cleo's finding it more and more difficult not to find the pair of them ridiculous.

Ursula can't hide how unsuited she is to these activities. She insists on wearing all her usual regalia of scarves and tights and skirts beneath her overalls, which makes her body shape even funnier than usual, and she applies full pancake and more, in spite of the inevitability that the whole carapace will be steadily sweated off all day behind a pair of safety goggles.

At the end of each day Ursula makes a show of retiring to the bathroom to soak off her fatigue, reappearing in some new ensemble later on to prepare one of her increasingly erratic evening meals. It's a wonder she has the energy for anything on top of all that, but she does: she's been writing letters with which she intends to flyer the whole town, telling every parent all about their proposed new school. The good thing about it is that all this activity is tiring them both out so much that they have no time to think about how the future is actually going to work. Then they'd really get panicky.

You've got to admire it, really. And Cleo does – even as she has to look down into her cereal to stop herself laughing over breakfast at the sight of lipstick creeping down the seams of Ursula's wrinkled lips as they part carefully to allow each spoonful of muesli, without ever touching the spoon. Cleo bites down aggressively on her own sugary spoonfuls, being sure to generate the sound of tooth on metal with each bite.

'The bank man's coming at ten,' says her father, between gulps of coffee. 'You should both be working by the time I show him round.'

'I'm not doing it today,' says Cleo, without knowing she was going to.

Ursula and her father exchange a look which she can't be bothered to examine.

'Okay,' he says, only mildly deflated. 'What are you going to do instead?'

'I don't know. Read. Be by myself.'

Which is her plan, until, when he is with the bank man and Ursula has tooled up with a blowtorch and gone off somewhere, there is a knock at the front door and an uncertain-looking courier arrives to deliver a van-load of educational supplies: desks, blackboards, exercise books, boxes of chalk. She directs the man to unload it all into one of the waiting rooms near the front entrance and then pockets some of the pristine sticks of chalk as a plan occurs to her.

She leaves the trail quickly, heading as deep as she can into uncharted territory, losing herself. When she comes across the beauty salon, she knows this must be where she installs herself. She sets out her book, a packet of gum and a bottle of water, and waits.

She reads, and relaxes into the building rain. She puts in one piece of gum, then another, then a third. She tries to chew the wad of gum in time to the rainfall. She positions a paint pot underneath a leak in the roof, and settles back to see if he or she or it will come.

This will be one of her most persistent memories: lying in this tattered salon, closing her eyes to the rain and the pinking of drops in the paint pot, chewing and waiting. Starting to doubt herself. To think she has imagined the whole thing. When her chewing gets a little too enthusiastic, and her molars accidentally catch the insides of her mouth, and she feels the pain and tastes rusty, salty blood, she spits out the gum to enjoy the taste. She feels her teeth straying back to the insides of her mouth, trapping bits of flesh and biting until she tastes it again. *You're not stupid. Just keep swallowing. Just keep swallowing and everything will be okay. You're not stupid.* Her thumbnail starts to press into the back of her hand over the cover of the book, poised to deliver proper hurt if it isn't true. Because it must be true. Her leg muscles tense, and the rain begins to sound like laughter.

Then, with a little shift of broken glass, her ghost announces himself. She feels a hot swell of relief that he came. She put up a signal and he came.

She's back in time to catch the banker on his way out, her father nervously seeing him off at the front door, and saying something about *getting in proper exterminators before we open.* Her father's shit-eating grin would be maddening under normal circumstances, not least because it would never work with a guy like this – a small man in a suit, whose hands are tied – but for one thing that's not what you might call a *positive mental attitude*, and for another these are not normal circumstances.

She has no way of telling how the meeting has gone,

because he would be nervous either way, but she is in such a good mood that when her father introduces her to the bank guy, she sticks out her hand for him to shake, and says, 'So are you going to give us the money then? Because we're screwed if you don't.'

The two of them are laughing about it as she goes inside and her father leans into his car window to make a few closing remarks, so it wasn't a bad thing to do, and who knows, it might even have helped.

She waits on the other side of the front door, watching the hall carpet carefully, because it would be typical to screw up the day now with a careless footstep, and when the sound of the banker's car has retreated he comes in, and she shoots him raised eyebrows intended to enquire and reassure simultaneously, and gives him a hug.

'Hard to tell,' he says. 'But I did the best I could.'

'And that's all you can ever do,' she says. 'What shall we eat to celebrate?'

She opens cupboards and tries to think what would be good for a rainy, optimistic evening. Something cosy but summery, because in spite of all this water there's a feeling of it in the air that can't be denied.

'Cheese on toast?' she says.

'Now you're talking,' he says.

They are bustling round the kitchen together and even dancing, and he sticks on the radio so the thing is more choreographed, and they are singing at each other using wooden spoons as microphones, so loudly that they don't hear the sound of Ursula's screams until they are really quite loud.

He turns off the radio so they can listen properly. It's coming from outside somewhere. They hear Ursula's voice getting closer and closer, and now it's settled into scandalised muttering, interjected with the occasional *Jesus Christ*. The door is thrown open, and she is standing in the doorway in her overalls, smelling of bonfires, with bird's nest hair and a long red mark down her right cheek.

It takes her some time to catch her breath. Then she looks at them both and says, 'I'm lucky to be alive.'

Cleo and her father exchange a quick glance, and she has to work hard not to laugh.

'I was doing what you told me to do,' says Ursula. 'Making a proper start on the building. I'd been stripping paint in that room on the end of the Enfield, but it was starting to make my head spin, so I decided to do something else. I went up to Occupational Therapy, and you know how cluttered it is up there, so I thought I would make a start on it, and clean it out a bit. I made a little fire in that sheltered bit outside of all those old woodwork projects and unfinished models and drawers full of paintings and things. And the fire must have attracted her.'

'Who?'

'A completely crazy woman. She came at me out of nowhere and started stamping on the edges of the fire trying to put it out and screaming at me about patient rights, and telling me I was destroying people's lives.'

'So what happened?'

'I told her that this is private property now and she had to leave or I'd call the police. She didn't take any notice, so I tried to move her.'

'And?'

'She went *berserk*. She attacked me. Scratched down the side of my face, and started hitting me. Then she ran off back towards Wreaking. She's probably in there now, beating at the door of the dispensary, looking for her medication.'

'Should we look for her?'

'I don't think she'll come back. When she wouldn't leave I had to threaten her with the blowtorch. I think it gave her quite a shock.'

Cleo can feel the blood rushing to her face, but she won't say anything, even though what's hammering through her head is the thought that if it turns out that the person Ursula has hurt is Cleo's hidden friend, she will be *very* upset.

In the morning it's still raining, but the mood of the house is different, and nobody comes beating up the stairs to her room with cups of tea or instructions. She hears the phone ringing, and knows it will probably be the call he's expecting from the bank manager, and so she waits a reasonable amount of time before heading downstairs to check on the outcome. There is no need for anyone to say anything.

That afternoon, for the first time since the move, her father loads his self-published books into the back of the car and sets off for one of his habitually humiliating experiences trying to get people to buy them on the corner of a local high street. These excursions were frequent in the past. They are a good barometer of how doomed he is feeling. Cleo knows the drill, and it is far too important for her to allow Ursula not to follow it. Never do you suggest that he take fewer boxes. Never do you make a single remark when all the boxes arrive back in the evening after he has spent the day being sidestepped and disregarded. Never do you say anything unless he talks to you.

'I suppose there is a bright side,' says Cleo, after he rattles off down the drive. 'At least he's not focusing on the setbacks. He's not moping, or dwelling on the past.'

Ursula sniffs. 'He's living in the future. Which could end up being a hell of a lot worse.'

30

He is coming to adore the approach. He goes as early as he can in the mornings, taking a line of attack over the water meadow. He loves how the building shape-shifts with changes in weather or approach. One minute it is a gothic cityscape, the next it resembles something more organic, its buttresses and walls looking as if they have grown from the ground. This morning, at dawn, a corner gable of one wing was cutting out like a ship's prow over the mist, its gargoyles like ornaments. When he got in closer, the same wing seemed to have more than the usual number of rusted loungers lying around under ivy-clad awnings, which combined with the marine freshness to conjure the fleeting atmosphere of a seaside villa.

They seem to have noticed it, too, this changeable quality. They seem to play up to it. At times he can't get close enough to Revenant House to work out what's going on, but he always feels he can discern quite definite moods. Sometimes they sit peacefully together, the woman and the man and his daughter, lolling with books. Sometimes there are purposeful assemblies, where they don overalls and face masks, and the father assigns everyone duties for the day. There are grand briefings by the front porch. These often turn out to be the happiest days, from what he can see.

Sometimes they look trapped, as if the madhouse were still in business and they were its last inmates, conferring anxiously among the shrubs about how to make their escape. Sometimes they can't be seen at all, and Roland is forced to imagine what's going on inside. He sits, or lies there, sometimes with a bag of food, watches the windows, and imagines the charge and flex of their emotions. He finds that he can sleep more deeply at the hospital than he ever has at home, sometimes waking up in the mornings with the shuffling of birds in the room with him, sometimes surprised by the weather if he has slept outside.

It's a bright morning, and he's been up for hours, so he scrounges some eggs for breakfast from an honesty box outside a farm on his way back into town, picking out a couple of pound coins from the tin as well so he can get a packet of bacon. There is a hum to the air, and a haze on the horizon that makes the tankers look precarious. He's in a good mood as he gets home, cooks up and takes down the food. Only when he's full does he start wondering where everybody is.

He hears quiet muttering from behind Carol's closed door as he climbs the stairs. He knocks quietly, and waits, listening to a reaction of some kind from within.

Mona's shorn, bullet-head appears in the doorway. 'Where have you been? Don't bother telling me.'

'Is everything all right?'

'Carol's having a bad day. The best thing you can do is leave us to it.'

'Can I talk to her?'

Mona's firm hand comes across the doorway. 'That's not a good idea.'

'Why not?'

She lowers her voice. 'Because I think you might be part of the problem.'

'Don't be silly. I want to talk to her.'

Mona comes on to the landing, and shuts the door behind her. 'Did something happen at the hospital the last time you took her there?'

'No.'

'It was just a normal walk? Nothing from the past upset her?'

'Of course not. Let me talk to her.'

'I really don't—'

'Trust me, will you?' He pushes past her into the room.

It's hot, and smells of unwashed bodies. Carol sits on the side of her bed, still in her nightgown. He can see her body's fragile, intimate creases down its front, which embarrasses him, so he stares at her face. Her right eye is violently inflamed, so swollen that she must have trouble seeing out of it. As he stands there he understands why. She is compulsively rubbing it, slapping her right hand on to the socket and pressing very hard on the eyeball with frantic, scratching fingers.

'I told him you weren't having the best morning,' says Mona. 'But he wanted to see you.'

'Not my best self,' she says, quickly. 'You know how it is.'

'Why don't you get up, and we'll go out for some air,' says Roland. 'Talk about it.'

Carol responds by rubbing her eye even more frantically. 'I can't do that, Roland, much as I'd like to.'

'Why not?'

'The authorities wouldn't hear of it.'

He turns to Mona. 'Why won't you let her come out? Just for a walk on the front?'

'You don't understand,' says Mona. 'Tell him what you told me.'

Her fingers are back in the eye socket. 'You know some of it already. How the authorities wouldn't have it, the idea of me taking my paintings away from up there, even though it wasn't going to do me any harm, was it? They've had it in for me for such a long time though, I don't know what I was expecting.'

'Who have?'

'The authorities. The *powers that be.*' She looks away in exasperation. 'And now they're *burning them up.* It's wiped me out, I can tell you. So sad. All that hard work people did going up in flames. And none of you *care.* Not really. I mean you say you do, but you don't really. I heard her talking to you, before we even went up. Saying I'm not your friend. And I'm not, am I?'

'Of course you're my friend,' says Roland. His face is breaking out in pins and needles of embarrassment and hurt and unreality.

'You can't trust anyone,' she says, to herself, with bitter amusement. 'And nobody's going to look after you when the authorities come out in their true colours. Screaming nurses with blowtorches burning all the hard work and telling you to leave your own home and nobody around when it matters because they're all off looking out for themselves.'

'I'm very fond of you,' says Roland.

'Well, you shouldn't be. And you're not, anyway. You're a liar. Oh dear, look at him now, looks like he's going to burst into tears. Big boy like you. When are you going to grow a bit of backbone? And what are you *doing,* creeping around in old hospitals? Is it true what she says about you and the women's undies? It *is,* isn't it?'

Mona's grim expression settles into determination. 'I think we've had enough now.'

'Vicious boy,' says Carol. 'Taking me up there. You knew what they were doing, didn't you? The whole thing makes sense now. Don't think I don't see it. God, did you lot think it would be that easy? Think I wouldn't see it?'

Carol makes a swift dart for Roland's face with her left hand, and with a speed and a deftness that astonish him, Mona intercepts it and returns Carol's hand to her lap. He feels sick. There is another feeling as well, like vertigo. Like the house is tipping over.

Something occurs to Mona, and she lifts the mattress of Carol's bed at one corner. There is a neat pile of blue pills, at different stages of staining from her saliva, where she had popped them in and kept them there before popping them out again. It feels like lifting a stone and finding an infestation of something.

'You can go now,' says Mona. 'Carol and I have things to talk about.'

He leaves the room, goes downstairs and straight outside. He stands on the seafront, looking down on the beach. He has been standing for some time when he becomes aware that Mona is beside him.

'She's gone to bed now. But you can never really relax with them. I remember a boy we had up at Wreaking. Everybody thought he was fine. Years, he'd gone, without any funny business. Then one morning he was on a day trip down here in the town, and got loose of the party, and the next thing anybody knew, he'd run off down the Ness with some poor little girl. God knows what he'd have done to her if we hadn't found him.'

'But she's not like that. She's not, *mad*, like that.'

'Don't be so naive. All that talk about the authorities is classic paranoid delusion. I've seen it all my life.'

31

'If you're going to leave, just leave,' says Cleo. 'There's no need to put on a display of how bad you feel for doing it.'

Ursula's streaming, cow eyes look down on her, shedding floodwaters of emotion, of sympathy, of regret for being the one to abandon her to him. This lavish display is even more annoying than her cowardice, and it's the last thing they need. Her father is bringing the car round to take Ursula to the station, and Cleo is standing between her and her packed suitcases in the hallway, as if she might limit the damage Ursula can cause, even at this late stage, by keeping an eye on her.

Ursula looks as if she might be about to say something, then she shakes the words out of her head and holds out her arms to Cleo as if yet another one of her hugs will say the unsayable – as if a great clamp of clothes and perfume is the only adequate response she can muster to the situation.

But Cleo has had enough of Ursula's embraces, and her forearm stops this one in its tracks. 'I put up with you because I thought you were going to make him happy. You're useless now.'

She is nothing but a useless display of streaming, avalanching eye make-up. And with every step she takes towards Cleo, she is driving her across the hall carpet, towards several clusters of the more vivid and dangerous flowers.

'Stop it,' she repeats, trying to sidestep the advance. 'He's the one who should be crying, not you.' The car is pulling up outside. Feeling cornered, Cleo steps forward and pokes Ursula in the chest, which forces her into taking another step backwards because Ursula is so immovable. 'Stop crying now. He doesn't need to see this.' She holds up her hands. 'I *command* you.' This seems to get through. Cleo holds out a handkerchief, and hands it to her with a swift, vicious mime. 'Clean yourself up.'

When the handkerchief comes away, the face behind it has taken on a harder expression. Ursula doesn't look back as she walks out of the door. She even lifts her own suitcase for once in her life. Which only goes to prove that all she was looking for was permission to leave.

Cleo watches the front door close, and stands listening to the two of them outside, exchanging awkward practicalities about luggage and train times: the sad epilogue to a lot of overheard pleading and shouting. It's nearly over. She will just wait until she hears the car actually leaving.

His voice, wary. 'Are you ready then?'

'She can be quite poisonous, that girl of yours.'

'I can send on anything you've forgotten, of course.'

'I mean it.'

'She's just protective of me.'

Sound of car boot slamming. Footsteps. 'I know it isn't my place to say this under the circumstances.'

'But you're going to say it anyway.'

'It's important. You know what makes it worse? Her not understanding. Not knowing properly about her mother. You owe it to—'

She hears the car doors clunking shut, her father's first excruciating gear change, and the crunch and hiss of wheels on gravel as the car drives away.

Oh, terrific.

She looks down at her scuffed trainer, dusted with dry dirt.

And of course. There it is. There is Ursula's parting shot.

She doesn't even try to move her foot out of the way, the inevitability of it is so tiring. She has trodden on a red flower. Her foot is just there, on the edge of one of those pungent blooms. And no amount of telling herself it doesn't count because it's Ursula's fault is going to take away the consequences. You can't make up rules one day then forget you have broken them the next.

When he gets back from the station, she takes his coat silently and directs him to the sitting room. She has laid out two trays in front of the television. A bottle of wine and a jug of water. He sits down and they watch together with beans on toast and grated cheese. He sighs from time to time, but there doesn't seem to be any great need for conversation.

Before bed, she makes him hot chocolate. On the stairs they share a lingering hug, and she thinks he might cry, but he doesn't, and there's no sound of sobbing in the night that she can hear. She leaves the childish cloud of fairy lights on above her bed, and, after staring into them for so long that they have imprinted themselves on her vision, she goes to sleep.

'Painting!'

What now, she thinks, her heart pumping with panic, her head hauling itself from a dim, exhausted dream. He's in the room.

'Today, it's all about painting.'

Of course. Ursula. She is already missing the state of forgetting she had gone.

She half opens one eye to watch him padding round the room, desperate as a caged gorilla, wanting her up so he will feel less alone and more purposeful.

'What's this? More water come through in the night? Never mind.' He grabs her bath towel from the radiator, chucks it on the floor and plants his foot on it before quickly moving the foot from side to side and leaving the towel crumpled under the window, soaked with dirty water and bearing a footprint. 'So anyway. Painting. We'll start at the far end of the Enfield and work backwards. Try and hit the centre by lunchtime. Window frames first, then walls. And you know what else?'

'What?'

'I had an idea in the night. What about making this building a *conference centre* instead of a school? Eh? No need for pupils or teachers or anything. We'll just rent it out to people for their meetings, get caterers to do food. It will be great. The history of the place will probably give it *cachet*. It will be a talking point.'

'I didn't get much sleep,' she mutters, burying her head back into the pillow.

'That's okay,' he says. 'You can go back to bed this afternoon. For now, though, it's all about the painting! See you downstairs in ten minutes?'

She turns over the pillow when he's gone and there's a coolness to this new side that is irresistible. He can start the damn painting on his own.

'Painting!' He's all the way back downstairs now. Let him shout, if that's what he needs to keep himself propelled.

As she dozes off again, even from all the way up here she can hear the way he's walking around, singing the word 'painting' in a tuneless, obsessive way.

She can see underwater.

Fine bubbles file upwards from under the leaves of plants.

Fish bat their tails once or twice to remain stationary against the current.

She has never been able to see underwater like this before.

She feels a cold patch on her forehead beginning to spread as she pushes her head in further, to see more.

The cold patch expands as her face goes in deeper. It's freezing cold.

Somehow heavy, too – as if the water had great mass.

She isn't trying to do it but her face is steadily being pushed downwards.

And then she cannot breathe. She is choking, and panic is rising. And her head is cold. And her nose is obstructed. And it stinks of fumes.

What is so difficult to take when she thinks about it later is the fact that paint does not tip fast out of a pot. That when you pour paint, you have ample opportunities to think twice.

She screams and coughs and waves her arms to try and stop him, but the damage is done and he flings the paint pot to one side, where it clatters to the floorboards. The mark will be there for many years – unassailable evidence that this is not something either of them imagined.

He's still standing there. Her pillow is covered in heavy, cold paint. It clings, coating her hair and making her blind and stinging her eyes. She doesn't need to see his face to imagine the intent blazing from them.

When she manages to wipe her eyes the first thing she sees is his red tool belt, which makes her panic even more. Next she thinks he might go for the blowtorch as well, because nothing seems off limits at this point. Then, thankfully, he leaves.

She had forgotten how his rage is a bully in itself. How when it is around everything has to be charged with the mood. Just as when he's up, everyone has to go with him too, when he is angry, everything turns to bile.

She dismantled her weapons in good faith. She believed them when they told her the war was over. But now she must re-arm as quickly as possible, or she will be destroyed.

The scale of it is always surprising. And what other word is there for what's in these actions, what other word than *hate* can you reach for?

When she has scrubbed at her hair, shampooed it four or five times and put her sheets in to soak, she goes downstairs, concentrating on keeping her breathing steady. She is determined not to speak with a quavering voice. Determined to show him up for it with shaming calm and composure. She can't find him at first, then when she goes outside she sees his feet sticking out of one of the waterside pavilions, and she thinks at first that it's going to start in the way she has always imagined it would – one shoe off, dangling from rafters or a light fitting somewhere, the creak of a noose as he rotates gently round.

The surface of the lake is coated in pollen that makes her think at first that he's managed to tip paint all over the water as well. Will this be the colourful thing that is pinned to the terrible memory? Then one of his feet moves and she knows he's still alive, and she turns to go somewhere else, to let him carry on thinking about what he's going to say to her to begin the process of reconciliation this time.

That evening he cries, kneeling by her bed, trying to explain himself. She's heard it all before – though not, it must be said, for a while. She gives him a discerning ear, open to the discovery of whether or not he has any new tunes. And she stares at him, not letting him off the hook, wanting to watch him squirm like an insect stuck with a pin.

'Try and imagine being trapped under snow,' he says. 'It's cold, and muffled, and dark. I can't feel anything at all in the real world, even though I'm still meant to be in it. Try and imagine what that's like. You'd want to punch your way out, wouldn't you? You'd do anything to fight your way through and back to the real world. To be able to breathe again.'

'It must be hard,' she says.

'And that's what happens. It's like with those superheroes you love. I have to change in order to get out from under the snow, because only my temper gives me the energy to break out. See?'

'Yes.'

'And then sometimes, you're on the other side of the snow, and I end up hitting you accidentally because I don't see that you're there. Do you understand? At that moment, I'm not myself. It's not because I don't care about you.'

'So what am I supposed to do about it?' she says. 'If it isn't my fault, that means there isn't anything I can do to stop it. I just have to live with you being mean to me when you aren't happy.'

'I promise it will never, ever happen again,' he says.

As he leaves her under her fairy-light halo and closes the door, she knows that even he can't possibly believe that one.

They get through some deliberately dull, calm days. He tries to keep things on track by disappearing, though she has no idea now whether he's building a school or a conference centre, or when she will return to a school of her own.

She gets into the habit of walking past his door at night, to hear if he is crying. At one time, long ago, hearing the sound made her sad. Then for a short, nasty period, it made her happy. Then she simply tried to avoid hearing it. Now she patrols, on the lookout for it, as much because it's a barometer of incoming weather as for anything to do with solicitude.

When, one evening, she knocks on his door, enters, and

finds that both he and his bedclothes have gone, it alarms her. She keeps on walking, and eventually, in a record office lined with high metal shelves, she finds him. This is how she comes to understand that he has started moving at night.

One morning, feeling kind, she decides to take him breakfast of tea and a boiled egg. She looks around in several of his favourite sleeping places, carrying the egg and the cup and starting to feel stupid. Eventually she finds him in his study. His hair sticks up at an angle from the back of his armchair. She rounds the chair and he stirs. She looks around for somewhere to leave the breakfast among all the paper.

'Morning,' he says, opening one eye, his throat slightly blocked by sleep. He smells.

'Have you been here all night?'

He taps the egg on the arm of the chair, and begins peeling it, dropping bits of shell on to the floor. 'I slept here. It was fine. And now I don't need to get up, because I'm up already.' There's a funny catch in his throat, and his breathing sounds laboured.

'Try and go to bed sometime. You know what happens when you're tired.'

He bites down into the egg and waves her away. That evening after dinner, she sees the lights of the study blazing again, and realises that habits are starting to form.

Since he seems to have given up work on the building, she decides to take some of it on herself. She spends a morning grappling with stairwell cages, unscrewing them and pulling them out, and making a pile of them in the garden. At first he comes out simply to see what the noise is and retreats. Later, he appears in his overalls, with his bag of tools, and silently starts working beside her.

They make their mark on the building. When they have decided which is to be their principal bathroom, they rip out the partitions between the cubicles, and keep one big bath which has a crane arm suspended over it that makes Cleo think of the teddy-bear graspers they have at amusement arcades. They contemplate leaving the limb in place as an object of interest, then take it down and chuck it out of the window. He says he will clean it up later. (It will be there, rusted and broken, a robotic amputation, for years to come.)

Then he produces his showpiece: a mirror he has stolen from the superintendent's house. It takes effort for both of them to set it up on the marble shelf where a set of basins had previously been, and when it's up, they know it will be up for a long time. The mirror is cloudy and dark. It makes her look different. If she takes a step backwards then comes forward again into the light it looks like she is emerging from a foggy night. The surface of its glass is etched with scratches, scarred by polyps and scabs and gaps, and she gets to know the details of every one of these imperfections during afternoons spent staring into the mirror, waiting for something to happen, trying to watch herself grow old.

Bruises are hatching on her arms from a day of taking down fire doors in the Enfield wing.

'Won't the school need fire doors?' she said.

'It won't be that kind of school,' he replied.

Her goodwill is being put to the test. Opening up these corridors is making them less oppressive, but she still doesn't know what the place is going to be used for. There has been little talk of the school since Ursula's departure. Instead it is just a question of embracing every positive impulse he has, inhabiting it with him, and never stopping to ask why something might or might not be a good idea.

Sensing her fatigue, he announces that he will cook dinner. She sits, nervously watching television, hearing clattering and occasional soft curses coming from the kitchen but knowing she mustn't go and help. The one thing you don't do when he's cooking is try to get involved.

Soon they are at the table staring down at what he has produced, which she has resolved to love no matter what: blackened chicken legs with baked beans, fried mushrooms and boiled potatoes. The potatoes are undercooked, the mushrooms are overcooked and the chicken is both under-cooked in the middle and overcooked on the outside. Blood wells in the flesh as she cuts into it, reminding her of what it is: something's limb, severed from its corpse, seized into place by heat.

She is so distracted by the analysis of what is on her plate, and by the effort of devising reassuring lies with which to praise it, that she doesn't notice until they have already been in conversation for some time that he is drunk. He must have been nailing the wine while cooking, and the bottle he's on now has too much left in it to be his first of the evening.

'Are you enjoying this?' he says, sawing away at his pink-fleshed chicken piece with dogged exuberance.

'Delicious,' she says, holding up a forkful of mushrooms to confirm it.

'It's not bad, is it?'

She keeps her eyes on her food through the pause that follows, because she can tell it's one of those pauses where he's preparing something big to say. She can spot them a mile off. They are excruciating – as is the pained, emotional face he always tries to put together.

'You remind me of her tonight,' he says.

Oh God, here we go. Cleo knows who he means but she can't believe he's going to be quite this predictable.

'Your eyes are just like hers were,' he says. 'All that's missing is the mole.'

'What?'

'Your mother had a mole just there, on her right cheek.' He stands up messily and picks up a pen from the counter. 'We could draw it on.'

'Please don't do that.'

'Go on,' he says. 'For me. Just so I can see what it looks like.' He lunges at her face with the pen, sticking it roughly into her cheek, where it pulls at the skin, narrowly missing her eye.

She grabs the pen from his hand and flings it away. 'What are you doing?'

But he's just standing there, leaning over the table, swaying. So, in her hurt and shock, she shouts at him some more. And tells him what she really thinks of his cooking. So disappointing how quickly it happens. How fast they can both go up. They have lost the habit of being kind to one another completely.

When she has fled the room, with its bean-strewn floor, its mushroom-stained walls and its shattered plates, she grabs a torch from her room, and a blanket to sleep in. She sets off for the hydrotherapy suite, a place on the far side of Wreaking that she has been saving up for when she wants to disappear properly. She plans to bed down for the night amid the dangling loops of harnesses and clusters of bathing chairs.

The tanks and baths are empty and the needle-point shower cubicles no longer work but there's still a chlorinated taint to the air. In daylight these walls are a glacial blue, the colour of slab ice, but tonight there is only the beam of her torch. She sits in an empty pool with her blanket wrapped round her, trying to read her book.

She hopes he's fucking worried, and fucking ashamed, and fucking scared. It's all fake. You can't say you care about one thing and then just say you care only about another when it lets you down. How can he go from saying Ursula is the answer, to saying it was her mother all along? Just because Ursula has let him down, what, that's *completely* changed the way he feels? Or was he just lying about how he felt about Ursula before? It can only be one or the other.

She is still determined to see the night out here, but she is getting bored, and because most of her meal ended up on the walls she's getting hungry. Then, a brainwave: she remembers that by the entrance to this building, as at several other places throughout the hospital, there is a vending machine. Maybe it's not too much to hope there might still be something in it.

Wrapping the blanket round her, she sets forth, following her torch beam through the double doors past a dead pot plant, and there it is, a hulking brown rectangle with adverts for chocolate bars on the side.

The front window has been comprehensively smashed, revealing the inner workings of the machine. She shines the torch on its interior, letting light play over the zigzag delivery system. There! At the back. She can just make out the end of a chocolate bar that none of the vandals was able to reach. No surprise, either – the wrapper is only just visible. But with her little hands . . . Securing the torch in the crook of her left armpit to keep light trained on the relevant area, she leans forward and thrusts her arm deep into the machine. She is so intent on reaching as far into its guts as she can that she does not notice until the damage is quite serious that a jagged shard of glass is cutting into her arm.

She manages to jostle the torch out from her armpit to her left hand so she can direct light on the situation. The blood is stark against the white of her skin. She puts the wound back to the glass spike that created it. The glass is cold against the skin – but when she reunites the wound with its maker, when the shard is touching flesh and blood and not skin, it seems to hurt less. Moving very slowly, aware of how loud her breathing is, she moves her arm against the glass again, pressing hard, making the cut longer and deeper.

The pain is sharp and clean. She can turn it up or down. The blood is soaking down her arm so much that there's more dark than light. Which means that she is still staring at it in the light of her torch beam when her wrist is snatched by a powerful hand, and she is grabbed and spun around.

'Don't do that,' says Roland.

32

He stands there, breathing heavily, holding her wrist, staring at the floor, wondering what will happen now. He feels a tackiness on his fingers, between his skin and hers, which he realises is her blood.

Later, perhaps as soon as the next day, he will bloom with pride in his bed at having saved her. He will resound with it, like a fingernail-flicked glass of water. Later still, it will occur to him that maybe she didn't need to be saved – that what she does is none of his business, and he exposed himself as the creepy voyeur that he is for no good reason. For now, he stares at the floor, awaiting developments.

Her midriff is in his sightline, flickering with the intermittent light of her torch. He allows his gaze to settle on the mole he likes, trying not to make it too obvious, freaked by its proximity, still wondering what to do. Her wrist feels fragile, almost bendy.

'It's okay,' she says, quietly. 'You can let me go. I'll stop.'

But she doesn't scream or call him weird, or anything like that. Which is . . . relaxing.

He lets her go, embarrassed by the strength of his grip. And soon they are together, walking and talking, and the fact that the world has made this possible is enough to make him want to punch holes in the ceiling tiles, or heave a chair through a window.

They leave the hydrotherapy suite and walk down a long corridor that is orange shading to yellow, and past its junction with another in which the orange washes to red.

'The colours were to help people get around,' he explains. 'Nurses. Patients as well, if they got lost. The corridors are so long, and there are so many of them, that people got lost easily. You follow a certain colour and it leads you back to your ward.'

She smiles. 'My dad will like that. You know a lot about the building.'

His skin prickles. Already he is boring, geeky.

She doesn't remember what is actually said first between them, but she will not forget the urge to communicate to him that it's okay, him being there. Even as she is still coming to terms with its dimensions, his face is dawning with animal panic.

For someone so fast, he's awkward. His body seems unfamiliar to him, almost unusable. Parts of it are outsized (feet, legs, arms). Others are still the features of a boy (shoulders, trunk). He wears a grown man's trousers that don't fit him well at all. She will find out later that he rescued them from his mother's clutch during a bonfire of his father's clothes.

'Have you seen the children's ward?' he suggests, with the polite tone of a tour guide. She says she hasn't so he takes her. He moves quickly and quietly round the building.

The walls here are a bold, bright green, which have been decorated with low, scrawled drawings: animals, stick people, clouds, spaceships. There are posters of alphabets and pictures of animals with their names underneath. The toilet stalls are divided by heartbreakingly low partitions.

They sit together on a bench, under a long row of hooks with alphabetised names beneath them that stretch the length of the wall. Their heels squeak on the chequerboard floor. There's no electric light anywhere, but miraculously a battery-powered clock on the wall above them is still going. The laboured advance of its sweeping second hand is the loudest noise they can hear.

'It's just the two of you over there now?' says Roland.

'Yes.'

'Was that your mother I saw before? When you used to dance under the water?'

She laughs at how much he has seen, and at how willing he is to admit it. 'No, that was Ursula. She's gone now.' She sees him looking scared by the bad news and not knowing what to say. 'It's okay. They come and go. They can't face having to look after me. I scare them off.'

He looks down. 'I can't believe that's the only reason.'

She makes a slicing gesture with the side of her foot on the floor's black and white squares, hoping it will squeak to break the mood, but it doesn't.

'No,' she says. 'It's not. It's mainly because of my dad. He's hard to live with sometimes.' Right on cue, they hear the distant sound of Scriven's voice, calling her name. 'He's getting worried. We had an argument.'

'You should get back,' says Roland.

'I will. But you should come to our house sometime. When he's in a better mood, he likes the idea of old patients being around.'

Roland speaks quickly. 'I'm not an old patient. I just like coming here.'

'Why?'

'I don't know.'

He is looking down again, embarrassed. Here is another

one, she can tell, who she is going to have to tread carefully with. Why does everyone have to have their own private minefield of things you can and can't step on?

'You should get your arm bandaged up, too,' he says. 'That could get infected.'

'Okay,' she says. 'So I'll see you again sometime?'

'Yeah, if you want.'

'I was born under a witch's curse,' she says, a couple of days later, in a matter-of-fact way.

They are exploring a ward corridor, stepping over the long, limp snakes of pulled-out fire hoses. The walls are part panelled in warm wood, and part painted in honey-coloured orange. The atmosphere of enforced happiness is completed by the daffodil optimism of a yellow noticeboard wall.

'What?' says Roland.

'My mother couldn't get pregnant for ages. Then she and my dad met this magic old woman on a train somewhere in Europe, and she blessed my mother's stomach so that I could be born. So I was born under a witch's curse.'

He nods earnestly, wondering what she's talking about. 'My dad used to keep me in cardboard boxes,' he blurts out, and explains.

'Really? Box tunnels? Like a big hamster?' Her laughter disconcerts him at first, then his frown wilts into a smile.

'It sounds weird when you say it like that.' He starts laughing too. 'They just did it because they were afraid of something happening to me.'

'I expect something probably did happen to you,' she says. There is a pause, during which they both hear her father's lonely, bellowing call. And this time she says it – and there's no way he can say no. 'Do you want to meet him?'

'I don't know if this is the right time,' he says, following her anyway as they head across the Wreaking maintenance yard towards the fence that separates it from Revenant House.

'You'll have to do it sooner or later. But don't worry: I know he's weird too. He can just disappear right in front of you. It doesn't mean anything. Just don't try and find him again if he does. He'll come back eventually.'

He wants to stop her and ask what that means but it's too late, because they're crossing the gravel sweep of the driveway, and the shape of Revenant House is looming in the spring air. She opens the front door and they cross the lobby's wild, floral carpet. They approach the kitchen, and he can hear her father moving around in there, radio on, saucepans banging. Roland hangs back instinctively, with the result that her father doesn't see him when she pushes open the door, and he thinks Cleo has come in on her own, which means he hears a more intimate moment than he should have.

'There you are,' says Scriven. 'We haven't talked about the other day, and I want to say sorry. Can you let me make it up to you, my poppet?'

She waits calmly for him to finish before speaking. 'There's somebody else here.'

'What?'

'I'd like you to meet my friend Roland.' She pulls him into the doorway, and into sight.

For the first time Roland sees her father seeing him. His legs feel like pile drivers plunging his feet into soft sand, and at the same time they are losing mass and taking him away from the ground, into the air. He is swelling with strangeness at the kitchen and its smells, at glimpsed details of pots and condiments. At hostility to this man. At not being able to hide. At having stepped out of the scenery and become part of the play.

Her father wears a dirty white jacket with thin blue

pinstripes. Up close, his face is more lined than he had imagined. The hair is thinner, too, but that makes it fizz up above his head in a way that looks young rather than old. But he looks unwell: his skin is puffed up, livid, as if some noxious substance were bulking out the skin from beneath. Broken red veins crackle on his upper cheeks. He looks straight at Roland and the look is insolent, penetrating. It is the look that Roland will come to know as the signifier that he is on top – ready to say yes to anything, to take anything on. Or maybe that's because Roland has already been used by Cleo as a weapon. If he's embarrassed he tries not to show it. He wipes his hands on a dishcloth, and walks right over, into Roland's space, to shake his hand.

'Well,' he says. 'Nice to meet you. You'll stay for dinner.' He seems to go vague at this point, and look away. To decide that a mask of distraction is the best way to combat these unforeseen circumstances, and any embarrassment they have caused him. 'Assuming we have enough to eat.'

'What about these pears?' says Cleo.

'Damn the pears,' says her father.

'You're in a good mood,' says Cleo. 'What about the fridge?'

'I wouldn't look in there if I were you.'

Cleo goes over to him and touches him affectionately on the arm as the two of them stand together in the mouth of the fridge. There's something affected about it. A posture that says, *We're the kind of people who don't really know what's in our fridge, and when we do look it's likely to be something we've forgotten about.*

'Good Lord, look at this,' says Scriven, taking out a pungent sheet of cardboard into which something fishy has liquefied. 'Was that smoked salmon?'

Stuff past its sell-by date. Well, Roland is used to that. 'Let's have a look,' he says, with authority. But at a glance, it's clear that even for him the fish is too far gone. 'Do we need money?' says Roland. 'I have a few pounds.'

They don't laugh for long, but they laugh long enough for it to be the thing he remembers most that night.

She sees it. She sees it well before Roland does, if indeed he sees it at all, so distracted is he by the endearing fruit conversation, the eccentricity of the rotten salmon.

She sees the way her father is looking at him, and she knows instantly that he is hatching some plan for Roland. Planning to put him to use. That Roland is meant to help him try and make her happy here.

She watches him appraising her new friend. She sees his eyes going cool and measured, no longer out to impress or communicate but to analyse and test for weakness. Nothing he loves more than a new opponent.

She feels a kind of danger at that moment – a danger she will only be able to define properly much later in life, when more has happened, as she looks back on moments like this: it's the danger of an adult who doesn't draw any distinction between himself and children. Because they are still only children at this point – aren't they?

Her suspicions are confirmed during the scratched-together meal that ensues, when her father begins probing in earnest. They are sitting at the long refectory table, with candles in jars, and cans of beer, one of which was offered to Roland, who declined.

'Your mother was a nurse here?' says her father. 'I'd love to talk to her about the history of the hospital.'

'She doesn't like coming back,' he says, folding bread round a piece of old cheese. 'Or talking about it much.'

'Really?' says her father. 'Why not?'

'She's too busy, I guess.'

'What about your father? What does he do?'

'He doesn't live with us any more.'

'I see. And is your mother happier or sadder without him?'

To try and create a distraction, Cleo goes to the freezer and returns with a tray marked *Samples*, in which wooden sticks sit up from melting frozen blocks of white, yellow and purple.

'Lolly?' she says. 'They're lemon, orange and blackcurrant. We made them ourselves.'

Roland takes an orange one and sits there with it, looking dubious, as if he thinks nobody else is going to eat one and is wondering if there's a test going on.

'You were saying,' says her father. 'About your mother.'

She wants to help Roland out of this. He's probably not met an adult like this before, who wants to test him in a playful way, and get to him, and push his buttons. He probably doesn't realise how much of a joke it's meant to be.

'Probably sadder,' says Roland. 'She's more of a worrier now he's gone.'

Scriven is picking about in the tray of lollies. 'Anxiety,' he says, 'can be put to many good uses. In sheepdogs, it is indispensable.'

She can see the confusion on Roland's face, the feeling of having betrayed his mother, as he stares at the ground to avoid having to look back at her.

'Do you ever talk about your father at home?'

'Never.'

'Do you want to?'

'I don't know.'

'Exactly how anxious is she?' says her father.

'I don't know. I just meant, she worries a bit, that's all.'

'The main thing *you* should be worried about,' Scriven goes on, 'is the old pendulum effect. Don't let her anxiety rub off on you, but don't let it send you too far the other

272

way either.' He slams a hand on the table, making the tray of lollies jump. 'Now these are melted. And who's eaten all the blackcurrant ones?'

Cleo speaks in a soothing voice. 'There's one, see?'

'Hardly.' Her father sees the purple block in the corner of the tray in a pool of its own meltwater, grabs it petulantly and sticks it in his mouth.

'Make it last,' says Cleo. 'There aren't any more.'

'But it's fine, really,' says Roland. 'She's had to put up with a lot since my dad left.'

He's feeling guilty. Her father doesn't seem to have noticed the guilt, which is a sure sign that he wants to exploit it.

'Families get decapitated by bereavement,' he says. 'Loved people are evoked through repetition of their habits and expressions long after they have been mourned. By talking about your father more, you'd keep him alive. Keep his place as a keystone in the wall.'

She doesn't like the way this conversation is going. The way Roland keeps looking at the door.

'Wait a minute – my father's not *dead*,' says Roland. 'He just ran off.'

But already she can see that he feels like he has lost ground. She will have to explain to Roland that this is how it always is with her father. Every conversation with him is about winning or losing. And every conversation is about himself, rather than the person he's talking to.

When he leaves, she follows him outside.

'Sorry,' she says. 'He always finds a way to make everything about my mother. Even when he doesn't think he's doing it.'

'It's okay,' he says. He looks hunted.

She suspects that what she has said won't make him feel any better on the walk, or make the laughter from every creaking gate and hooting owl any less piercing. And she can see him getting worried about it, that he ought to be

273

thinking about it, and she wants to take away the worry too. So she leans up and gives him a kiss on the cheek. As he blunders off into the darkness she wonders whether that hasn't made things worse.

33

'Do you want my bath?' she calls, lying in soak.

'No, I can't be bothered getting wet.' His voice carols up from downstairs as his attention deviates momentarily from whatever he is concentrating on: refurbishing a bit of hospital equipment, or following through some barmy impulse as to what it can be converted into.

She is becoming a fearless explorer. Her legs and arms are covered in the scratches and bruises of climbing and falling and restricted entry. The wounds light up one by one in the hot water as she lowers herself in. She lies, transferring her attention from one injury to the other, reflecting on the latest adventures of her and her strange new sidekick. There are still bits of the hospital she hasn't seen but Roland has made a good fist of showing her round. Wreaking no longer feels infinite. She rubs some of the bath bubbles on to a long, yellow bruise down her left forearm, grazing it with her thumbnail in a way that she knows will do something to the nerve endings of the yellowy-blue skin, generating a maddening, tingling feeling somewhere between pain and itching.

The days are getting longer. It's no longer as cold at night as it was. She allows herself to feel a kind of indulgence at the prospect of summer. Nesting birds in the ivy outside allow her to believe that the future can be reasonable. She lies, poaching, listening to their flits and starts.

How much did Roland hear during all that time he spent listening and watching? Does he do it still? Whether or not he's seen it, she has not yet told Roland about her father's anger. She hasn't decided yet whether or not she will.

Maybe she won't have to. Having someone else around, even this peripheral, strange person, has allowed her and her father to get closer again. They leave doors open so one can hear what the other is doing. They call out to each other from room to room. Their intimacy has been refreshed.

'When might you be ready to eat?' he says, and she realises he's standing right there, in the doorway. She can see his shoes. She sinks down into the water and tries to arrange fistfuls of foam to cover herself.

'In a minute.' She raises her voice to try and put distance between them, to hint to him that he should be further away.

'Did you see Roland again today?' She can see the awkward jiggle of his trousered leg, though he's angled deliberately to communicate that he's looking away at some fixed point.

'Yes,' she says.

'I like that boy. Though obviously he is rather odd.'

'Can you close the door? It's draughty.'

She submerges her head quickly, and when she comes up again she can hear him back downstairs. She hauls herself out of the bath and stands dripping and steaming in front of the Decision Mirror, shifting from side to side to make its scratches cover different bits of her body, to try and make them correspond to her own. So the school idea is back on the march. She asks herself whether she should take this cue to ask him whether he has considered the possibility of any more education for his daughter, given that he's meant to be a teacher and all that. The mirror tells her quite unequivocally that the answer to that question is no. Which is good, because it fits with her own thoughts. She isn't going to become the kind of person who actually *asks* to go to school.

The next day she and Roland meet up as arranged in the remnants of a small chapel not far from the operating theatre. You can see where the altar was because there's a raised area with a little bar round it where Communion was given out. Beyond that, there's not much to it.

'We should try and get into the big chapel,' says Roland, scanning the walls. 'I think there's a way in through the service tunnels.'

'I'm bored,' she says. 'I think we should get out of here.'

'Out?' he says.

'Isn't there anything in town we could do? Anyone else we could see?' She regrets it almost as soon as she says it.

'Well,' he replies, looking miserable. 'There is someone you probably should meet.'

This is how it changes.

Within the hour they have pitched up at Arcadia, which she has seen before but not up close. It's a glaringly lit single-storey hangar overlooking the beach. Chill North Sea air drives in a constant smell of chip fat and vinegar from the café next door, where a cheery woman known inexplicably as Bertie spends her days frying doughnuts and chips, and kicking people out when they linger. Roland tells her about this as he leads her to the doors, under the rising shriek-fits of herring gulls overhead.

The tatty neon sign outside hints at a kind of exhausted madness, an eternity of mechanised entertainment. Inside, it smells of carpet and popcorn, and the banks of machines strobe and burble and sing and give off a constant synthetic promise of riches. Every so often one of them shoots its bolt for no obvious reason, going berserk with light and sound, and producing nothing. A shortish, dirty-looking boy is kicking the side of a fruit machine.

'That's him,' says Roland.

And Oliver turns in their direction, and locks on to her, and everything speeds up.

Within hours the three of them are mixing juice with cheap vodka down on the beach. The juice has no brand name, nor is its fruit of origin identified. They're just blank yellow cartons with red, joined-up writing on them that says *Juice*. The contents don't taste of any single recognisable fruit, and combine with the vodka to generate instant acid indigestion. Cleo has some change and she offered it to Roland to buy something better, but was ignored. She has noticed already how these boys are in the habit of committing to their ideas.

Saturday afternoon is bleeding into Saturday evening, and the town is at its most glaring: the shrieks from the ghost train actually sound animated; one of last night's condoms floats in the surf under the pier – a promise of more romance to come. Cleo is aware that this is already as much alcohol as she has ever drunk.

'He kept you a secret,' says Oliver, smoking a cigarette furiously, as if it was a race. 'From his best mate. Why would he do a thing like that?'

'Maybe he didn't think I was worth telling you about,' she says. She is still thinking of the way he saw her across Arcadia. The way the machine he had been kicking was irrelevant in a second. The way he shot Roland a look for having the nerve to hide someone from his attention.

'Now I know you don't believe that,' says Oliver, happily.

Belatedly, she looks around, wondering where Roland has gone.

It is every bit as unbearable as he knew it would be, but there was nothing else to be done. They had to meet eventually, and when they did everything was always going to change. Well now it has. All he can think of to keep hold of her is to suggest they do more of the same, so they stay there, drinking, as the night wears on.

They sit together in the fresh seafront air, passing round the lukewarm booze. At some point Oliver produces a pair of binoculars, and the three of them start watching a courting couple in a bench booth on the pier who think they cannot be seen. They are cast in a pool of yellow street light, closeted, while end-of-pier illuminations shimmer behind them.

Oliver is grumpy because he's just returned from unsuccessfully trying to blag weed off some twenty-somethings standing round a brazier, so for the moment, nothing pleases him, including this lacklustre display of affection.

'They're not really *doing* anything,' he says. 'I mean, he's sort of grubbing around between her legs but she keeps moving his hand away. It's crap.' He hands the binoculars to Roland in disgust.

It's true. The couple are coiling and bucking, but in a cyclical, back-and-forth way – they are working against each other, not towards a common goal. It makes you wonder whether she wants to be there at all, or whether she is struggling to get away. As Roland adjusts the binoculars to get them in focus he looks again at the guy, at his suit, at the nasty, persistent way he's moving.

'Wait a minute. I reckon that's Victor.'

Oliver grabs the binoculars. 'Well *now* I'm interested. So it is! Filthy boy. He must be back for the weekend. Nice of him to tell me.'

'Victor is Oliver's half-brother,' Roland explains. 'Lives up in town. Makes a living stripping out people's houses of stuff and flogging it all off, especially when they die.'

'I didn't know that was a job,' says Cleo.

'It sure is,' says Oliver. 'And you should hear about the

cash he makes. You do this deal where you buy everything in the house, right? And that means that whatever you find, even if it's something the sons or daughters of whoever's died don't know anything about – whatever you find, it's yours. He found fifty grand in cash in the base of a wardrobe once. And a mate of his found a Roger Moore statue bricked up behind a fireplace.'

'Amazing,' says Cleo.

'It's Henry Moore,' says Roland.

'It *is* amazing,' says Oliver. 'And as soon as we're done with this place I'm going up to town to join in.'

Roland has the binoculars back. 'Oh dear me, Victor,' he says. He carries on talking, trying to say what he thinks are the right things to say about Victor, about how disgusting he is, and what's he doing to that poor girl, and so on, to keep the conversation flowing, and stop time from doing its nasty work. He is waiting for a reply from either Cleo or Oliver, but none comes.

He can't take his eyes off the binoculars, because that would mean that they'd know for sure he had seen them, which would be worse. But he doesn't have to take his eyes off the binoculars, because he can tell anyway that Cleo and Oliver are kissing. Properly sliding around on each other's mouths, and sharing smiles in between, in a way that he knows he will have to be cool about. While he is condemned to watch a mutant, half-brother version of it playing out in the boxed-in booth on the pier.

'Yeah,' says Roland. 'It's definitely him.' He plunges the binoculars deep into his eye sockets, so hard that he can feel them hurting his eyeballs, and his view is blacked out into nothing at all.

She leaves straight after breakfast, not bothering to seek out her father. He will be dozing somewhere, ratty after yet another failed night's sleep. From the minute she left the boys last night, the feeling that she might have hurt Roland has been swelling inside her, and she needs to see him before it gets any worse. She had allowed herself to assume the belief that all she has to do is say his name to the walls, and he will appear. She is worried that she might have jeopardised that protection. She goes from room to room, checking his favourite places: the back of the assembly-hall stage; the suitcase room; the nurses' common room with its comfy sofas and floor-to-ceiling panelling. There is no sign. She pays a last-ditch visit to the hydrotherapy suite, where she hears noises. Clattering and sawing and buzzing, above, in the ceiling. Voices in conversation.

She calls his name, to no response, and follows the sound into an adjacent corridor to investigate further. When she calls a second time the noise in the ceiling stops, and there is whispering. A ceiling tile is swatted down in a cloud of dust and fragments, and, in the resultant square aperture, a pair of vicious eyes appear on a face otherwise hidden by a thick dust mask.

'Hello again,' it says, pulling the mask down to the neck to reveal the upside-down face of Victor.

She notices for the first time that up and down the length of the corridor are coils of copper, ribbons of it in the gloom, set among chunks of something grey and fibrous.

'What are you doing here?' she says.

'Just tidying up. Only don't tell anyone – some people might not approve.'

'Okay,' she says.

'You shouldn't be walking round here without a mask on. Lot of nasty shit coming down out of these walls. Understand?'

'Okay,' she says.

'Stuff that will make you cough for life.'

'Okay.'

'Off you go then – and don't breathe a word, okay? Say hello to the little brother.'

She hears Victor and whoever he is with laughing in the rafters as she wanders off, and she is reminded of the appraising look he gave her when Oliver took them over to the pier to find him last night. It was not a good look – nor did she like the proprietorial air that Oliver assumed. There was an ugly feeling of being shown off. She's sad to find that Roland is no longer hiding in the walls, looking out for her, and has been replaced by these creatures instead.

34

Now they are three. And with Oliver on board, they get to grips with the building in a serious way. Even though Oliver knows it of old from the parties, Roland is conscious of wanting to communicate his ownership of the place, to release it to Oliver at his own pace. But Oliver isn't ready to do it at anybody else's pace. He runs ahead, and whoops, and throws open doors. He shouts and gabbles as his imagination gets to work, repopulating the hospital with his own personal cast of nutters.

There's another problem: Cleo seems to have adopted some new, sultry manner – a way of walking and talking that is all about sex. A knowing insolence. A desire to shock. Roland is determined not to rise to it, although he knows that this is precisely what he is being invited to do.

The three of them go over it, coming to know the place in detail – even its spookiest, most forbidden areas. They take turns lying on the slab in the morgue. They experiment with the machinery that remains in engine sheds and work-shops, trying to get things started again, and when they fail, smashing them up. They plot out the building's darker purposes, filling in the gaps, of which there are many, with the vivid substance of their imaginations.

Then there are the spaces they can't understand however

hard they try, like the mossy chasms between wings that allow them to look into rooms they don't yet know how to reach. It seems perfectly possible that some invisible part of the hospital might still be in business. That if they look in the right place, they might find some clerk taking calls in an office, or a nurse doing the rounds with a medicine trolley. The building still feels like it could spring that kind of surprise.

One hazy afternoon, they are staring across a courtyard into a ground-floor window where they can see what looks like exercise equipment: straps and bars; harnesses; poles. It's a room that none of them have been in, but they can't work out how to get there. Oliver is on one of his favourite rants – the one about being locked up and medicated and electrocuted until you are as mad as they want you to be.

'Imagine being locked up in one of those padded cells. You'd tell them again and again, *I'm not mad, I'm not meant to be here. There's been a mistake.* But they wouldn't believe you.'

'I know how to get in there,' says Cleo to Roland. 'You just have to go round to the end of the dining hall, past that big set of scales where they weighed the food.' She points across the yard. 'We could get to it right now.'

'That's not where that goes,' says Roland. 'Where you're pointing is the corridor that ends up in the walk-in chillers. And the dry stores. This is somewhere different. None of us have been anywhere near that room. Maybe we should start drawing a map.'

He shifts uneasily. When he is beside her like this, he feels persistent worms of desire, working at his thigh muscles, seeking to bring them closer – or even projecting the fantasy that they are touching, and that it means something.

'Then you'd get frustrated,' says Oliver. 'You'd start to get angry. They'd have to restrain you. But you wouldn't go quietly. Of course you wouldn't. You'd swing at them and thrash about, and tear at their eyes and say *I'm not crazy, I'm not*. You'd play right into their hands. They'd love it. *You're not crazy? Of course you're not crazy! At least . . . NOT YET. Ha ha ha ha ha ha ha.*'

'What about the back airing court? Isn't there some little office off there?'

Something else that's started to happen is that he keeps finding himself mirroring her. He can't help it. He wants to establish it between themselves, their compatibility. When she eats, he eats. When she touches her hair, he touches his own. He can tell that Oliver has noticed it.

'You must be blind. There's no way that's there. That's right round the other side.'

'They'd be shocking you from the off. That would be a given. Before you'd even got your bags unpacked, they'd be giving you the shocks. Then there'd come the drugs.'

'I can't understand it. It's like there's a whole corridor missing.'

'And then the next thing you knew you'd be taken off to some *room* we don't even know about, maybe the place you're looking at right now. And here it comes. The big one. The one from which there's no turning back. They'd sharpen their scalpels to make those little incisions and then whisk the points around in your brains, scrambling them up like eggs.'

Cleo looks over at Oliver with an exasperated look. Roland cuffs him lightly round the head.

'I still don't really get what the point of a lobotomy is,' says Cleo.

'Neither did I,' says Oliver. 'So I looked it up at the library. Not nice.'

'But what does it do?'

'I don't know. But I think what happened is that they worked out where the place is in your brain that makes you mad. And they worked out that if you stuck a knife in it, and messed it all up, like, I don't know, like sticking a screwdriver into a computer, then you were just all calm and stuff.'

Cleo runs speculative forefingers down the sides of her temples. 'Through the sides of your brain?'

'Devil horns,' says Roland, still trying to work out how to get to the room. 'I read that somewhere. The scars you get are called devil horns.'

'Yeah, but that isn't the only way in,' says Oliver. 'There's another one, called the trans-orbital.'

'How does that one work?'

'It's easier, and you can't tell when someone's had it done.'

'Why not? Where does it happen?'

'Round the side of the eye.'

Later they are drinking in the laundry block – a large, galleried space with hydraulic lifts and a giant dumb waiter for transporting the linen.

Oliver disappears for a while, and appears above Roland and Cleo in the gallery. He's wearing some clothing he has found up there – a dusty green coat with white piping round its lapels, and beneath it, a torn, floral dress.

'I'm Mona,' he screeches, in high falsetto. 'Don't say blimey, or I'll cut out your brain.'

Cleo passes her can of cider to Roland with a grimace. 'Has he always been like this?'

'You've calmed him right down. He's usually much worse.'

They pause, watching Oliver as he acts out a sort of electrocution dance on the balcony. Roland watches her staring up at him. The smile on her lips. The way it hesitates as it waits. The way it breaks out again at the least thing Oliver does. She is lost to him, and he doesn't know what to do.

'What are you talking about down there?' says Oliver.

'You,' says Cleo.

'Good,' says Oliver. He pounds down the stairs to their

286

level, picks up a mud-caked mop and charges Roland with it, narrowly missing a burned-out hole through which the basement can be seen. Standing there, teetering on the edge, Oliver looks into Roland's eyes, and crosses himself. Sunlight springs behind him, fretting the edges of his features.

'In the name of the Father, and the Son, and the Holy Ghost,' he says.

Roland looks on in terror, knowing that Oliver is a monster, certain of it, just as certain as he is of his own inability to stop him. And Cleo, drunk, not yet sixteen, has stopped worrying about how close he was to falling down the hole, and is laughing in a way that Roland knows he could never elicit from her in a million years.

Eventually they run out of cider, so they shamble over to Revenant House in search of food and amusement, Cleo telling them not to act drunk, and giggling and stumbling as she says it. Roland has a headache.

There's no sign of her father so the three of them start rummaging around the ground floor, and Cleo is sensible enough to find something for Oliver to do to stop him ransacking the place. She leads them to one of the waterside pavilions where she knows there's a wooden trunk of games equipment, and soon Oliver has collected up a load of flags, golf clubs, wooden racquets and tennis balls, and is instructing the other two on how to play a hybrid game he is inventing on the spot which he has decided to call Madball.

They hack around in the overgrown lawn with their various kit. A competition develops to see who can hit a ball closest to the water without it going in. Roland keeps asking what the rules are but the other two are insensible, and seem to be competing with each other to see who can behave in the stupidest way possible. Throughout, Oliver lurches nearer and nearer to the water's edge, and eventually he finds a way to hurl himself in. Cleo doubles over with laughter.

'That's a goal!' she says. 'I've scored a goal. The game is over!'

'Never!' Oliver shouts. 'The game of Madball is *never over*.'

'Good Lord,' says a voice from the direction of the house. 'They're multiplying.'

'Dad,' says Cleo, the joy still on her face.

'And who's this one?' says Scriven.

'Oliver,' said Oliver, flopping forward out of the water and stumbling across the lawn with a hand outstretched. 'I like your wreck.'

Scriven glances at the building behind him. 'Some lovely things live on wrecks. Lobsters scuttling about in the hulls of sunken ships. *Those are pearls that were his eyes*, and all that.'

'Couldn't agree more,' says Oliver, dropping the hand quickly and looking away with an undisguised smile of contempt.

And there it is. Just as with every other significant adult Oliver has met in his life. Immediate suspicion. The light of goodwill swiftly extinguished, and her father is wary. Is it the close weather that's making Roland so hot that sweat is running down his back, or is it the feeling that accompanies these two worlds in collision?

'Anyway,' says Scriven. 'I fully expect that you are someone who knows this place of old from being up here trashing it, but thanks for pretending that you're seeing it today for the first time.'

'You're welcome,' says Oliver, amazingly managing to get away with this remark, and with the cheeky grin that follows it. But he doesn't see the look he gets in return.

35

Cleo. The name is latching on to him, like something sticky. Like someone grabbing your shoulders and pulling you irresistibly down. He wonders if he might start to hate her. If it was just a case of leaving them to it and going away, he could swallow it. But it isn't. They claim to want him around, and protest when he says he's going elsewhere. They won't let him go, as if they have made a pact that he must be on hand to watch their steady co-absorption. And then, regardless of all their crap, there are the times when he knows he's meant to disappear completely. He doesn't know what they suppose he is doing in the meantime.

They find five bicycles in a corrugated-iron shed. They are cranky machines, but three of them don't have completely flat tyres.

'Let's go for a spin,' says Cleo. 'The estuary.'

Oliver is wobbling around, taking off already, but Roland turns away. 'I'll see you down there,' he says.

Cleo grounds her feet unsteadily. 'Why?'

'I don't want to ride a bike, that's all. Tell me a place and I'll meet you.'

But when he is sitting by the rushing expanse of the river two hours later there is no sign of them. And he's been there for at least another half-hour before he sees them emerging from the concrete pillbox near the beach that he knows to stink of piss, not that this will have dented Oliver's resolve, or given him pause about taking her there. And as they walk towards him they are doing stuff to their clothing, straightening things out, and wheeling the bikes slowly rather than tearing about on them in the eager way that they had before. Roland has to pretend that he's only just arrived, that he enjoyed his walk, and that it has not been a nightmare for him, and that he's good old Roland, and that he didn't run half the way here to cut down on the amount of time the two of them would have alone together, cursing himself to the end of time for never having learned how to do something as elementary as ride a *fucking bike*.

'Now, you – buy us all a drink,' Cleo says to Oliver when they are finally all together and walking back into the town, as if to make it up to Roland by coquettishly bossing Oliver around.

'He can't buy us a drink. He's too small. He never gets served,' says Roland.

'And that's why we need good old Roland,' says Oliver.

As he's buying the drinks he's aware of them outside, touching each other, laughing, having obviously concluded that there had been no harm done to good old Roland. He can't help the thought. It is building in him, and he knows it's only going to get worse: STOP TAKING MY FRIEND. It is flashing in his head like an emergency alarm. STOP TAKING MY FRIEND. The problem is that he doesn't know which one of them he wants to say it to more.

It's happening again. He watches them through the clear vinyl doors of the operating theatre. Roland is concentrating on the bold yellow segments of the RADIATION WARNING sign, to try and avoid the silhouette show taking place behind the mildewed curtain. But the commingling of the two shapes cannot be ignored. The way it reaches a pitch of sound and movement, and then stops, and slows. He cannot help but watch it.

He will come to understand that what tortures him most is the fact that they linger afterwards, not hurriedly dressing as you might expect young, inexperienced lovers to do. They keep on kissing after the event, still hungry for one another. That's how he knows it is real.

When they come out, he steps away to spare her the shock and spare himself the embarrassment, and he overhears them as they head out to find him.

'We should find Roland,' she says.

'He's probably been watching anyway, the big pervert.'

The laughter hurts less than the way she leans into him as it bursts out of her.

Cleo and Oliver have settled into a studied routine of lying around ostentatiously in each other's arms, hoping to scandalise her father, who sulks indoors between sporadic bursts of renovation and hours closeted in his office. Cleo's theatrical laughter bubbling over Oliver's muttered words has become Roland's most hated sound.

Leaving them outside, Roland walks into the kitchen, so sun-blinded he can barely see the table. Jealousy on a hot day: the retinal image is there, a blue inky patch in his vision, of the shape of them out there. Flies swerve and settle on a plate of curling sandwiches. He can still hear their voices.

'What is he even doing in there? Staring at the walls as usual?'

Laughter.

A vase is soaking in the sink – rotten stalks floating in the stagnant water. He plunges his arms in it up to the shoulders to try and cool down. The water brims and comes over the edge, splashing down his legs and hitting his feet. He wants to leave. But leaving will make it worse. He has to stay, and endure this, even though it feels like the temperature is being turned up and up and there is nothing to be done.

When he re-emerges, they call to him, wetly intertwined on the grass.

'Why don't you come for a swim?' they say. 'Cool down a bit. You never go swimming.'

They mean it in a friendly way. But something has flipped in him and he can't take it at face value. In Roland's mind the invitation to swim is a taunt aimed at him by those who are not big and awkward, and zip around on bikes, and glide through water.

'If he doesn't want to swim, he doesn't have to,' says Cleo, instantly making things worse.

'You think I don't want to?'

She looks worried. 'I just meant you don't have to, that's all.'

'Fine.'

He hurls himself in, and the cold is like something being switched on inside him – some species-old, dormant system, shocked into action, lighting up his blood and organs, seizing them into life. His heart threatens to split itself. He is electrified, cannot take a breath. He is ungainly. The underwater footage would be like that of a wading elephant. He dives to hide himself from the beautiful couple on the bank. From Oliver's infuriating over-spasm of hilarity. Reeds. Bubbles. Cold. The seizure of the cold is good. He will leave. He will go home and pick up some of his criminally neglected duties at the Golden Sands. He will see how Carol is. Carol! The thought of her brings sharp pangs of regret. And gives him an idea.

He surfaces and quickly beaches himself, and slops away in his soaked clothes across the lawn. They're calling his name, but there's no way they will catch him in Wreaking if he wants to be lost. A few unexpected turns, and he's alone in the hospital. If they followed his wet footprints they might track him, but he suspects they're happy to give up and revert to sunning themselves.

He makes his way to the record office. The corridors are damper than he remembers, and since the party much of the ceiling has fallen in. The room itself is overflowing with waves of paper and records. Some of the filing cabinets have been tipped on to their side, and many have been emptied, but much remains.

Some of the records are so old that he struggles to read the writing. Some are more modern and typewritten. He takes out a few files at random. He browses the notes and recommendations concerning families in peril, suicidal mothers, anxious fathers, damaged children. Once he's worked out the storage system, it doesn't take him long to find her.

He opens the cardboard folder with her name on it, and finds thin sheaves of A5 pages inside, typewritten, addressed to a GP somewhere in suburban south London. He picks one at random, and reads.

Dear Dr Bell,

I saw Carol again this morning. She has been undergoing a sustained bout of depression for some weeks now, and confided in me that she fears she might harm herself. It has now been nearly a year since her last episode, and nearly five years since her initial attack, which came on as you know following an episode with her father, which she still won't go into detail about fully. There was certainly some violence, and while she won't admit to any sexual abuse I would certainly not rule it out.

Dear Dr Bell,

There has been little improvement in Carol's condition and I must add that unless some improvement is seen we may

*have to consider certification and another prolonged stay here
at Wreaking. I have put her on a heavy course of*

Dear Dr Bell,
*I regret to inform you that Carol's situation has deterior-
ated, and she violently attacked a matron last week. For her
own safety and that of those around her, I fear we must*

He cradles the folder to his chest, and tucks it carefully
inside his shirt.

He makes a short excursion back to Revenant House,
where the lovers are still messing around in the garden. On
the kitchen table he sees her father's car keys, along with a
fistful of pocket change and a couple of crumpled banknotes.
Roland quickly takes a twenty and leaves before anyone
realises he's back.

His clothes are nearly dry from the walk by the time he
reaches the supermarket. He spends Scriven's money on an
extravagant meal of smoked salmon, brown bread and white
wine. He imagines they will all sit together, eating it and
thanking him.

Back at the Golden Sands, he lays out his wares on a grand
platter, with the salmon laid out in drapes and folds, and
scattered red onion, and capers, and quarters of lemon. He
watches Carol, unsure of whether or not he should tell her
what he has found. Which means that Mona hasn't really
been getting any of his attention at all until he notices what
she is eating.

Ignoring the fish and the bread, she has selected a piece
of lemon from the plate, and is doggedly sawing it up with
her cutlery and putting pieces in her mouth. She looks
confused, but bites on, through peel and flesh, without even
wincing.

Nobody speaks, aware that to contradict her version of

the world would be to open a door to something they aren't quite ready for.

'Enjoying that?' he says, shooting Carol a glance across the table.

'Lovely,' says Mona. 'Lovely.'

36

A morning of hot sunlight on the water. She is in the lake up to her shoulders, reading, her bare feet just retaining purchase on the slime-green glass dome underneath. Tiny movements lead to agreeably uncontrolled slippage. Her arms are resting on a thin, low-hanging branch that reaches just far enough from the bank, enabling her to keep the book raised up. She is unmoving, enjoying the chill on her body together with the heat of the sun on the top of her head, the insects clouding around her, the dank smell. Dragonflies, cellophane-shiny, are dipping in the lake, settling on lily pads, curling like beckoning fingers. She takes her eyes off the paperback to watch them skimming the pollen-coated surface. Tiny diamonds of light shift on the outskirts of her vision.

From somewhere, she hears a whispered question.

Are you getting this?

The words are faint on the air. They are spoken and replayed in her head before she realises that they came from her own mouth. It takes considerable self-interrogation, and a lot more staring at the water, before she realises she was addressing the question to her mother.

When she has thought about it some more, she realises that this is a good sign, because it means that something is making her happy. But what could have gone and done a thing like that?

The stranger realisation comes later – years later – when she looks back on this, and understands that the thing she was talking about, the object of the question, was Oliver. That in that moment, she was asking her dead mum to check out her new seventeen-year-old boyfriend.

Because there is an urge there, isn't there, to tell someone about it? About the revolution that has happened to her way of processing the world? And who better to tell?

'She was a superstitious one, your mother. She even believed in angels, do you know that?'

Her father has said that to her more than once. The remark is usually accompanied by a wistful smile, but also, if you look closely, a hardness that can only be anger. It was years into her childhood before Cleo understood that there were still complex feelings there. She thinks the idea of angels is fine. In her more whimsical moments, she allows herself to think that her mother may even be an angel too.

The story of the train journey has been drilled into her so many times that it has taken up a position among her memories. It is something she can actually feel nostalgic for. And as such, it is something she feels she can relate herself. She knows there are some details she hasn't got right in her version, but it is hers. This is how she sees it.

The train clatters down a blinding coastline. Tunnels of warm darkness alternate with bright blue skies and sea spray flying up from the walls of fishing villages. Her mother is always perfect, always beautiful.

She was recovering from the latest of several miscarriages. The two of them had gone away together to try and forget all about it. The old woman was already in the carriage when they got on.

The old woman looked across from feeding her little grandson and asked whether Cleo's mother was pregnant. And her mother put on a brave face, and replied that she had been, but was not any more. And the woman smiled with her crinkly eyes and said how sorry she was, and offered them boiled eggs.

Her mother became pregnant so soon afterwards that she began to believe that the old woman was responsible. And that there was therefore something magical about the child within her. Which made it very obvious to Cleo's mother what she had to do when the test came – as she had known all along that it would.

She knew she was unwell almost as soon as she was pregnant. Cleo doesn't know how it really went, but she describes it in her version as a feeling under the armpits – a kind of crippled weakness that made it impossible for her to lift any weight, a stabbing pain, a feeling in her body of panic and desperation that made her want to sob. But she told no one. She waited for confirmation from the doctor of one condition before she enquired about the other. She wanted it that way round.

She told Cleo's father, smuggling it into the good news: she was pregnant, and if they were lucky she would live long enough to carry the child to term. In so doing she set up a confusion which has persisted in him for the whole of his life, and will live in him to the end. (So she said to Oliver.)

Without the baby, he said, she could have treatment that might save her. And then they could continue. At which she looked at him, and said, 'You know full well that's not going to happen.'

He pleaded with her. She was throwing life at the situation, she said. Could he not see that? She would live on in that way.

It wouldn't be her, though, he said. It would be someone else. It would be her *killer*.

(We don't know if he definitely said this, Cleo said. But he might have done.)

The stage was set for his hatred of Cleo. From before she was even Cleo.

This is the story she told Oliver, more or less. She knows there were one or two embellishments, but since it's her story she can tell it how she likes.

Oliver didn't offer judgement, or – which would be worse – sympathy. He just nodded, and seemed to understand.

'Do you wish she'd got rid of you and saved herself?'

'Of course not,' said Cleo. 'I just wish my dad hadn't told me there was ever a choice.'

At this, Oliver leaned towards her, so that she could smell the cider on his breath. It started to happen, the thing that had been threatening to happen for months now, which she wanted to happen but which she had thought they would have to plan in advance carefully in order to make sure that Roland or her father weren't around. They started kissing, and they were on her bed, and it happened. And it was good. The nakedness was good. She was closing her eyes, and beginning to see the point, when she felt Oliver tense inside her, and then she was scrambling to get out from under him in time, and pull herself away and on to her knees, but it was too late, because it had happened, and now it was everywhere, cooling on her thigh and who knew where else.

She looked at Oliver, shocked to start with, and then laughing along with him. She wasn't afraid of anything he could do to her, because she knew that although he would do anything he wanted, she also knew that anything he did would be interesting.

'Sorry,' he said, looking down at himself, still twitching, at his bunched trousers which hadn't made it lower than his knees. He laughed along with her, and as they laughed at this thing he couldn't control, more drooled out of the end of it, and she took another swig of the cider and fell backwards and started to think about when they might be able to do it again.

She had known from the first time she saw Oliver that this would probably happen. And she wasn't unhappy about it because what's more it was funny, but now she had an urge to get him out of here as quickly as she could, because this was potentially dangerous territory.

Right then, just at the point that Oliver had started to do a dance because it made the sight even funnier, right then was the moment her father's too loud voice came bouncing up the stairs. Oliver half leapt, half fell off the side of the bed, and hid there, silently laughing, as she threw herself at the door to stop her father opening it and yelled that she'd just got out of the bath. She heard him then, poking around in the bathroom, checking to see how dry and unused it was.

Later, she had to find some way to explain to him why she'd decided to have a second bath after that one. Because her imagination was firing fully, the sperm seemed to be everywhere, and going without a bath simply wasn't an option.

Nor is this the only area in which her imagination has been overreaching. As she stands on the underwater dome, seized by cold water, talking to her mother, she realises that having told Oliver a few invented facts to retain his interest has made her realise just how faint her understanding is of what *really* happened.

'Lunch,' shouts her father from the house.

She splays the book open, and balances it like a pitched roof over her tree branch, before letting her feet slip off the glass and plunging into the water.

37

Her father is spending more time with them. It's not something Roland particularly understands, but it has a beneficial diluting effect which he isn't about to challenge. Scriven seems to have decided to lock horns with Oliver in pre-arranged skirmishes, as if a gentlemen's agreement were in place over how their war should be prosecuted. Roland worries about things at home, but leaving is not an option.

Today, their peculiar band has assembled in and around one of the waterside pavilions. Sunlight has heated the cabin, bringing up sweetness from a coil of fly paper that spirals lazily in the window. The walls bleed with resin. Scriven is in a canvas chair, hulling strawberries at speed with quick clockwise twists, eating them, and chucking the stalks into the water. The artwork in here has almost faded to white, but you can just make out versions of the lake in bright colours, many with inflated scale, and fanciful features in the background, like mountains and airships. Cleo and Oliver sit beside each other in the doorway. Roland is hiding his embarrassment at the ongoing confrontation by lingering at the water's edge, pulling out blanket weed, slime turning fibrous as he pulls it.

'Tell me again about that dilemma of yours,' says Oliver.

'I won't,' says Scriven, through a mouthful of strawberry. 'You're just trying to be difficult.'

'I'm not being difficult. I just don't think it's a fair question. The Nobel prize-winning scientist is drowning in the same river as my father? Why? And why can't he swim? My dad can't swim because the bicep was ripped out of one of his arms by a stallion, but what's wrong with the scientist?'

Scriven sighs. 'For God's sake. It's not meant to be a real scenario. It's a *moral* dilemma. Do you save someone you love, or the person who will be of most benefit to the race as a whole? Do you get that?'

'I get it,' says Oliver. 'But I still don't see why the scientist can't swim. He's not much of a *scientist*, is he?'

'Enough!' Oliver always knows how to push him over the edge in the end – not that the edge is ever very far away. 'Don't take it seriously, then. You're a tourist. You can never engage with anything long enough to learn. It's no wonder they didn't want you in the sixth form.'

Oliver blows a slow, defiant raspberry.

'I rest my case,' says Scriven, turning his attention back to the strawberries.

'No, okay,' says Oliver, sitting up straight. 'Let's talk about this one some more.'

'There's no point.'

'We're talking about sacrifice, right? Deciding to do something for somebody else and not for yourself.'

'Yes.'

Right there, right in front of her dad, he's doing it. Letting his hand stray on to the skin of Cleo's arm. He's good at ignoring it, but there's nobody here who doesn't think Scriven is noticing the way that the two of them are always touching at least slightly, with one bit of their bodies.

'So it's a bit like what Cleo's mother did, isn't it?'

Scriven stares silently at the pile of blanket weed that Roland has been building on the bank.

'I mean, she decided to save her daughter rather than save herself, didn't she?' says Oliver. 'I'd say that was for the good of mankind.'

Scriven blinks, but doesn't move his head. Roland stands by the water with a long strand of weed dangling from his hand.

'I think we should talk about something else,' says Cleo.

'Why? I thought he wanted me to *engage* with the question. Isn't it a good example?'

Scriven speaks quietly, his hands at rest in the strawberry bowl. 'Cleo been talking to you about that, has she?'

'Yes.'

'Okay. Well, you're right, I suppose. It was a self-sacrificing thing to do.'

'Wasn't very nice to you though, was it?' says Oliver. 'Hasn't left you in a very good way.'

Scriven brings a strawberry to his mouth and gnaws at it, trying to separate it from its stalk, but the two seem to be stuck fast, so he bites forward on the stalk as well, swallowing the whole thing down, and has to suppress a little cough in the process.

'Some people think everything means something,' says Scriven. 'Other people think that things just happen. I spend my life desperately trying to persuade myself I am in the latter camp, but sometimes I'm not sure I am. When I miss Cleo's mother, for example. And then you get people who think that the world means *too much.*'

'Say that again?' says Oliver.

They are back at the house now, the same afternoon, and rather than retreating, as Roland had assumed he would, her father has re-emerged hungry for battle.

'Some people call it saliency syndrome,' he says. 'The inability to distinguish between what matters and what doesn't. Everything has to mean something. Why is everybody wearing a black coat? What is it about the number five? To a greater or lesser extent we all suffer from it. We all think everything relates to us, even when it doesn't.'

'What's this got to do with anything?' says Oliver.

He closes his eyes. 'It explains why so many people ended up in places like this. And why for the most part they really aren't so far away from the rest of us. You must have all thought at one time or another that what was going on around you had some higher meaning, or significance? Haven't you? Or do you all just think life's completely random, with no one in charge at all?'

'I don't follow you,' says Oliver.

'Okay. Let's try another one. Have you ever been really unhappy?' says Scriven. 'I mean, so unhappy that you're in danger. I'm talking out-on-the-window-ledge stuff.'

He asks the question so casually that Roland seems to decide that a casual answer is the best response. 'I've felt sad sometimes, yeah.'

'I don't mean that. I don't mean just sad. I mean so stuck in it you can't tell which shoe is which in the morning, let alone be bothered to put one on. I mean so depressed you can't get out of bed.'

'Then, no,' says Roland.

'Imagine what it was like for that lot. Hey! What are you doing with my pen?'

Oliver found it on the table, the stainless steel biro that Scriven always uses, and unseen, has been handling it with his usual, destructive nervous energy.

He snatches the pen from Oliver's hands. Its clip is bent at a catastrophic angle, and there is no way it can be put back. 'Are you going to apologise?'

A shrug from Oliver. 'It's just a pen.'

'This was a present.'

'From your lovely wife – I know.'

'Wait,' says Cleo. 'You're being cruel.'

Now Oliver turns on her. 'Who's being cruel? I've seen what he's like. He's totally hung up on the dead, and takes no notice of the living.'

'Is that right?' says her father. 'What about you? With all your talk of being trapped by this town. What if you're not trapped here by anything other than your stupidity? I don't see you wanting to do much to get out of here. You just want to sit around getting drunk the whole time, and touching up my daughter.'

'Dad.'

He walks right up to Oliver, staring him in the face. 'You're cross because you know you're never going to get out of this place, or places like it. Aren't you? You know you're going to end up working here in some shitty job. Because you don't actually want to learn anything.'

Oliver brazens it out with a smile, but Roland knows he's never been spoken to like that by an adult before.

'And since you are so against the idea of my being in mourning for my late wife, you'll be pleased to know that Cleo and I will be going away the day after tomorrow to pay our respects to her, and you are not invited.'

'I could come if you wanted,' says Oliver.

'I don't think that's appropriate, old man,' says Scriven, placing a sarcastically patrician hand on his shoulder. 'It's more of a family occasion. You can come along next year, after you've married her.'

Roland sees her looking to Oliver for some reassurance at this point, or even an affectionate look, but all you can see is the anger blazing in his eyes towards Scriven as he laughs at his own joke.

'Besides,' he adds, 'I think you two could probably do with a cooling-off period.'

Roland tries to go with him, but Oliver is off, marching away in the direction of the path to town.

Roland decides to leave him to it, and takes a quick walk around the chapel before heading home, to put some distance between them. He imagines bells calling the disturbed to prayer on Sunday mornings. He thinks of all the lonely funerals. The noise of crickets in the waist-high grass seems to him to be saying the name of the place, over and over again: *WreakingWreakingWreakingWreakingWreaking*. It has got to them too.

38

The act of driving is terrifying him as much as ever. He swears whenever he has to change lanes, and obviously doesn't trust his wing mirrors because he keeps whirling his head to one side then the other, with such violence that she thinks he might get whiplash.

She is, of course, thinking about Oliver. The skin of her thigh feels pinched where his latest delivery has dried in her blonde, downy hair. If she moves in a certain way she can feel it tug. She loves knowing that they're off on this sorry pilgrimage with some of him hitching along for the ride.

Her father is staring straight ahead, and she knows he's thinking about Oliver too – or trying not to. The main reason she knows that her father hates him is that he never mentions his name. He doesn't want to risk hearing something he doesn't want to know. There was relish in the way he told Oliver that the two of them were going away. And a hint of pleasant desperation in Oliver's implausible request that he tag along.

She is pondering all this as they make their way up the motorway on their annual pilgrimage to her mother's river-bank. Lanes are switched. Service stations frequented. Petrol acquired. All the dismal obligations of travelling round this small, sour island. And because they never travel now, this is another situation where he overlooks how far she has moved on, and insists on distractions that expired as relevant things to her years ago. I Spy. Number-plate games. She hates it all. The smelly car with all its familiar things. The ragged scroll of a road atlas. The tin of caustic, fluff-caked travel sweets. At least if Ursula or her mother was around she'd be able to drift away on the back seat. But then they wouldn't be doing this journey, would they?

Something about being side by side together staring at a common thing rather than each other means that they can talk. The windscreen wipers are on, and she imagines what they might be saying as they equivocate. *On one hand, on the other hand, on one hand, on the other hand.*

'She'd be fifty soon, your mother.'

What is she supposed to say to that?

He stares ahead, grimacing into the rain.

'When?' she says.

'You don't know when her birthday is?'

'Course I do. September the eighth.'

'Well there you go then. That's next week.'

There are times when she looks or speaks in a certain way when she can tell she is reminding him of her mother. Or at least – that he is trying to access the memory of her mother through her. She knows she is right about this because she's found evidence of it in some of the things he writes, on bits of paper lying around in his study.

The way she laughs. The curiosity. The way she asks questions. The way she judges my answers. The way she is in the world. The way she negotiates with it. The similarity. The unbearable similarity.

'Sometimes when you look at me you miss Mum, don't you?' she says.

He glances at her, then shoots his eyes back to the road. 'Not because of anything you do on purpose. And you know I wouldn't trade you for anything.'

308

The conversation is supposed to end here, but she's not in the mood for that. 'I don't know if you believe that.'

She watches the wipers' steady sweep in the shocked silence.

'I mean, I know you want to believe it. Except that if you still had Mum and not me, you could make hundreds of other children. You wouldn't miss me if you'd never met me.'

'But I did meet you.'

'Shall we have some music?' she says, jamming whatever cassette is sticking out back into the machine, which turns out to be something they both like, so she starts singing, and he joins in after a while.

They stop at a B&B with pink chintz in the windows, on the outskirts of the town. After they've checked in and left their bags in the room, they get back in the car and set off. He pulls up at a flower shop on the way, leaves the car idling and returns with a bunch of roses wrapped in newspaper.

'She loved roses,' he says, again. She had been wondering whether he would manage to produce that bit of information for the third year running, and sure enough, here it is.

The riverbank is just as bleak as she remembers it – unworthy of all the significance it receives. She stares into space, as usual, waiting for him to decide that enough time has elapsed. They lay down the flowers, and she knows she isn't supposed to talk. She feels scraped of her joy, like a zested lemon.

'I've got a bit of a surprise for you,' he says.

'Yeah?'

'Wait here.' He goes back to the car, and she can see him reaching into the boot for something. He comes back carrying something large and metal under his arm. As he gets closer she sees that it is what can only be described as an urn. She sees that there are tears in his eyes.

'Is that—'

'I've been waiting for the right moment to do this,' he says. 'I think we should do it now, don't you?'

'Are you serious?'

'We should do it quickly,' he says. 'I think you're supposed to ask the council's permission.'

When it is done they go to a pub for dinner, and he allows her one glass of wine while he sets off on the rest of the bottle. She is embarrassed by the volume of his voice. She imagines that other diners are listening to their conversation.

It wasn't until Oliver pointed it out to her that she realised how much his voice had been ringing off the walls at home. 'Have you never noticed it?' he said. 'The sheer *volume*? Why can't he just turn it down?' That's all it takes: for someone to walk in and point something out, and then your whole world can start changing.

'Tell me again,' she says. 'How it happened. How she died. Because when I was trying to tell it to Oliver, I'm not sure I remembered it properly.'

'Okay,' he says, looking awkward.

He begins to embark on a familiar story of the train, and the illness, some of which she has heard before, and some of which is new. And all of which, she knows, is somehow wrong. She waits for him to finish all the same.

'Tell me something else,' she says. 'Why have you been telling me all this time that this place was where her ashes were scattered if they weren't?'

'What do you mean?' he says.

'And your story. It changes a bit every time. Don't you think I'm old enough now to be told whatever it is you haven't been telling me?'

He sets his glass down on the table, and puts a hand to his eyes, screwing them up tight, and rubbing them with his fingers. 'Okay,' he says. 'You're right. I should have done this before.'

She reaches for the bottle of wine between them, and pours herself a full glass. 'Do it now.'

'I've told you before that your mother believed she could see angels, haven't I?'

'A bit. Not all that much.'

'This wasn't just something whimsical. It wasn't a joke. To her, they were real, living people, who talked to her, and got cross with her, and kept her company. There were different ones, with different personalities. There was one called the Drill Sergeant, who gave her the courage to do things. Another was called the Sniggering Aunt, who helped her laugh at the world, and made it less scary. Sometimes she could only hear them. Other times, she said that they were right there, with these big creaking wings that were so high above them that she wondered how they ever got through doorways. She said they smelled, too. They smelled of leather and sweat and candle wax and feathers.'

Cleo nods, wondering where this is going.

'What I haven't told you is that after you were born, the angels started to speak a little louder.'

He smiles, as if this was an appropriate time for a fucking joke, to make light of it, and when he sees the expression on Cleo's face, his smile drops and he resumes his story very quickly, with no smiling at all.

'Okay, okay. Sorry. Here goes. We'd been an item for nearly six months before she came clean about them. At that stage she was wise enough to know not to come straight out with it, but to take my temperature first, to see what kind of person I was. And I was keeping a secret of my own. My secret was that I was so in love with her that she could have told me there were aliens in her basement and I'd have believed it.

311

'I'd noticed it from the beginning in some of the things she said. *They say it's going to rain next week. They told me the traffic would be bad today.* But I missed it the first few times. Then, I don't know, I thought it was some kind of verbal tick she had. Then one Saturday morning we were in the car, driving out somewhere for the weekend, as we did from time to time. And I made some remark about how happy she made me. Something sentimental like that. *They told me you'd be the one for me*, she said, and smiled.

'*Who told you that?* I said.

'*You're going to think I'm completely batty*, she said. *You're going to finish with me.*

'*No*, I said. *Whatever it is, I'll love it.*

'*I warn you*, she said. *You're going to laugh at me.*

'*Try me*, I said.

'*The thing is*, she said, *that they talk in lots of different ways. They always have. They've done it since I was a child. The radio is one way I can hear them. You see, if I turn the dial now, there are certain frequencies that enable me to tune into them. Does that sound strange to you?*

'*No!* I said. *Not in the slightest.*

'From then on, they were out in the open. She told me how they had talked to her since she was a child and advised her on everything in her life. How they had always been there. Later, she told me how they had spoken to her through the old woman on the train. And I grew to love them. To me they were simply her own charming way of expressing what she was feeling and thinking. In the third person, if you like. And then you were born.

'She had told me through the pregnancy of how the angels were talking to her about you. As you grew inside her, the angels were telling her all along what you were going to be like. They knew far in advance that you were a girl, long before we did.

'One day, I came home to find her lying back in an armchair while you cried your eyes out in the next room. You hadn't been changed all day, and the smell was awful. Then at night, I heard something, and went in to find her standing over your cot with a pillow in her hands, talking to the Drill Sergeant. And that was how I first started to understand that the angels had changed their tune. There's a reason why I keep coming back to the story of that train journey. It's the last time I can remember her being herself.

'We went to see the doctor. I thought there might be some medication they could put her on. It was post-natal depression, I thought. That was all. There was no need to mention the angels. But she came straight out with it. And you should have seen how his ears pricked up at the sound of that.

'*Angels?* he said, and looked at me. *You knew about this?*

'And there it was.

'*There is somewhere I think we might just check you in for a few days*, he said. *Until you feel better.* And he gave the name of the local psychiatric hospital.'

'Wreaking?' says Cleo. 'She was at Wreaking?'

'No,' he says. 'Somewhere similar, near where we are now. What I'm getting at is that after you were born she became very ill indeed. So ill that it was thought she might harm herself. Or you.'

He sighs. 'They're called command hallucinations. People think they're being talked to by the radio, or wherever, and told to do things. And she started to think that the angels were telling her to hurt you. Everyone from the Drill Sergeant to the Sniggering Aunt to all the others.'

Cleo drinks her wine, and tries to remain composed.

'And so she went to hospital, to try and get better. And they put her on a kind of medication called anti-psychotics. And the medication took away her angels.'

'So what happened then?'

'What happened then is that she was so sad and angry at me for having taken away her angels that she said she didn't want to live with us any more. Which she probably couldn't have done anyway. She was far too ill to leave the hospital. And that was why we used to come here every year, to this riverbank. So she could watch you from the other side.'

'What?'

He carries on, sadly, realising there's nothing else for it now. 'They used to bring her out for the day. It was the only way she would consent to seeing you. I wanted her to see you growing up.' He fiddles with his napkin. 'I wanted to see her, too. But she never really forgave me.'

'And that's the reason we keep coming here?' She wants to drink more of her wine, wants to ask him to fill up her glass, but her hands are shaking in her lap and she knows that if she tries to lift anything then it will all go horribly wrong. 'For that reason?'

'Yes.'

'So.' Keep hold of the voice. Just keep hold of your voice and you won't cry. Try to control this tentative smile. 'So. She's still alive?'

'She died three years ago,' he says. 'I'm sorry.'

A long pause.

'How did she die?'

'She took her own life.'

He's gone. She knew he'd go first. It disgusts her how he's always ready to cry at the first available opportunity.

'Why did you do this?' she says, eventually. 'Why did you make up this stupid story? Why didn't you just tell me?'

'Because I didn't want you to feel responsible. I thought it would be nicer for you to believe that she died trying to protect you. I thought it would mitigate against any feelings of abandonment.'

'What?'

'I thought it would make you feel better.'

'Well, it didn't,' she says. 'At all.'

'You don't know what it was like. She was hurting herself whenever we went anywhere near her. She couldn't be left alone. She took a fork from the kitchens and tried to put it through her cheek.' He's crying so hard now that it's affecting his voice.

'Well. This explains where the money came from that enabled you to make your *brilliant investment.*'

'There's no need to be cruel.'

'Isn't there?'

Nobody speaks for a long time.

'If all of that is true,' she says, finally. 'Then why on *earth* do we have to keep on coming back to this stupid place?'

'I'm sorry,' he says again, pointlessly. 'On the other hand – her ashes *are* actually scattered here now. So I suppose you could call it a self-fulfilling prophecy.'

What she will remember more than anything is her rage that he could be cheap enough to shell out only for one twin room for the pair of them. But of course this is what he does – to contribute to the fantasy that this ritual might ever conceivably be an experience that brings the two of them together.

She lies beside him, cringing at every clearing of his throat, every fart, every shift of his bedsprings. She wishes she could go somewhere to cry for real, and begin to understand what he's told her in peace, in her own time.

An alarm clock's digits flash infuriatingly in crystal blue. Finally, he speaks.

'Why do you suppose my chickens keep disappearing?'

'What?'

'I just don't get how it's happening. It's not a fox, because there's no sign of one getting in or out. Who's taking my chickens? I replace them and then they disappear. If it wasn't ridiculous you'd actually think someone was coming up just to *steal* them from me.'

'You didn't tell me about that,' she says.

'I've had new fences, locks on the coop, ditches, the lot. Everything to try and keep the damn things safe. It's like *dark magic*, the way they keep disappearing.'

She turns to the wall just in case he can see her, and grins into the darkness of the fluffy pink room, and beams out love for Oliver that shoots up and out of this place. Which means that he's here, right now. And he's achieved a miracle, because even though her mother's not here and neither are her angels, Oliver is.

On the drive back, he tries to bring it up again. 'You can see, can't you, why I tried to protect you?'

'Yes,' she says. 'You didn't want me to feel bad.'

'Exactly. I didn't want you to feel bad. I've only ever tried to do things in a way that didn't make you feel bad.'

'You didn't do a very good job of that, did you?'

He knows better than to try and keep talking after she has said that, and they sit in silence throughout the drive home, right up to the point at which they see the fire engines.

And, as they get in closer, the smoke that is rising in dark billows from the Enfield wing.

'Well, what have we here?' she says.

Her father, hands bunched at the steering wheel, says nothing at all.

39

'He's a total shit. And if I have anything to do with it, he's going to get his comeuppance.'

Since they can't seem to summon the imagination to do anything else, the two of them are back at the hospital. Roland wanted to go to Arcadia for the afternoon – anything to get away from here – but Oliver insisted they come back, because he said he had a surprise. Roland is dreading the surprise.

'What are you going to do to him?' says Roland. 'He's pretty pathetic. There's not much you can do to him that he isn't already doing to himself.'

'I don't know,' Oliver says. 'But he better watch it. Anyway. Look what I've got here.'

Roland looks down and sees that Oliver is holding a ziplock plastic bag containing a pair of nasty-looking green pills. 'Whatever those are, you must be joking.'

'I don't know what they are,' says Oliver. 'But I nicked them off Victor, so I bet they're good.'

They're in a room full of shining broken glass. Every single windowpane in it seems to have been smashed, and the glass is so evenly distributed that it looks strategically placed to make sunlight spread all over the floor. Roland shifts his feet forward, making splinters and shards crunch and pulverise. Oliver has one of the pills in his palm and is holding the other one out for Roland.

'Down the hatch,' he says. 'Anyway. My point is that he's dodgy. I don't think we know the half of it when it comes to how nasty he is to her. He might even be feeling her up for all we know.'

'Yeah right,' says Roland.

'I'm serious. I tell you, I've got a good instinct for these things.'

'You're full of shit.'

They have stopped at a row of baths full of standing water. The little green pills are working fast. Things are starting to happen to the light, and Roland is sweating in waves that are alternately hot and cold, flushing down his back. Oliver throws a bit of plaster into the gloom and it lands with a wet plunk.

'Why do you think they shout at each other so much?' says Roland.

Oliver sits knees up in a window, casually dismembering a daddy-long-legs. 'She thinks he wishes her mother was alive instead of her.'

'And does he?'

'Dunno.' He releases the limbless insect, which spirals to the floor. 'But if I was a betting man . . .'

'Which you are.'

'Then I would put good money on the chance that somewhere inside – yes, he does. After all that, what do you expect?'

'After all what?'

Oliver sits up straight. 'I thought you were a bit quiet the other day. Do you mean she's never told you the story of what happened with her mum?'

Roland hates himself almost as much as he hates Oliver.

All the time he wasted, talking about his missing father and his stupid ring pull business and his cardboard tunnels and making her fucking aeroplanes instead of finding out about her. Leaving Oliver to march on in there, as he always does, and get the low-down. *You never thought to ask how her mother died? Is that right?* He thumps himself on the tensed muscle in his thigh, discreetly so that Oliver doesn't notice, but hard, and carries on doing it until the leg is dead and he knows there will be a big bruise, to remind him not to be so stupid in the future.

'She had cancer or something, but she refused to have any treatment so she could have Cleo. Then she died. And he's hated her ever since.'

Roland continues to pound the flesh of his thigh. He blinks, trying to keep focused, but his eyes seem to want to go all over the place, and the waves of warm and cold are still running up and down his back. Moving on, they pass through a room lined with rows of bedside anglepoise lamps that hang dead like swans with broken necks.

'I'm bored,' says Oliver.

'What about the water tower? We've only done that once.'

'Fuck the water tower. Let's get into the Enfield, and have a look at his so-called *school*.'

'Please let's not do that,' says Roland.

Which is about the worst thing you can ever say to Oliver.

Against all the odds, the Enfield is looking pretty good. The rooms have been cleared, the floorboards stripped, the walls painted. There's a chance this thing might actually work.

Oliver sifts through the boxes of school stuff lying around: packets of chalk; brand-new blackboards; metre rulers. 'Poor bastard,' he says.

The sun has nearly gone, and they're wandering the long,

echoing rooms on the second floor when Roland becomes aware of how cold he feels. He tears up the packaging from a carton that a blackboard came in, rips it into little pieces, and starts setting a fire in a green-tiled hearth. It makes no difference to the temperature. Roland scouts around, collecting more old newspapers and a few bits of wood, and adding them to the fire in the grate.

'Good work!' says Oliver. 'Let us sit like gentlemen, and drink the rest of our vodka.'

They pull up two chairs to the fireplace and sit there passing round the drink.

'You're not serious, about him . . . hurting her?' says Roland.

'I bloody am. I'm almost positive of it.'

'But she hasn't told you anything.'

'She doesn't have to.' Oliver's grin gleams in the firelight, snarling at the edges. 'I can tell something's not right.'

'God, I'm shivering,' says Roland. 'What are these things anyway?'

'Who knows what Victor has lying around? I'm shivering too. What else can we burn?'

Roland gets on his knees, blowing the fragments of paper, getting them going. Looking around for more stuff to put in. Eventually, he picks up the chair he was sitting in and smashes it up on the floor, feeding the pieces one by one to the fire. Still, he feels freezing. This fire isn't doing anything, with its miserly little flame there in that dismal institutional grate.

'I'll see if I can get anything from outside,' says Oliver.

Roland is kneeling down in front of the hearth, for what feels like hours. Why won't it go, this fire? Even the cardboard boxes he finds don't seem to want to go. The skin of his hands is rippling, and why won't this fire burn? He adds several newspapers, a magazine, a flip-chart pad, all sorts, but the cold is unbearable. He's been on his knees here for hours, with no results. What is he supposed to do to get it going?

It is at this point, Oliver will tell him later, that Oliver is in one of the overgrown yards, watching the networks of black on sycamore leaves, and crushing berries in his hands, sparks behind his eyes, when he becomes aware of the light at the windows of the wing, glowing fiercely like a sunrise.

These things are amazing, he thinks, staring at the glow.

And then he is breathless to get back inside.

The wave of flame as Oliver opens the door nearly takes his face off.

Roland is on his knees at the centre of the room, frantically stoking an inferno of chairs and tables that is building around him. His fire has consumed half the room, and he is feeding it. He's put chairs in a heap to make them burn. The floor is being eaten in front of them.

'Better,' says Roland. His hair is smoking, and looks as if it is about to catch at the edges. 'Is this happening?'

Oliver screams. 'What do you mean, is this happening?'

'Is there someone else here?'

'Concentrate,' says Oliver, laughing. 'Concentrate. We've got to go.'

'Hoover,' says Roland, seeing a large industrial vacuum cleaner leaning against the wall. And for a second he actually tries to hoover up the fire, which leads to the sight, if anyone were outside to see it, of a flaming machine, exiting the window and falling to the ground.

'Sorry,' says Roland. 'Sorry, sorry, sorry.'

They run down the stairs feeling the fire on their backs, then stop outside in the courtyard to take in the full implications.

'Sorry,' says Roland, and falls over, smashing into a discarded bottle on the ground with his face.

'Stop saying sorry,' says Oliver, who is still laughing. 'Come here, there's glass in your face.'

He leans forward and pulls a curled green shard from Roland's cheek. Blood is wet on his skin. Oliver is a devil and an imp and he has horns and doesn't. Their cold, sweaty foreheads briefly touch. And there is a moment of such honesty between them that nothing will ever really need saying again.

'Come on then,' says Oliver, leading him into the darkness. 'Best be off.'

PART FIVE

40

Not for the first time in her life, she wishes this journey took longer. The trains now – they just hum along. There's no clatter of rolling stock. And even if there were, you couldn't open the window to let it in. You're just trapped inside with this stuffy, sanitised zing.

The mainline service dispenses briskly with all the city's outer layers of high-rises, warehouses and car yards: familiar to her, but not close enough to her destination to be more than anonymous. She changes to the branch-line train, which sets forth through a haggard landscape of farms slashed up by motorways, and here she enters the realm of the painfully known. Beside a drainage ditch stands the windmill that she has watched deteriorate on its spindly tripod over the years, now so rusty that its fins are dropping like petals. In the middle of a field of stark, yellow rape linger the remains of a once-proud brick barn, whose blackened ribcage of roof timbers today recalls some massacre footage she reviewed last week, most of which couldn't be edited into anything fit for broadcast. Cleo the Bad News Filter, defending others from the ugly truth for so long that her whole perception is tainted: everything she sees is affected by the snagged, trapped disasters she has saved others from, and this familiar sight is no exception. Charged with awful association like so much else in her life, the barn glides past at speed, which means it is time to start getting her bags together for arrival.

She swigs water by the exit door, and when the bottle is empty, she crushes it and lays it on top of the contents of the overflowing bin. This one-way single track is the home stretch, its sidings bursting with blackened cones of buddleia that paw at the carriage windows as you shuttle in. She knows precisely when the Wreaking water tower will come into view, how it will float over the town's roofs, how it will sink away again as the train reaches the station.

And here is that familiar little pavilion, which no amount of fresh advertising or smart benches can dress with modernity – a place that will forever welcome her with a loaded baggage carousel of association. Whatever else may happen here, it will always be the venue for every awkward arrival and departure that characterised the middle years, after relations had been re-established but remained dangerously undernourished. He always met her, but never dropped her off – a habit that seemed emblematic of what a finite resource his hospitality was, of how much the welcome seemed to dwindle as the weekends wore on. When it was over, after the latest in a long line of botched conclusions, this was where she would end up, always early for the train beyond all precaution. She would smoke in the face of Sunday evening, fronting up to the bad feeling. She would drink on the train. When she got back into town, she would feel the rush and warmth of the city, with all its people, and start plotting to destabilise someone's night, and working out who to call with her irresistible offer of abandon.

She steps on to the platform, and into the smell – something zesty and timeless like samphire, moderated as usual by the weight of soil and manure. She snares the only taxi in the rank, and directs its incredulous driver to Wreaking. She can see him watching her in the rear-view mirror, trying to work out what her business is – whether it's legit, or whether she's up to something she shouldn't be.

'Here?' he says, at the gates.

'Here.' She is surprised by a feeling that is not just excitement, but – really? Yes: it's pride.

The taxi driver is still looking at her with suspicion as he takes her money. As she gets out, a blue Renault 5 speeds away down the hill.

She doesn't stop to peer into the boarded-up lodge, or clock the gatepost griffins. She ignores the long stare of the driveway. She doesn't even try the gates. Instead, she flings her bag round the side of the tight ranks of iron bars and through a gap so familiar she could find it with both eyes gone. This is her resolution: to keep moving, and take new angles of attack.

Her fingertips stray on the trunks of beeches and oaks, on thickets of diseased sycamore. She finds that she knows individual trees, can make out how they have changed. Here is the conifer that grew in a crazy U-shape thanks to the proximity of an adjacent tree that had since been felled, leaving an appealing seat that you could lie in and watch the sky. Here is the giant beech where Roland tried to hang a swing, and up there is the wisp that remains from the moment the rope snapped and sent him crashing into a laurel. The heartbreak of things changing. The heartbreak of things staying the same.

The closer she gets to Revenant House, the more she can smell the too-still, pond murk of that summer: an atmosphere nurturing of subaqueous fronds, and creatures that favour stagnation. He used to boast that the lake had its own unique ecosystem, and now that she is back she remembers having seen plants and animals here that she has never seen anywhere else: towering golden rods, pungent mushrooms, and, if you disturbed the earth in the right places, nests of slow-worms that writhed obscenely in the soil.

To further delay her arrival, she veers off in the direction of the vegetable garden, and finds the grounded, overgrown relic that is the tomato bus. Its yellow paint has cracked off, and the plants inside have all but devoured the vehicle. Now, it's a bus-shaped forest on piles of brick. Only the *aking* can be made out on its side panelling, in curly, seaside lettering. She finds the door and forces it open. The tomatoes are planted in wooden boxes on the cream-coloured plastic seats, but it's impossible to tell now where any individual plant begins or ends. Most of the plants have yet to bear fruit but she can see one or two that look ripe enough. She picks one from near the door, twisting it away and rubbing it against her front. She brings it to her mouth, punctures the skin with her incisor and sucks a rush of seeds and juice and flesh into her mouth. She stares into the leaves, lost in the sweetness and savour of the tomato.

A smell of rotting draws her away from the bus and over to the chicken coop, which is in a terrible state. The feathered lumps of two birds remain, sinking into pecked mud and scrub – the ones too emaciated to be worth picking off. She puts her head around the door of the outhouse feed-store nearby, and sees a rat's tail slithering into a sack of corn.

The house keys are hot in her left palm. She lets them drop into the outside pocket of her jacket as she walks round the lake. Creatures fillip, breaking the surface. Quick darts of activity in the slow-moving organism. She tries not to look too early, but it's no good. There, presiding over the water, is Revenant House, with its white gables, its high windows, its lawn and pavilions. Its condition has worsened shockingly even since her last visit. The burnt-out side is now a proper ruin with trees growing through it, blurring its edges. It looks like the haunted house of a dead plantation owner.

She arrives at the front door, trying desperately not to

join the dots of past and present. There are countless painful changes and deteriorations, countless stumbling blocks tagged with memory. She must resist them, or the house will barge in and mess with her intentions. Just looking at the base of the boot scraper, she sees Oliver asking what it was one hot, hectic afternoon, and hears their laughter as he plonked his foot down and snapped the thing off. She remembers his look of dread as he realised he'd broken something else, and Roland frowning as he knelt to put it right, but made things worse because he was too strong. She told them it didn't matter, and the three of them went foraging inside and found nothing to eat but crackers and jam. She looks at the bell push, and remembers it getting stuck one morning when her father was trying to work, and his temper going off, and having to take a book and hide in Wreaking until it had all blown over. She reaches into her pocket and brings out the fist of keys.

She has never even known this door to be closed, let alone locked. After some effort, she shoves it open. The porch's parquet floor moves in all the right places as she steps forward. The smell of his house: damp apples, musty clothes, boot mud. If it was autumn there'd be a box of rotting fruit round here somewhere that you could blame for that smell, but it's not, it's springtime, all cut grass and dew, and that orchard-rot smell is here all year round. She draws it in deeply, then looks beyond the threshold into the hall, at the umbrella stand he made from an old sharps disposal bin. His walking stick stands among the brollies, its silver spaniel's head top worn away over years by the pressure of his palm. She touches it, conscious already of the reassurance she is deriving from the physicality of the building, from its smells, from the fact that things are where they should be. Her defences are crumbling and she hasn't got beyond the porch.

She leaves her bag outside and advances on to the hall

carpet. She contemplates its flowers, taking strange comfort in their harsh curls, their dangerous toxic waves, which have never stopped seeming otherworldly to her. The smell in here: dust, food, damp. And, somewhere, him. Some hint of aftershave, sweat and scalp. This is what remains.

'My deepest condolences to you,' said the policeman, on the phone.

This was the first call. The news it contained was strong, unsweetened, a shot of strangeness that arrived as she stood there, in her apartment, assessing her new furniture, trying to work out what was happening. Phone clamped to the side of her head, because this is how big things happen now, they arrive through hot little objects in your hand. The news seemed both perfectly in keeping with the prevailing levels of weirdness and also to be a kind of bracing antidote to them, because what was more unreal, or more real, than this?

'My God,' she said. 'You did that well.'

The policeman was young. Maybe it was even his first time doing anything like that. It felt important to praise him for it.

'Really?' he said, unable to hide his pride.

'Really. That was a very difficult thing to do, and you did it brilliantly.'

'Well, I am sorry. Would you like more details now, or would you like to spend some time taking it in, and then call me back?'

'More time,' she said. 'I'll call you back. If that's convenient.'

'Anytime,' he said.

Her bright, empty flat had lost all relevance. Even with its new dining table and new artwork, it was the most banal place in the world. She looked again at the painting, getting up close to examine the brushstrokes that went into the composition of the water. She went to her wardrobe and took out the holdall she uses for smaller trips away, set it out on the bed, then thought again and got out a larger suitcase. She returned to the kitchen for her phone, and called the policeman back.

'Sorry – me again,' she said.

'That was quick.'

'I couldn't think of anything else to do.'

He cleared his throat. 'What else would you like to know?'

'I guess, how did he get there?' she said. 'That far down the Ness. It's nearly three miles long, isn't it?'

'He wasn't quite at the end,' said the policeman. 'But you're right – it's a mystery. He was a tough old man, but there's no way he could have done it by himself, given the state he was in. The short answer is, we don't know. I'll tell you one thing, though – we'd much like to speak to whoever it was who placed the 999 call from the phone box on the seafront. We wondered whether you might be able to help us there.'

'Me?'

'We've literally no idea how to find her, and she said some things that suggested you might know who she is.'

'Like what?'

'Like, *Tell Cleo I'm sorry.*'

'Yeah. I see what you mean.'

They laughed at that, before both wondering whether it was appropriate, and stopping abruptly. Assuming a more businesslike tone, he said that if it was okay with her, he would get an undertaker to call her, to take her through *the options*. After the call ended, she folded up the piece of paper on which she'd written the policeman's number, and put it in her purse.

She was packing when the undertaker rang. What did you

pack? She normally knows what to pack in any given situation, but this one was tricky. You resorted to learned behaviour. That was what you did. You read the manual that was out there, in books and films, in the way that people were said to behave.

'I am sorry about all this,' said the undertaker.

'Everybody keeps saying that. There's no need. It's not your fault,' she said brightly, realising as she said it that she didn't have to put on an optimistic voice for him, because he dealt with miserable people all the time.

'We don't have to cover all the arrangements now,' he said. 'I just wanted to introduce myself, and let you know that you can take your time. There's no great rush.'

'No rush?' she said. Which forced the man to be more specific about what he meant. Her father, he said, is *on ice*. He wasn't making light of it, but there was a sense that if she had wanted to crack a joke at that point, the option was there. He was good for it. She let the moment pass. She didn't feel quite the same connection she had felt with the policeman.

'Just get in contact when you're in the area, and we can talk about whether or not you want to come and see him, and how to take things from there. It's completely up to you how we proceed.'

There were still things to be done to organise her temporary exit from normal life. A period of reckoning was due, and its terms had to be drawn up. Which meant calling Emma at work. She dreaded this, because she feared that Emma would bring out her dead husband again, and try to imply some sort of kinship in grief, which was the last thing she wanted to navigate. Luckily, Emma had decided in advance that comforting practicality was the order of the day.

'So you'll drive down there?' she said.

'No,' said Cleo, fiddling with her eye and totting up in her head the number of times she has told Emma over the years that she doesn't drive. 'I'll get the train.'

'Quite right,' said Emma. 'Driving's probably not a good idea in your condition. And you're sure you wouldn't like me to come with you?'

'I'm sure, but thanks. Just don't give my job away while I'm gone.'

Cleo thinks she's tough. Thinks she knows. But how will she fare when it's *real*? The editing suite has shown her how the worst bit of death is the way life accommodates it. The way that those who are left behind tidy up the bodies and carry on. It's always the most chilling part of the execution – the way the hangman carries on moving, or the lethal injector, or the man in the mask who bends down to busy himself with slashing the throat. One carries on, one does not. And the one who does had better not have anything they wish they had said or done differently when the moment has passed. But it isn't like that for them, is it? For her and her *late* father. Because they were realistic about their affection for one another, and always have been. That was when it struck: the sudden terror that all this time she has been telling herself the two of them didn't get on so that it would be easier to see him leave.

She's known women whose proximity to their fathers is a primary form of sustenance. Declaring it to the world gives them definition. Whatever disappointments and failures life may throw at them, they always have that crutch to lean on: at least *he* never let me down. The trait is all the more pronounced, of course, in those whose fathers are dead. Cleo has seen it in friends and colleagues with lost parents, and lost fathers in particular. They bow their heads in showy remembrance whenever the abstract idea of fatherhood comes up in conversation – remembrance that becomes a form of demonstrative communion, intended to transmit, to all who may be watching, the message that *nobody knew him like I did*. Will this be the moment when she becomes one of those people? She can't imagine herself in that mould. But she is afraid of finding out that she will miss him after all. That she miscalculated badly on this one. That she was, even to an extent, Daddy's Girl.

His coats and jackets in the hall are stained: every one in the row has horizontal streaks of brown and yellow across its tails and arse. The stains are tough and hardened. She wonders to herself what on earth they might be, but cannot bring herself to smell them.

Why wait. One by one she unhooks each garment and lays it down on the floor. Each is familiar, heavy with association. Each gives up a powerful blast of his smell as she breaks its hanging shape and pats it down on the floor. The quilted green one, branch-torn, impregnated with bonfire smoke. The tweed walking jacket, with acorns and cobnuts in its pockets to be poked into the ground with his stick when he was on the move. There's one of hers, too, hidden, flattened against the wall: a pink Puffa she wore the year they came here.

She is ambushed by his fishing waders. The sight of them, and of the shoulder straps with three of his brightly feathered, hand-tied flies still attached – it's a gut punch. She sees herself down in the underwater room, watching her father's shadow teeter clumsily on the surface of the glass above them as he tried to fish, and remembers how hard she laughed when he slipped into the water, rubber trousers filling up and dragging him down. The waders seem to contain an invisible version of their former occupant. They are holding out for a shape that no longer exists.

She is shaking. She squats low on the carpet, staring into

the space between her knees. She has been protected until now, but in minutes the past has undone her.

There is a noise: the soft drop of something down the wall. Her eye just catches the rush of a mouse. Somehow her legs find the energy to right her. She walks over slowly to check behind the sharps-bin umbrella stand to make sure she was right, and sees the tiny, quivering ball. She moves away to let it calm down. She is grateful to the mouse for snapping away her attention.

She sits on a stair, watching a cobweb flutter in air she has newly disturbed, and an amount of time goes by. She doesn't know how much. She is just being here again, allowing the atmosphere of the place in, accepting the inevitability of the feelings that will come. Facing down the whole house like this will take forever. She needs to take his best shot right now, while she's still strong. She flicks on light switches, and strides down the hall to his study – as if it were a case of putting up a front to the building, of showing it who's boss.

It has several names: Diogenes syndrome, or syllogomania, or squalor syndrome: the loss of the ability to throw things away. She knows about it because of a feature she edited where they could barely get the cameras into the guy's house because it was stacked to the ceiling with decades of yellowing newspapers. The loss of the distinction between rubbish and possessions. The inability to abstract. The insistence on every object's value. The absolute embodiment of the truth that being able to forget is a *very good thing*.

At the centre of the room is what must be his desk, but it can't be seen properly because everywhere, there is paper. Toppling stacks. Swirls and eddies. Patient records, his own writing, magazine clippings, newsprint. You'd think the room had been used as some kind of dump but for the fact of his armchair in the middle, and a channel, a route through the mess that must have been his animal track in and out. On the arm of the chair is the book he was reading, its bookmark painfully halted, never to proceed. The oxygen concentrator squats nearby. Its long plastic hose snakes away from the machine and loops over the chair's other arm, hooked into place over a knife that is embedded in the upholstery. So that he wouldn't lose it. She sees his coping mechanisms, and guilt throbs inside her.

'I want to talk to you about my will,' he said, sometime last year.

'I don't want to talk about that,' she said. 'It's maudlin.'

'It's not a long conversation. But it's important. One minute someone's walking around and talking, and able to keep you abreast of their wishes. The next, they're an object, without any wishes at all.'

'For God's sake.'

'Just listen. All I want to tell you is that if I die suddenly, you'll find it. My will.'

'Where?'

'It will be obvious. It will be lying around.'

'Where?'

'In the study.'

She has to try and concentrate on one fixed point, or the scale of the mess will overwhelm her. Her eyes centre in on the fresh pad that sits in front of the armchair, and on his silver pen that sits on its top, throbbing with harm. He may be gone, but this pen probably has a half-life of thousands of years. She thinks of touching it, even of daring to pick it up, but is not quite ready for that.

And then, floating up out of the mess, there it is: an envelope, addressed to her. In his handwriting. That might be the will, or might be something more powerful. It's recently written. She has a strong suspicion that the best thing to do when it comes to this envelope is to keep it near her and live in hope. To let her unconscious write its contents for her. *Let's not look at this now*, she thinks. *Let's maybe never look at it at all.*

Behind the chair, on the wall, familiar boxes are stacked. The boxes he used to take back and forth to the high streets of towns on Saturday afternoons, hawking his self-published books. The two completed ones were called *Babylonia* and *Insomnia Ward*, and here they are, in stacks of brittle, yellowing volumes. She sat and read them dutifully once. Now she finds she can hardly remember them at all. She picks one from the carton and opens it, to find handwriting between the printed lines, in a variety of inks. Checking another, she finds a different set of edits, made at some other time. How long did he spend in here, going over himself like this?

She knows that in this room are the best clues she will ever have, but the thought of having to plough through it all in search of him is exhausting. It feels like a puzzle she hasn't the will to solve. This is the time when she should be getting to know her quirky, difficult old man, and finding out that he had a heart of gold in spite of one or two rough edges. She's just not that sure she can be bothered. She drops the books into their box, closes the flap with the toe of her shoe and leaves the room, pulling the door shut.

41

She climbs the stairs to her attic bedroom to find much of it in pieces, its constituent parts giving the impression of an exploded diagram. Even the bed is half dismantled. Some boxes of things remain, but the room isn't how she remembers it. There are long-forgotten toys. There are childhood objects that she feels she has never seen before, as if someone had put them up here to trigger false memory. There are notes from Roland and Oliver that revive long-dead jokes and arrangements. There are handwritten letters addressed to her father that explain why *this time* she has run away for good. It all seems so melodramatic now.

She remembers. She is allowing herself to, for what feels like the first time (though of course it is not). How Roland stepped out of the fabric of the building and stopped her hand. How the three of them bled into one another, slowly at first, then urgently rushing to get combined. The effect that had on her father. And how the resulting unstable compound finally combusted one September day that refuses to be seen clearly, and changes with every new attempt she makes to recall it.

It starts with her staring into the Decision Mirror and thinking of her mother. Her new mother. The only-just-deceased mother; the locked-away mother; the banshee who wasn't even good enough for the attic. Not the gentle ghost on the bright metal train, nor the angel too long past to be remembered with anything but love. This mother was more recent, and might have been available to her all this time, or some of it, had it not been for someone thinking he knew better. The conversations they could have had!

She positioned the mirror's shadows over her eyes, her chest rising and falling with dark energy. All this time, Cleo had been talking to her mother as if she were dead and therefore somehow within reach. And all this time, she wasn't. He had let her believe that. And now he wouldn't even talk to her about it, because the Revenant House fire had burned off the last few flecks of pride he had left.

And today, this was her decision: not to let it go. Not to let him get away with it. Because he'd had more than enough years in hiding, and it was time for him to stand up and justify himself. And if he even dreamed of saying that he had done it for her, rather than just admitting that he was weak, and couldn't face doing anything else – if he did that, then she would stand right there before him and say it to his face: *liar*.

A handful of gravel sprayed the bathroom window. She looked out and saw Oliver at the front door, holding a bag of shopping in one hand and a can in the other. She flung out her arm in a frantic, repelling gesture. Nothing he loved more than creating agitation. He set off on a calm, convincing saunter towards the front door, which made her slap the window, and mouth as violent a *Fuck off* as she could manage in silence. His shrug and the swig of his cider that followed were a calculated threat, and when he walked off in the direction of Wreaking she knew she had to follow him or he'd be back.

'You must be mental,' she said.

He sat on a wheelchair ramp leading up to the ward entrance, his legs dangling into a ragged clump of nettles. One spent, crushed can was beside him on the concrete, alongside its open successor. His hands were down in the nettles, picking around for any flowers that remained so that he could raise them to his mouth. Sucking nettle nectar was something he had taught her at the start of the summer. How you twisted off the little white blooms without getting stung. Which bulbous bit of them you had to graze with your front teeth in order to free their cargo. The way the morsel of plant matter when you nibbled was followed by a tiny burst of sweetness. At the time it had felt like precious, secret knowledge. Today, it was the posturing gimmick of a boy.

'What?'

'I said, are you mental? Coming here. He thinks you burned half his house down.'

Those pale blue eyes. The distance they could generate when required. When someone dared to oppose him. When he became sufficiently aware of, and interested by, an opponent.

He held her gaze, and sniffed up a drip from the end of his nose. 'That's what he thinks, is it? Because of what – because he doesn't like me? Maybe I should go in there and have a word.'

'Don't even think about it. I want to talk to him myself, about stuff that actually *matters*, and I don't need you around making things more complicated.'

'What am I supposed to do in the meantime?'

'You can wait. I'll meet you over here in a bit.'

Now there was a smile. 'And what if I get bored?'

'Then you can drink.'

'And then what?'

'Then I'll be back.'

That was what he did. He held his boredom over you like a threat. And she knew him well enough by now to know that the threat was real.

'Before I go,' she said, 'where's Roland?'

'Stuff to do. Carol's in a state, or something.'

'Right.'

He took a long swig from his can and kicked at the rusting nettles. 'What? Don't you believe me?'

She took a longer way home than was necessary, trying to rebuild her determination. Rediscover her outrage. She let herself imagine the compound lies that had accumulated over the years. She ran through all the questions she was going to insist he answer, and promised herself she wouldn't leave him until he did. *Where do you get off letting me take the blame for a made-up version of my own mother's death? How many girlfriends did you get through while she was still alive and locked away?*

At least it explained his panicked relapses in the old days, whenever someone couldn't handle him and left. He defaulted back to Cleo's mother because, for all of his temporary amnesia, she had never gone away. She felt foolish. She felt behind. All this time she had been denied key information, not just by him but by Ursula too, who wasn't even part of it. Everyone laughing at her, at her small thoughts, at what she didn't know.

She skipped contemptuously over the flower-mines of the hall carpet, through the blank, self-reflective corridor of empty noticeboard cabinets. She saw the light in his study, and rehearsed some of her bigger questions. *Did it never occur to you that I might have wanted to meet her? That remembering my mother was something I'd have liked?* The study light drew closer. She stepped forward, unsure of her objective beyond knowing that she wanted something to happen that could never be undone.

He might be asleep. She opened the door, and knew quickly that he was anything but. Even from behind the chair she could see that he was scratching away with his pen, doing a sort of muttering thing he sometimes did in here. There was an enclosed fug in the room, of old coffee and damp wood. A log hissed in the grate. Her footfalls made floorboards creak. Constellations of afternoon dust were lit up above his head, and his thin red hair stuck up, as if both hair and particles were charged, under the control of some unseen force.

In the memory, she rounds the chair and there he is. She is rounding the chair still. She is always reaching the front of the chair, and his red hair. The red hair. The green chair. *If you loved her so much why lock her up? If you hated me so much why not get rid of me and keep her?* The tilt of the head as she saw him hearing her, and the soft thud as he dropped the pen on to the pad.

He didn't even look up. He just carried on staring down at the useless, idiotic page in front of him, working an old button around between his teeth and lips. And what *was* his work anyway, when it came to it?

'Can I ask you something? I'm sorry to bother you, but it won't take long.'

'I'm working, Cleo,' he said, in his most infuriating, patronising-parental voice. A voice determined to put all recent events neatly behind them. 'Can't it wait until later?'

'I want to ask you something. It's important.' Red-faced, determined, a little out of breath. Ready to hold him to ransom, just like Oliver held people to ransom. Happy to do it, if that was what it took to get what she came here for.

'Ask me later.'

At this point in the memory, more recent levels of sympathy threaten to direct things, and she has to remind herself that at this point his health was not compromised. This was not an invalid with an oxygen machine, but a dangerous, unpredictable force. She remembers the fear as she approached the chair that he might just drop the pen and come at her. And she knows that the fear was real, because she feels it still.

'But I might not want to later.'

'You'll be the same person, won't you?'

'Dad, can I just—'

'PLEASE. Why do you have to be so selfish?'

His eyes locked on to hers for one dangerous moment. She turned and took careful steps out of the room, concentrating on her breathing, trying to stay upright in the flood of new chemicals that were surging into her brain. Trying to understand what he had just made her do.

All he had to do was say *yes*. She knows that her hostility would have melted away. Her first question would have been something wonderful that surprised even her, like: *Will you please accept my apology?* They would have talked properly about all the things they were meant to be talking about. And she would have explained to him that she was not cross with him any more, and that she understood why he had done what he did. But no.

Try again later, he seemed to be saying. *There will always be another chance for us to patch things up. The moment will always come again.*

And this part is very clear: the way she thought to herself as she walked to the door – *Oh yeah?*

Light shines through the broken shutters, throwing jagged patches on to the bathroom floor. The fittings are full of dead flies. The thick, enamelled bath is dusty. A low tide of murky water sits in the toilet bowl. On a table is a pile of creased, watermarked copies of the *Milan Review*, so that he could enjoy the fruits of his brief editorship at leisure when he sat in here. There are mustard-yellow streaks on his towels that she doesn't even want to think about.

She finds the Decision Mirror leaning against a wall, facing away from the room. She pulls at the top of it, and hears the slump of falling glass as she slowly inches it round. The mirror is cracked into segments, and shards have fallen away, but much of its surface is still intact. The hours she spent staring at this thing. She pauses for a while looking at herself, mildly shocked by how she now looks in it, as if she hadn't seen herself at all since the last time she stood in this room.

She chucks the towels on to the landing in a heap, intending to burn them. Maybe she'll burn it all. She feels an urge to fire up the great boiler cylinders over at Wreaking, and feed the entire contents of this house into its gaping mouth, until it is flaying her face just to look at it. And this thought gives her a shove. Not wanting to waste more time, she storms downstairs and outside to look for wood to fire up the range. In the kitchen she cleans out the air intakes and empties the ash pan, then she lights a clumsy, choking fire. Patiently she builds the flames and listens to the hums and clanks of the house as it wakes up. When enough time has passed she heads back to the bathroom with some detergent and a scrubbing brush and turns the hot tap.

The sound is as if someone has shot the house in the heart: the thunk of a depth charge hitting the hull of a submarine. Followed by a lurching creak as the vessel rolls over. Then the sound of an orchestra tuning up to a note bending upwards to a note and coming into a great single humming NOTE in the pipes. Cleo lets the brown water run for a while hoping it will go clearer, but it's obvious this is as good as things are going to get so she heaves the brass handle that drops the plug in its cage – no risky lengths of chain in this building.

When the taps are running and steam is creeping across what remains of the scabby, pockmarked mirror, she opens the wall cupboard looking for soap, and finds his shaving kit: the razor, caked with cells; the sandalwood soap bowl; the brush. The exoticism of his shaving brush always fascinated her: its perfumed smell; the lettering on its base, worn away by years of brisk morning lathering, that reads *Real Badger*, the flecks of matter adhering to the hair – *brock hair*, he'd called it – hair that is now frozen into the shape in which it was left by the last swipe he ever made across his face.

She picks up each shaving item in turn, and sets them down on the corner of the bath, looking down through the gaps in the shutters at the front door, where her bag is still standing in the porch. She could swear she hadn't undone the zip. And is it her imagination, or is it facing a different direction to the one she left it in?

That first day she stood in the gloom of the doorway staring up at a window on this floor and saw someone calmly regarding her. Tonight she stands here looking back at the fearless, curious girl she was then, the skinny girl with her canvas trainers and her tatty jeans, and she wonders whether what she saw then was the ghost of her future self. She wants to wave but she knows that if she breaks her concentration by moving, that girl will be gone.

She undresses and gets in the bath with the taps still running, lying flat to get under as much of the warm, stained water as she can. The steam highlights the dusty light beams that burst through holes in the broken shutters, as if someone has been hacking at them with an axe. She is unconsciously keeping her leg out of their path, as if the light might cause her to singe like a movie vampire.

Do you want my bath?

No, I can't be bothered getting wet.

The ritual of passing on their bathwater, because the range only warmed so much. Calling down one to the other when you got out: she thinks of it now, watching the water rise. She remembers how she would refrain from shaving her legs if he had announced his intention to get in after her. Except when she was cross with him. Then she would shave them anyway, and perform so many other ablutions that by the time she came to hand it over, the water was a porridge of soap and scum and hair. Once or twice she peed in it as well.

She stares at the shaving brush perched precariously on the corner of the bath. She wonders how many of his skin cells are contained within it. She picks it up and holds it to her face, turning it, smelling it. She replaces it on the side of the bath. Then quickly, with the back of her hand, as if she were trying to pretend she hadn't meant to do it, she knocks the brush sideways and into the water. The hairs wave. The last flecks of soap disperse. The heat liquefies what remains, soaking the shape of that final swipe away. She retrieves the brush and whisks it round in the water, watching old soap cloud between her thighs. She lathers up with his shaving bowl, and begins scraping away at her strong, peppery leg hairs.

She didn't return to Oliver straight away. She knew he was waiting, but she also knew what seeing him in isolation would entail, and wanted something else beforehand, some pause in the afternoon's momentum. So she went up to the wardrobe where she knew her father kept her mother's clothes. Where, she now knew, he came whenever he needed a fresh button to pop in his mouth, a moth in search of fetish-food.

She looked through the garments, hoping for some

sustaining clue, some message that she could seize on and take out into the world. There was nothing. It was just a rack of musty old clothes. She might as well have been browsing a charity shop. She selected a fitted white shirt and a pair of jeans. She pulled on the jeans, zipped them up, moved her legs a little to settle into them. She put on the shirt, checking in advance to make sure it still had its buttons. She finished things off with a green silk scarf that she tied around her neck. She left the house and set off into bright, cold sunshine.

She knew it wouldn't take long to find him. This was not Roland. Sure enough, a sequence of deep, wobbling booms created a sonic trail to the kitchens. After checking a couple of walk-in chiller units, she found Oliver standing in the middle of a cavernous, white-tiled space vacated by the removal of some large-scale catering equipment. He was throwing rocks at a metal cage set in a blue dish that hung on a chain from the ceiling – what remained of an industrial-sized insect zapper, a great chandelier of death, presiding over the food preparation areas.

Oliver's head snapped round as he heard her coming in. He saw her, and dropped the stone in his hand.

'You look older,' he said.

'Do you like it?'

'What do *you* think?'

Without taking his eyes off her he rummaged in his bag and chucked a can of cider in her direction. She caught it clumsily, and held it out in front of her as she opened it so as not to get spray on her mother's clothes.

They ended up in a loft space above the laundry. The floorboards were laid in light that burst up in thin, scorching lines along the length of the room. Swallows chattered and hovered about their heads in protection of their nests.

He made a crude pile of laundry bags for them to lie on,

and with the familiar tools of cider and cheap vodka, they fell to their usual, urgent business. Oliver unpicked the buttons of the shirt with fascination, as if he thought he really was going to find an adult woman inside. She kissed his smoky, boozy mouth. She was ready to do whatever he wanted, just so that she didn't have to keep thinking about the failure of her grand confrontation. But he could tell that she wasn't interested, and that interested him.

'Now then,' he said, taking his hands away and sitting back. 'Something's just happened over there, and I think you better tell me what it is.'

She buttoned herself up. 'It's been happening for some time.'

And this was how she first came to tell the truth about her father to someone else. Or some of it, anyway. Oliver sat in silence, relishing every detail.

'Ha!' he finally said. 'That explains one or two things.'

'Yup,' she said, and drank.

'So what does he want from you? What's his problem, exactly?'

'Who knows? Maybe it's not the sort of thing you can try to explain. I haven't told you half the messed up things he's done, because I've been trying to be loyal to him.'

'Like what?'

'Like he poured paint all over me when I was asleep. Like he tried to draw a mole on my face when he was drunk to make me look more like my mother.'

'Seriously?'

'Seriously. Stop laughing. It wasn't funny.'

'Well,' said Oliver. 'If it's his wife he wants, I think his wife is what you should give him. It's getting cold out here. Can't we go back to your house for some food? Maybe watch television, or something? The things people do?'

She stood up. 'I suppose so. But let's stay out of his way. I don't think he's very predictable.'

Inside, they stood in the silent hallway, looking down the corridor towards his study door.

Cleo spoke quietly. 'You want food, then?'

'Course not,' said Oliver. 'Show me the clothes.'

She was climbing slowly up the stairs, trying to minimise the sound of her footfalls, when he overtook her two steps at a time.

'In here?' he said, steaming down the landing.

'Wait,' she said. 'I don't think we should.'

But he had already thrown open the relevant door and she could hear him inside, going at every cupboard and drawer he could find. They were soon standing together in front of the open wardrobe. For the first time, she felt she was getting some kind of personality off these clothes. She thought they felt scared.

'You know the way he often has a button in his mouth? Well it turns out they come from in here. He's been nibbling away at little bits of my mother, all this time.'

Dishing the dirt on him felt good. She wanted this. Wanted Oliver in on his nasty little secrets.

'Fucking weirdo,' said Oliver, holding up a pretty blue summer dress to his front and turning in the light to see how it might suit him.

'Let's go. We shouldn't be in here.'

'Why not? These are yours as much as they are his. More, probably. I'm serious. If it's your mum he wants, then maybe that's what you should give him.' Now he was trying on a long, red skirt. 'Wear her clothes. Do your hair like hers. Draw on the damn beauty spot. See how he likes that.'

She laughed. 'Don't be an idiot.'

'Seriously.' He turned in her direction, holding a straw hat over his head, and pouting. 'Don't you think it would be interesting?'

Which was how he came to be standing behind her in front of the Decision Mirror, watching her make herself up, the half-bottle of vodka on the counter beside them. She could feel the heat of him behind her. Could smell smoke on him, and boy's sweat.

'I don't see the point of this,' she said, when she had applied lipstick and eyeshadow as best she knew how.

He turned her round slowly, ready with the eyeliner pencil, a look of concentration on his face. 'Just tell me again where that mole was, will you?'

'Where's Roland?' she asked, trying to catch his eye.

'Keep still,' he said. 'Or this might hurt you.'

42

Roland drives in silence, which is all you can do when the van is going flat out, with its bellow, its rattle, its worrying smell. He is smoking with the windows closed, alternately ashing on his own thigh and punching it, as memories surface of things he wishes hadn't happened. Victor being the latest, and most pressing. He glances down at Victor's briefcase on the passenger seat, at its busted chains, and exhales heavily.

Nice to get out of town, though. He never was built for the city. He can feel his pulse slowing the minute he leaves. He likes big skies. The sight of magpies bouncing in fields with twigs in their beaks. The way a jay sometimes falls messily out of a hedgerow, like it's being ejected from a nightclub.

Nightclubs. Victor. Shit.

He pulls off the motorway and into a service station, coasting the van to its usual, unnerving, *will-it-won't-it* stop. Inside, he finds a payphone near some kids playing on video games, and checks to make sure he isn't on CCTV before making the call.

'There's a man trapped in a shipping container under some railway arches,' he says, when he's been put through to the relevant emergency service. 'You should get there fast, 'cause he isn't all that well.' He gives the address.

'I don't suppose you're going to tell us who we have to thank for this information?'

'When you find him, I imagine it will be the first name on his lips.'

'I see. Crisis of conscience, is it?'

'Feel free to have a look around when you're there. See what you see. No telling what might be lying around.'

And that is that. Whatever they find in there, Roland's bridges are burned. Before leaving the service station, he checks a large plastic bin behind the restaurant for any on-date food, but finds it empty. On the way back to the car, he passes a couple who are arguing over which one of them is going to pick up the shit their dog has just done on the verge, leaving coffee and a bag of croissants on the roof of their car. Which at least gives him something to be going on with during the next leg of his journey.

But placing the call wasn't enough. As he guns the van up to speed, and prepares to get back on the road, his thoughts turn inevitably to Oliver. He'd know what to do in this situation. Or, at least, he'd say that he knew, which would be almost as good.

He looked different. That was the first thing. The disarming beauty of his, which had saved him on so many occasions when it looked like he might finally be held to account for something – it had left him. Even from a distance, when Roland was arriving at the campsite and saw the figure in the torn T-shirt shambling out from under the pine trees to greet him, he could tell. He knew what that walk was supposed to look like – knew it better than any other, probably – and this wasn't right. It was still Oliver, but when he got up close, his eyes were set in hollows so deep that they looked like bruises, and his energy seemed now to be spent in repetitive tics instead of the compulsive bursts that had characterised him before. Was it geography that had done it? Being too far away from Victor, or some other source of confidence at home? Or was it just being too close to whatever it was he had been doing out here? Maybe it was something simpler and more inevitable to do with running out of time.

They had spoken to sort out the arrangements, which involved Roland calling the site reception desk from the phone box near Victor's tunnels, and hoping someone English-speaking would answer. When the babbling voice came on, Roland realised how much he had missed it.

'I should warn you, you're going to throw up with jealousy when you see this place. I never even have to leave. All I have to do is be around to fix stuff when it goes wrong. Which is fine, because to be quite honest with you I wouldn't *want* to be anywhere else. We're right on the beach here, with clubhouse, restaurant, you name it. Basically, I'm on permanent holiday.'

You had to take a train down the coast to get to the resort from the airport. Roland hadn't been abroad much before, which was possibly the reason why the journey reminded him not of one of his own memories, but of the stories Cleo used to tell about her mother and the witch's curse. He remembers sitting there, trying not to think about her. It was a painful time to consider the past, because at this point he had no idea where Cleo was.

On the plus side, business with Victor was taking off, and it was starting to look as if, with a little dedication, and the shedding of one or two scruples, they could make some serious money. Part of Roland's job in coming here was to tell Oliver that it still wasn't a good idea for him to return home, without letting him realise that they had come to that conclusion for the good of the business, as much as for Oliver's safety. He had been away for nearly a year, and even though Roland hated Victor for pointing it out, it was undeniable that with him gone they were making more progress. Things were more professional. Less inclined to hysteria. With Oliver around, things turned agitated far too quickly. Which was, of course, how he came to be in trouble in the first place.

The site, which comprised fourteen six-berth tents with self-catering annexes, was one of several dotted up and down this coastline that were run as franchises by the individuals in charge – meaning that in theory, any profits that Oliver made went straight to him personally.

It smelled of piss under the pine trees. The toilet block, which was the only brick-built construction on the site, had to occupy a central position, equidistant from every tent, so that nobody could complain about being too far from the facilities. There was a bar area built of wood with a thatched roof, a cluster of picnic tables in a central clearing and a reception hut where Oliver hung out during the day, fielding complaints to do with missing crockery or unsafe appliances or insufficient soap.

'Do you like the name of the bar?' said Oliver, dumping Roland's bag in the dirt and pointing to a handwritten sign above his head. *GOLDEN SANDS.*

'Nice,' said Roland.

'You'll be staying in my tent,' he said. 'But they're big, so you needn't worry. It won't be too intimate.'

'Nothing I haven't seen before.'

'Food? Drink?'

'Food. Water. Please.'

They sat at one of the picnic benches. It was hot. The sound of children and families enjoying the afternoon filtered through from the beach. Oliver went over to the bar area, where UHT milk was stacked in a shrink-wrapped cube on a pallet. He pulled a brick of milk from the stack, snipped off its corner and brought it to the table with two plastic tumblers and a bottle of rum. He poured himself a large glass, then added a spike of rum and left the top off the bottle. Roland helped himself to water from the tap.

'Sure you don't want a drink? You don't have to have what I'm having.'

'I've given up booze,' said Roland, trying to find a way of saying it that didn't sound preachy.

'Why?' said Oliver.

'I just don't want to any more.'

'Bloody hell, you must be hungrier than ever.' He went back to the bar, opened a chest freezer and pulled up a plastic sack labelled *Tapas*, which he slashed open with a Stanley knife before shaking its contents into a deep fryer. Roland ate steadily as they talked from the ensuing plateful of ham and cheese croquettes.

'They're not bad, are they?' said Oliver, not touching a single one.

As afternoon wore on into evening, families came and went from the beach, occasionally requiring something from Oliver, who barely bothered to conceal his irritation at being interrupted. His one concession to their appearance was to put the rum under the table. Later he pulled a second brick of milk from the pallet, and moved on to whisky.

'All I need is a bit more capital, and this place could really take off,' he said. 'I don't suppose you can help me?'

'What could you do that you aren't already doing?' said Roland.

'Are you having a laugh? Proper restaurant with a barbecue, maybe put in a swimming pool, more room for motorhomes – all sorts of stuff.' He plunged his cigarette into the mound of butts in the red plastic ashtray on the table, and pulled another from the packet. Roland lit it for him, which created a natural pause in the conversation.

'I know you probably think it's something we've talked about enough,' said Roland. 'But I want to ask you about Cleo.'

Oliver took a big drink, and looked away. 'What about her?'

'Excuse me,' said a voice with a German accent.

Oliver got untidily to his feet. 'Can I help you, sir?'

A fair-haired man stood before them, wrapped in a beach towel. 'Some money has been stolen from my tent.'

'Money?'

'Over 200 euros. I was only gone for an hour. I left it wrapped in a bundle of my clothing, and now it is gone.'

'It does happen, sir, much as we try to stop it. Kids coming in from the beach. Gypsies.'

'This campsite is meant to be secure.'

'I know sir, but when you're under canvas, you know, all that freedom has its price. Don't worry, though – we have a system. I'll fetch you a report form, and you can apply to the company for a reimbursement. They're pretty good about it.'

Oliver shot Roland a wink as the man turned to leave, his expression congealing again instantly as the man had another thought and turned back around.

'I almost forgot – two of the toilets are blocked as well.'

'Forgive me, sir. I'll get on to that straight away.'

He returned twenty minutes later, throwing his plunger into a bucket beside the bar. 'Jesus, these people. They want to get some fibre in their diets.'

Roland watched him for a while, smoking, and waited for him to drink some more and calm down. 'Do you ever hear anything from home?' he said, finally.

Oliver looked out over the tents towards the beach. 'Not much. Victor never goes down there, I suppose.'

Roland shook his head. 'Not lately.'

'How's he doing, anyway?' said Oliver.

'Same.'

'Bad luck.'

They smiled.

'Listen,' said Roland. 'He says you can't come back yet. He says they won't take it well.'

'I don't want to come back, so that's great news, far as I'm concerned.' This cigarette butt he ground firmly into the pine needles with his foot. 'What was that about Cleo?'

'Yes,' said Roland.

'Well?'

'I still don't really understand what happened.'

'What do you mean?'

'You know what I mean. The accident.'

Oliver held out his hands in a shrug. 'I've told you as much as I know. I don't remember much of that day beyond the afternoon, anyway. It was an accident. They happen.'

'That's not good enough.'

'How many times have we talked about this? I asked her myself. She said I knew all I needed to know.'

'What's she letting you off the hook for?'

Oliver lit another cigarette. 'It's better to leave it. I think something happened that she doesn't want to go on thinking about any more than she has to. And that should be enough for us to stay out of it.'

'That might be one of the most slippery things I've ever heard you say.' Important to try and stay calm at this point. Try to keep a hold of his voice. Try not to say anything he didn't mean. 'Tell me this, then: why did you tell me to keep away?'

Oliver's face settled into a different expression – one that Roland knew very well. Readiness to fight. 'What do you mean?'

'From their house. I was going to come over there with you, and you told me not to.'

357

Oliver set down his glass and put a hand to his eyes. 'Their house? You'd *burned down* their house, for fuck's sake. And as far as I can remember you were pretty upset with yourself about that. Don't you think it was a good idea for you to steer clear of them for a bit?'

'You never worried about pissing him off at any other time. Why that day in particular?'

He held his hands up. 'If you want me to say it – all right: I wanted her to myself. Without you.'

'And look where that got you. Look where it got her.'

'I don't know what more you want me to say.'

'Neither do I,' said Roland. He took a long drink of his water and moved a thumb around in the dish of croquette crumbs.

Oliver spoke quietly. 'How is she, anyway?'

'I don't know. I've lost track of her for the moment.'

'What about her dad?'

The last time Roland had seen Scriven was about a week after the accident. Roland had gone to Wreaking and found him sitting in the garden, in a wet deck chair. When Roland asked him about Cleo, he replied very simply that she had gone, and would not be back. *And if you have any sense*, he said, *you'll stay away from your friend Oliver for good.*

'I haven't seen him either,' said Roland.

'That's probably for the best. Now everybody can just get on with their own lives. Have a drink.'

'No,' said Roland. 'I told you I was worried about her. You told me not to come. And you promised me you'd take care of her.'

'For fuck's sake! It wasn't *my* fault she got hurt.'

'Who says it wasn't your fault? Where were you when it happened?' Roland stood quickly from the picnic bench and walked off in the direction of the beach.

He had known for some time that what he had thought

initially couldn't be right, that Oliver hadn't actively *done it* himself. But the conversation seemed to confirm something he had always suspected, which was that he hadn't done anything to stop it either. It made it even more difficult than it had been to get rid of the feelings he had on the morning after the accident, when his mother, having heard about it, threw open the curtains and made her grim announcement. *I warned you about Oliver, didn't I? Well, now it's happened.*

Roland spent the next few days helping Oliver fix things around the campsite, which meant fixing things while Oliver got on with the day's business of medicating himself with powerful, milky drinks. He mended showers. He secured several tents that were half falling down. He treated a girl who'd been stung by a jellyfish.

Oliver waited until there were only a few hours left of Roland's visit before he started asking seriously for the money. There was something contemptible about seeing him so reduced. At seventeen, Roland would have done anything for Oliver. Oliver at seventeen had been glorious, unstoppable. Oliver at twenty-six dealt with blocked toilets and shorn-off guy ropes.

'Please,' he said, in the end, on that last night. 'Please help me out.'

And Roland looked away, embarrassed by how unattractive he found the desperation.

'That's a no, then is it?' said Oliver.

'Let me think about it,' said Roland, realising that Oliver probably didn't even know why his request was being declined. And finding that more contemptible than anything.

You shouldn't go up there today. We don't know what kind of mood they'll be in. Let me go. I'll check the place out. I'll take a reading on the lie of the land. It's for the best if you stay away for now. Nobody's going to blame you for the fire, but keeping your distance is probably the best idea.

'All right. When I get back, I'll wire you some money,' said Roland, remembering what he had said to Oliver in return, that day. *What about her? What about Cleo?*

'You promise?' said Oliver. *Don't you worry about her. I'll protect her. You know that. I'll watch out for her.* 'How can I be sure?'

How can I be sure? That was what Roland had said too. That day. Which made his reply all too easy – because it was the same reply Oliver gave him back then.

'Trust me.'

Just trust me.

Roland left him dead drunk at the back of his own bar, with a queue of guests muttering about overflowing toilets, and he hasn't seen him since.

It's not your fault. He thinks of Oliver's desperate look, and of Mona telling him on the day of the accident that it had happened.

It's not your fault. He drills it into himself, punching his own thigh, shaking his head along with the van's jerks and shudders.

43

Over the next two days the building comes alive in unexpected places. Flies stream from taps when she turns them. She can't seem to drink from a glass without having to pick a soaked moth from her mouth. When she puts a hand to her hair, it comes away with a bug every time. The lake is hatching with thread-like creatures so small that Cleo isn't sure she is even seeing them, or whether they are only tiny ripples in the current.

His bedroom, by contrast, is the deadest place she has ever known. Even when she throws open the windows, goes away for two hours and returns, she is stifled by the sheer deadness of the place. Desiccated insects litter the floor. The remnants of trashed cobwebs billow lazily near the ceiling. When she pulls back the covers of his bed she finds an atrophied mouse nest, months abandoned, in the horsehair mattress. How did things get this bad?

After this particular discovery she begins sweeping Revenant House systematically, trying to get the measure of things. Every room brings its quirky little surprise. In the kitchen there's a patina of grease on the wall you could write your name in. A crop of mushrooms grows under the table. In a sideboard she finds a drawer full of photographs of eggs. Not Polaroids, but whole films of stills, that he must have bothered to go into town to get developed. Eggs in every possible style. Boiled ones in cups. Fried on toast. Messy scrambles. Omelettes indecorously heaped on unwashed asylum china, with the *NHS WREAKING* logo round the rim of each plate.

Delving deeper, she finds shoeboxes, meticulously labelled:
GLUE.
LONG STRING.
NAILS.
CASTORS.
SHORT STRING.
ADHESIVE TAPE.
STRING TOO SHORT TO USE.

She finds mundane remedies for piles and bunions – ailments about which she knew nothing. She finds Warfarin – was there a thrombosis he never disclosed? At one point, she finds herself reading his clothing drawers as if they were a book she is hooked on: his socks; his shirts; the clunking shambles of his shoe-pile.

Something in the squalor, in seeing him so undefended like this, makes her loyalty kick in, marshalling better memories that rise up to his support. Memories of him as a younger man. Of feeling safe with him. Of laughing on car journeys and listening to music together and huddling in front of the television. The kind of stuff that needs a powerful soundtrack. What you might call Montage Memory.

Her own instincts annoy her. What kind of perversity is this? He's no longer around to be his old, disappointing self, and so *now* her sympathy kicks in? In the interests of balance, is she now supposed to remind herself of the ways in which he fell down, having spent all these years trying to remember him kindly? Well, fuck.

'I'm not sure this is acceptable,' she says, to the air.

This is the devastating thing that she longs to have told

him if she had had the guts: that the most crushing thing about his unhappiness, the thing that made it hardest to bear, was how boring it was. She used to tell herself she was saving that one up for when she really needed it. But like most of those who devise last-resort weapons, she had always known she would never have the heart to use it. The aftermath would be too bleak, and the status quo could always be endured another day. She had favoured instead the slow death, by silence, that felt guilt-free at the time, but, she now suspects, was preparing to drop an unearthly payload when it was all too late, and there was no more talking left to do.

In other words, now.

She tells herself that the temptation to see him in every proximate living thing will come to seem naive, but she doesn't care, because she's enjoying it. Everything from birds that linger longer than normal, to dragonfly nymphs that scamper in pond-mud, territorial and cagey. Even as she tries to reject the thought, she wonders whether he dispersed himself favourably in her direction, whether it works like that. Could he be the shield bug preening on her pillow? Is some portion of his energy powering the moth on the kitchen counter, that shuts up its wings and curls its proboscis when she gently blows on it? Is he so diluted? And if it is like that, wouldn't it have been more sensible to connect with him when he was all in one place, concentrated, reachable? Remembered particles of superstition would seem to suggest that when you leave one place, you can be in any place. She knows it will seem ridiculous that anyone should actually believe this, just as it's ridiculous that anyone should believe in angels, but here she is, starting to believe it, as the old boilers of her imagination fire up again.

And yet. Just as in the past, when her feelings soured from pity to fear to quiet satisfaction at the sound of him crying in the night, now her attitude to these possibly innocent insects adapts too. Standing in her bedroom window on the third night, she finds herself watching a ladybird, and fancying that it might be him, trying to get back to her and make amends. She eliminates it quickly before it can fly away, with a pinch of her finger and thumb.

'It's getting light,' she said, standing right here, on this spot.

Her voice was close in the window, so close it sounded unreal. A dampened acoustic. And it was: cold daylight was soaking the sky, defining the spidery fingers of trees. The sun was coming up over the weed-snagged car parks and outbuildings of the derelict hospital. It felt dangerous. Nobody was in charge. Nobody cared that they had beaten the night, or that she and Oliver had been doing what they had been doing. Nobody would care if they didn't even get up today.

She looked back at the bed to see if Oliver had heard her, but he was asleep, at a spooky angle across the bed that made him look dead. His last cigarette was still burning in one hand, and he was clutching a bent cider can to his chest in the other. She felt cold. The mineral reek of recent sex hung in the air. She was still wearing items of her mother's clothes. The flush of contact had been and gone, leaving her only with relaxation and a slight headache.

She felt a shot of pity for her father down there in his chair, fronting up to things, or imagining he was. She pulled on more of the clothes, and made the decision to go down and talk to him. Not in the hectic, confrontational way that she had the previous afternoon. In any way that he wanted. Just as it was feasible for him to be fast asleep in the afternoon, it was equally likely he would be wide awake now, as the sun came up. She plucked the cigarette from Oliver's hand, took a deep drag and dropped the butt into a spent can on the side. She covered him with a blanket.

She didn't stop off at the bathroom to see what she looked like, or question whether he might care that she smelled of smoke and sex. Instead she stopped off to look at the remains of the burned-out wing: scorched boxes of chalk; ruined chairs and desks.

He was asleep in his chair, though had clearly been writing for hours. She thought about just turning to leave, but thought again. She wanted to know he was okay. To tell him she was too. Softly she put a hand on his forearm, trying not to wake him too abruptly.

His eyes opened, and she saw the confusion in them as he tried to focus on what was in front of him. Then he leapt upwards, a look of terror on his face, and pinned her to the wall with his left arm across her chest.

'No,' he said.

On the morning of the third day, she walks into town and buys food from the supermarket. As she gets out of her taxi, a little blue car that was waiting at the end of the drive disappears at speed. When she gets home, she chucks the spoiling food from the fridge, and replenishes it. She fills a big bowl with apples and puts it on a windowsill she has scrubbed clean.

She makes a bonfire in the garden, and burns his towels and some of the more egregiously stained clothing. She is no closer to understanding the origin of those strange horizontal swipes across the seats of his jackets.

She goes into his study, heaves the green armchair outside, and throws it on to the fire. It catches quickly. She is shocked by the high-pitched squeals, and by the panicked mice that hop out of it one by one and streak for the long grass by the lake. The fire spreads dangerously beyond the area she had allocated for it. She jogs to the kitchen for water, to arrest the spread of the flames, and also because she has the idea that if she finds any smouldering mice she will be able to douse them for their own safety.

She returns grappling with the weight of a large silver cylinder which she thinks is part of a catering-sized tea urn, and which she has filled nearly to the brim with cold water. But when she reaches the fire it is not as out of hand as she had thought it was, and seems to have tidied itself, and settled into a more compact shape.

'The phantom gardener,' she says, narrowing her eyes, and scanning the edges of the wood.

Finding that she has no appetite for anything but comfort food, she makes spaghetti hoops on toast. She takes her plate out from the kitchen, past the coat rack in the hall and into the sitting room, eating her meal in the company of the familiar, beaten-up old television in spite of the fact that she can't get it to work. On her way back to the kitchen with her dirty plate she sees a bright orange streak across the back of her jacket where the plate of spaghetti had brushed against it on the way out. It makes her laugh.

She takes herself back outside. It smells like rain over the bonfire smoke. She ambles through the woods over to the border with Wreaking, to see how things are looking. She scans the length of one of the long, outer walls, and can't see a single intact window. She can just make out peeling blue paint on an upstairs wall. As she heads back home around the lake, the rain arrives. For now the lake is only simmering but it feels like there is more to come.

The waterside pavilion has all but lost its roof, so she seeks shelter inside the tomato bus instead. The drops ping on the roof of the clear plastic hatch above her head, clear discs exploding in the dust. Water starts to coat the skylight's surface as the rain beats down in earnest. She lies down on the floor of the bus, enjoying the rhythm, taking deep lungfuls of the smell, and quietly, she becomes aware that there is breathing in the bus besides her own.

Calm breaths, working smoothly.

'Roland,' she says.

44

He wakes up in the night thinking something's wrong, then the confusion lifts and he remembers that he is not in the back of his van, but in a building, and not just any building, but Revenant House. The change feels dangerous, vertiginous – but it's happened. He has seen her, and she's seen him, and all is supposedly okay. And now he is bedding down on a tiny, crippled sofa in one of the waiting rooms by the front door as the rain continues to fall outside.

She set him up in here, and brought him sheets and a pail of coal. She explained that the only room apart from her own that has a bed in it is her father's, which, she said, is uninhabitable. She said this was a good place to sleep because the room is small and the fireplace doesn't smoke. It didn't occur to her that a fire might not be required. And so, even though it's a mild night, Roland has lit a fire, because Cleo wanted him to have one. Because for anyone to want him looked after is something to be treasured. Especially her.

He's sinking so heavily into this toy piece of furniture that he fears his impact will permanently destroy it. The skin of his face is hot and tight from the fire, and his body is sweating under the packing blankets that he heaped over himself out of habit before closing his eyes. But there is comfort in following her instructions, because it proves to him that she was here. So long as he's too hot, then it's true.

They sat in the kitchen together feigning comfortable silence, as if there was nothing they needed to say – and maybe there wasn't. She drank wine while he heated up two ready meals and quickly devoured them. He kept trying to remind himself that although he has seen her lately, it's a long time since she saw him – not that he can on any account tell her that. Into the silence, she announced that they had better find him somewhere to sleep.

He brought his van up the drive, and stood behind her in here while she tucked in the sheets, looming, aware of his breathing. She apologised for installing him somewhere so basic, talking over the strangeness of seeing him again, of him *being here*, and the compound strangeness of the fact that they were both acting as if it was all quite normal.

'We can get you fixed up somewhere else tomorrow,' she said. 'If you're staying.'

'If you saw what I'm used to,' he said.

They agreed to talk more in the morning, and she was gone. And now here he is, watching faces flare and dwindle in the fire, the little devils of cartoons, Oliver-shaped, taunting him for daring to breathe the same air as her, hissing doubts at him about what she must think of him that his life still hasn't gone anywhere, and that he is *still* creeping around her like this, even after all this time.

He swings his feet to the floor and rubs a hand up and down his face, sinking his features into the thick flesh of his palm. Even now there is an embarrassment, a flush that overtakes him at the mere prospect of being seen by her. No wonder he has kept out of her sight for so long. No wonder it unsettles him that they should be co-inhabiting this new reality of sitting together at tables, and talking – a reality in which there's no watching through windows, or foraging through bins.

He goes upstairs to piss and have a drink of water. He suppresses the urge to climb the spiral staircase that leads up to her room. Standing with the light of the waxing moon throwing hard contrast on to the textured walls of the building, Roland waits for the wave of feeling that he knew must surely come next. He lets it in, and gives it oxygen, because this has to happen, and he might as well get it out of the way now, while it's dark and he has time on his hands.

It was inevitable: now that he and Cleo are formally reunited, the missing component is all the more apparent. The fact that it's dark makes the pain more acute. The guilt at not having done more to help Oliver when he was asked to. Back in the waiting room, he slips another shovelful of coal on to the fire, knowing that he will be awake now, and he might as well have the company. He stares at the coals, remembering Oliver's pleading face, lit up by the firelight of a beach brazier, equally redundant, and his own calm refusal to help.

In the morning he climbs the stairs to her room to look in on her and she's still sleeping: deep, steady breaths and snorts. It's 9 a.m. – as late as Roland can remember getting up.

He stands over her, watching over the precious space she takes up in the world. There are a few less regular breaths, cut with sighs, and he thinks he has disturbed her. But she buries her head back in the linen, and her tidy little snores are once more rasping into the room. Her glass eye stares up at him from the bedside table. He looks away. Poking out of the bottom of the bed is a foot. There's a white sticking plaster on her toe, to stop her shoes from rubbing. He notices a shaving cut on her ankle. He sees the tone of her skin, dusky against the white of the bedsheet. Next to her he is bone-headed, knuckle-grazing, a primate.

He had forgotten this: how watching Cleo sleep is like

going on a great adventure. How all you want to do is watch over her while she makes the journey.

He goes downstairs and gives the cupboards a once-over to find a tightly packed twist of coffee in the bottom of a foil packet. He boils some water, and fixes up a strong brew. With steaming mug he pulls at the back door, which scrapes a contribution to the storm of white lines on the stone slabs.

'We can sort that for starters,' he says.

He drinks his coffee by the lake, too much of it, enjoying the taut, headachey build of the caffeine. Yesterday's rain is already steaming off the flagstones. It's going to be hot.

The yard by the maintenance sheds smells of fresh shoots and pollen. He roots around until he has found a screwdriver and a hand drill. He lifts the kitchen door up on its hinges, shouldering it easily and driving the screws in deep, getting real bite on the wood.

'You won't sag again in a hurry,' he says.

He takes the last of the coffee to Cleo's room in a fresh cup, treading carefully as he climbs the stairs. He can hear her, snoring still, from outside the door. He goes in anyway to leave the cup by her side in case she wakes up. She has moved so he can no longer see her face, but a clump of hair has made it out between the pillow and the sheets, like vegetation struggling through Arctic tundra. The drowsy sound of a bee zones in and out at the window. She is so deeply asleep that to interrupt it would be to risk something terrible. He leaves the coffee, knowing it will go cold, but wanting her to know that he thought to bring it to her.

He goes downstairs, and finds a newspaper. He tries the crossword, but the paper is old and yellow and he doesn't get the clues. He looks around for more obvious stuff to do but there is so much that he would not know where to start. It is only a matter of time before he finds himself at the door of the study. Scriven's great storm of papers and mess.

371

The place she has not yet dared to look at or rationalise.

The papers are all mixed up, with bits copied from one to another, some typewritten, but most done in his looping black handwriting:

> . . . when I think of all you have missed. She became such a lovely girl, our daughter. So adorable as a child: red cheeks, a kind of breathlessness, a concentration on everything, a seriousness. And you missed it. You missed it all . . .
>
> . . . so tell me, somehow, if you can, what I am supposed to do with the knowledge that my memories of you from before are fading? That I can't now remember how much we laughed, or at what? It's KILLING me. Please. If you can send me any kind of signal, I'll be watching – I'll pick it up . . .
>
> . . . patient is inconsolable over the fact that the medication she has received in our care has caused the demise of what she calls her 'guardians' or her 'angels'. This has plunged her into a chronic depressive state, which we have been treating to no obvious avail . . .
>
> . . . and how was I supposed to explain to you then, at that age, that it was better for you not to see her? That she actually wanted to HURT you? If you can think of a way I should have done that without making things worse, then . . .

Roland feels the shame spreading across his face, the hot feeling of a busted voyeur. He needs something to work this away, the excess of caffeine, this nauseous, awkward feeling. In the yard near the old bus he finds wood to chop. He splits logs for what must be an hour, until well after 2.30. A warm, carpentry-shop smell rises up off it. Shavings and chips with the glaring freshness of new wood accumulate on the ground. The callouses in his palms start tingling. It feels good to be active. Stretching is delicious: the confirmation of the existence of healthy muscle has never felt so good. The smell of warming wood reminds him of busting doorframes; of the smoke that sometimes comes out when you stick in a crowbar and lever something open. The outrage of the dumb materials.

He senses Cleo watching him as soon as she is there. He knows that she is waiting for a natural pause between his axe-blows so that she won't distract him and risk harm. He adores her for this worry, though he would feel her coming a mile off, and his aim is always true. He could split a hair on her head with a sharp-enough axe, and would know exactly when to pull back. She has no idea how powerful he is. He likes that too.

Eventually he sets down the axe and turns to her. 'I forgot how much you can sleep.'

She steps forward on the tips of her toes, frowning at the rough bits of the ground, puts an arm around his waist, and gives him a dry kiss on the neck. Her breath smells of sleep – complex, strong, intimate.

'I have never slept like that,' she says, 'in my life.'

A nerve is jumping in his shoulder from all the chopping. It feels like someone is insistently tapping him to get his attention. He tries to shrug it off.

'I'm going swimming,' she says.

45

Green apples in a bowl: Roland sniffed them out, and now he's selecting them one by one and cutting them into segments with his pocket knife. Somehow he has revived the television, and the two of them are sitting side by side in front of the early evening news, as the number of apples dwindles. Regardless of whether a new segment is destined for Cleo or for Roland, its piece of core is tossed into the pulping machine that is Roland's mouth and devoured. He's not on her blind side, but Cleo is trying not to look sideways too intently, in spite of her fascination at this, the adult version of him – so self-possessed that it almost scares her, but so sad that she almost can't bear to be near him.

They have, she remembers, seen each other since the accident. When was it? Years ago – a chance encounter. One of the street coincidences of big cities, that seemed quite natural at the time, but which she now finds herself questioning – for all the good it would do her to find out the truth. Some information is more troubling than it's worth.

'So I just bobbed along all that time,' she is saying. 'And then I sort of drifted into finding what I wanted to do. It might just as easily not have happened.'

The news being on, with all its stock phrases leaping out from the headlines, is giving her the pretext she needs to tell him about her job. Not that he's asked her about it. He hasn't asked her a single question, but she is babbling away all the same, furnishing him with information in order to ask him for at least some of the information she wants about him.

'How long have you been in your job?' she says.

'Forever. But it's not what you'd call a normal job.'

sharp rise in the number of

'What is it?'

'You remember Victor? Oliver's brother. Nasty character. I work for him.'

radical preacher of hate

'I remember him.'

He passes her a segment of the apple with a sad smile that makes her wonder for a second whether she should be heading off to the kitchen to get the hot chocolate on. Then she looks at him again, munching his apple cores. Who knows how he's really feeling? She doesn't know him any more now than she did when he first stepped out of the walls to stop her arm.

will give a speech later tomorrow in which he is expected to say

'I'm sorry about your dad,' says Roland. 'I've been meaning to say something, but I didn't know what.'

'Thanks. In a way I'm glad it's over. I can get on with remembering him now.'

body of a man has been found in a

'Don't you want to know, then?' he says, his eyes fixed carefully on the screen.

'Know what?'

'Where he is. What's happened to him.'

So that's what's on his mind. Or *who* is on his mind.

'I don't know,' she says. 'Do I?'

He passes her a segment. This apple is sharper than the last. She curls her feet up under her legs, and resettles herself. 'I always thought that if there was any reason for he and I to contact each other then we would have done it.' She smiles. 'I did try to find him, once.'

Roland chews slowly, running his thumb forward and back over the knife blade. 'Yeah? When was that?'

'A couple of years ago, after I got out of something. I was down. I thought seeing him might cheer me up.'

'And?'

'None of the numbers I had for him worked. Even his mother didn't know where he was. Anyway, it never happened. I met someone soon after. And then things went a bit haywire for a while.'

He shifts in his seat, chewing slowly. He reaches for a drink of water and takes a large gulp. He reaches for a cigarette that sits pre-rolled on the arm of the chair, and lights it up. 'It might surprise you. To see him now.'

She clears her throat. 'So – you do know where he is?'

'Roughly. It's been a few years.'

'Is he okay?'

'You know him. Always lands on his feet. He's running a campsite in Spain.'

'Really?' She finds herself laughing.

'Yeah.' Roland smiles too.

'No!' she says.

Just the idea of him, present in the conversation, seems to have cheered them both up. He always had that effect.

'He got it into his head that the thing to do, once you'd *got out,* once you'd escaped, was to get to Spain. He'd built it up in his head. *We'll do this, then we'll get out to Spain.* I don't know what he thought he was going to find when he got there. But he did what he said he would.'

'I always had the feeling that he would just burst back into my life one day,' she says. 'When he felt like it. When he had something to impress me with. Do you know what I mean?'

'Sure.'

'Maybe I'll go and find him,' she says. 'When I've sorted everything out here.'

'He's got quite the little empire out there. You should see it. He's on permanent holiday.' Roland transfers his cigarette to his left hand, and his right hand brings the knife in towards her mouth, bearing another apple segment.

She shakes her head, and looks away. 'No more for me, thanks.'

He gets to his feet with the empty bowl in his hands. 'I said I'd try and make that hot water run up to the bathroom better before I went. I better do it now, or else I won't have time.'

'You're going?' she says.

He nods, without looking at her. 'Tomorrow.'

'Okay,' she says. 'Isn't there someone else you ought to be paying a visit to before you leave?'

'I'll do that on my way out.'

He goes without looking back at her, dragging his sadness along with him. She is crossing the hallway after he's gone when she hears a sound from the direction of the front door, and sees something being forced insistently through the letterbox. A fat, blue brochure, folded in half to get it through, drops down and lands on the carpet. Cleo looks out of the window and sees a man in a suit striding away down the drive. She looks down at the brochure and reads: *A Development Of 600 Luxury Homes.*

While he's off somewhere with his spanners, sending groans through the pipework, she has an idea. She collects his bedding from the mashed-up sofa in the waiting room, and one or two other key items, and puts herself to work.

She finds him again just after 9 p.m., standing out on the moon-shocked lawn. The light is so bright it could give you a headache. They stare at the hard shadows, speaking quietly for no good reason.

'I don't know if it's something to do with bereavement,' she says. 'Or something about this house that dulls the brain. But being here makes me feel, sort of, *detuned*. I can't tell how long we've been here.'

'This place always did make your compass spin,' says Roland.

'I keep meaning to tell you. There's this car I keep seeing at the end of the drive.'

'What kind of car?' says Roland.

'Little blue one. An old Renault. I've seen it a couple of times now. Just parked by the lodge, with someone sitting at the wheel. And whenever I get anywhere near it, the car revs up and speeds off.'

'I see.'

'I wondered if it was someone who knew him. A friend, or something.'

'Wouldn't you know if he had any friends? Wouldn't they be getting in touch?'

'I don't know,' she says. 'Isn't that awful?'

'I think you're all right,' he says.

'Come on,' she says.

'Where?'

'I hoped it might be like this tonight,' she says. 'After today.'

'Why?'

'Don't you remember? What clear nights are good for here?'

She leads him back into the house, and straight down the cellar steps. As they reach the bottom he sees the candles in jars she has put along the corridor, that cast flighty yellow light on to the damp walls.

He laughs. 'When did you do this?'

Their feet crunch on the desiccated bodies of frogs. She thinks of the first day they came here, Ursula in tears upstairs, and her father coasting on diminishing reserves of enthusiasm. She sees him now, leading her round on his tour of the future.

She stares at the spread of Roland's flexing back. The idea of it ever being massed against you is terrifying. She feels sorry for anyone who might have crossed him over the years, and even momentarily wonders what she is doing, leading him down here by herself.

As they walk the length of the corridor she extinguishes the candles one by one, and darkness clots behind them. At the entrance to the underwater room, she picks up the last lit candle in its jar, and hands it to him.

'In you go.'

He steps inside, and sees the nest she has made with her mattress, his blankets and as many cushions and pillows as she could find in the house.

'It's damp.' His voice has a cold, subaqueous echo.

'That's why I brought us all these layers.' She steps forward, trying to find her footing on the uneven surface beneath them. 'Lie down,' she tells him. 'Get comfortable.'

He hands her the candle as he lies down to try and settle himself. She watches its light bouncing unsteadily around the deep green glass of the dome.

'Ready?' she says.

He nods into the candle, staring up at her face, and she blows it out with a quick, sharp breath and a whiff of waxy smoke.

On a clear night like this, when the moon is powerful enough, the curved glass walls of the underwater pavilion act as a magnifying glass for the constellations. The two of them lie, staring up at the bright white patterns, which are intermittently wobbly when the surface of the water moves overhead. It's like looking into phosphorescent water.

He lies still and tense beside her, and hesitates when she moves herself closer.

'You can move, if you need to,' she says.

'I'm fine like this.'

'Well – you can move anytime.'

'Are we going to sleep down here?'

'It would be a bit of a pain to take all this crap back upstairs now.'

'Yeah, okay. Sorry.'

'So,' she says. 'What do you want to know?'

'About what?'

'You know what I'm talking about.'

'What is there to know that I don't know already?'

'That's what we're here to find out.'

'Okay then,' he says. 'Tell me.'

'Sometimes I think I've tried so hard to forget it that I've remembered it *too much* – so much that I can't trust the memory any more. And I'd had a lot to drink, thanks to our friend.'

'Go on.'

'It's embarrassing, because it's so stupid. But I guess in that moment, I thought I could sort of, *be* my mother for him. In a nasty kind of way. To make the point that he should be concentrating more on me. Because I had just received this shock. Found that she had been around, until not that long before, and I could have known her. I was hating him for that. I'd been messing around with Oliver – trying on some of her old clothes, putting on make-up. And I had the idea of drawing on this mole she used to have. The one he seemed so fond of.'

'You had the idea?'

'Yeah.' She clears her throat, shifts, and resettles herself, careful not to give Roland the impression that she's trying to get away from him. 'I wasn't in a very good mood with him, remember? It had quite an effect. He was fast asleep in his armchair when I came in. It must have been like waking up in a nightmare.'

'Why? What did you do?'

'I think I said something provocative to wake him up. *Is this what you wanted?* Something like that. Then just stood there. Over him. Not saying anything. Maybe even . . . pouting a bit. I was drunk. I'd been with Oliver. My mind was full of sex.'

Now it's Roland's turn to shift awkwardly. 'And?'

'He'd hardly taken it in when he went for me. Leapt up out of the chair. His voice was groggy from sleep. He was probably drunk, too. He was scared. He kept shouting. *Take it off. Take it off.* He pinned me to the wall with his left arm, and he had his pen in his right hand, poised in the air. Like he was about to write graffiti on the wall, or sign papers on someone's back. He came in with it to . . . draw over the mole, as if he'd forgotten in that moment that it was something you could just rub off with your finger. In that moment, he saw something else. It's like . . . I had a morbid thing about plane crashes for a while once, because . . . it doesn't matter. I've edited crash footage. And looked it up online. The reason why it's so important to pay close attention to the security briefing is that the more it's drilled into you what to do, the more likely you are to do the right thing when logic deserts you. Because all logic fails. I read one account of a man who was found stuck in his seat in a crashed plane, frantically grabbing at the armrest of his chair thinking it was somehow going to undo his seat belt. I've come to think that by dressing like that, I did something to my father that sent him down a blind alley in the same way. All he could think of to do was try and rub it out.'

'That doesn't explain how he came to hurt you so badly.'

'Not a lot does,' she says. 'But you're right – at this point he was just scratching my eyelid. That very fragile skin, right on the edge. And then something changed. It was over very quickly, but there's no doubt it happened. I felt his left arm tighten up across my chest to make sure he had me. The pen moved with more intent. Once. Quickly. And it was done. I didn't scream.'

How to communicate to Roland the other thing? The fact that however impossible it would be to understand, however much her inability to understand it would define what she could and couldn't think about from that moment on, there was also a sense of inevitability to it. A feeling that this was always where the two of them were going to end up.

'What about Oliver? Where was he when this was going on?' She can feel him tensing up with anger beside her.

'I tried calling for him, I think. But he couldn't hear me. He was right at the top of the building. It wasn't his fault.'

Of all her alterations, this one is the most significant. But there is nothing else to be done. No good can come of telling him that it never even entered her head to call for Oliver, because she knew what a useless state he was in. Or that in fact, even though she knew he was nowhere near, the name she called, and more than once, was Roland's.

'So what did he do?' says Roland. 'When he realised he'd hurt you?'

'He was just vacant. He was there, but he wasn't there. He put the pen back in his pocket, as if he'd just completed a document, and he left the room. I had no idea what to do. So I lay down in a bay window, on a rug, and tried to close my eyes, and ignore the fact that I couldn't see through my right eye, and there was liquid on my cheek. I decided to wait for him. That there was nothing else to be done except wait for him to catch up. I was in shock, obviously. But I think I knew then that trying to talk about it was something that was never really going to be possible. Especially when I saw the look on his face when he came back in, and realised what he'd done. It seemed to have erased almost everything that had happened before. Shit, I don't know. Who knows whether I'm even remembering it right?'

'Did it hurt?'

'I can't remember. I remember bits and pieces of the aftermath – a doctor trying to explain to me what the procedure was, what surgery they had to do to make things better. I remember telling some nurse to alert social services, because I wanted to leave home. And someone asking me directly whether he'd done it. I remember trying to think of a way to imply that Oliver was to blame, without directly getting him into trouble. Everyone was very ready to believe it was him, of course. Wondering whether that was right, but knowing that I couldn't think of anything else. Wondering how I could possibly tell you. Knowing that I couldn't. But no – I don't remember any pain.'

'That's it?' says Roland.

'I've never told anyone any of that.'

'It wasn't Oliver's fault.'

'No.'

'Why did you let me think that it was?'

'Because I thought if you knew it was all my father, you might have hurt him. And I might even have wanted you to.'

He lies beside her in the underwater pavilion staring at skewed, magnified starlight, and, like something liquefying, she feels him relax. She congratulates herself once more on her talent for consolation. She stares up at the white light that has travelled all this way, only to be modified right here above their heads. She tries to think of another topic of conversation so that they don't dwell in this particular place, but Roland has already fallen asleep.

46

He can't find a space for the van on the seafront so he parks up round the corner and heads for the Golden Sands on foot. He wishes he hadn't lost the old sign – it might have been a good present to bring for her. Something to stir a memory or two. Not that she seems to need them.

The building isn't even called the Golden Sands Guest House any more. Under the expansion programme that has forced it to spread out sideways, assimilating the houses on either side, it is now simply called Sands.

On the ground formerly occupied by his hallway, where Mona would fret in front of the television, a resplendent reception desk has been set up. The private health-care company that led the acquisition of the two adjacent houses and knocked them all into one has its own house style, of light wood and white painted surfaces. Bright orchestral music is piped in at all times. A fishbowl full of business cards sits on the reception desk, next to a sign advertising a prize draw for a week in one of the *boutique* beach huts on the seafront. There is a noticeboard in a glass case nearby, in which group activities are advertised: painting and sailing; theatre trips and other cultural events. And all under the stewardship of the stalwart, reliable figure who was running this place when the initial offer of a buy-out came through – whose real identity has thus far remained miraculously unearthed, through a combination of bluffing, luck and dodgy paperwork. It wouldn't be possible if they didn't live under the same roof. But to the casual visitor, what has changed? Mona and Carol are still here. There's just a little confusion as to which is which. Neither of them ever got out that much in the town, so nobody's about to march in here and point the finger. The Mona they interviewed for the job was every bit as well informed about the ins and outs of caring for psychiatric patients as the real one – and these days, is far better suited to it.

'Can I help you, sir?' asks a cheerful male nurse in a pressed blue shirt.

'It's Roland Lamb,' he says. 'Mona's son.'

'Of course it is. We haven't seen you for such a long time.'

He smiles. 'I'd like to see my mother, if she's around.'

'She's in her office. You know the way, don't you?'

He can see Carol through the open door, staring at her desk, frowning down at papers, one leg going up and down like mad, a shoe tapping on the floor. She looks up when she hears him coming.

'You're here,' she says, getting up to embrace him. 'I've been losing my mind.'

'I know,' he says. 'But you didn't have to keep driving up and going away again. I told you I'd be there. You could have just come in.'

She shakes her head. 'Not until I knew you'd seen her.' She sits back down at the desk, and fiddles absent-mindedly with a ball of elastic bands. 'I don't know what to say. There was nothing I could do. He *planned* it, the toad.'

'It's not your fault. And nobody would think that it was, even if they knew. Which they aren't going to.' He puts a hand on her wrist. 'Do you understand?'

Her foot stops tapping, and she looks a little relieved. 'She's not too devastated?'

'She's fine. Okay?'

Carol nods. 'I knew it was coming, but the way it happened was a terrific shock.'

Roland still isn't sure exactly how they found each other, but he can picture it happening. He supposes at some point she just ended up there, on one of her trips, and one thing led to another. As ever when it comes to Carol, the important thing is not to ask her too many questions. And he will owe her forever for what she's done for Mona.

'Anyway,' she says. 'You'd better go and see her.'

'I was just about to.'

He walks down an immaculate, squeaking corridor, through two sets of fire doors. He admires the pictures on the walls, many of which he can tell are painted by Carol herself. They have been simply framed, in glass and oak.

He reaches the door, knocks once, and enters, closing the door behind him. He's given up fighting it now. At the beginning he used to want to break the carapace, and say *Look! It's me! Remember? Can you be you now, too?* Now, he just takes what he finds.

Mona sits in the bay window of what used to be her old knitting room, looking out to sea. As usual her right hand is resting on the wrist of her left, feeling for a pulse. In the last five years, her hair has gone from salt and pepper to pure white. She looks positively angelic.

She looks up at him as he comes in, and as usual there is a pause before the kick of recognition takes place. And a further pause while she tries for his name, which does not seem to be within reach today. The names went early. It was a crucial factor in enabling the plan to work.

'It's Roland,' he says, sitting beside her. 'You've been

leaving me phone messages, haven't you? And here, you see – I came to see you. You called me, and I came.'

'So you did,' she says. 'How have you been keeping?'

He can sometimes keep her on track long enough for a reasonable conversation, and so it proves today. 'I'm sorry I haven't been in to see you for such a long time.'

'Well, I know you're very busy.' It is an automatic response, based on nothing but politeness.

'Not too busy to see you. I thought we could go out for a cup of tea.'

She looks worried. 'Out?'

'Just for a bit. Get some air.'

There's a place three doors down called the Southern Café. He takes her there every time, and every time she says she's never been before. Arm in arm, they make their way down the seafront.

'I notice they've done up the pier,' says Roland.

'So they have,' she says. 'You wouldn't recognise it, would you?'

The café is overheated, and decorated with old utensils on shelves: copper kettles; cast-iron saucepans. They've just taken their seats and are beginning to look at the laminated menu when a black cat with a white flash on its front scampers in from behind a counter, and settles itself on a chair near their table, beside a radiator. The waitress scolds the cat, and offers to take it away, but Roland sees the look on Mona's face, and tells her to leave it.

'Here, Kitty,' she says. 'Come and say hello.'

The cat exists out of time. It's a stand-in for every other cat Mona and her son have ever experienced, which makes it something the two of them can interact with. Mona is fascinated by it. The only thing that irks Roland is that she keeps on whistling for it, to try to attract its attention.

'You don't whistle for cats,' he says.

'Come on, Kitty,' says Mona, whistling again. 'There was a time when cats loved me, you know.'

'You don't whistle for cats.'

The cat, and the fact that it won't respond to her whistling, make it impossible for her to relax at first. Eventually she forgets about it, and stops looking over her shoulder.

'It's lovely to have you back, anyway,' she says. 'You were gone such a long while!'

'Not all that long,' he says. 'I came a few months ago.'

'It's years,' she says. 'Feels like years, anyway. I talk to you sometimes. I know it's silly. You left *me*, after all. Why would you want to talk to me? But I do it anyway. Do you ever speak to Roland?'

'I – no. Not for some time.'

'You should get in touch. Drop him a line, at least. I expect he'd love to hear from you.'

'I'll give him a ring.'

'That would be nice. He missed you so much, when you'd gone. I didn't know what to do with him. It used to break my heart.'

'Do you remember how we used to box him up in all the cardboard left over from my business?'

'What?' She looks a bit shocked, as if he's said something untoward. 'What do you mean?'

'I was thinking about it the other day. Don't you remember? All those spare boxes lying around? And we'd make him these big hamster runs that he could get lost in. We never knew where he was half the time.'

'Don't be daft,' she says. 'You've dreamt that. I don't know what you're talking about. We never did anything of the sort. It would be cruel.'

'But I can remember it,' he says. 'I remember it happening.'

'You don't know everything, you know,' she says. 'Now what am I going to have, a scone or a sandwich.'

'Have both,' he says.

She looks at him, worried. 'We did all right, didn't we?'

'What do you mean?'

'We looked after him. Set him on his way.'

He puts the palm of his hand on hers. 'Yes,' he says. 'Of course you did.'

'Good. You find him, and say hello. And remember me to him when you do.'

Back in her room, he gets her settled in her chair again, by the window, right hand on left wrist. When she's looking outside, he takes out his wallet and leaves a healthy stack of Victor's cash in her bedside drawer.

He plants a kiss on her forehead and she puts a hand to his wrist as he does it, and just for a second the smells of detergent and age recede and there it is – the smell of his mother.

'I've left Carol some money,' he says to the nurse. 'Make sure my mother knows about it, will you?'

The nurse looks up cheerily from his forms. 'Of course. Have you got far to go?'

'Bit of a way,' says Roland. 'But travelling relaxes me.'

The nurse points to the fishbowl full of business cards. 'I don't suppose you have a card on you? Only we're raffling a week in a beach hut. That would give you a reason to stay longer next time.'

'I don't carry business cards.'

'And where are we off to now?'

'It's looking like it might be Spain.'

'Very nice too,' says the nurse.

It's not the past you mourn, thinks Roland, so much as the future. He steps on to the front and looks out to sea, where incoming waves are bumping up spray into rainbows. He turns into the wind, wondering if the van has it in her for one last good start.

Acknowledgements

Clare Alexander and Michal Shavit

Nick Armstrong, Rebecca Carter, Louise East, Sarah Flax,
Liz Foley, Sam Gilpin, Henry Hitchings, Rory Kinnear and
Dan Light

Harry Boothby, Chris Brotherton and Mark Simpson

Rose Grimond

Thank you.